POOL OF SOULS

Cheryl Landmark

For your enjoyment!
Cheryl Landmark

Cover Design: Ed Tsunoda

DEDICATION

To Rachel Baker, whose infinite patience,
commitment and advice were invaluable in helping me
hone this book into a source of pride.

ACKNOWLEDGMENTS

Thank you to my husband, Mike, for his unwavering love, support and encouragement as I strive to achieve my lofty dreams. And, to Rachel Baker, whose dedication and commitment to helping me is awe-inspiring and touching. I am humbled and grateful. Thank you to Ed Tsunoda for his design of the awesome cover. And, to my fellow former Asylett authors whose advice, encouragement and support have been incredible. I may have written the story, but I was definitely not alone in making it a book.

CHAPTER 1

The mare sounded apologetic but urgent. *I'm sorry to disturb you, Caz, but I think you should know that someone is trying to steal me.*

Cazlina Narzin became fully awake but didn't move. She kept her breathing quiet and steady, as though still in the rhythm of sleep, but every nerve and sinew in her body tingled with alertness. Her hand tightened on the hilt of the dagger tucked into the waistband of her trousers.

She spoke to the mare through the telepathic link that bound them. *I'm awake, Miris. Where is the scoundrel?*

She heard the mare snort gently. *He's near my head and about to grab my halter. I really think you should do something, and fast.* The mare's tone suddenly changed. *Oh, my, Caz, he's a handsome devil!*

Miris! Cazlina thought, reproachfully. *Now is not the time to admire the rogue's looks.*

Sorry.

Cazlina opened her eyes cautiously. In the pale moonlight, she could dimly make out the shape of a dark figure standing near the mare's head.

Miris, move closer to me, Cazlina instructed. *I want him where I can reach him easily.*

The mare tossed her pretty head and sidled away from the dark figure reaching out for her. Cazlina heard a soft curse from the would-be thief and then his low voice trying to coax the mare back to him. Miris pranced skittishly toward where Cazlina lay silently on the ground under the big oak tree, staying just out of reach of the figure and forcing him to follow her.

This is fun, Caz! Miris said. *I've never had anyone try to steal me before.*

Well, don't enjoy it too much, dear one, Cazlina replied, dryly. *Just move a little closer now.*

When she judged that the thief was near enough to take him by surprise, she jumped to her feet, drawing the dagger out at the same time.

"Touch that horse and I'll slice the fingers from your hand," she said, coldly.

Caz, such violence!

Quiet, Miris. Let me handle this my way.

The figure stopped dead when she suddenly rose from the ground in front of him. Then, he straightened to his full height, which was well over six feet. In the light of the moon, his keen eyes scrutinized her closely, and a faint smile tilted the corners of his firm mouth. He wore dark clothing and a shabby cloak.

"I mean you no harm," he said, holding his hands out to the side.

Cazlina stared accusingly at him, the point of the dagger just under his chin. "You were trying to steal my horse."

He chuckled and shrugged. "She's such a fine specimen. I couldn't resist taking a closer look at her."

Miris pricked her dainty ears forward. *Well, Caz, he can't be all bad. At least, he appreciates splendid horseflesh when he sees it.*

Never mind, Miris. He's still a scoundrel and a thief.

The mare snorted delicately. *Yes, but what a handsome thief.*

Choosing to ignore the comment, Cazlina glared at the tall stranger.

His faint smile bloomed into a wide grin. "Why, you're a young woman!" he exclaimed and leaned closer to get a better look.

She flicked the dagger upward, the sharp point nicking the skin on his neck. A small drop of dark blood appeared. "Don't come any closer," she warned, "or I'll stick this dagger in your throat."

Pulling back, he raised his hands in false submission, the amused grin still on his face. He completely ignored the small cut under his chin. "Ah, the lady has spirit. I admire that."

"I don't care what you admire," she snapped. "You were trying to steal my horse. I don't appreciate that."

"You know, I really thought you were a boy, at first," the man said, as though he hadn't heard her. "With your short hair and rough clothes, who would have guessed there is a beautiful young woman under there?"

She glowered at him, resenting the bold examination of his eyes.

Impervious to her indignation, he asked, "Well, my lady, what can I do to atone for my rather *enthusiastic* admiration for your mare?"

Eyes narrowed in anger, she said through gritted teeth, "By all rights, I should cut off a finger or two just to teach you a lesson."

Throwing back his head, he laughed, the deep sound startling in the quiet of the clearing.

She frowned; annoyed that the stranger didn't seem to be taking her threats seriously, even though she secretly had no intention of carrying them out if she could help it.

Miris, dear one, do me a favor, please. Give this scoundrel a small nip to let him know I mean business. He's enjoying this far too much.

The mare threw her a mildly reproachful look. *Must I always do your dirty work?*

Just do it, please.

Miris dipped her head and inflicted a small, but painful, nip on the stranger's left arm. A startled yelp replaced his laughter. Then, it rang out again. "By all the gods, you even have your lovely mare trained to keep horse thieves in line!"

Cazlina glared at him. "You seem to find this all very amusing. I don't. Trying to steal someone's horse is a serious crime, especially when it's *my* horse."

"But, I failed in my attempt," he complained, plaintively. "My reputation as a horse thief in these parts will be forever stained by the fact I was bested by a mere slip of a girl."

"How unfortunate for you," she snorted. "But, I don't intend to stay around here long enough to besmirch your so-called reputation."

"Are you leaving so soon, my lady? I thought maybe we could get to know one another better, especially since we share an appreciation for such fine horseflesh."

He reached out a hand as though to stroke Miris' sleek red neck and Cazlina flicked the dagger point. "I wouldn't touch her, if I were you," she warned.

He drew back his hand with an apologetic shrug.

She contemplated him. "Perhaps, I should do you a favor and cut out both your eyes. That way, you won't be tempted anymore by the sight of a splendid horse."

White teeth flashed in a maddening grin. "I like you. You remind me of me, full of spice and vinegar and willing to take on the world."

"Don't insult me further," she muttered. "I may just cut your damnable throat."

He pretended to look shocked. "What language, my lady!"

"Stop calling me your lady!"

His hands lifted in mock surrender. "Forgive me if I have insulted you once more, my lady--oops, sorry."

Sighing faintly, she found herself tiring of the exhausting game. Sleep this night had been fitful at best, and she still felt the vestiges of fatigue from the long, hard ride that day. All she wanted to do was get rid of this smug, silk-tongued devil and be on her way. She had to reach Terrangay before General Viadon's army left the walled city.

The stranger seemed to sense her restlessness and started to back slowly away. "Well, I guess I'll be going now, too," he said, bowing from the waist. "You have my undying gratitude for leaving my fingers and eyes intact. Good luck to you, my lady."

In the next instant, he slipped away, melting into the shadows.

Cazlina blinked, her heartbeat tripping a little faster. She was certain the horse thief was still watching her from the shadows. Her skin prickled with the anticipation of a sudden attack. Striding swiftly to the saddle under the big oak tree, she picked it up while keeping a constant lookout for any movement among the trees and shrubs.

Silence reigned in the clearing. Still, her pulse thudded rapidly as she slipped the saddle on to Miris' back and cinched it tightly.

I think he's gone, the mare's quiet voice tried to reassure her.

Maybe, but, I don't trust him for a second. The sooner we're gone from here, the better I'll feel.

She finished saddling the mare and glanced around once more. The small clearing remained still and silent. The confrontation with the man might never have taken place, except in her imagination.

Tucking the dagger back into the waistband of her trousers, she swung hurriedly up into the saddle. With a last quick look around, she urged the mare away from the clearing, expecting at any moment to see a figure burst out of the underbrush and drag her from the saddle. The adrenaline and anger that had kept her going earlier seemed to drain away in a rush. Now, she wanted only to put as much distance as she could between herself and the horse thief.

As Miris cantered away, Cazlina swore she heard a chuckle float out of the air behind her. The mare whickered softly as they galloped through the dark landscape. *Well, that was exciting.*

"I'm glad *you* think so," Cazlina said, out loud. Instead of excitement, a weak, drained feeling pervaded her body. "I can't believe I actually faced down a horse thief much bigger than me and threatened to cut out his eyes."

The sheer audacity of her actions stunned her. The stranger could easily have knocked the dagger out of her hand and overtaken her. Why hadn't he? She wondered.

Perhaps, he's really a kind soul at heart, Miris said, helpfully.

Cazlina snorted. "Miris, you are far too kind-hearted yourself. You see virtue in everyone, even if they don't deserve it."

Well, someone as handsome as he and an admirer of fine horses couldn't be all bad, now, could he?

Cazlina gave the mare a gentle slap on her sleek neck. "His *admiration* nearly took you away from me, dear one. Would you have liked that? As I recall, *you* were the one who urged me to do something to stop him from stealing you."

The mare flicked her ears and snorted delicately. *I certainly would not have wanted to leave you, Caz. Not even for one as pleasing as he.*

"I'm glad to hear that."

But, if he was truly bad, why didn't he just overpower you and steal me? Why did he give up so easily?

Cazlina felt a flicker of annoyance. "Well, I *did* have the dagger pointed at his throat. Perhaps *that* acted as somewhat of a deterrent."

I'm not trying to belittle your courage, Caz. You were indeed very brave, and I'm proud of you. But, you must admit, he was much bigger than you.

"Of course he was. But, just because he didn't try to wrestle the dagger away from me doesn't prove any honorable intentions on his part. Maybe he was terrified but didn't want to show it."

Caz!

"All right, all right, I admit that's a little farfetched. He certainly seemed anything *but* afraid of me. Maybe I surprised him by openly confronting him and that's why I was able to get away so easily. He didn't expect a 'mere slip of a girl' to stand up to him."

Perhaps.

"Anyway, we're away from that scoundrel now and we have much more pressing matters to concern ourselves with. General Viadon's army will be leaving Terrangay soon and we must reach the city before he marches out."

CHAPTER 2

Two days later, Cazlina guided Miris toward a line of low, smoky mountains on the horizon. The sun blazed down on them with extreme vehemence. Heat waves bounced off rocks and the dusty ground, and tiny puddles of tepid water in depressions seemed to be the only source of water for miles.

Cazlina dozed fitfully in the saddle as Miris kept to their course.

After a few more hours of riding in the sweltering heat, Miris' tired voice sounded in her mind. *Caz, I think I must stop now and rest.*

Cazlina became fully awake, straightening up in the saddle with a small moan. Her neck and shoulder muscles were cramped and stiff. She squinted against the blazing rays of the mid-afternoon sun. "All right, Miris, let's stop for the day and get out of this heat."

They found a small stand of straggly trees with narrow, speckled leaves that provided a meager amount of shade and prepared a camp. Cazlina took a currycomb out of one of the saddlebags and began to brush Miris' dusty, sweaty coat back to its former glossy shine.

As she worked, she said teasingly, "If that horse thief could see you now, he wouldn't be so anxious to steal you."

Miris snorted and tossed her head. *I'm certain he would still be able to see the fine horseflesh beneath all this dust and grime.*

Although the shadows beneath the spindly trees afforded scant protection against the sweltering sun, the air seemed to grow a little cooler as the huge, yellow orb sank toward the western horizon. Cazlina finished grooming Miris and then, after a supper of bread and cheese, settled back against the gnarled bark of one of the trees, staring out at the darkening mountains on the horizon. *What am I doing here?* She thought, bemusedly. *Gareth will kill me when he finds out I've followed him to Terrangay.* She grinned in the gathering darkness, picturing her brother's eyes blazing as he ranted on and on about her pig-headed foolishness.

She shrugged. Gareth should know her well enough by now to realize she could never quell her thirst for adventure, or her impulsive nature, which, in fact, he shared to a great extent. After all, did he really think she would stay submissively in Rothtown while he fought to protect the domains of Regalis from Queen Saranor's greed? He, more than anyone, should know his sibling was no weak, helpless female. She had given him enough bloody noses and bruises to make him realize that, underneath a deceptive slimness and pixie-like face, his little sister possessed a toughness and strength that matched his own.

She shifted against the rough bark of the tree.

No doubt her big brother would be upset with her, but she knew how to get around his anger. Only two years separated them in age, and, since their parents' deaths ten years earlier, their relationship had grown very close. Finding themselves bereft of both beloved parents at the same time, she and Gareth clung to each other for mutual support, love, and protection.

After he left Rothtown, heading for the walled city of Terrangay to join General Viadon's rebellion army, she grew restless and irritable; missing him terribly and worrying about his safety.

Tales of the rogue queen's barbaric and aggressive exploits against the lands to the south ran rampant through Rothtown. In the past few months, with the aid of a powerful mage and her army, she had carried out bloody raids into Lattica, the western domain bordering her own domain of Janix. Her soldiers had attacked Lattica's capital city of Bolgar, killing King Antol and the entire royal family. Villages and towns in the surrounding countryside had been decimated, leaving hundreds of men, women and children dead and many more taken captive.

The queen had grown increasingly greedy and discontent with ruling only the domain of Janix. She had decided that subjugating all of Regalis suited her ambitions more. When the commander of her troops, General Darnellis Viadon, opposed her orders to lead his men against the citizens of Lattica, Saranor threatened to have him imprisoned and tortured. He barely managed to escape with his life from the queen's castle in the capital of Vendor, taking several of his best officers with him, and making his way to the western city of Terrangay, where he began to organize a rebellion to fight against Saranor's tyranny.

The inhabitants of Rothtown, situated in the remote northern region of Janix, far removed from the center of Saranor's power, heard the tales of their queen's brutal atrocities and were shocked and horrified to learn of the extent of her evil in her quest for world dominance. Many of the young men in the small town, including Gareth, who were bored with their mundane, provincial life, welcomed the news of General Viadon's rebellion and eagerly set out for Terrangay to join his army.

After a weary traveller brought word that Saranor's raids were now extending into Xenad, the domain of the aging queen, Mariel, Cazlina began to seriously consider joining Gareth in Terrangay as well, not only because she wanted to see him again, but because she believed the wicked Saranor could not be allowed to wreak chaos and death on the world. The more she thought about it, the firmer her resolve became. A plan to travel to Terrangay and offer her services in General Viadon's army began formulating in her mind.

Gareth won't like that you will be putting yourself in danger, Miris had warned before they left Rothtown. *Remember, he told you to stay here in Rothtown where it's safe.*

Cazlina had bristled in annoyance, "Gareth is far too fond of telling me what to do. If he can join the general's rebellion, so can I. Besides, once I'm there, he won't have any choice but to accept my decision."

Miris had snorted. *That poor boy has never stood a chance of dissuading you once you get a notion in your head.*

"I can't help it if I'm so much stronger-willed than he is," Cazlina had replied.

Now, here she sat, with a line of mountains and a dark belt of trees separating her from the sprawling, walled city of Terrangay.

A discomfiting thought tickled her mind. What if Gareth's regiment had already left Terrangay to attack Queen Saranor's troops elsewhere? Since his departure from Rothtown two weeks earlier, she had heard no word from him.

She shrugged irritably. *He has to be there,* she told herself, firmly. *I didn't come all this way to join him, only to have him off somewhere playing soldier.* Nevertheless, she resolved to quicken the pace the next day.

Early in the morning, she took as little time for breakfast as possible and headed out once more on her journey.

As she and Miris approached the forest near the foothills of the mountains, Cazlina began to experience an increasing sense of apprehension. The tree trunks were blighted with strange, fungus-like growths; sharp-toothed, yellow leaves laced with gray sickly moss drooped toward the ground. The forest had an ominous, claustrophobic feel to it.

Miris' pace faltered. *I don't like this place, Caz.*

"I don't either, dear one. Something doesn't feel right."

Cazlina wondered if it would be possible to skirt the forest and find another route to the foot of the mountains, except, the thicket of trees seemed to stretch endlessly to either side. Too much time would be lost trying to find an alternate course to follow.

Miris advanced reluctantly to the edge of the trees and stopped. Cazlina stared into the dark, murky shadows. Up close, the gnarled trunks were even thicker and more crowded than they had appeared farther away, and an eerie silence pervaded the dank woods. No cheerful bird songs or reassuring patter of small animals in the underbrush lightened the gloomy atmosphere.

Must we go in there? Miris asked.

Cazlina let out a slow breath of resignation. "It seems we have no choice if we want to reach the mountains. Maybe the forest doesn't extend as far as it appears to and we'll be through it in no time."

She urged the mare forward. Reluctantly, they entered the murky gloom beneath the tangle of leaves and hanging moss. Almost at once, the foreboding they both felt became stronger, slipping from apprehension into alarm.

Cazlina heard a faint sound directly behind her, like a giggle quickly suppressed. She spun in the saddle, her pulse accelerated to a racing beat, but she saw nothing in the shadows.

Miris danced skittishly. Cazlina wanted to reassure the mare, but her own panic was rising to higher levels. She thought she saw quick, furtive movements in the underbrush. The creature, whatever it was, seemed small but incredibly fast. The sense of danger intensified.

A scream wrenched from her dry throat as an object suddenly dropped from above and landed on her right shoulder. Tiny, sharp fingers, like claws, dug painfully into her flesh. Turning her head, she found herself face to face with a small ugly creature. At first glance, it looked like a tiny child, but leathery green skin covered its knobbly-limbed body, and bright, cruel eyes sparked with an evil that was not even remotely child-like.

"Human!" It hissed at her and grinned, revealing needle-like teeth. Claws dug deeper into her shoulder and she flinched. The wicked grin widened.

Cazlina drew in her breath, fighting down sour fear that rose up to choke her. She swiped awkwardly at the creature with her left hand, but Miris' prancing threw her off-balance. The vile little beast easily ducked the blow and hissed loudly in her ear, "Foolish human."

Before she had a chance to strike at the creature again, another one landed on her thigh, clinging cruelly with its sharp claws. She cringed and swatted it, sending it flying through the air. It landed spitting on the ground near Miris' flashing hooves and the mare kicked out. The hideous creature emitted a high-pitched squeal as a hoof caught it on the side of the head and crushed its skull.

"Not nice, human," the one on Cazlina's shoulder growled and raked sharp claws down the side of her neck.

Gasping at the sudden pain, Cazlina struck out. This time, her hand caught the creature full in the face and the thing screeched, tumbling from its perch. It bounced off the back of the saddle before hitting the ground and lying still.

Another of the foul creatures sprang from the underbrush and landed on Miris' sweat-stained neck. The mare whinnied in terror as the tiny fingers tore into her flesh. She rose on her hind legs, eyes rolling in panic. Cazlina nearly slid from the saddle and clung desperately to the pommel to keep from falling off. She managed to dislodge the tiny monstrosity clinging tenaciously to Miris' neck, and it tumbled to the ground where the mare pounded it under her hooves.

The horrid creatures seemed to be everywhere. Cazlina felt dizzied by the effort of trying to keep them off her and Miris. The instant she dislodged one, another sprang from out of nowhere to tear at their flesh. A foul odor permeated the air and several small bodies littered the ground, obscene green blood soaking into the carpet of leaves and needles.

Cazlina felt herself weakening and her entire body throbbed with pain and exhaustion. Rivulets of blood ran down Miris' neck and flanks, and the mare's mind screamed with fear and pain.

Cazlina cried out as another one of the creatures landed on the back of her head, hooking its claws into her hair and yanking her neck back until she thought it would snap. She tried frantically to pull it from its roost, but the thing clung stubbornly, hissing and giggling in her ear, "Foolish human, you can't get away!"

From the periphery of her vision, she caught sight of a lone figure on horseback rushing toward her. Before she could ascertain who he was, he galloped down her left side. The creature on the back of her head emitted a harsh squeal as the man ripped it from her hair. Cazlina twisted around in the saddle in time to see her rescuer hurl the creature against a tree while reining his mount in a sharp arc around Miris' back side. He galloped past her, snatched up Miris' reins and pulled the mare swiftly forward.

Cazlina clung tightly to the pommel and bent low over Miris' neck. The mare did not need any urging. She ran as though all the demons from hell were after her.

At last, the nightmare dash took them out of the darkness of the forest and into the blazing radiance of the sun. Cazlina gulped in a lungful of the open air, finding even the scorching heat welcome after the ghastly murk under the trees. She finally raised her head and sought out her rescuer, wanting to thank him for helping her to escape those repulsive little creatures back in the forest.

Ahead of her, a man on a big roan stallion turned in the saddle, and the words died in her throat.

The horse thief she had left far behind in the clearing two nights earlier stared back at her.

CHAPTER 3

W hat in the name of all the gods were you doing in there?" he demanded, before she was able to find her voice again.

She stared at him, confused and startled. "Wha-What?" she finally managed to say.

Now in the daylight, she could see his features more clearly. Fine lines crinkled the corners of brilliant blue eyes set in a deeply tanned face. Reddish-brown hair, thick and wavy, curled over his ears and down to his shoulders. *A handsome rogue indeed,* Cazlina reluctantly conceded. The soft lines around his mouth indicated a man who obviously laughed a great deal. At the moment, however, his eyes were darkened with anger, not amusement, as he glared at her.

"Don't you know that you *never* venture into the Windles' forest?" he growled. "Whatever possessed you to do such a foolish thing? You could have been killed back there!"

"I have no idea what you're talking about," she told him, shakily.

He released Miris' reins and urged his stallion a little closer to her. The anger in his eyes faded and was replaced with a concerned expression. "You really don't know about the Windles, do you?"

She shook her head, feeling weak and drained. Burning pain from numerous cuts and scratches on her body seeped through the temporary numbness brought on by the shock of the attack and her sudden escape. Bright flashes of Miris' fear interwove with her own subsiding terror. The mare's head drooped and her bloodied sides heaved as she struggled to bring herself back under control.

"Those repulsive things are called Windles?" Cazlina asked.

The man nodded gravely. "They inhabit that particular forest and love to tease and torment unwary travellers before killing and eating them."

She shuddered, flicking a quick glance back at the dark edge of the forest, still too close for comfort.

The stranger followed her gaze. "It's all right. We're safe here. The Windles never leave their home."

Somehow, that did not entirely reassure her, but, presumably, he knew what he was talking about.

"What are *you* doing here?" she asked.

He assumed the role of dashing rogue once more. "It appears I'm rescuing my lady from terrible danger."

She stared blankly at him, unable to summon the anger and suspicion she knew she should be feeling right then. At the moment, she didn't care what his unscrupulous motives might be. Gratitude at her and Miris being alive after their horrific experience in the forest kept all other emotions at bay.

The discomfort of her wounds was becoming more noticeable as the shock wore off. She winced at the stinging and burning from the deep scratches on the side of her neck and her right shoulder. The back of her head felt as though the hair had been ripped from her skull, and warm blood trickled down the nape of her neck.

The man seemed to sense her pain. He dismounted and strode to her side, reaching up with both arms. "Let me look at those wounds."

She didn't object as he lifted her from the saddle and set her on the ground. *Miris, dear one, are you all right?*

The mare lifted her head, blowing softly through flared nostrils. *I think, perhaps now, this handsome horse thief might be a little more skeptical of my fine qualities when he looks at my present condition.*

Cazlina smiled inwardly. *I'm glad to hear you still have your sense of humor. Are you in much pain?*

A little, but now that I'm out of that terrible place and know you're safe, I feel much better.

Cazlina turned to the stranger, who had produced a rag and water-skin in preparation for cleaning her cuts. "Please, look after my horse first," she said. "I can wait until you have administered to her wounds."

He gave her a mildly sarcastic look. "You're granting me permission to touch that magnificent animal of yours? She's not going to bite me again, is she?"

Cazlina smiled weakly. "I promise she won't bite you, but don't get any ideas about jumping on her and stealing her away. I may be injured, but I can still throw my dagger quite accurately."

He pretended to look hurt. "My lady, you wound me grievously. Such an utter lack of confidence in me cuts me to the heart."

"I'm certain you'll live."

His firm mouth twitched and he turned to Miris, running his hands gently up and down her neck and sides to determine the extent of her injuries. As he worked, he threw Cazlina a mischievous glance over his shoulder. "I have a splendid mount of my own and have no further need of yours," he said.

She looked at the beautiful roan stallion standing a few feet away. The animal's large, intelligent eyes stared calmly back at her.

"I presume some gentleman of means is now walking around horseless," Cazlina said, dryly.

The stranger chuckled softly.

Obviously recognizing her ability to communicate with animals, the roan's droll voice resounded in her mind. *I assure you, the loss of my former owner is not great. This master has proven to be more kind and considerate in a matter of hours than my previous master was in three years. I hope I can continue to serve him for a long time.*

Cazlina stared bemused at the broad back of the man who gently cleansed Miris' wounds. What kind of horse thief concerned himself with being kind to the animals he stole? She would have thought monetary compensation would be his only objective. However, from the looks of his shabby, dusty clothes, it didn't seem to be a particularly lucrative occupation for him.

"I need to get some alimum leaves to put on these cuts. They'll soothe the pain and heal them faster," he declared, interrupting her baffled contemplation.

She nodded silently and sank to the hard ground, trying to find a position that was not painful for her aching body.

The stranger disappeared into the tall grasses at the edge of a shallow gully.

Miris rested her chin lightly on top of Cazlina's head, taking care not to touch the bleeding wound on her skull. *Do you agree he is a pleasing human, Caz?*

Miris, he's a rogue and a thief!

True, but he did rescue us.

Cazlina sighed heavily. *Yes, he did, and I'm grateful. But, that doesn't mean I have to like him.*

The man returned a few minutes later with several bunches of an odd-looking plant with narrow red leaves.

He promptly made a fire and boiled water in a small tin bowl. Cazlina watched his quick, efficient movements as he stripped the strange plant of its leaves and dropped them in the boiling water. A sweetish, pungent odor rose from the bowl.

"Are you a healer as well as a horse thief?" she asked, curious despite herself.

He flashed a grin at her. "Not really, but when you lead the kind of life I do, you learn a few tricks from the land." He bowed. "Permit me to introduce myself. Jorin Montrill, at your service."

Reluctantly, she said, "Cazlina Narzin."

"Pleased to meet you, *Tanil* Narzin," he said, using the informal greeting normally reserved for close friends and acquaintances of the female gender.

Cazlina stiffened at the familiar tone of his voice and said icily, "I'm not certain I could say the same, *Tan* Montrill." She pointedly emphasized the formal greeting for a male stranger.

He reacted with another maddening grin.

As he administered the pulpy mass of leaves to Miris' wounds, Cazlina's sense of suspicion, dulled by the experience in the forest and the pain of her injuries, came to the fore once more. With a narrowed gaze, she asked coldly, "Have you been following me?"

His eyes flashed at her as he applied a thick mass of warm, damp leaves to her injured shoulder. She felt an immediate relief from the throbbing pain of the deep cuts. "Now, why would I be following you, my lady?"

Her lips tightened. "It seems rather convenient that you were here to rescue me from the Windles."

He shrugged nonchalantly. "I travel this country quite extensively. It's pure coincidence that I happened to be in the neighborhood when I saw you entering the Windles's forest. I knew you would be in trouble, so I galloped in on my great steed to rescue you from danger."

She sighed wearily. "I *am* grateful to you for saving our lives, but I don't trust you in the slightest. I would appreciate it if you would let us continue on our way without interference."

"I know we met under rather unfortunate circumstances, my lady, but I really don't mean you any harm. I must admit, though, I'm intrigued to find a young woman riding a magnificent animal out here alone in this forsaken country, obviously bent on a mission of some kind. My curiosity has been aroused."

Her nostrils flared with annoyance. Unfortunately for him, his curiosity would remain unsatisfied. She had no intention of telling him the nature of her mission.

When she remained stubbornly silent, his eyes twinkled with amusement. "I should warn you. This country is very rough and holds many dangers like the one you just experienced with the Windles. Perhaps, you should consider hiring a guide to take you wherever you're going."

"*That* won't be necessary. I can take care of myself."

"Whatever you say. I do believe you are quite capable of protecting yourself against even the most terrible of monsters in this land."

Her pulse skipped a beat. "Monsters?"

"Oh, yes, there are several horrible kinds of creatures lurking about in this country." He shuddered. "I have had to turn tail pretty quick to escape some of them."

She peered closely at the handsome face near her own. Although he looked serious, she had no doubt he was teasing her and the knowledge made her bristle with annoyance.

"Well, I suppose, if you doubt your own courage, the best policy would be to run," she said, acidly.

This time, he threw back his head and laughed the deep, rich laughter she remembered from two nights earlier. She glared at him, sorely tempted to have Miris bite him again to shock him out of the great pleasure he seemed to be getting from deliberately irritating her.

She shifted away from him and rose from the ground. The boiled leaves of the alimum plant had numbed the pain of her wounds, and she found she could move much easier.

Are you all right to travel, Miris?

The mare bobbed her head. *He has wonderful hands, Caz. My wounds feel much better now.*

Wonderful hands or not, I have no great faith in his integrity.

Caz, I really do believe you are being much too harsh on the poor man.

She gave the mare an exasperated look, which the animal returned with a mild one of her own.

Cazlina turned back to Jorin. "I appreciate your help," she said, ungraciously, "but I really must be going now."

The stranger, completely unaware of the exchange between her and Miris, rose and towered above Cazlina, looking down at her with amusement.

"Well, my lady, should you have further need of my services, I am perfectly willing to help out," he said, with a mock bow. "You'll find me somewhere in this wilderness, keeping a sharp eye out for any splendid horses that happen to be wandering around."

"No doubt," Cazlina huffed, and he chuckled.

She moved over to Miris and ran her hands gently down the mare's neck and sides. Jorin's administrations seemed to have worked wonders on the animal's injuries, and Miris assured her she didn't feel much pain.

Cazlina swung up in the saddle and looked down at him. He watched her with a smug, amused expression that made her want to slap it off his face.

"Don't follow me anymore," she warned. "I'm quite capable of damaging you severely."

"I have no doubt of that," he chuckled. "Rest assured I *do* value my life, poor as it may be."

She snorted in disdain and urged Miris forward. Flicking a final glance over her shoulder, she saw him standing there, hands on his hips and watching her departure with disturbingly interested eyes.

CHAPTER 4

The mountain range was actually further away than Cazlina thought prior to entering the forest. Stars began appearing in the sky by the time she and Miris reached the bleak, barren foothills.

Cazlina saw no sign of the horse thief, but that did little to reassure her. His chosen occupation, no doubt, made him quite capable of blending inconspicuously into the landscape and escaping detection when he wanted to.

She regretted now not asking him if he knew the location of the pass through the mountains to reach Terrangay. He seemed to be quite familiar with the land hereabouts. However, her stubborn pride denied her the ability to ask for assistance from a horse thief, especially one who seemed to so thoroughly enjoy annoying her.

When she expressed her doubts about finding the pass, Miris said loyally, *I'm certain you'll have no problem, Caz. You're very good at that sort of thing.*

"Thank you, dear one. I hope you're right."

They rode in silence as she vainly searched the darkening landscape for signs of a pass. It occurred to her that perhaps they should stop for the night and continue in the morning.

A movement off to her right caused her heart to thud painfully. A terrifying thought invaded her mind—what if Jorin was wrong and the Windles had left their home to follow her and Miris?

She frantically searched the deepening shadows. Out of the darkness, a long sinewy four-legged body appeared in a patch of pale starlight and stopped to regard her with slanted, golden eyes. The starlight revealed a big cat of some kind, with sleek muscles rippling under a coat of black and white stripes.

Realizing movement could cause the dangerous-looking animal to attack Cazlina froze in the saddle. He must have come down from the mountains, she decided, looking for prey.

She reached for the handle of her dagger and was reassured by its presence. The small weapon would probably be of little protection against the big and powerful animal should he decide to attack, but perhaps she could slow him down enough to allow her and Miris time to escape.

The tip of the cat's long black tail twitched faintly as Cazlina stared into his yellow eyes.

Time seemed frozen.

Then, the animal opened his mouth in a wide yawn, revealing sharp white fangs, and sat down, curling his tail around his front paws. A voice with a hissing inflection infiltrated Cazlina's mind. *Follow me. I will lead you where you want to go.*

She gaped at the creature and he gazed back impassively, the tip of his tail still twitching. *What do you mean?*

The cat's eyes glinted in the starlight. *You are a stranger here. I will help you to find your way.*

Do you mean you'll show me how to get to Terrangay?

The way is dangerous. You will need a guide.

Miris trembled at the proximity of the huge, powerful cat. *Caz, we must flee this place immediately!*

I don't think he means us any harm, Cazlina tried to soothe her.

Strange as it seemed, it did indeed feel as though the animal did not harbor dangerous intentions toward her and Miris.

What kind of creature are you? Cazlina asked, curiously. *You don't seem like an ordinary mountain cat.*

The animal's tail twitched. *I am one who is of the night and I go by the name of Yanan. You do not need to be afraid. I will guide you safely.*

Mystified, Cazlina could only stare at the strange cat. Her journey had certainly taken on a distinctly peculiar air, what with the horse thief and Windles and now a mountain cat that wanted to be her guide.

The creature watched her impassively, waiting, it seemed, for her consent to lead on.

I must be crazy, she decided, *but I'll follow you, Yanan.*

Immediately, the cat rose and moved gracefully off into the shadows. Cazlina saw the glitter of his eyes as he looked back over his shoulder at her.

She touched her heels to Miris' side and the mare reluctantly started forward after the cat. *Are you certain this creature isn't going to eat me, Caz?*

I don't think he wants to hurt us, Miris, Cazlina replied, reassuringly. *I don't know for certain just what his intentions are, but he seems to want to help us.*

The cat's lean, sinewy body slipped in and out of sight ahead of them. Cazlina couldn't help but wonder if she was only imagining the phantom-like creature. What kind of mountain cat ignored such delicious prey as Miris and offered instead to escort them safely to their destination? It was definitely no ordinary animal.

The cat blended in perfectly with the black shadows and patches of starlight. Whenever Cazlina thought she had lost sight of him, she'd find he had stopped to wait for her.

The foothills rose steadily. Yanan seemed to know exactly which path to follow to avoid the most dangerous and jagged ground. The higher they climbed, the cooler the air became, and Cazlina found she had to don her woollen cloak as protection against the cold.

The ride through the mountains passed in a blur. She concentrated so intently on keeping the cat in sight that she paid little attention to the landscape around her, except to note its barren and melancholy atmosphere.

They rode through the mountains for perhaps two hours before Yanan led them down a narrow defile surrounded on two sides by jagged black rock. Loose stones rolled and shifted under Miris' hooves. Cazlina focused on keeping the mare from losing her footing on the rough ground and failed to keep her eyes on the cat up ahead.

She heard a sound and looked up, expecting to see Yanan, but nothing stirred on the path in front of her. The mountain cat had disappeared.

The sound came again, this time the unmistakable click of a horse's hooves on the stony ground ahead of her. At the same moment, she heard a similar noise from behind. A sense of peril assailed her. The steep sides of the narrow corridor prevented Miris from climbing out, and danger seemed to block the way ahead and behind.

Where had Yanan gone? She wondered. The creature had promised to guide her safely, and, now, at the first sign of danger, he had disappeared.

Horrible visions of tiny, ugly bodies with sharp teeth and cruel eyes raced through Cazlina's mind, and the panic and terror she had felt in the Windles's forest rose up once more. What terrible creatures threatened her this time? Perhaps, the horse thief had not been merely teasing her about monsters. Perhaps, they really did exist.

Miris pranced nervously, aware of the sounds from ahead and behind, as well as picking up on the thin threads of fear that Cazlina was beginning to exude.

A dark figure suddenly loomed up in front of them and Cazlina gasped. She couldn't see it clearly, but in her panic-stricken mind, the figure assumed gigantic and monstrous proportions.

"Halt! Who goes there?" A loud, masculine voice boomed out of the darkness. "Be you friend or foe?"

From behind her, another rough voice demanded, "Tell us your name, stranger, or we'll kill you where you sit."

Panic prevented her from speaking immediately. In response, the figure in front of her moved close enough for her to see the unmistakable glint of light on a bladed weapon.

"Start talking or I'll slit your throat."

Miris trembled violently and instinctively tried to back up, but the second intruder blocked the way.

Cazlina could see now it was a man on horseback who confronted her and not a monster. A heavy fur cloak contributed to his huge bulk and he held a wide-bladed sword in his right hand. He moved a little closer.

Cazlina decided to take refuge in bravado and straightened in the saddle. "I am on my way to see General Viadon," she said, in a commanding voice. "Let me pass immediately."

"Whoa, Kesel!" the man behind Cazlina exclaimed. "It sounds like we have a young lady here, or a lad whose voice hasn't broken yet."

"How do we know you're not a spy for that murderess, Saranor?" the first man demanded. "Or, maybe even Saranor herself."

"I give you my word I'm not a spy or the queen. I'm going to join General Viadon's army."

The man behind her snorted derisively. "What does a little lady like you want to join an army for? You plan on being a camp follower? We sure could use some soft female bodies to warm our beds at night."

She stiffened. "Of course not! General Viadon has need of soldiers and I wish to become one."

Kesel gave a bark of laughter. "A soldier now, is it? Did you hear that, Farzi? This young lady wants to become a *soldier*."

"Go back to wherever you came from and stick to playing with your dolls," Farzi growled. "An army is no place for a girl."

"I insist you let me pass," Cazlina demanded.

"Insist, do you?" The man in front flicked his sword at her. "Trying to give us orders, are you, girlie? Well, I have news for you. *We* will decide whether or not we'll let you pass."

"Wait a second, Kesel. What say we take a chance on her?"

Cazlina relaxed a little in relief, but his next words made her tense once more.

"If she agrees to show us both a good time, maybe we could just kind of look the other way and let her go afterward."

Kesel chuckled. "That sounds good to me. I was getting bored staring at these rocks. What do you say, girlie? I think that's fair enough payment for allowing you past this point."

Under the cover of darkness and her cloak, Cazlina reached for the dagger in the waistband of her trousers. The small weapon would be no match against the men's broad-bladed swords, but at least she wasn't totally defenseless.

Miris, I think our best bet is to make a run for it. They won't be expecting it.

I agree, Caz. These men don't mean to let us pass without trouble.

Cazlina's eyes searched the darkness. She could see a very narrow opening between the horse in front of her and the jagged wall of the corridor. It would be a tight fit, but, if she took the man by surprise, she might be able to push him far enough out of the way for her and Miris to squeeze by.

Before she could make her move, scrambling noises came from the top of the defile. The man behind her gave a startled shout.

"What the..."

Cazlina glanced over her shoulder in time to see a black, sinuous shape detach itself from the shadows along the top of the steep corridor and drop down on the dark figure on horseback behind her. A pair of bright, golden eyes gleamed in the darkness.

Taking advantage of Yanan's sudden reappearance, Cazlina pulled the dagger from her waistband and dug her heels into Miris' side. The mare leaped forward and bolted by the man directly in front of her. As she passed him, Cazlina struck out with the dagger, aiming for his sword arm.

Her sudden dash for freedom caught him by surprise. He yelped in pain as the weapon sliced through the sleeve of his jacket. His hand jerked and the sword fell from his fingers to land with a clatter on the stony ground.

Miris plunged down the narrow corridor, stones rolling dangerously under her flying hooves. Behind them, Caz heard the man she'd stabbed curse loudly, but she heard no sounds of pursuit from him or his partner.

A striped shadow raced by her and she saw a flash of golden eyes. Yanan's sibilant voice sounded in her mind. *Hurry! You are not safe here.*

"I think I've figured that out for myself," she muttered, bending low over Miris' neck. "You picked a fine time to disappear. Those men could have killed me. Who are they, anyway?"

Yanan glanced back at her. *Sentries, posted to guard the passes.*

"I assume they're General Viadon's men, since they took me for a spy of Queen Saranor's?"

They are Viadon's men.

She fervently hoped she had seen the last of the two men for they wouldn't be too pleased with the way she had extricated herself from the tense situation. Perhaps, their intentions had been entirely harmless and they had simply been hoping to relieve the boredom of sentry duty by trying to frighten, what they took to be, a young defenseless girl. Perhaps, they would have let her pass without any further intimidation. Still, whatever their true motives had been, she had no desire to stick around any longer to find out.

CHAPTER 5

It wasn't until the slopes began to dip down into a valley on the other side of the mountain that Cazlina felt some relief and finally allowed herself to believe the two men had not followed them.

Hundreds of stars glittered in the heavens above, spreading faint, ghostly luminance over the landscape. She saw the flickering flames of several campfires dotting the foothills in front of her and wondered if they indicated the presence of more of General Viadon's sentries.

Yanan led her away from the campfires, staying in the black shadows and skirting widely around any areas where there seemed to be guards. Cazlina followed, only too happy to avoid the soldiers. She had no wish to experience another encounter like the one she had with the men up in the mountains.

She wondered what General Viadon's reaction would be to her request to enlist in his army. Would he scoff at her as his men had done and send her on her way, believing she could not possibly be of any use to him as a soldier, because she was a young woman untrained in formal battle? She would have to make him see beyond her small, boyish appearance to the strength and determination inside and convince him she would be a valuable addition to his army. She knew she couldn't expect much help from Gareth in her quest, for he would be determined to send her back to Rothtown, where she would sit, safe and bored, and chafing at the bit to do something worthwhile with her life.

Her ruminations ended as Yanan led her around an outcropping of black jagged rock and stunted trees and out onto a flat plateau. There, before them, on the slope of a wide, shallow valley, lay the walled city of Terrangay.

Accompanied by the dim light from the stars above, the glow of hundreds of lights from within Terrangay enabled Cazlina to see the enormous size of the city, sprawling up and down the slopes of the valley. A high wall entirely surrounded the area, with small towers situated along it in specific intervals. Light flickered from those towers, as well.

She stared at the sight in amazement. She had never seen such a big city before, and could not imagine the number of people who must populate the one sprawling endlessly before her.

The thought evoked a flutter of apprehension. How in the name of all the gods would she ever find Gareth in that teeming metropolis?

Yanan glided silently down the stony slopes of the plateau and into the valley. Not wanting to lose sight of the cat in the darkness, Cazlina urged Miris forward.

Travel across the valley bottom proved easier than through the mountains. The black and white mountain cat chose an invisible path among the stands of trees and skirted the reed-choked banks of a narrow river. At one point, they came across a dirt road that seemed to lead directly toward Terrangay, and Cazlina started to turn toward the city.

Yanan bounded in front of her, forcing Miris to stop. His golden eyes flashed at her. *Wait! This way.* He disappeared silently into the underbrush at the side of the road.

She stared after the creature. His voice had held a note of urgency and she wondered what had caused his alarm. Yet, she didn't question it for long. Yanan had already proven to be a valuable ally, and she knew there had to be a good reason for concealment.

She urged Miris off the road and through the underbrush where the cat had disappeared. The incandescent glitter of his eyes showed her where the creature poised motionless on top of a fallen log.

Do not make a sound, Yanan warned. *Something comes.*

Cazlina did not like the sound of that rather cryptic announcement.

She slid quietly from Miris' back and led the mare around the fallen log, concealing both of them behind the tangled mass of branches and leaves. Yanan leaped silently from the top of the log to the ground and blended perfectly into the shadows beneath the tree.

Cazlina strained her ears for unusual sounds in the night as she searched the darkness past the underbrush for any movement on the indistinct road. A faint breeze sighed overhead, rustling the leaves of the trees. Nothing out of the ordinary seemed afoot.

She looked toward the shadows under the log where Yanan had hidden and could not see the big cat. Her heart skipped a beat.

As though to reassure her of its presence, the sibilant voice said, *I feel no magic in the air. The mage is not with them.*

What are you talking about? Cazlina asked, bewilderedly.

Saranor sends a scouting party. But, Nostrimus is not with them.

Cazlina's pulse skipped a beat.

Saranor? Here, so close to Terrangay?

Her palms were suddenly damp. There was tightness in her throat, and she had to work to keep her muscles from tensing up at this realization.

This scouting party, is it very big? She asked Yanan, a bit more apprehensively than she would have liked.

She still couldn't hear anything coming down the road. Surely, there would be hoof beats or the jangle of bridles to give away the presence of a large scouting party.

Suddenly, Miris pricked her ears forward. *Something is here, Caz!*

At the same moment, Cazlina glimpsed blurred movement on the road in front of them. Wraith-like shadows slipped past her line of sight. She counted at least half a dozen of them, their passage eerily silent. If she had not known to look for them, she would not have detected their presence. Although she couldn't clearly identify them, they didn't seem to be humans on horseback as she had expected.

She dared not breathe for fear the mysterious creatures would sense her presence and rush to attack. Beside her, Miris rolled her eyes. Cazlina pressed a hand gently against the mare's flaring nostrils, trying to calm the animal's rising panic.

It seemed as though an eternity passed as they remained hidden behind the fallen tree and Queen Saranor's scouting party slipped noiselessly by. Cazlina's chest hurt from the effort of holding her breath, but she dared not release it.

At last, the scouting party disappeared out of sight and she breathed freely again. Yanan assured her their presence had gone undetected.

What were they? She asked, still rather shaken by the close call. If Yanan had not been there to warn her, she would have ridden unsuspecting down the road, and the creatures would have been upon her before she knew it.

You do not want to know, Yanan replied. *I must go now, but you must warn the general of this.*

Cazlina stared into the eyes of the cat. *Aren't you coming with me into the city?*

The animal's whiskers twitched. *I am of the night. I cannot enter the cities of men. You must continue on into the city on your own. Be careful on the main road. There are patrols, which might delay you or prevent you from reaching the general. I do not think Saranor's scouting party will venture too close to Terrangay, but be alert.*

She saw a dark shadow detach itself from under the fallen tree and melt away into the night. "Wait!"

She felt a sense of loss and anxiety. What if she ran into Saranor's scouting party again or encountered a different one? How would she be able to detect their presence without the big cat to warn her ahead of time?

Tell the general my name and that I still live, the sibilant voice sounded faintly from a great distance.

He knows you? Cazlina asked, nonplussed.

She heard an almost inaudible hissing, as though the huge striped cat was chuckling. *He knows.*

Where did that creature go? Miris asked. *Has he gone for good?*

I think so, dear one.

I'm not certain I like this adventure anymore, Caz.

I'm not crazy about it myself, Cazlina answered, wryly, as they struck off in the direction of the walled city.

I wish that strong, handsome horse thief were with us now, Miris said, plaintively, as they pushed their way through the tangled branches and bushes.

We don't need him! Cazlina flared at once. *We are quite capable of looking after ourselves.*

Of course, you're right. The mare's tone became apologetic and soothing.

Cazlina sighed contritely. *I'm sorry, Miris. I didn't mean to shout at you. It's just the mere mention of that ruffian seems to make my blood boil.*

I wonder why he bothers you so much.

Cazlina leaned over the mare's shoulder and gave her a reproachful look. The animal gazed innocently back at her.

As they approached more open land, Cazlina could see the glow of the city lights off to her left. She found the road leading to Terrangay, and plodding along, she and Miris came across fences and pastures and silent, dark houses but saw no signs of people. A hushed, eerie stillness lay over the land, as though all life had been drained from it. No animals stood in any of the fields and pastures they passed, and Cazlina began to wonder if she and Miris were the only living beings in the whole countryside.

Signs of habitation became more evident as they neared the towering wall of the city. Tents and makeshift buildings had been set up outside the wall, making it seem as though a second, hastily erected city had sprung up overnight. Dark figures moved against the light of campfires and flickering torches, and Cazlina guessed the inhabitants in the outlying areas must have left their homes in order to be closer to the protection of Terrangay.

Cazlina hurried forward, hoping a patrol would not stop her before she reached the city gates. This turned out to be an unfounded concern. Although several other people travelled the main road leading up to Terrangay, no one seemed to give her more than a passing glance.

Up ahead, she saw two guards stationed on either side of the enormous closed gate. Massive iron lamps set into brackets high up on the wall flanked the wooden gate and brightly illuminated the road leading up to it.

As Cazlina neared the city, the towering wall overwhelmed her. Constructed of a pale brown stone, the wall stretched off into the distance on either side of the enormous gate, losing itself in the shadows outside the illumination of the lamps, and rising upward at least a hundred feet to meet the black sky. She could see two small guard towers directly over the gate on top of the wall, each manned by two soldiers. Points of flickering torch light further along the wall indicated the presence of even more towers and guards.

The city resembled a well-guarded fortress. She gazed worriedly at the daunting structure, wondering how difficult it was going to be to gain entry into it.

CHAPTER 6

The two guards eyed her suspiciously when she rode up to the gate. Their long lances came down at an angle, blocking her forward progress.

"What's your business here?" one of the burly men asked, curtly.

Cazlina drew herself up in the saddle, refusing to be intimidated by the guard's brusque manner. "I have very important news for General Viadon," she said, firmly. "It's imperative I be taken to him immediately."

The two guards exchanged glances.

The one who had spoken smirked at her and said, "What's so important that the general must be disturbed at this hour of the night?"

"My news is for his ears alone," she replied, coolly.

The other guard scowled. "Oh, really? And what makes you think he wants to hear it, boy?"

"I'm not a boy, and if I'm not allowed in to see General Viadon and tell him my business, I certainly won't hesitate to let it be known you refused entry to a messenger who carried vital information for the revolution."

The two men exchanged glances once more. This time there was a trace of uncertainty in their looks. They seemed to be weighing the possible consequences of refusing her entry into the city. If they dismissed her as a prankster and it was later revealed she did indeed have in her possession news crucial to the general's campaign, they would both be in deep trouble. On the other hand, if they allowed the general to be disturbed for no good reason at all, they would be punished as well.

"Where did you come by this news?" one of them asked.

"That doesn't matter," Cazlina said. "What matters is the general will be very unhappy if he doesn't hear what I have to say immediately."

"How do we know you're telling the truth?" the other man demanded.

"I give you my word. General Viadon must hear what I have to say, or Terrangay may be in very grave danger. We can stay out here for the rest of the night arguing, or you can let me into the city to deliver my news before it's too late."

Her serious manner seemed to be having an effect on the two guards. Although their demeanors suggested they still harbored suspicions, they also appeared on the verge of admitting her to the city. She held her breath, hoping for the best.

"You'd better be telling the truth, girlie," one of them growled. "If you're not, my friend and I are going to be very unhappy, and you really would not want that to happen. Is that understood?"

Cazlina nodded. "You don't have to worry. On the contrary, General Viadon will probably reward you for being alert and sensible."

Although they both stared at her as though questioning her sanity, she saw that they lifted their lances and reached to open the huge wooden gate.

"Where will I find the general?" she asked, as the gate slowly swung open on well-oiled hinges.

One of the guards shrugged. "Just ask anyone you meet. They'll direct you to him."

"Thank you."

She urged Miris forward, anxious to enter the city before they changed their minds.

You handled that very well, Caz, Miris said, as she trotted through the narrow opening. *I'm proud of you.*

Cazlina smiled smugly. *Thank you, dear one. I was rather persuasive, wasn't I?*

Despite the lateness of the hour, the city streets bustled with activity. She could hear music and loud laughter from several taverns that lined the main road.

Her first impression was that Terrangay was a fairly prosperous city, with paved streets lined not with the unstable, flickering light of torches, but with bright, steady lamps set high on black iron poles. Houses painted in various pastel shades of blue, green and pink and rising two or three stories high flanked the road.

The streets themselves followed the slope of the valley, winding in a seemingly haphazard manner between the rather closely set houses. Several huge impressive buildings, built of the same pale brown stone as the city wall, loomed out of the darkness. The buildings looked very official, and Cazlina could only speculate as to their purpose. Certainly, no such structures existed in the small village of Rothtown. Only the two-story, gray stone office of Barcas Frond, the town leader, could really be considered the most impressive building there. Until she had seen Terrangay, she had always found that building quite magnificent. Now, it seemed rather ordinary and commonplace in comparison to these grand structures, resplendent with carvings and balconies and manicured grounds.

As she rode down the paved street, gazing about in awe and wonder, she began to see evidence that not all in the great city was splendid and beautiful.

Loud, raucous music and drunken laughter spilled out of the extraordinary number of taverns that lined the street, and the pools of yellow lamplight revealed alleyways filled with refuse and rats between the buildings. Women in low-cut dresses that left little to the imagination hung on the arms of soldiers staggering down the street or stumbling in and out of the taverns. At one point, Miris had to step around a man lying in an intoxicated stupor in the middle of the road.

The shabby, appalling display of the men and women on Cazlina assumed was the main street of Terrangay tarnished her first impression of the city. She had to remind herself that this was a city filled with soldiers. Perhaps, such behavior helped them to cope with the stresses and worries of upcoming battles.

A woman in a tight blue dress hurried by, her dark hair tangled over her bare shoulders. Bright light from a street lamp brought out the harsh, taut lines in her heavily made-up face.

Cazlina called out to her. "Please, could you tell me where General Viadon has his headquarters?"

The woman glanced back at her, a faint scowl on her face. "What do you want to know for, boy?"

Cazlina didn't bother to correct her. Her appearance often led people to initially mistake her for a young male. Although the misconception annoyed her, she let it pass this time.

"I need to see him immediately. Could you please direct me to him?"

The woman stopped and then sidled forward, a sly expression on her brittle features. "Never mind the general, lad. How about you and me have a little fun together?"

Cazlina sighed. "It's very important I meet with General Viadon. Do you know where he is?"

The woman pressed against Cazlina's leg and peered coyly up at her. Her darkened eyebrows drew together into a frown. "Why, you're not a boy, after all! You're a girl." She licked bright red lips and smiled. "But, never mind. I'm not fussy, as long as you have money to pay for some fun."

Cazlina made a sound of disgust and pulled on Miris' reins, urging her away from the dreadful woman. Her strident voice followed them down the street.

"What's the matter, girl? Think you're too good for me, is that it? Think Luby is too old and can't do her job anymore, do you? Come back here, you young pup, and I'll show you what I can do!"

People turned curiously to look at the screeching woman and the object of her derision. Cazlina kept her gaze straight ahead, feeling her cheeks burning with humiliation.

What an awful woman, Miris said, in a shocked voice.

Yes, Cazlina agreed, grimly. *We must find General Viadon, Miris. I don't want to be out on these streets any longer than we have to.*

An old, white-haired man appeared on the street ahead of them and she approached him cautiously. He, at least, gave the impression of respectability, although he was somewhat deaf. When he finally understood her request, he proved to be more than cooperative.

He pointed down a street that curved off to the right. It seemed to lead to one of the official-looking buildings Cazlina had first noticed when she entered the city. "His headquarters are right there. Just follow that street. You can't miss it."

Cazlina thanked him and proceeded in the direction he'd pointed.

As she approached the well-lit, three-story building with its splendid statues of marble and bronze flanking the paved pathway to the entrance, she could see a lone guard standing at attention by the wide paneled door. Wryly, she wondered how long it would take to convince him she must see the general. Although she could understand the need for such stringent security measures, each delay meant that Queen Saranor's army could be moving closer to Terrangay without warning.

The guard glanced at her as she rode up to the entrance and dismounted. "Move along, lad," he said, dismissively. "You have no business here at this time of night."

She sighed inwardly. How many more times would she be mistaken for a boy this night?

She tried to look serious and credible. "Excuse me, sir, but it's imperative that I see General Viadon at once. I bring him news that is very important."

The guard's look of skeptical disbelief reminded her of the two guards she'd encountered outside the city walls. "Sure, that's what they all say," he said, bored. "Run along now before your mother and father wonder where you are."

She refused to budge. "Terrangay is in grave danger. Queen Saranor has a scouting party not more than a few miles from here. The general must be warned."

The guard gave her a hard glance. "What kind of nonsense are you trying to hand me?"

"It's *not* nonsense. I saw her scouting party on the road just east of here. There were maybe a dozen creatures in it and they were headed this way."

The guard stared at her earnest face. "If you're stringing me along, lad..."

"No, it's true! The general must be told at once. If this is an advance scouting party, then it must mean Queen Saranor's army is not far behind."

The guard hesitated and then said, "Wait here. I'll see if General Viadon will see you."

He tapped on the door behind him with his lance and a small flap immediately opened at head height. A round, pale face peered out.

"Someone is here to see the general. Claims to have seen a scouting party for Queen Saranor," the guard said.

The face in the opening nodded and the wooden flap closed.

Cazlina waited impatiently at the foot of the steps. The guard completely ignored her now, his duty done.

She wondered what she would do if General Viadon refused to see her. She'd have to find another way into the building, even if it meant forcing her way in. The general had to believe her story. She knew what she had seen and what Yanan had told her.

After what seemed an eternity, the wooden flap in the door opened again and the same face peered out. "The general will see the person now."

Cazlina exchanged a relieved glance with Miris and tied the mare's reins to a railing at the left of the door. *Wish me luck, dear one!*

CHAPTER 7

The guard opened the paneled door and Cazlina stepped inside.

A round-faced man, a sergeant from the looks of his uniform, stood waiting for her. His expression was neutral, neither hostile nor friendly. "This way," he said, turning to lead her down a long hallway.

The interior of the building proved to be every bit as impressive and elegant as the outside. Rich tapestries and paintings hung on the walls and splendid sculptures of marble and bronze filled several niches. *A rich man's palace hastily converted into an army's headquarters,* Cazlina thought, as her boots clicked sharply on the highly polished golden tiles of the floor.

Despite the lateness of the hour, she saw many officers and soldiers poring over maps and official-looking documents in several rooms along the hallway. They glanced up as she passed by, then promptly dismissed her and bent once more over their work.

Never had she been in the middle of a battle campaign. The general's headquarters hummed with muted activity and voices. In several places, huge maps had replaced the tapestries on the walls, and officers gave orders in crisp, authoritative tones. Passing soldiers glanced curiously at her as she followed the sergeant, staring around her in awe.

The sergeant led her up a wide staircase at the end of the hallway and along another corridor carpeted in deep, rich burgundy. Several feet down the hallway, he stopped and tapped on a pair of ornately carved doors.

Cazlina heard a deep masculine voice say, "Come in!"

The sergeant ushered her into a large, airy room. Rich draperies of white cloth patterned with pale roses hung from the ceiling to the floor along one entire wall, no doubt hiding several large windows. A huge desk covered with documents and maps sat in the middle of the room on a carpet of pale green as soft and plush as a thick lawn of grass. Off in one corner, a large canopied bed reclined behind partially closed curtains of the same white material that adorned the windows.

A man sat behind the desk, his dark head bent over a piece of paper in front of him. He looked up as the sergeant approached with Cazlina in tow.

General Darnellis Viadon was a handsome man with a neatly trimmed, gray-flecked brown beard and sharp brown eyes. Despite the lateness of the hour, he appeared alert and impeccably dressed in a steel-gray uniform. He had a reputation of being a very intelligent and shrewd man, and a strict leader, who expected and received the very best from the men and women who served under him.

His eyes regarded Cazlina coolly. "You claim to have seen a scouting party for Saranor," he said, without preamble. His tone suggested neither belief nor disbelief, but the fact he had consented to see her at all gave Cazlina encouragement.

She had no idea whether to bow to him, salute him, or offer him her hand in greeting. His reputation and military bearing intimidated her, and she found herself uncertain of the proper behavior to employ in his presence. In the end, she opted for standing as straight and tall as she could and assuming a persuasive expression.

"General, I'm sorry to disturb you at this hour of the night, but, on my way to your city, I spotted a scouting party for Queen Saranor and thought I must bring you this news immediately. They were no more than a few miles east of here."

He leaned back in the chair, his impassive expression unchanged. Beside her, she heard the sergeant make a low, derisive sound, and she narrowed her eyes, refusing to be discouraged by the lukewarm response to her news.

"You may go now, Sergeant," the general said curtly, and the man immediately saluted and left the room.

Viadon leaned forward once more, resting his clasped hands on the desk in front of him. His penetrating eyes caught and held Cazlina's. "These are perilous times," he said, gravely, "and I'm a very busy man. My time is too valuable to be wasted."

She kept her gaze locked on his. "I realize that, General," she said. "That's why I knew you would want to hear my news as soon as possible. The scouting party consists of at least a dozen members. I don't know what the creatures are, but they're definitely not human. They were travelling from the southeast, and, if it hadn't been for Yanan, I wouldn't have detected them at all."

The general glanced sharply at her. "Yanan?"

She hesitated, biting her lower lip and wondering how to tell him about the mysterious mountain cat that had appeared to her on the other side of the mountains. The general would certainly think her insane and throw her out on her ear.

Finally, after some internal debate, she opted for the unvarnished truth, sensing the shrewd man before her would immediately see through any fabrication or evasion.

Taking a deep breath, she said, "Yes, General. A mountain cat named Yanan was my guide through the mountains. He warned me of the scouting party before I ran right into it."

His keen eyes stared at her. She couldn't tell from his shuttered expression if he believed her or not. "How do you know the creature's name was Yanan?" he asked, in a neutral voice.

She hesitated again, trying not to shift under his penetrating gaze. "The cat told me his name," she said finally. Her body tensed in anticipation of the general's ire at being told such a ludicrous tale.

He frowned. "Told you?" he repeated, in a dangerously quiet voice.

Cazlina took another deep breath. "As implausible as it may sound, I'm able to communicate with animals. I can talk to them telepathically."

He stared at her silently. Finally, he asked, "Where are you from?"

"I'm from Rothtown. It's a small village in the northern part of Janix. My name is Cazlina Narzin."

"How long have you had this ability to communicate with animals, *Tanim* Narzin?"

"All my life. I discovered my powers when I was a very small child."

He leaned back in the chair and tilted his head to one side, contemplating her with his disturbingly direct gaze. "Are you certain this mountain cat said his name was Yanan?"

"Yes. I'm positive that was the name he gave." She plunged ahead, encouraged that he had not yet shouted for the sergeant to throw her out of the building. "The creature also said that you knew him."

Viadon did not respond at once. He tapped one finger on his chin, apparently lost in deep thought. A moment later, a faint smile twitched the corners of his mouth under the gray-flecked beard. "So, my old friend, you are not dead after all," he murmured.

"I beg your pardon, sir?" Cazlina was not certain if he spoke to her or to himself.

He didn't seem to hear her, his eyes staring thoughtfully off into space, and then he stood up suddenly. "*Tanim* Narzin, show me on the map exactly where you saw this scouting party." He beckoned her over to a huge map that completely covered one wall of the room.

Cazlina stared helplessly at it. "I'm sorry, General, but I'm not familiar at all with this area. Could you show me where Terrangay and the mountains are on the map?"

When he had pointed out the walled city and the range of low mountains to the east of it, she bit her lip, trying to remember exactly where she and Yanan had encountered the scouting party. After all, it had been dark, the stars her only light, and she had a very vague idea of how far from the city she had been.

Tentatively, she placed a finger on a section of the dirt road that led from the mountains toward Terrangay. "I think it was about here," she said, hesitantly. "But, I don't know for certain. I didn't see where the scouting party went after they passed. It was dark and the creatures were difficult to detect. They made virtually no noise at all."

"Saranor would make certain of that," Viadon said, grimly. "She would have chosen her creatures well for a scouting party." He gave Cazlina a sharp glance. "I trust that what you have told me is the truth, *Tanim* Narzin?"

She nodded. "Yes, sir. I have no reason to lie to you."

"Then, I thank you for bringing me this news. I will have the sergeant see you are given food and lodging for the night."

"General, there is one other thing. My brother has joined your army and I wondered if I could see him."

The general nodded. "Sergeant Zandorin can find out what regiment your brother is with and take you to him later this morning."

He started to turn away, but when she still hesitated in the middle of the room, he raised an eyebrow. "Is there something else, *Tanim* Narzin?"

She hesitated and then plunged on rapidly before she could lose her nerve. "I would also like to join your army."

"Oh?"

"I'm quite skilled in the use of a sword and dagger, even if I don't look very strong. And, I thought, perhaps, you could somehow use my ability to communicate with animals to your advantage."

He gazed silently at her. Finally, he said quietly, "War is a dangerous and bloody business, Cazlina Narzin. It is not a game."

"Yes. I'm fully aware of the dangers."

His eyes regarded her thoughtfully. "How do your parents feel about this decision of yours?"

"I have no parents. There's only my brother and me."

His lips twitched. "I presume your brother is unaware you have come here with the purpose of joining my revolution?"

She felt a flush of guilt stain her cheekbones. "I haven't been in touch with him since he left Rothtown two weeks ago, but I'm sure he'll understand when I explain to him I couldn't stay safely in our little town while Queen Saranor spreads her tyranny over the world."

The general gazed at her when she finished speaking. "There are going to be very dark times ahead, *Tanim* Narzin. Are you certain you want to subject yourself to the horrors and dangers of war?"

"I only know I can't hide under my bed while Saranor ruthlessly slaughters the people around me. I'm not foolish enough to believe I might not be killed, but that doesn't stop me from wanting to do my part."

The general clasped his hands behind his back and tilted his head, gazing steadily at her. She tried not to fidget.

"I will make certain you are reunited with your brother later this morning, *Tanim* Narzin," he finally said. "In the meantime, I would suggest you get some rest."

Before she had a chance to say anything further, Viadon strode briskly over to the ornate door. He opened it wide and spoke to the sergeant posted outside of it. "See that this young lady is given food and lodging for the night and then ask Captains Petros, Spargus and Belledar to come to my quarters."

The sergeant saluted smartly. "Yes, sir."

"And find out what regiment her brother is with." The general's eyes flicked to her. "What is his name?"

"Gareth. Gareth Narzin. But, General, what about...?"

He held up his hand. "I must deal with this news you have brought me, *Tanim* Narzin. Go with the sergeant now, please."

He turned on his heels and strode back over to the huge map on the wall, clearly dismissing her. Cazlina had no choice but to follow the sergeant out of the room.

CHAPTER 8

The sergeant led Cazlina and Miris to a stable situated directly behind the general's headquarters. The tantalizing, pungent smell of clean hay and horses greeted Cazlina as she entered the barn, and Miris whickered a soft greeting to the other animals, which poked their heads over the stall doors to peer curiously at the newcomers.

The large building housed several horses in clean, roomy stalls. Obviously, the previous owner had owned a great many horses and had taken good care of them. Now, the general and his senior officers kept their mounts in the stable.

The sergeant left Cazlina in the care of an elderly stableman, who talked constantly as he led her to a stall at the far end of the stable. She listened politely to the garrulous old man, but what she really wanted was to be left alone with Miris and to curl up on the sweet-smelling hay and fall fast asleep. The night had been a long one and she found herself exhausted.

The old man brought her bread and cheese to eat and a jug of cool water to wash the simple meal down. While

Cazlina munched tiredly on the food, he filled an oat pail to the brim for Miris, who gratefully sank her nose into it.

"You're a stranger around these parts, ain't you, young lady?" the stableman asked, watery blue eyes avidly curious. "I don't recall ever seeing you before tonight."

"Yes, I am new to this area," Cazlina replied, but did not elaborate. She simply felt too tired to engage in conversation.

The old man forked more hay into Miris' stall.

"My name's Grogan, by the way, Norbo Grogan," he said, cheerfully, totally oblivious to Cazlina's reluctance for talk. "I'm too old to serve in the army, so they put me in here to look after the horses. I don't mind. I want to help the general any way I can. He's a fine man, General Viadon, and he's going to send the wicked Queen Saranor running back to her castle with her tail between her legs, mark my words. She doesn't stand a chance of winning over the general."

Cazlina had to admire the loyalty of the old man. It served to reinforce her own decision to join General Viadon's cause, even though she had no idea if she would be allowed to do so. The general had been very noncommittal, giving her no clear indication of whether or not he would agree to her request.

She certainly didn't look forward to engaging in bloody combat. The thought of facing enemy soldiers terrified her--she could quite easily be killed. But, she couldn't simply cower in Rothtown while the world was plunged into bloody chaos. Gareth's concern for her safety was understandable, but, at the same time, she wanted to do her part to stop the wicked queen.

"You joining the general's army, miss?"

Cazlina started, having almost forgotten the presence of the old man in her ruminations.

He continued without waiting for her reply, "We've been getting new recruits in here every day, hundreds of them, all wanting to join the general's rebellion. His army is growing by leaps and bounds. There must be at least two thousand by now." The old man grinned, revealing several missing teeth. "This army ain't just for men, you know. You'd be amazed at how many pretty young things like yourself have joined, too."

Before she had a chance to respond, he moved on to another topic. "Pretty mare you have here," he said, admiring Miris' sleek red coat as he expertly ran a currycomb over her flanks. "Take good care of her, too, I see."

"Don't compliment her too much," Cazlina warned, wryly. "She already has a big enough ego."

Miris gave her a mildly reproachful look and mischievously rubbed her head against the old man's arm. *At least he appreciates my finer qualities.*

You are extremely spoiled, dear heart. Don't let it go to your head too much.

Grogan chuckled hoarsely. "They do tend to get that way sometimes, don't they? Lovely creatures, though. They don't give you orders or talk back and, as long as they get food and water, they usually don't bite you or step on your toes."

I only bite when I'm told to, Miris said, primly, and, then, only with the greatest reluctance.

Cazlina smiled inwardly at Miris' comment, and at Grogan. She rather liked the friendly stableman, but she could see he would stay there and talk for the remainder of the night if she did not politely ask him to leave.

"Thank you for taking such good care of us," she said, grasping his arm and guiding him gently but firmly out of the stall. "You're very kind."

She closed the stall door behind him and he looked disappointed.

"Well, if there's anything else you need, just let me know," he said. "I've got my own room down by the front entrance."

"I'll be sure to do that. Thank you."

He reluctantly made his way down the dim centre aisle of the stable, looking back over his shoulder at her with inquisitive eyes.

She sighed and sank to the floor of the stall, revelling in the sensation of the fresh, clean hay crackling around her. Despite being exhausted, a feeling of buoyant happiness pervaded her tired body. In a few hours, she would see her beloved brother once again. She had been terribly lonely and worried since he had left Rothtown. Even though he would probably be very angry with her for following him here, the sight of his dear face would make this strange and dangerous journey worthwhile.

She curled up in the hay, pillowing her head on her saddle. Within moments, she fell sound asleep.

When she finally awoke, feeling refreshed and revitalized, sunlight was streaming through the dusty windows in the stable. Miris contentedly munched on more oats in a corner of the stall. Her large, intelligent eyes rested lovingly on Cazlina's face. *How did you sleep, Caz?*

Very well. How about you?

I spent some time talking to the other horses, but then I had a nice nap. I like this place, Caz. I wish we could stay here.

I wish we could, too, dear heart, but I have a feeling we might be leaving soon, either because the general is going to kick us out, or because he may be engaging in battle with Saranor shortly.

Cazlina rose and brushed hay off her clothing. She wondered if there was a bathhouse close by where she could wash away the dust and grime of the last few days. It would not do for Gareth to see her in such a disheveled, unkempt state.

Norbo Grogan came down the centre aisle with a pitchfork in his hand, and Cazlina greeted him over the partition of the stall.

"Well, good morning, little lady. How are you this fine day?"

Cazlina smiled, more willing to engage in small talk now that her fatigue had been banished by sleep. She assured him she felt well and asked where she could find a place to wash.

"There's a fine bathhouse just behind the stable," Grogan informed her. "It's got fancy taps and tubs where you can get a hot bath. It's what the servants of the great house used to use, and the general allows all of us stable hands to take a bath there as often as we want."

"It sounds wonderful."

She picked up her saddlebags. "If Sergeant Zandorin comes to get me before I'm back, will you please tell him where I am and ask him to wait?"

"Sure, no problem."

She gave Miris a gentle slap on her sleek neck and left the mare happily munching on her breakfast.

Emerging from the dim interior of the stable, Cazlina blinked in the bright sunlight.

The yard between the stable and the building that housed the general's headquarters bustled with activity and noise. Soldiers on foot and horseback paraded up and down the extensive grounds to the shouted orders of commanding officers. Blacksmiths pounded on anvils and thrust newly made swords and lances into buckets of water, sending noisy clouds of steam into the air. At first glance, it seemed chaotic, but as Cazlina watched, she could see the discipline and organization that underlay all the frenetic activity.

Overhead, she heard the loud beating of wings and looked up to see at least a hundred huge birds darting back and forth in precise V formations. On closer examination, she realized, in astonishment, they were not birds at all, at least not in the strictest sense. Although they did possess wings, they had multi-colored, iridescent scales instead of feathers covering their bodies and a head similar to a horse, although narrower, on their long necks. The wings themselves were strikingly beautiful, transparent and veined with thin membranes of black, gold and blue. Each creature carried a diminutive woman upon its back, strapped into an elaborate harness that enabled her to keep her hands free to wield a long, strange-looking tube of shiny metallic material.

As Cazlina watched in amazement, one of the creatures swooped low to the ground and the tiny woman on its back pointed the tube at a small bush. Astonishingly, orange flame leapt from the tube and completely disintegrated the bush.

Cazlina grabbed the arm of a passing soldier. "Excuse me, but what are those creatures up there?" she asked.

The young man grinned. "You've never heard of the Fire Birds?"

She shook her head.

"They're hydriths from the Yaltez domain," the soldier explained. "Those women on their backs are soldiers from the same area, who train the hydriths for combat from the air. I've heard they're very impressive in battle, and, from what I've seen so far in their practices, I can believe it."

"They're beautiful!" Cazlina breathed.

"And deadly," the young man said. He gave her an apologetic grin. "Sorry I can't stay and talk longer. Sergeant Brayth wants me to load up one of the wagons. He gets pretty grumpy if you don't hop to it when he gives an order."

He hurried off, leaving Cazlina to watch in fascination as the hydriths performed elaborate maneuvers in the air, guided expertly by the tiny women on their backs.

After a few more minutes, she realized she was wasting time. Sergeant Zandorin would probably be coming to get her soon and she still needed to take a bath.

She searched for the bathhouse and spotted a small stone building behind the stable. A few men and women were entering and departing the building with articles of clothing in their hands. That must be it, she reasoned.

When she entered the humid, steamy building, she saw a long hallway with several rooms opening on either side. The rooms had carved wooden doors, which gave her a sense of relief. She had been afraid there would be just one large room with several tubs and no privacy. The same sandy-colored stone that was prevalent throughout the city had been used for the walls and red clay tiles lined the floor of the hallway. People passed her in the corridor, giving her no more than a cursory glance.

Cazlina stepped into an empty room and closed the door behind her, latching it against the possibility of someone barging in on her. A large oblong tub with ornate gold faucets almost filled the small room. An oval mirror hung on one wall, and a wooden bench provided a place to put her saddlebags.

When she turned the faucets on, hot water gushed out, filling the room with steam. She saw several jars of bath oils and soaps lined up on one corner of the large tub, and a fluffy towel hanging on a hook on the wall.

While the tub filled with water, she opened a glass jar with green liquid in it and sniffed. It smelled like fresh summer breezes and flowers. She dumped a generous amount into the steamy water. In seconds, the room filled with the wonderful scent of the bath oil.

The hot water felt like velvet on her skin when she slipped out of her grimy clothes and into the tub. She sank into delicious bubbles up to her nose. She could have stayed immersed in the tub the whole day, but she was anxious to see Gareth. In addition, she wanted another audience with the general to convince him she would make a valuable contribution to his revolution.

Reluctantly, she finished bathing and stepped out of the tub, feeling considerably more human than she had earlier. She pulled clean clothes out of her saddlebags and hurried through her dressing, giving her short chestnut hair a quick combing with her fingers.

Critically, she surveyed her image in the steamed-up mirror and frowned, wishing her pixie face and pert nose did not make her look quite so young.

Her chin rose resolutely. Despite her unimposing appearance, she *would* convince the general she possessed considerable skills that she could bring to his cause.

CHAPTER 9

As she returned to the stable, she saw Sergeant Zandorin standing just outside the double doors with another man beside him. She almost didn't recognize Gareth in his steel-gray uniform and knee-high black boots. His chestnut hair, grown longer than when she had last seen him, framed a face deeply tanned from the sun. He looked tired but fit, and, even from this distance, she could sense the pent-up energy and excitement in him.

He had never been one to be content with just sitting and doing nothing. In Rothtown, there had been very little to challenge an adventurous spirit such as his, so, when he had heard about General Viadon's rebellion against Queen Saranor, he had leaped at the chance to do something worthwhile with his life...even if that something proved to be extremely dangerous and liable to get him killed.

Eyeing him critically as she approached the stable, Cazlina had to admit soldiering suited her big brother very well.

"Gareth!"

He looked up at the sound of her voice and his blue eyes widened in delight. "Caz!"

He strode forward and enveloped her in a hug that almost crushed her slim body. She didn't mind one bit. It felt good to see him and touch him once more, and she snuggled against his chest, breathing in the heady odor of horses and manly sweat pervading his uniform.

After a few moments, he set her away from him, his eyes beginning to darken with the anger she had predicted he would react with upon sight of her. "What in the name of all the gods are you doing here, Caz? I couldn't believe it when the sergeant told me you were in Terrangay. What kind of foolish, hare-brained...?"

She held up her hand. "Before you go spouting off righteous indignation, dear brother, hear me out first. I was worried about you. I wasn't even sure if you had made it safely to Terrangay since you never bothered to let me know when you arrived."

To her secret delight, a guilty flush stained his tanned cheeks. "I'm sorry about that. I should have sent you word before now, but it's been absolutely mad around here. I guess I forgot."

She smiled inwardly. That was one way to deflect his anger, make him feel guilty first.

Crossing her arms, she sternly looked him up and down. "Here I've been worrying myself sick about you, and you look like you're having the time of your life."

However, this time, her offensive stance failed to distract him.

He frowned at her. "Never mind me. What about you? I thought I told you to stay in Rothtown. By Donar's breath, girl, don't you ever listen to me? It's not safe anywhere else right now with Saranor running around the countryside with her godforsaken army." He ran his hand distractedly through his hair. "Honestly, Caz, sometimes I wonder where your brain is."

She started to bristle. "Now, wait a minute, Gareth. I have just as much right to be here as you do. What makes you think you're the only one who can fight against Saranor?"

He stared at her, horror dawning in his eyes. "Don't tell me you've enlisted in the army?" He grabbed her shoulders. "You didn't, did you?" He shook her gently. "Tell me you didn't do something so stupid!"

She pulled away, frowning. His patronizing attitude tempted her to say she had done just that to punish him, but she couldn't bring herself to tell an outright lie. "Not exactly," she said.

As his face registered relief, she continued, "I intend to enlist. In fact, I've already spoken to the general and told him I wanted to join his rebellion." She deliberately omitted telling him General Viadon had not yet accepted her request. Then again, he hadn't outright rejected it, either.

Gareth's eyes turned a deep sapphire blue as they blazed in anger. "Are you crazy?" he exploded, and several nearby soldiers looked their way, curious about the commotion.

"Hush, big brother," she admonished, putting a restraining hand on his arm. She certainly didn't need him creating a scene in the general's courtyard. "I'm not crazy," she said. "I've thought long and hard about this. It wasn't an easy decision, especially since I knew you would be upset."

"Damn right I'm upset," he exclaimed, but kept his voice lowered this time.

"General Viadon needs all the able-bodied men and women he can get to fight against Saranor's army. You said so yourself. No place is safe as long as she's out there spreading her evilness. Not even Rothtown. In fact, I'm probably safer here than in Rothtown." She waved her hand at the bustling activity going on around them. "This is a trained army that can defend itself against Saranor if she attacks. There is no such army in the village. What chance would I have if Saranor came there?"

"That's not the point," Gareth growled. "I don't want you here in the middle of the action. You could get killed!"

She glared at him. "So could you! Do you think I would feel better hiding under my bed in Rothtown, not knowing if you were alive or dead? At least, being here I am aware of some of the goings-on."

His face looked stricken. "I love you, Caz. I don't want anything to happen to you."

Her demeanor softened. "I know. I love you, too. That's why you have to let me do this. I would sooner die with you by my side than without you."

He grimaced and pulled her tightly against his chest once more, his voice muffled against her still-damp hair. "I swear you have a stubborn streak in you the size of the Telagor Sea."

"Matched only by your manly ego," she teased, smiling against his chest.

She pulled away and looked up at him, serious once more. "Please don't be angry with me anymore. I'm here and I intend to join General Viadon's army. Make it easy on both of us and accept it."

He remained silent for a moment, looking down into her earnest face. Then, he finally shook his head, his face settling into lines of resignation. "I should know better by now not to try and change your mind when you have it made up," he said, wearily. "Besides, if you try to go back to Rothtown now, there's no telling what dangers you might run into. At least here, I can keep an eye on you."

She hid a smile. Little did he know of the dangers she had already faced on her way to Terrangay. She wanted to tell him about her adventures, but now did not seem like a good time. She would wait until his irritation with her had cooled down a bit more.

The droll voice of the sergeant sounded beside them, and Cazlina started, having forgotten the presence of the other man in her tumultuous reunion with Gareth.

"If you two are done shouting at each other, the general would like to see both of you in his office," Sergeant Zandorin said.

Cazlina stared at him, her heart thumping. What did this summons by the general mean? Did he intend to berate her for being foolish, as Gareth had just done, and send her packing home? The stubborn streak Gareth had complained about made her narrow her eyes in anticipation of a battle of wills between her and the general.

Gareth, too, looked startled by the sergeant's words. "Wha-What for?" he stammered.

The man scowled. "How should I know?" he said. "I don't question his orders and neither should you. Now, come along. You don't want to keep him waiting, do you? He's a very busy man."

Cazlina and Gareth exchanged uneasy glances and then followed the sergeant across the busy courtyard, dodging the platoons of soldiers practising their drills. The Fire Birds swooped overhead, their swift shadows racing across the dusty ground. Every now and then, a bush would erupt into flame and Cazlina would jump, her nerves tautened in anticipation of the upcoming audience with the general.

A different man guarded the entrance to the general's headquarters this time. He saluted smartly and opened the door when the sergeant approached him with Cazlina and Gareth trailing reluctantly behind. Sergeant Zandorin ushered them into the same upstairs office-bedroom where Cazlina had met with the general earlier that morning. This time, Viadon stood at one of the tall windows at the end of the room, gazing out at the activity in the courtyard below. Sunlight crept across the pale green carpet, and the general still wore his neat gray uniform. Cazlina wondered if the man had even been to bed yet.

The sergeant left her and Gareth standing by the huge wooden desk and exited the room. They kept silent, waiting for the general to acknowledge their presence, and Cazlina tried not to fidget nervously.

Finally, Viadon turned from the window to face them. His penetrating gaze fell on her, and she felt her cheeks redden. "Ah, *Tanim* Narzin. I trust you slept well and enjoyed your reunion with your brother."

She refused to look at Gareth as she said, "Yes, sir, thank you, I did."

A faint smile touched the general's lips, and Cazlina wondered if he had witnessed the turbulent reception she had received from her brother.

Viadon's gaze moved to Gareth standing tensely at her side. "*Tan* Narzin, no doubt your sister has told you of the invaluable news she brought to me earlier this morning?"

Gareth looked startled and glanced at Cazlina. "No, sir, I was not aware of any such news."

The general raised his eyebrow. "Oh? Well, perhaps she didn't have a chance to tell you in the excitement of your reunion."

Before Cazlina could respond, he continued, "Cazlina encountered a scouting party for Queen Saranor on the road leading to Terrangay, and, with a great deal of courage, made her way to the city to warn me of the presence of these enemy soldiers. Her bravery and quick thinking in eluding the scouting party and bringing me this disturbing news has enabled me to send out a squadron of my own troops to intercept Saranor's creatures before they can do any damage. You should be very proud of your sister, young man."

Both Cazlina and Gareth stared at him in astonishment.

Cazlina had come to this meeting fully expecting to be lectured for being a nuisance and ordered to return home to Rothtown. She certainly had not been prepared for the lavish praise the general heaped on her. She searched his face carefully for signs of duplicity, but could detect none as he gazed sternly at Gareth.

The young man gulped and stammered, "Y-Yes, sir, I-I'm very proud of her."

He stole a bewildered glance at Cazlina, but she could only shrug.

Eyes unreadable, General Viadon continued, "Because of the important contribution Cazlina has already made to my campaign, I have decided to accept her offer to join my army."

Gareth's face paled. "But, sir, I-I don't think that's a good idea. She-She's just a girl!"

Cazlina tightened her lips and jabbed him sharply in the side with her elbow. He winced.

The general looked at Cazlina. "How old are you, *Tanim* Narzin?"

"Twenty-two, sir."

He nodded. "Old enough to make your own decisions, I would surmise. Do you still wish to enlist in the army, or have you changed your mind after having had a chance to think it over?"

Aware of Gareth standing tensely by her side, she didn't look at him as she shook her head resolutely. "I have not changed my mind. I still wish to serve in your army."

"Caz, don't be crazy," Gareth whispered, fiercely. "It's too dangerous!"

"We've already been through this," she hissed back. "The general is right. It's *my* decision."

From across the room, Viadon spoke up. "It's quite understandable that you are worried about your sister, *Tan* Narzin. War is a bloody business and the harsh reality is that she, or any one of us, for that matter, may not survive it. Unfortunately, Saranor has left us no choice. I need a large, able-bodied army if I wish to defeat her, and I'd be foolish to turn away anyone willing to help me achieve that goal."

"But-But..."

The general's sharp gaze quelled the objections rising up from Gareth and the young man subsided reluctantly. If the situation had not been so serious, Cazlina would have smiled at the miserable expression on her big brother's face. He wanted desperately to argue with the general but knew it would be a losing battle on his part.

"Cazlina, you will become a member of my immediate staff, reporting directly to me," General Viadon said. "I believe your abilities will be best served in the capacity of scout."

Cazlina felt an absurd mixture of relief and annoyance.

It annoyed her that the general, despite his earlier praise for her, probably thought her too young and inexperienced to be of much use in battle and wanted to keep her out of the action as much as possible. Scouting, although dangerous, would probably be relatively safer, provided she remained vigilant and careful at all times. On the other hand, the thought of participating directly in bloody battle certainly did not appeal to her, either.

"That's all for now," Viadon's voice interrupted her thoughts. "I will be scheduling a meeting with my senior officers later this morning and will send for you then, Cazlina."

He contemplated the two young people standing by his desk and his eyes twinkled faintly with amusement. "In the meantime, I would suggest you both take advantage of the short time you have to catch up on each other's activities. I intend to leave Terrangay shortly and there won't be much opportunity for socializing after that."

CHAPTER 10

After leaving the general's headquarters, Gareth did not take Viadon's advice and spend more time with Cazlina. Instead, he stated tersely that he had to get back to his regiment and stalked off, his back stiff with anger and resentment.

Cazlina watched him go with a heavy heart. She wanted to run after him and try to explain once again the reasons for her decision, but she knew it would be pointless. He needed time to cool down and perhaps then he would be able to listen to her with a more open mind. She took solace in the fact he could never stay angry with her for very long. Of course, she had never deliberately placed herself in such danger before today, so it might take some time for him to get used to the notion. She had known her coming to Terrangay would not sit well with her brother, but she had hoped their reunion would have been more joyful and less confrontational.

Sighing faintly, she returned to the stable where Miris waited.

The mare bobbed her head when Cazlina approached. The animal's eyes shone with sympathy as she picked up on her mistress' unhappiness. *Gareth is worried about you. He thinks your actions are foolhardy, because he's afraid of losing you.*

I know, Cazlina sighed, *but I'm tired of being treated like a little girl. He's just going to have to understand I'm an adult now and responsible for my own actions.*

Give him time. I'm sure he'll come to that realization. For now, you're still his little sister.

Cazlina laid her cheek against the mare's warm sleek neck and smiled wryly. *You know, Miris, for all my bluster to Gareth and the general about how brave and grown-up I am, I suddenly do feel like a very small child. In a little while, we're going to be facing Queen Saranor and her army and the thought terrifies me.*

Miris rubbed her cheek against Cazlina's short chestnut hair. *Don't despair, Caz. As long as we have each other, we'll never have to face danger alone.*

When the summons from the general came two hours later, Cazlina couldn't help experiencing a jolt of panic that left her heart tripping erratically in her chest. Now that she had officially become part of the general's army, the cold reality began to seep through the impassioned fervor that had led her to leave the safety of Rothtown and travel across a strange, unknown country to join a revolution. The days ahead promised to be dark and dangerous, and she wondered if she really possessed the courage necessary to survive them.

After being shown into General Viadon's office, she noticed three other men in the room besides the general. From the looks of their uniforms, she assumed them to be high-ranking officers and felt rather intimidated by their presence.

The general came toward her, sensing her hesitation. He took her by the elbow and gently guided her toward the waiting men.

"Cazlina Narzin, may I present my senior officers, Captains Kadan Spargus, Malak Petros and Reedis Belledar. Gentlemen, this is the young lady I was telling you about."

They nodded politely and regarded her with curious, probing eyes. She fidgeted a little under their speculative gazes, wondering what the general had said about her.

Captain Spargus, a lean man with a rather angular, sharp-nosed face, said with a trace of skepticism, "General Viadon tells us a mountain cat calling himself Yanan appeared to you last night."

She glanced at the general and he nodded his approval for her to answer.

"Yes, sir, that's right," she replied, as calmly as she could.

"I understand you talked to the animal?" Captain Petros asked. Short and a little plump, he had dark hair slicked back over a round skull. From the lack of expression in his voice, Cazlina couldn't tell if he believed her or not.

"That's correct, sir. Since I was a small child, I've been able to connect telepathically with the minds of animals. I can understand their thoughts and they can understand mine. I have no idea how or why I can do this, but I can."

"So, this Yanan was able to communicate with you?" the third man asked. Captain Belledar was tall and muscular and had a shock of white-blond hair curling over his ears. He seemed the least suspicious of the three and she turned eagerly to him.

"Yes. Yanan was my guide through the mountains, and he also warned me about the scouting party before I ran into it. Then he disappeared back into the night."

"As I told you, gentlemen, *Tanim* Narzin has come to us with quite a tale," General Viadon said, eyes flashing to where she stood rather uncertainly in the middle of the room. She tried not to shrink under his shrewd gaze and wondered if now would be the moment when he would laugh uproariously in her face and condemn her in front of his officers for daring to come to him with such an outlandish story.

Once again, the general surprised her when he continued on in a serious tone, "I, for one, am inclined to believe her story. It may sound far-fetched, but I don't believe she's making it up. Are you, Cazlina?"

She shook her head vigorously. "No, General. What I've told you is the absolute truth."

"But, Mattius Yanan as a mountain cat...?" Petros asked. "How is that possible? The last we heard, he was dead."

"So we believed, Malak." Viadon nodded. "Maybe Saranor didn't kill him as we first thought. Maybe, she punished him instead, by having her mage turn him into the animal Cazlina saw last night."

"That's possible, I suppose," Petros mused. "But, if it really is Mattius Yanan, why hasn't he come to Terrangay? Surely he knows we're here."

Cazlina listened to the conversation with growing astonishment. The officers seemed to be implying the black and white striped cat named Yanan was actually a *man*!

She recalled the words of the animal when he had urged her to warn the general about the scouting party, and she spoke up tentatively, "Excuse me, but, perhaps, Yanan *can't* come here."

"What do you mean?" Viadon asked.

"When I asked him about coming into the city with me, he said he was of the night and didn't belong in the cities of men. Maybe he meant he can't enter populated areas, because the spell prevents him from doing so. Is that possible?"

"You may be right," Viadon said, thoughtfully.

"This is none of my business, but--who exactly is this Mattius Yanan and why would Saranor turn him into an animal?" Cazlina asked.

The general didn't seem to resent her question. "Yanan is--*was* an advisor of Saranor's. He was also a very good friend of mine and shared my aversion for her campaign of terror. He fell out of favor with her and suddenly disappeared shortly before I was forced to leave the castle. It was widely believed Saranor had killed him. Now, it appears that might not have happened at all."

He walked over to his desk. "Gentlemen, for the moment I would suggest we accept Cazlina's story and get on with more important matters."

He motioned toward the comfortable chairs arranged in front of his desk and then sat down in his own chair. He clasped his hands on the desktop and leaned forward. "I have not yet heard anything from the troop I sent out earlier this morning to search for Saranor's scouting party. That doesn't surprise me, as I'm sure the queen has chosen creatures that will be difficult for our soldiers to detect. But, I don't want to wait any longer. If she's sending scouts this close to Terrangay, she's getting bolder. We must prepare to move the troops out today."

Spargus nodded. "I agree. The squadrons are ready. I can have the commanding officers briefed and prepared to depart within an hour."

"I've already sent messages to the troops in the mountains," Belledar said. "They are to maintain their positions until told otherwise."

Viadon nodded. "Good. Malak, what news have we received from our forces in the west?"

The plump man leaned forward. "So far it's been quiet, but I did get word that flashes of light have been spotted on the horizon in the direction of the Telagor Sea."

The general pursed his lips thoughtfully. "Nostrimus' magic, no doubt." And added for Cazlina's benefit, "Nostrimus is Saranor's mage."

He stood up and moved over to the huge map hanging on the wall, pointing to several locations. "I want troops stationed here, here and here. All the passes to the mountains must be blocked completely. One squadron of five hundred soldiers is to be sent west to the Telagor Sea to join with the forces already there. Another squadron will be sent north toward the Lorrin Plains. Malak, I want you to join the western forces with your group, and, Kadan, the northern troops. Reedis, you will continue to be in charge of the eastern forces. I will take command of the southern squadron and Cazlina will accompany me. Kadan, I also want you to see to the dispersion of the Fire Birds. Split them up into four squadrons to accompany the four regiments on the ground. I want the troops ready to leave in one hour." He nodded at his officers. "That will be all."

The three men rose and saluted, then hurried out of the room.

Cazlina also stood up, feeling shaken by the rapidity and urgency of the orders issued by General Viadon. Within an hour, she would be at the forefront of an attacking army. The knowledge felt like an anvil hanging precariously over her head, ready to fall on her and crush her. She had barely arrived in Terrangay and already events had accelerated so rapidly she felt as though the very breath was rushing from her body.

The general glanced at her. "Are you ready for this, Cazlina?"

She felt a flush stain her cheeks as she realized he had probably seen every doubt and fear cross her face. She straightened her shoulders. "No, sir," she confessed, honestly. "But, I promise I will do my best for you."

He smiled. "That's all I ask of any of my soldiers. Prepare to leave in an hour. We'll meet in the courtyard by the stable."

She nodded and left the room.

Back at the stable, she leaned weakly against the stall door and said, "Well, this is it, Miris. Tell me again I'm doing the right thing."

The mare gazed at her with sympathetic eyes. *You can always change your mind, Caz. I'm sure the general would understand.*

Cazlina shook her head stubbornly. "No, I've committed myself to this venture and I won't turn tail and run now. I could never live with such cowardice."

A coward you are definitely not, Caz. I will be very proud to carry such a brave heart into battle.

Cazlina felt tears prick the corners of her eyes and laid her cheek against the mare's warm sleek neck. Miris had always been such a loyal and loving friend. Cazlina only hoped she wasn't leading the mare to a certain death just to prove something to herself and to Gareth. She shook off her morbid mood and saddled the mare.

Earlier, she had been given enough rations and water to last for several days and she slung the full saddlebags over Miris' back. She had also been given a freshly forged sword to strap around her slim waist. The blacksmith, upon observing her slender frame, had handed her a finely honed weapon that was remarkably lightweight and shorter than a regular sword.

"She may feel as light as a feather, my girl, but she's got as keen an edge as any larger sword and she'll stand you well in battle."

She hardly felt the weight of the weapon around her waist, but the brush of it against her left thigh somehow reassured her. Her own dagger was still tucked into the waistband of her trousers.

Even with having the physical weapons to fight the upcoming battles and the stout heart of a loyal friend to carry her through whatever perils awaited her in the dark future, she couldn't help but wonder if she possessed the moral strength necessary to control her fear and act boldly in the face of danger.

CHAPTER 11

Cazlina led Miris from the dim, peaceful stable to the chaotic courtyard awash with bright sunlight. Several squadrons of troops were already lined up in preparation for departure. The many faces staring straight ahead carried a mixture of expressions ranging from fear, excitement, panic and anticipation. Several also had the glazed, woebegone look of someone in the throes of a nasty hangover. No doubt, many of them had frequented the noisy taverns Cazlina had observed on her entrance into the city the night before and now suffered from their over-indulgence.

The jingle of bridles, the stamp of hundreds of feet and hooves, and the shouted orders of the commanding officers rang out in the dusty air. Overhead, the measured beating of the Fire Birds' wings added to the din of the huge army.

Cazlina urgently searched the faces of the soldiers filling the courtyard, hoping to see Gareth one more time before the army left Terrangay. The abrupt way they had departed earlier weighed heavily on her heart, and she didn't want to leave their disagreement unresolved before it proved too late.

Her wish was answered a moment later when she heard a resounding, "Caz!"

She spun around, her gaze widening in relief. "Gareth, there you are! I was hoping to see you before we left."

He ran his hand through his tousled hair. "I'm sorry I shouted at you earlier. I shouldn't have been so hard on you."

She shook her head. "No, I'm the one who should apologize. I tried to bully you into accepting my motivations for coming to Terrangay without giving you a chance to adjust to the idea. I'm sorry for causing you so much worry."

He enveloped her in a hard hug. "I think you were *born* to cause me worry, dear sister," he gruffly teased.

As he pulled away, his face twisted in a slight grimace. "As the general so clearly pointed out, you're old enough to make your own decisions. As much as I would like to be able to keep you hidden away in some secret place safe from all dangers, I've come to realize that isn't possible, especially now with Saranor spreading her poison over the world. And I think the general has a soft spot in his heart for you."

"What are you talking about?"

He grinned. "I've just found out my regiment has been assigned to the general's command, which tells me he realizes you need your big, brave brother around to protect you."

Cazlina's heart leaped with happiness at the prospect of not being separated from Gareth as they marched off into the uncertainties and perils of war. The knowledge boosted her spirits so much she didn't even react to his comment about her needing his protection.

"That's wonderful, Gareth."

He gripped her shoulders. "Since I won't be by your side every minute, you have to promise me you'll be careful. Don't go taking any foolish and unnecessary risks."

"I don't want to be a hero," she said, quietly. "I just want to help the general defend the world against Saranor."

"All right, because if I hear of you pulling any idiotic stunts, I'll personally thrash you within an inch of your life."

She smiled with amusement. "With a brother like you, who needs enemies? Seriously, Gareth, I don't intend to put myself in unnecessary danger if I can help it. I have a feeling the general will make sure that doesn't happen, either, when he gives me my assignments."

Gareth scowled. "That's the only good thing about this whole mess. I'm glad the general took you under his wing."

She frowned at him. "You make it sound as though I need to be sheltered like a child."

He held up his hand. "Don't go getting all defensive on me again. I know you're not some weak, helpless female. I still have a sore rib from when you jabbed your elbow in my side in the general's office. I only meant you'll probably be a little safer under his command than if you were placed in the common rank and file."

She sniffed. "Well, I'm glad you have a sore rib. You deserve it for calling me 'just a girl'. I'm twenty-two and quite capable of looking after myself. After all, wasn't that what I was doing in Rothtown when a certain someone decided he had to rush off to become a soldier in Terrangay?"

"You're absolutely right," he conceded with a sheepish grin.

"Well, well, if it isn't my lady and her splendid horse."

Cazlina thought she was hearing things at first. The deep, masculine voice that came from directly behind her sounded remarkably like that of the horse thief she had left on the other side of the mountains the day before. She pivoted on her heel, startled to see that the tall man with the curly hair and maddening grin standing behind her was indeed Jorin Montrill, whom she had completely forgotten about in the excitement of the last day.

Her first instinct was to lash out at him in anger for having followed her again. Then, she remembered there had been no time to tell Gareth about her adventures on the journey to Terrangay. She hesitated for a moment and then decided that telling her brother the whole truth at this point would only serve to make him more upset than he'd been earlier. His protective attitude toward her might even lead him to physically attack Montrill, which she definitely did not want to encourage. One scene in the general's courtyard was more than enough for one day. Besides, her uneasy relationship with the frustrating horse thief was her problem, not her brother's.

Her lips tightened as she fought to keep her voice calm. "Gareth, will you excuse me for a moment? I need to talk to this man."

Gareth glanced from her to Jorin, his eyes narrowing a little. "Sure, I'll be over here." He walked off a short distance and stood watching them behind a suspicious frown.

Cazlina turned back to face Jorin. "What are *you* doing here?" she demanded, trying to keep her voice down.

He pretended to look hurt. "Now, now, Cazlina, is that any way to greet an old friend?"

She placed her hands on her hips and glared at him. "You followed me again! Didn't you take my warning seriously the last time? I thought you said you valued your life, pitiful though it may be."

"I believe I said *poor*, not pitiful."

"Oh!" She stamped her foot. "If you don't stop plaguing me, I swear I'll wipe that silly grin from your face."

He stepped back a pace and held up his hands. "I certainly wouldn't want that, my lady. I'm rather partial to my face the way it is, thank you."

"Then stop tormenting me," she said, coldly. "Or you'll be sorry you ever laid eyes on me."

"Please, can't we put the unfortunate incident with your mare behind us and be friends? After all, we'll probably be spending a great deal of time together and I would rather not have to watch my back the whole time. It'll be enough to have to do that with the enemy."

She stared at him. "What are you talking about?"

He bowed, sweeping one arm across the front of his body. "Behold the latest recruit to General Viadon's army. I signed up this morning."

"What?"

His eyes danced with mischief. "I've been assigned to the general's command, which I believe is where you've been assigned, as well. So, you see, my lady, it appears we'll be fighting alongside each other."

Oh, how splendid! Miris exclaimed.

Cazlina felt too shocked to even respond to the mare's apparent delight. She could only stare dumbfounded at the man in front of her, unable to believe her ears.

He surveyed the activity and noise going on around them and seemed oblivious to her stunned silence. "I certainly never thought I would ever be a soldier. I hate being told what to do," he commented and then shrugged.

"Oh, well, I guess it's time for a change. Besides, I always was the adventurous sort."

His twinkling gaze swung back to her. "So, this is the mysterious mission you were bent on. Rather unusual, isn't it, for a young woman like you to join a revolution? Not many would be so brave or so foolish."

At last, she found her tongue and said caustically, "You know nothing about me, and it's none of your business whether I'm being brave or foolish." Her temper snapped as she took one step closer. "Stay out of my way, Montrill," she warned, "or you shall find yourself on the receiving end of *my* sword instead of Saranor's."

"My, my, who would ever think such violent tendencies exist in you."

Her lips tightened. "If I were you, I wouldn't be foolish enough to test those tendencies."

"Rest assured, I may be reckless, but I am not suicidal!"

Caz, surely you don't mean to follow through with any of your threats? Miris asked, in a surprised tone of voice. *I've never seen you so angry and upset.*

Cazlina sighed inwardly; feeling shocked herself at the intensity of her emotions. *I would never actually attack him,* she conceded guiltily, *unless, of course, I had a very good reason.*

The mare rested her chin lightly on Cazlina's shoulder. *I think you're being too harsh on him. I don't believe he harbors any ill intentions toward you.*

Well, maybe not. But he's still aggravating! He admits to being a horse thief. How can I possibly trust him not to steal you away from me some night while I'm asleep?

She sighed in frustration and stole a glance at Jorin Montrill, who was regarding her with amused eyes, seemingly unperturbed by her heated threats.

"Wouldn't it be better for both of us if we were to learn to get along instead of fighting each other?" he asked, plaintively. "After all, we'll soon be involved in conflict against Saranor and her troops. I would much sooner have your sword put to use against the enemy than against me."

"Oh, don't be ridiculous," she snapped. "Of course I wouldn't really kill you."

"No apology needed," he said, cheerfully, even though she had not apologized. "On the contrary, I admire your tenacity and feistiness. It'll do you in good stead during the battles ahead." He grinned. "From what I observed in the mountains, you are quite capable of handling yourself in dangerous situations."

She glanced suspiciously at him. "What do you mean, from what you observed in the mountains?"

"I'm referring to those two fellows in the pass. You know, I actually felt a little sorry for them when they chose to tangle with you. The poor fools had no inkling of what they were getting themselves into."

"You *were* following me! Otherwise, how would you know about those two men?"

He shrugged. "I just happened to be in the neighborhood," he said, innocently. "I was too far away to be of much help when I realized you were in danger, but when I *did* reach the pass, I could see my service weren't needed, after all. One man was out cold on the ground and the other was cursing about some wild animal attacking him." For a brief moment, the amusement in his eyes became replaced with concern. "If I were you, Cazlina, I would watch out for those two men. That fellow, Kesel was in a very dangerous mood, and I don't think either one of them would be too happy to see you again."

Cazlina wanted to retort sharply that she could take care of herself, but, reluctantly, she had to concede the wisdom of his words. She hoped, as well, never to see those two men again, but, since they were part of General Viadon's army, it might be possible she would encounter them once more. If she did, she would have to be careful.

"Thank you for the warning," she said, grudgingly, and his wicked grin appeared once more.

"Truce?" he asked, holding out his hand.

She stared at it for a moment, tempted to completely ignore the gesture. She didn't want him to think she had forgiven him for his attempt to steal Miris from her. On the other hand, perhaps Miris was right and she was being far more harsh and querulous than she should be. Even though friendship was definitely out of the question, she supposed she could at least attempt to be civil to him.

Placing her hand in his, she felt his strong fingers close over hers in a firm grip.

"Truce," she said, curtly. "But remember, I'm still quite capable of discouraging you from bothering me."

He chuckled merrily. "You have my word. My first priority is to see that all of my bodily parts remain intact."

"Cazlina, what's going on?"

Gareth's voice sounded behind her and she turned to see his face creased with worry and suspicion. He glared distrustfully at the stranger.

"Gareth, this is Jorin Montrill. *Tan* Montrill, my brother, Gareth Narzin."

The two men eyed each other silently, neither one making an effort to offer his hand to the other. Gareth scowled blackly, looking like he would leap on the bigger man at any moment, while Jorin Montrill stared calmly back at him with a faint twinkle in his eye.

"How do you know my sister?" Gareth demanded.

Jorin's amused eyes flashed to Cazlina's face. "We met while Cazlina was on her way to Terrangay. I was able to offer my assistance a few times when she needed it."

"What do you mean?"

The horse thief chuckled. "Perhaps your sister should tell you. I'm sure her version of the events will be much more colorful than mine."

Gareth turned to her, his eyes narrowed suspiciously. "Caz?"

She frowned, irritated at them both. Gareth's overly protective big brother attitude had once more come to the forefront, ready to defend his little sister against what he perceived as a threat to her, while Jorin Montrill continued to be his usual insolent self.

"I'll tell you all about it later, Gareth," she said, dismissively. "It's neither important, nor very interesting."

She narrowed her eyes at Jorin, daring him to contradict her, but he merely raised his eyebrows in amusement and remained silent.

To her relief, a sergeant rode by then and gestured abruptly, saving her from further explanations. "All right, soldiers, get in line! We're about to leave. Come on, move it."

Jorin grimaced. "I've only been in the army for a few hours and already I don't like it. At least, they haven't forced me to wear a uniform, yet. Well, my lady, this is it. I hope you know what you're getting yourself in to."

"I can take care of myself."

"I hope you're right. After all, who will look after your pretty mare if you get yourself killed?"

Instantly, she flared, "Don't you even *think* about touching my horse, Montrill! I shall live forever just so *you* cannot have her."

He laughed his deep, rich laugh. "That's the spirit, my lady. Hold on to that thought when you're in the midst of battle."

He swung up into the saddle on his big roan stallion and looked down at her. "May the gods be with you, my lady," he said, "and, hopefully, with a poor wretch like me."

He grinned at her once more and then turned his horse to move into the waiting line of soldiers.

CHAPTER 12

W ho the devil was that man, Caz?" Gareth demanded. "Why were you so upset with him? It almost looked like you were going to punch him or kick him at one point."

Put that way, her empty threats to the horse thief sounded rather ridiculous and Cazlina had to smile wryly. Her actions imitated those of a small cornered animal baring its teeth and growling ferociously to show it was not defenseless. By no means did she trust or like Jorin Montrill, but she had to admit honestly to herself that, if his intentions toward her were indeed unscrupulous, he had already had plenty of opportunity to carry them out. As highly irritating as he had been so far, he'd also been relatively harmless.

She gave her brother what she hoped would pass for a reassuring smile. "Never mind, Gareth, it's not important. Let's just say *Tan* Montrill and I started off on the wrong foot when we first met and have had a few unfortunate misunderstandings since then. But, it's something we have to resolve ourselves. You don't have to worry about it."

Her brother narrowed his eyes. "He didn't hurt you in any way, did he?" he asked, his voice dangerously quiet.

She hastened to diffuse his growing agitation by speaking in a deliberately flippant manner. "Not unless you count insulting my pride. He, like certain other males I could name, made the mistake of thinking I was a helpless woman in need of protection and guidance. I set him straight on that score. I suppose it was a blow to his enormous ego. Anyway, there's no time now to tell you about it. We'd better follow the sergeant's orders and prepare to move out."

He frowned, obviously still unconvinced by her placating manner.

She sighed inwardly. He would not be satisfied until she had told him about her encounters with the horse thief. But, she wondered if it might not be better for everyone if she downplayed the tale. Gareth's quick temper might lead to big trouble with Jorin Montrill, who, if she was honest with herself again, had really done nothing wrong after that first failed attempt to steal Miris. True, he aggravated her to the point of wanting to punch him, but, if the truth be told, she owed him a debt for saving her and Miris from the Windles, much as she hated to admit it.

She saw General Viadon arrive in the courtyard and breathed a sigh of relief. The imminent departure of the army from Terrangay would postpone her explanations to Gareth for the time being and give her a chance to think about what to tell him.

Gareth gave her a quick hug and then mounted his horse to join his regiment. "Be careful, Caz."

She swallowed past a lump lodged in her throat. "You, too. Don't try to be a hero, all right?"

He grinned, his irritation with her momentarily forgotten. "I won't, if you won't."

She smiled. "I promise."

She mounted Miris and looked over to where the general stood. An older man, thin almost to the point of emaciation, had accompanied the general into the courtyard. He wore a dark brown cloak over a long robe of silvery gray. At a gesture from Viadon, a groom hurriedly brought forward a horse that had already been saddled and assisted the man to mount. After making certain he was comfortably ensconced on the horse's back, the general himself swung up into the saddle of a big chestnut stallion.

Cazlina wondered about the identity of the older man. The general seemed to treat him with great respect and deference. She urged Miris over to where Viadon waited. He gave her a quick glance as she rode up.

"Cazlina, may I present Pharon?" the general said, turning to the man beside him. "He is a mage of great power and will be assisting us in our campaign against Saranor."

A mage. That explained Viadon's courteous treatment of the man.

In all her years, Cazlina had never seen a mage. She tried not to stare at his gaunt, angular face and luminous green eyes.

He regarded her curiously. "General Viadon tells me you, too, possess magic," he said.

She blushed. "It is true I can communicate with animals, but that's all I can do."

He smiled gently. "Do not belittle the power you have, Cazlina. Any gift, no matter how small, shows the gods have touched you with their magic."

Cazlina stared at him. *Her?* Touched by the gods? What a ridiculous idea! The ability to speak with Miris ever since her father had given her the mare at the age of five had always seemed natural. She knew such a talent was not common, but the thought of why or how she possessed it had never really crossed her mind.

"Standards raised! Sound the bugle!" General Viadon shouted, cutting through her bewildered thoughts.

Four soldiers on horseback immediately raised tall lances with gray pennants flying from their tips. A jagged red line, like lightning running diagonally from one corner to the other, adorned the pennants. The loud, bracing sounds of the bugle split the air and all noise and activity in the courtyard ceased, with the exception of the slow beating wings of the huge hydriths in the sky above. Expectant faces looked toward the general seated on his chestnut stallion, awaiting his orders.

He raised his sword high in the air above his head and then brought it down sharply. "Battalions, forward!"

He started out of the yard at a brisk trot, flanked by the four soldiers carrying the standards, and followed by Pharon and Cazlina.

Glancing back, Cazlina saw Gareth's unit fall in behind the general's entourage and gave her brother a quick wave before facing forward once more. Her heart sang knowing he rode behind her, even though they were headed straight into the arms of terrible conflict. If she died this day, at least she would have Gareth by her side when it happened.

Dust swirled in the air as the hundreds of mounted troops and foot soldiers marched at a lively pace out into the streets of Terrangay. The Fire Birds flew above them, blackening the skies with their precise and highly disciplined V formations.

Cazlina found herself caught up in the excitement and drama of the moment. Hundreds of people lined the streets and cheered as the troops moved toward the huge wooden gates leading outside the city. Soldiers stood at attention on top of the walls and in the towers, saluting as the general's army passed below them.

We must be quite a spectacle, Cazlina reflected.

Behind her, she could see the squadrons led by Captains Belledar, Petros, and Spargus. The gray pennants of the rebel army waved above the heads of the marching soldiers. The paved streets echoed with the tramp of feet, the clatter of hooves, the shrill cries of the Fire Birds, and the cheers of the citizenry of Terrangay. A fervent, impassioned air infused the army's departure and Cazlina found herself responding with a quickened pulse and excitement thrumming through her body.

Outside the walled city, the troops split up into the various detachments, as the commanding officers galloped back and forth to keep the soldiers in proper line. The Fire Birds assigned to each detachment broke out of formation and flew off in their designated directions.

The general's regiment turned south toward Queen Saranor's castle located on the outskirts of the capital city of Vendor. Two of the Fire Birds, acting as advance scouts, flew ahead of the squadron, their shapes mere black specks against the cloudless sky. For the greater part of the day, the troop followed the dirt road that wound through the valley bottom and skirted the ragged slopes of the mountain foothills.

Cazlina could now observe the landscape more clearly in the full, bright sunlight. The valley was wide and shallow, its sides rising in rugged steps. The narrow river Yanan had led her past the night before bisected it almost in half. Tall weeds and cattails choked the riverbanks in places, and, in others, white sand spilled down to the rushing water. Stands of dark trees, intermingled with the light green of aspen and birch, followed the curves in the valley bottom. Cazlina could see fields, golden with wheat and corn, on some of the less rocky slopes.

The regiment marched well into the evening, encountering none of Saranor's army, and, finally, near dusk, the general called a halt. The troops immediately began to set up camp for the night and, soon, cooking fires and tents dotted the field where they had stopped. Guards took up posts around the perimeters of the camp and near the road leading to the south.

The hydrith scouts continued their reconnaissance flights around the surrounding countryside. The other members of the elite flying group descended from the darkening skies and landed near the outer fringes of the field, apart from the rest of the regiment. The tiny female warriors leaped agilely from the backs of the enormous creatures and prepared to bed down for the night.

The general's aides erected a large, roomy tent near the centre of the encampment and a smaller one right next to it for Cazlina's use. She tethered Miris with the other horses and then prepared a simple meal of stew and bread.

As the evening wore on, Gareth did not put in an appearance. In a way, she found it a relief. As much as she loved her brother, she felt tired and on edge and didn't want to have to deal with his questions and demands for explanations about Jorin right then. Thankfully, Jorin was also nowhere in sight, and she was grateful not to have any further confrontations with both men that day. Her already tightly strung nerves couldn't take any more tension without snapping completely.

She wondered what to do after she had eaten. The answer came when Sergeant Zandorin scratched on the door flap of her tent and politely informed her General Viadon wished to see her in his tent.

A small table and two chairs had been set up in the general's roomy enclosure. Pharon sat in one of the chairs beside Viadon.

"Cazlina, I have an assignment for you," the general said, when she stood in front of him. "Pharon believes Yanan may be somewhere close by. The touch of Nostrimus's magic is in the air, but it is not the mage himself who is the source. Both Pharon and I feel strongly it is my good friend, Yanan. He must have followed us from Terrangay. Your mission, Cazlina, is to try and contact him. He seems to trust you and may appear to you once again, if he is in the vicinity. If you are successful in finding him, Pharon will try to reverse Nostrimus's spell and change Yanan back into human form."

"I will do my best, sir," Cazlina said, trying to hide her dismay. She didn't have the slightest idea how to find the mountain cat, which had already proved he could vanish into the dark shadows like a phantom, and was suddenly consumed with fear she would fail the general in the first assignment he gave her.

Viadon seemed to sense her uncertainty, even though she valiantly tried to hide it.

"I realize this may be a difficult task," he said, gravely. "If Yanan fails to appear to you, I don't want you to feel you have disappointed me."

"Yes, General."

He contemplated her for a moment longer and then said, "That's all. You may go now."

She nodded and left the tent, followed by Pharon.

Outside, the mage raised his face to the warm night breeze and closed his eyes briefly. "I sense his presence nearby," he said, quietly, opening his eyes once more. "But, I also feel great conflict. There is the willingness and desire to enter the encampment, but the spell is holding him back. There are too many people and lights."

"Perhaps if we ride away from the camp for a short distance, he'll be able to come to us," Cazlina suggested.

Pharon nodded his agreement and the two of them made their way to the stand of trees where the horses had been tethered for the night. The mage went to saddle the brown horse he had ridden earlier, and Cazlina continued further down the line of tethered horses toward Miris near the far end.

The mare had her nose buried in a bucket of oats and bran. Her ears pricked forward at the approach of Cazlina.

Are we going on a mission, Caz? The mare's voice held a note of excitement.

Cazlina nodded. *The general wants us to contact Yanan again.*

The mountain cat? Miris asked, warily. *That creature frightens me.*

Cazlina stroked the mare's velvety nose. *I know, dear one, but I don't think you need to worry about him. If the general is right, Yanan is really a man who has been changed into an animal by a mage's spell. Eating you is probably the furthest thing from his mind.*

Well, I certainly hope so!

The general's mage is coming with us, Cazlina continued. *He's going to try to bring Yanan back to human form.*

She saddled Miris and swung up on her back.

Without a word, Cazlina and Pharon moved quietly away from the field and slipped into the lengthening shadows under the trees. The guard patrolling that side of the encampment challenged them sharply, but let them go when he recognized the mage.

Night had begun to descend, but the warmth of the day remained and insects chirred and clicked in the dusk. Cazlina could see the dark bulk of the two Fire Birds in the sky as they flew their guard mission above the encampment. A faint luminance on the horizon above the tops of the trees and slopes indicated where Terrangay lay.

Cazlina observed the mage and his horse ahead of her. She could feel the magic in the air as he tried to pinpoint Yanan's location, and wondered if this was the cause of his horse's agitated movements.

"Here," Pharon said, suddenly, bringing his mount to a halt.

They had ridden into a shallow gully with a narrow stream, no more than two or three feet wide, running down its center. Mossy rocks lined the banks of the stream and fallen trees littered one slope of the gully, victims no doubt of a high wind or lightning.

A shadow behind one of the fallen trees on the side of the gully moved, and a striped, sinuous shape flowed down the slope to stand a few feet away from the two riders. Cazlina saw the familiar golden eyes staring at her out of the dark.

CHAPTER 13

"Yanan!" Cazlina exclaimed, relieved. She dismounted and approached the creature. "General Viadon was right. You are here."

I knew the general would come this way, the sibilant voice resounded in her mind. *I have been waiting here since last night hoping he would stop somewhere in this vicinity.*

"Are you really Mattius Yanan, Queen Saranor's advisor?" she asked.

The cat gazed at her out of gleaming golden eyes. *I am he. Saranor placed a spell on me as punishment for my disloyalty. I can no longer live in the company of men, nor can I dwell in the sunlight. I can roam only at night, confined to a world of darkness.*

"That is so sad," Cazlina murmured, feeling pity for the creature. She could not imagine being imprisoned in a life of dark shadows and moonlight, unable to move freely in the daylight.

Who is this man with you? The striped cat asked. *I sense magic about him.*

"Your perception is correct," Cazlina answered out loud. "This is Pharon, General Viadon's mage. He's here to help you, if he can."

She turned toward the mage and found him standing right behind her, regarding her with shining eyes and a faint smile on his gaunt face.

"A wonderful gift," he murmured. "You are fortunate, Cazlina."

He stepped closer to the mountain cat, which sat watching him closely. "Yanan, the general has asked me to try to reverse the spell Nostrimus has placed on you. I cannot guarantee my efforts will be successful. Are you willing to take the chance and allow me to proceed?"

An emphatic agreement resounded in Cazlina's mind and she nodded at Pharon.

What must I do? Yanan asked.

When Cazlina relayed the cat's question to the mage, he answered, "All that I require is a clear image of yourself as you were before the spell. Empty your mind of all thoughts but that picture, so I may focus on it during the process. You may feel a strange sensation throughout your body. Do not be alarmed. My spell will require that I explore every bone and muscle and nerve in order to draw out the human body that lies buried beneath Nostrimus's spell."

Yanan's sleek black head bobbed up and down, acknowledging the mage's words.

"Then I will proceed."

Cazlina moved back several steps, curious as to how Pharon would transform the animal before them into the man he used to be. In her entire life, she had never witnessed magic at work and she found herself holding her breath in fascination. For Yanan's sake, she hoped the terrible fate bestowed upon him by Saranor could be undone.

Pharon withdrew a dark red pouch from a pocket in his robe. He approached Yanan until he stood only a few inches away. The mountain cat did not move, even though his eyes narrowed to mere slits.

Cazlina's unique link with the creature's mind revealed the fierce concentration Yanan was using to maintain an image of a black-haired man with hazel eyes and a black beard. She could also sense his trepidation and desperate hope, though he tried to control the emotions as best he could.

Pharon opened the pouch and withdrew a small quantity of silver powder. He began chanting softly in a strange language Cazlina could not understand. As he sprinkled the silver powder on top of Yanan's head, the mage's voice grew louder. The cat began to quiver and then to shake almost uncontrollably, his mouth opening to emit a rumbling sound that grew rapidly in volume.

Pharon said sharply, "Do not fight me, Yanan!" Then his voice fell to a soothing murmur. "Concentrate fully on the image in your mind. The discomfort will soon pass if you ignore it. Listen to my voice, Yanan, and do not resist my probing."

The animal visibly relaxed, his eyes fully closed now. The mage's hypnotic voice continued to wash over him like a calming tonic. The specks of powder glistened like tiny jewels on the cat's head.

Moments later, much to Cazlina's astonishment, Yanan's black and white figure started to shimmer and dissolve as though fading away into the dark shadows of the night. In place of the feline features, unmistakably human ones began to appear and disappear in intermittent flickers.

Cazlina stole a glance at the mage and saw the narrow lines of his face frozen in total concentration. His green eyes shone with a brilliant glitter as he stared down at the amazing transformation taking place in the mountain cat. His voice droned on, the repetitive incantation falling softly on the warm night air.

Cazlina stared at Yanan, incredulous.

No longer did the creature resemble a mountain cat. Instead, a bizarre combination of feline and human features stood before her. The sleek head bulged and shifted as more and more of his features became those of a man, and the body formed distinctly human arms and legs. Once the transformation process began, it seemed to accelerate rapidly. So fast, in fact, that Cazlina saw it all as a swift blur that passed like a dream in front of her astonished eyes.

She saw Pharon raise his arms, the sleeves of his robe falling away to reveal spindly limbs, and his voice rose in a thunderous shout to the dark skies above. A brilliant light accompanied a sudden loud crack and then deathly quiet fell with an abruptness that left Cazlina shaken.

She tore her gaze from the still figure of the mage, whose arms had fallen back to his sides, and looked back at Yanan.

The striped mountain cat no longer existed. In his place, a naked man with black hair and a black beard lay motionless on the ground, his arms and legs twisted into awkward positions.

As Cazlina stared at him in amazement, he twitched violently, and suddenly sat up with a loud gasp, as though striving for a breath of life-giving air. His eyes peered about in blinking confusion.

Pharon roused himself from his motionless stance and gazed down at the man, his angular face carrying a faint smile. "Welcome back, Mattius Yanan," he said.

A short while later, General Viadon looked up from his paperwork as Sergeant Zandorin pushed aside the door flap of his tent and Cazlina entered.

"Well?" the general asked, expectantly, his eyes searching her face.

"General, I believe you know this gentleman."

She stepped aside to allow someone behind her to move forward into the fitful glow of the lantern.

The man with the black beard had Pharon's brown cloak wrapped about his body and his eyes held an expression of undisguised warmth as he regarded Viadon.

The general stood up abruptly, his lean face suffused with delight. "Mattius!"

He came forward to clasp the other man in a hug of heartfelt affection.

"Darnellis, it's good to see you," Yanan exclaimed, leaning back to grin at him. "I thought I would never have the pleasure of your company again."

"Nor I yours. I thought Saranor had killed you, but Cazlina convinced me otherwise when she told me about your encounter in the mountains near Terrangay."

Yanan's eyes flicked to Cazlina standing quietly off to one side, where she had retreated to give the two old friends the opportunity to reunite undisturbed by another's presence. He inclined his head and smiled at her.

"Yes, it was fortunate I discovered Cazlina in the mountains," he said. "I had been wandering near Terrangay for several weeks, trying to find a way to let you know I was still alive. But, Nostrimus's spell prevented me from entering the city, and, even if I could come to you, there was no way I could let you know it was me inside that mountain cat's body. Finding I could communicate with Cazlina was a stroke of luck. All I could hope for at the time was that she would be able to act as a liaison between us. I had no idea you employed the services of a mage as well, Darnellis, and that the spell could be reversed." He turned to the mage, who had slipped into the tent behind him and stood silently by the door. "My eternal gratitude," Yanan said, bowing to the man in the silver-gray robe.

Pharon smiled and inclined his head. "I am glad I could be of service. I was not at all certain my power could counteract that of Nostrimus, but, as it turned out, it was a relatively easy spell to reverse."

Yanan grimaced. "Perhaps, it was easy for you, mage, but it wasn't an altogether pleasant experience for me."

The mage's eyes twinkled faintly. "Transformation spells do tend to cause some discomfort to the victims."

Yanan twitched his mouth wryly at the vast understatement.

"Mattius, I'll have the sergeant bring you some clothes and food," General Viadon said. "Then you must rest. We can talk further in the morning."

The black-bearded man shook his head, his face assuming an urgent expression. "That can wait, Darnellis. I have news for you regarding the scouting party Cazlina and I ran into the other night. The creatures managed to slip through your men and circle back around to the south. I think they might be returning to Saranor's castle to report the movement of your army. I followed them for a bit, and they passed through this area not more than an hour ago. They can't be far ahead. It's still possible they can be stopped before they reach her."

General Viadon nodded grimly and looked toward the mage. "Pharon, can you discover the whereabouts of the scouting party?"

"I can try. If the distance is not too great, I may be able to detect them, but I cannot guarantee it."

He closed his eyes, his angular face a study in intense concentration. Shortly, a satisfied expression crossed his face and he opened his eyes. They glowed brilliantly. "I believe I have located them. They are very close. Would you like me to bring them here?"

Viadon gave him a sharp look. "You can do that?"

"I believe so." He began to murmur in the same soft, hypnotic voice he had used when transforming Mattius Yanan back into a man.

A sudden deafening boom sounded outside the tent. Cazlina jumped, her heart tripping alarmingly in her chest.

The mage smiled. "Your guests await you, General."

Viadon strode rapidly toward the tent door and lifted the flap. The others followed.

Outside, hovering just inches above the field was an enormous, transparent globe of flickering light. Inside the globe, dark wavering shapes with ferociously gleaming eyes milled about in confusion. Soldiers in the immediate vicinity gathered around the globe with shock and astonishment on their faces at the sudden appearance of this strange phenomenon.

CHAPTER 14

G eneral Viadon approached the globe, stopping a few feet away from the perimeter. His face impassive, he gazed up at the creatures imprisoned within. "Where is Saranor?" he demanded.

One of the apparitions moved closer to the wall of the globe and Cazlina gasped. Around her, she could hear others drawing in their breath at the sight as well.

The creature appeared to be made of nothing more than smoke and shadow. Long, gray tendrils only remotely resembling arms and legs floated every which way, as though stirred by a gentle wind. An elongated white blur with dark, fathomless holes that might have been a nose and mouth showed where a face should have been. The only features of substance about the whole creature were burning orbs of orange fire that seemed to glare down at the general.

One of the deep black holes opened wider. "You will get nothing from me, Viadon," the creature intoned, in a hollow voice.

"You are my prisoner," the general said. "Talk and perhaps I will show you mercy."

The unearthly creature stirred, the tendrils of gray mist waving aimlessly in the flickering light of the globe. "Mercy is a pitiful failing of you foolish humans. *I* would show no such mercy to *you* if you were my prisoner."

"A sentiment I'm certain Queen Saranor will also echo when she hears you have been captured," Viadon said, mirthlessly. "Who would you rather take your chances with, me or Saranor?"

The creature's eyes flickered and the flimsy tendrils of its body moved more rapidly. The other creatures, similar to this one, stirred restlessly. Obviously, the general's reference to Saranor's wrath had struck a chord.

"I will not betray the queen's whereabouts," the creature hissed.

Pharon watched the exchange with his arms folded and an impassive expression on his face. He leaned forward and spoke to General Viadon in a low voice. Cazlina, standing nearby, could barely hear the mage's words.

"It knows nothing. It was sent to keep an eye on your army and to inform Saranor of your movements. But, the queen was clever enough to order the creatures to report to a second scouting party. No doubt, that scouting party has been ordered to report to another and so on. Saranor has made certain that if any of her spies are captured they know nothing of her exact whereabouts. However, I can pull the thoughts from the creature's mind and show you where this party was to rendezvous with the other."

Cazlina stared in astonishment as a shimmering curtain suddenly floated in the air near the globe. Against this backdrop, the image of an indistinct road slowly took shape, winding obscurely through the dark shadows of trees and underbrush. At the far end, where the road seemed to vanish into blackness, the top of a dark, conical shape suddenly erupted into brilliant sheets of red flame. Plumes of ash and smoke silently billowed up into the inky sky, giving the whole spectacle a surreal and eerie air.

"I recognize that area," Viadon said. "That's the Mountain of Death, which means they are only half a day from here."

"You are fighting a losing cause," the creature who had spoken earlier said. "Why not give up now and throw yourself on the mercy of Queen Saranor?"

The general smiled frigidly. "I know how benevolent the queen can be."

He turned his back on the globe and spoke in a low tone to Pharon. "Is there some way you can destroy these creatures? We can't allow them to contact Saranor."

Pharon smiled thinly. "That is no problem, General."

The mage lifted his arms toward the globe hovering above the ground and bolts of white light leaped from his fingertips. They penetrated the glowing walls of the globe and crackled about the inhuman beings inside. The streaks of light tore the creatures apart like foul mist blown to tatters by gale winds, their tortured shrieks splitting the warm night air. Pharon snapped his fingers and the globe of light with Saranor's minions in it suddenly disappeared. Gasps and mutters sounded from the enthralled audience gathered near the general's tent.

Sergeant Zandorin, gaping along with the rest of them, visibly collected himself and bawled at the nearby soldiers, "All right, everyone, move on! Back to your duties."

The men and women shook themselves as though coming up out of a dream and began to drift away, talking excitedly among themselves and glancing back over their shoulders.

"Thank you, Sergeant," General Viadon said. He turned abruptly and slipped back through the door flap of his tent, followed by the others.

Cazlina felt drained and disappointed by the encounter with Saranor's scouting party. Their capture had failed to elicit any helpful information for the general. The queen's whereabouts remained unknown.

As though sensing her despondent thoughts, Viadon turned to her and said, "Good work, Cazlina. Without your assistance in communicating with Yanan and bringing me word of the scouting party, we would not have known of its existence before it was too late."

"But, it didn't do us any good," she said, bitterly.

"On the contrary, those creatures knew everything about our movements and would have reported the information to Saranor. With Pharon's help, we have eliminated that danger. However, it would not have been possible if you were not able to communicate with Yanan. Your contribution to the revolution so far has been invaluable." His kind eyes rested on her downcast face. "Get some sleep, Cazlina. We leave by dawn tomorrow."

She nodded and left, hearing the general's voice take on a tone of quiet animation as he resumed his reunion with the friend he had thought dead by Saranor's hand.

She paused at the doorway of her tent and looked around. The camp had begun to settle down for the night. Many of the campfires had been extinguished, leaving only a few flickering in the darkness. The vague shapes of the huge Fire Birds in their corner of the field bulked against the dark sky. The moon just started to peek out from behind a slow moving bank of clouds, and, in the pale wash of its luminance, she could observe the movement of the guards along the perimeter of the camp.

Somewhere out in the waiting shadows, Saranor's army lurked, perhaps halted for the night as well, their tents and campfires scattered across a similar field. Nevertheless, for the moment, all remained still and peaceful, and Cazlina stepped across the threshold into the darkness of her tent.

The piercing blasts of the bugle awakened the camp early the next morning, even before daylight had crept over the horizon. In a very short time, tents had been dismantled and packed away in the wagons, and campfires thoroughly doused. Horses had been saddled and the foot soldiers stood in formation, yawning and rubbing their eyes, trying to chase the sleep away from their tired bodies.

Cazlina hurried through her breakfast and helped one of the general's aides take down her tent and pack the camping materials away in a wagon. Then she went to saddle Miris, greeting the mare affectionately.

The general emerged from his tent when Cazlina rode up. She never ceased to be amazed at how impeccable and alert he always was, no matter what hour of the day or night.

Mattius Yanan, dressed now in a brown shirt and trousers, and with his black hair and beard neatly combed, accompanied Viadon. The former Queen's advisor looked tired but animated, his eyes glancing about as though drinking in all the familiar sights and sounds denied him for so long under Nostrimus's spell.

Cazlina tried hard not to stare, but, despite herself, her gaze kept straying toward him. She had a difficult time accepting that the trim, black-haired man before her was real and not a figment of her imagination. She kept expecting to see his image shimmer and dissolve into the sleek, sinuous body of the mountain cat once more.

She blushed guiltily when Yanan's eyes flashed her way. Now that he had become human again, she could no longer read his mind, but it seemed certain, nevertheless, that he could correctly guess her thoughts, for his mouth quirked into a faint smile as he gave her a wink.

She smiled back and then turned her attention once more to the general, who was speaking to his sergeant.

"Sergeant Zandorin, tell the commanding officers we leave immediately."

The sergeant saluted smartly. "Yes, sir." He turned on his heel and hurried away, shouting orders as he went.

"I expect we might see some action today," Viadon said to Cazlina and Yanan. "Saranor will be certain to have the roads and paths to her castle heavily guarded, but it is imperative we reach it soon. We must destroy the Pool of Souls, or it may be extremely difficult to stop her."

Cazlina stared at him, uncertain if she had heard him right. "Pool of Souls, sir?"

Viadon nodded grimly. "I've wondered why Saranor has been taking so many prisoners in her raids and have discovered why. It seems the queen has more than the sorcery of Nostrimus to aid her. Mattius has informed me that, just before he was changed by Nostrimus's spell, he learned Saranor now has in her possession a talisman known as the Pool of Souls. A very appropriate name, apparently, for its powers are strengthened and renewed by human souls that are released into it and subsequently into the queen. She draws upon all the traits of her victims— beauty, youth, strength, and all the darker elements like greed and aggression and wickedness--to make herself powerful and invincible."

Appalled at the description of the talisman, Cazlina shuddered.

The general smiled mirthlessly. "My sentiments exactly. It seems there are no limits to the queen's evil or the monstrous lengths she will go to in order to rule Regalis. If she is allowed to continue to draw upon the tremendous energies of the Pool, it will be virtually impossible to stop her before long."

The sudden arrival of a hydrith interrupted him, landing several feet away. The beautiful, transparent wings sent up little clouds of dust as the creature settled to the ground.

Miris pranced nervously at the close proximity of the hydrith, but Cazlina could only stare at it in astonishment, her breath caught in the wonder of its beauty and strangeness. Its horse-like head turned toward her, regarding her calmly with large azure eyes.

A young blonde woman slid from the back of the Fire Bird and introduced herself to Viadon as Gemia, one of the Yaltez soldiers assigned to Malak Petros's western regiment. She barely came up to the general's waist and had to crane her neck to look up at him.

She apologized for disturbing him, but she had been ordered by the captain to bring an urgent message. Petros had already engaged in battle with some of Saranor's forces near the Telagor Sea upon his arrival late in the afternoon of the previous day. Casualties had been light on both sides, but the enemy had managed to retreat into the foothills of a range of mountains on the eastern shore of the sea. Unfortunately, the numerous passes and canyons in the mountains afforded Saranor's soldiers excellent places of concealment and opportunities to ambush Petros' troops. The captain was hard pressed to drive them out of there. He remained confident, however, that his regiment would soon be victorious and added, as a footnote, that Saranor's mage, Nostrimus, was no longer in the western area.

"Captain Petros believes the mage may be returning to Vendor with several prisoners who were taken before the captain's forces reached the Telagor Sea," the young woman said, her voice carefully impassive as she related this bit of news to General Viadon.

Cazlina listened to the message with dread. According to the general, Saranor needed human souls to replenish the power of her Pool of Souls. Cazlina feared those unfortunate prisoners would, indeed, be used for that fiendish purpose.

The general appeared to entertain the same thought, for his bearded face tightened into grim lines. "Tell Captain Petros to keep me informed of any further developments," he told the messenger.

Gemia saluted and vaulted on to the back of the patiently waiting hydrith. The tiny woman deftly strapped herself into the elaborate harness and urged the creature into the air in a graceful, effortless leap. The Fire Bird banked toward the west, disappearing into a black speck in the lightening sky.

CHAPTER 15

Cazlina pulled her rapt attention away from the disappearing hydrith and back to the general when she realized he was speaking to her.

"This latest news reinforces the importance of the mission I intended to assign to you this morning, Cazlina," he said. "I want you to ride ahead to the Mountain of Death and seek out the second scouting party waiting there for the one we destroyed last night. It is imperative Saranor's army remain ignorant of our movements, so we may get within attacking distance of her castle and prevent her from using her prisoners to replenish the Pool. Are you up to the assignment?"

She straightened in her saddle. "Yes, of course, General. I'll leave immediately."

"Wait, don't go, yet. I'm sending another soldier with you."

He regarded her rather quizzically, and she wondered if something was wrong.

"Do you know a Jorin Montrill?" he asked.

She started. "Wh-What?"

Viadon's gaze remained speculative as he noted the sudden flush in her cheeks. "This Montrill came to me late last night and asked that he be allowed to accompany you on any mission I might send you on. He says he knows you quite well and he also claims he is very familiar with the lands around here, whereas you are not. He feels he can be of assistance to you in finding your way around."

Cazlina's lips tightened. Jorin's impudence was totally unbelievable. To suggest to the general that she needed to be looked after....

"Is there a problem?" Viadon asked.

She tried to quiet the trembling rage shaking her body. "I have indeed made the acquaintance of *Tan* Montrill," she said, tersely.

Her use of the formal term for a male stranger was not lost on Viadon.

"Do you foresee a problem with having this man accompany you on your mission?" he asked, his eyes probing uncomfortably.

Cazlina bit her lower lip. Her dislike of Jorin did not seem sufficient enough of a reason for her to ask the general to assign another soldier to accompany her. She must not let her personal feelings get in the way of her duty to Viadon, she reminded herself.

"No, there's no problem."

He continued to gaze at her. "Very well, I would like you and Montrill to leave immediately."

"Yes, sir."

She turned away, still seething inwardly at the audacity of Jorin Montrill. The last thing she needed was the company of that arrogant rogue on her mission.

It might not be so bad, Caz, Miris said, soothingly.

You seem to have forgotten how we met him in the first place, Miris, Cazlina said, bad-temperedly. *How can I be expected to like a man who tried to steal my horse and who has been an abominable pest ever since?*

But, he did save us from the Windles and treat our wounds and....

That doesn't change the fact he is aggravating, rash, reckless, dishonorable, disreputable....

Cazlina, don't you think you are getting a little carried away? Miris' voice held an unusual note of sharpness, which brought Cazlina's heated thoughts to an abrupt halt.

She grinned sheepishly. *I suppose I am overreacting just a bit.*

Miris turned her head to give her a gentle, chiding look, but didn't say anything. Cazlina felt properly chastened. *All right, I'll try not to cut his damnable throat, but, if he interferes with my mission...* She stopped, meaningfully.

Just give him a chance, Miris said. *Perhaps, he will be a help to you and not a hindrance.*

"Hah!" Cazlina snorted, but didn't say anything further.

She saw Jorin standing several yards away. Having finished saddling his roan, he swung easily on to the horse's back, saw her approach and slowly grinned.

"Well, good day, my lady," he said. "Isn't it a fine morning to be going for a ride?"

She stopped when Miris stood nose-to-nose with the roan and stared coldly at the man.

"I want you to know, Montrill, I am only doing this because the general has ordered me to. If I had my way, I would have him toss you in the brig and throw away the key. But, since I can't prove you tried to steal my horse and have been bothering me ever since, I suppose that pleasure is to be denied me. *You* may have a pleasant ride this morning, but I most certainly will not."

His eyes twinkled. "Now, now, I thought we had a truce. Don't tell me you intend to go back on your word? I could have sworn you had more honor and pride than that."

She gritted her teeth. "I'm surprised *honor* is so important to you, considering the line of work you have chosen."

He chuckled softly. "I admire your honesty. I always know exactly where I stand with you."

She opened her mouth to make a snide retort and then thought better of it. Something about him always seemed to bring out the worst in her, and she *was* feeling edgy and uncomfortable. It was easy to blame him for that, but maybe Miris was right about getting carried away. "Let's go," she said, abruptly, and pulled Miris away.

She urged the mare into a gallop away from the encampment, not even bothering to see if Montrill followed.

The dirt road left the wide valley and meandered out on to a flat plain of scrub trees and tall grass. Cazlina felt vulnerable and exposed as she cantered along the road, her gaze constantly searching for any signs of the enemy. Jorin Montrill rode at her side, his own eyes alert and watchful.

They had spoken very little since leaving the general's camp. Cazlina tried to ignore him as much as possible, still irritated by the manner in which he had finagled his way into her assignment. To her surprise, he did not seem inclined to taunt and tease her as she'd come to expect. Instead, he was unusually silent and serious, so unlike the laughing rogue she knew.

A short distance down the road, she began to experience a strange tingling sensation. The air seemed to vibrate with invisible currents of energy and the shrubs and grass began to blur. She tried to blink them back into focus, but there seemed to be no edges to anything outside of the very space she occupied.

She glanced at Jorin, wondering if he, too, experienced the bizarre phenomenon, or if she was imagining it. He had a quizzical look about him. When he caught her staring at him, he grinned uncertainly. "Am I crazy, Cazlina, or is there something very strange about this part of the road?"

"You feel it, too?" she asked, her relief overriding annoyance at the familiar way he said her name. "I thought I was imagining things."

"What is it, I wonder? I've never encountered anything like this in all my travels around this area," Jorin said.

She shook her head in response, unable to even hazard a guess as to the cause of the odd phenomenon.

As they rode further down the road, the strange tingling and blurring sensation passed, leaving the flat plain and dirt road looking normal again. Cazlina shook off her confusion and focused once more on the mission at hand.

A few hours later, they entered a thick wood. Upon their approach, it reminded Cazlina of the ugly, dank forest the hideous little creatures known as Windles called home. However, this forest proved to be completely different. In contrast, the dappled shadows were cool and inviting, and the trees smooth and fungus-free. Under the canopy of leaves, there were pale flowers which infused the air with sweet perfume. The road wound gently through the forest, passing chuckling streams and clearings of ferns and moss. The protection of the trees gave Cazlina a measure of relief. She felt much safer riding through this dim, green tunnel than out on the wide-open plain.

She looked for signs that Saranor's army had passed this way, but there weren't any fresh tracks on the dirt road in front of them, nor any telltale signs that anyone had camped recently in any of the clearings they passed.

She stole a glance at her companion. To her astonishment, she found his presence did not feel as intrusive as she had feared it would. It was obvious he understood the gravity of the mission by the way his eyes searched not just the road, but deep into the woods on both sides of them. She disliked the man and his annoying effect on her, but she had to grudgingly admit he made a good companion in this situation. No doubt, his disreputable profession had taught him to be cautious and alert. She welcomed those qualities now, regardless of how they had been obtained.

As they approached the edge of the forest, she glimpsed a familiar, conical shape through the last few trees. "The Mountain of Death," she breathed.

Jorin nodded. "Aptly named, too. I've heard it blows its top on a regular basis, although I've never actually seen it."

Realization suddenly dawned on her. "I've just thought of a reason for that weird sensation we felt back there on the road. That area must have been where Pharon intercepted the scouting party last night. I'll bet we were experiencing the residual magic he used to capture them."

Jorin looked at her oddly. "Then, it wasn't just a jest going around the encampment? There really were creatures of some kind in a giant bubble of light?"

She nodded.

"Some of the men were talking about it, but I thought they were merely trying to pull my leg," Jorin said, shaking his head.

"No, it was Saranor's scouting party. Pharon was able to pinpoint where they were on the road and capture them in his globe of light. He brought them to our camp and General Viadon questioned them, but they couldn't tell him where Saranor is."

"Couldn't, or wouldn't?"

She shook her head. "They had no knowledge of her whereabouts. Saranor had ordered them to report the general's location to another scouting party located somewhere near the Mountain of Death."

She shivered, realizing how close the foul creatures had been to the camp. She stared at the sinister-looking mountain ahead. Somewhere near it, another group of Saranor's minions lay in wait. Did the second scouting party consist of more of those frighteningly insubstantial creatures of unclean mist? Or, could they be inhuman beings of even greater hideousness? Cazlina glanced about, her skin suddenly crawling. Not with the tingle of the mage's magic, but with dread and a sense of danger.

CHAPTER 16

Cazlina and Jorin stopped just inside the edge of the forest, unwilling to expose themselves out in the open until they could ascertain if immediate danger loomed nearby.

Cazlina eyed the enormous mountain ahead with trepidation. It seemed quiet now. No rumbles or explosions of flame and steam disrupted the silence around it, but a gray haze hovered above the ragged top. She could see where rivers of fire had coursed down the blackened sides, smothering and burning all the vegetation and trees in their path.

The mountain seemed to be waiting. Cazlina wondered if it was building up to another massive explosion that would rip into the heavens and send ash and flame raining over the surrounding countryside. She realized if that happened, she and Jorin would be in grave danger. The mountain was vastly closer than it had been last night when Pharon had conjured the projection on the shimmering curtain of air, and this time there would be no protection.

"Fascinating, isn't it?" Jorin asked, staring at the mountain.

Cazlina shivered. "I guess you could call it that. Personally, I find all that power and fire inside, waiting to explode, frightening. It could kill us."

The familiar twinkle appeared in his eyes. "Well, let's just hope it waits until we get past it before it decides to throw a temper tantrum."

"Where do you suppose the scouting party might be?" she asked.

"If I were them, I would find a good place of concealment in those outcroppings over there." He nodded toward the rugged land to the west of the mountain. Reddish rock that was a shade disturbingly reminiscent of dried blood thrust up toward the cloudless sky in peculiarly shaped spires and plateaus. "There would be plenty of canyons and boulders to use as hiding places, and, even if the mountain should decide to explode, I think someone would still be fairly safe there."

Cazlina stared at the red outcroppings. "You're probably right. But, they're certain to have posted a guard to watch this direction since they're expecting the first scouting party to come this way. How do we prevent them from discovering us before we discover them?"

He shrugged. "We'll just have to come at them from another direction, one they wouldn't be expecting."

Cazlina frowned at him. "What are you suggesting?" she asked, not at all certain she wanted to hear the answer.

He flashed a quick grin at her. "You probably won't like this idea, but I think it's the best one we have."

He pointed to their left. The forest extended in a narrow, curving arm almost to the base of the Mountain of Death. In the immediate vicinity of the mountain, the trees and underbrush had been reduced to charred stumps and sooty ash.

"We circle around to the left, keeping within the woods until we come to the area that has been burned. I think the bulk of the mountain will act as a shield from there. If we skirt the base, we should be able to slip into the outcroppings without detection. I doubt the scouting party would suspect anyone would be foolish enough to venture so close to the mountain, and, therefore, we would have the advantage of surprise."

She stared at him, certain the man had gone completely mad. "*Are you out of your mind? What if the mountain decides to explode just as we are directly underneath it? We'd be killed!*"

"True," he said, calmly. "But, I still think we should take the chance."

"There must be another way."

"I am open to other suggestions, my lady. Do you have any?"

She squirmed in frustration. The trouble was, his idea made a perverse kind of sense. The alternatives were either to take their chances out in the open or do nothing to find the scouting party and head back to camp, an option she certainly had no intention of considering. The general was counting on her and Jorin to find Saranor's spies.

Jorin waited for her answer, his expression unreadable.

She sighed at last. "I think I must be as mad as you are," she grumbled. "But, I guess it's the only plan we have at the moment."

She expected to see a smug, self-satisfied expression on his handsome face, but he only nodded gravely.

Cazlina glanced apprehensively at the Mountain of Death. As though taunting her, a small puff of gray smoke and steam belched from the top, and she heard a low ominous rumble. It seemed as though the mountain was laughing at them, or perhaps, warning them not to attempt such foolishness. "Let's go now before I lose my nerve."

Jorin grinned at her. "That's the spirit."

They reeled their mounts around, retreated down the road for several hundred yards, and then pushed through the underbrush in an easterly direction. They remained silent, intent on making as little noise as possible as they made their way toward the mountain.

They lost sight of the enormous, conical shape almost as soon as they left the road, but sporadic rumbling ensured Cazlina remained uncomfortably aware of its brooding presence ahead of them. The closer they approached the forbidding monster, the more nervous and anxious she became.

She couldn't help but wonder if Jorin could be wrong. The scouting party might not be anywhere near the vicinity of the reddish outcroppings. They could be risking their lives for nothing. Although, she had to admit the weirdly shaped plateaus and canyons offered the best place for concealment and defense for miles around, and the approach she and Jorin took seemed the likeliest possibility for surprise. She hoped she had made the right decision in trusting her life to the one person in the world she least expected to entrust it to.

They covered the distance at a rapid pace. The trees began to show signs of charring and death, their stark, defoliated limbs reaching helplessly toward the sky. Black soot clung to their branches and coated the ground in ever-increasing depths. The smell of burned wood and grass hung strongly in the air.

Only death and destruction abounded in the place where a vibrant, green forest had once flourished. Even the birds and animals had been chased away or killed by the rain of fire from the mountain looming only a mile or so away. Cazlina found it to be a very depressing place.

Miris and the roan picked their way carefully over the charred ground. They tossed their heads in dismay at the rank smell of fiery death. Cazlina soothed them both telepathically as the need for silence and stealth was imperative.

The sun hung low in the sky when they finally reached the edge of the blackened forest and saw a stretch of open, ash-covered ground between them and the scorched base of the massive mountain towering above them. Jorin had been correct. The bulk of the mountain acted as a shield against any watchful eyes that might be lurking among the spires and rocky plateaus on the western side.

As if in warning, the mountain suddenly rumbled deeply and Cazlina jumped in her saddle, her heart beating rapidly in her chest.

"I think it's telling us we are not welcome here," Jorin said, in a low voice. Although he spoke in an amused tone, he glanced alertly up at the mountain looming menacingly against the sky and quickened the pace of his roan stallion.

Cazlina followed closely behind, her pulse racing as they picked their way carefully over the broken ground. In places, the rivers of fire had pooled at the base of the mountain, creating hazardous obstacles that smoked and spit at them as they edged by. Miris told Cazlina the ground felt very warm and uncomfortable, but not so hot it burned the bottom of her hooves.

Thus far, their approach had not been detected. No monstrous creatures spilled out of the reddish outcroppings to swoop down on them and rend them to pieces. Of course, Cazlina thought caustically, that could be because there *were* no hideous beasts concealed among the boulders and canyons.

She glanced at Jorin. He seemed calm and unperturbed. She wondered if he maintained a brave front for her sake. She began to realize she did not know this man at all. Her first impressions of him had not been flattering. She had thought him smug, shallow, outrageous, cowardly, and thoroughly unscrupulous, but it seemed he might possess depths she could not even begin to fathom.

As though sensing her befuddled thoughts, he glanced at her and his mouth quirked in the amused smile that seemed to come so easily to him no matter what the situation. "Didn't I tell you it was a pleasant day for a ride?" he whispered, wryly.

She caught herself smiling at his jest and tried to regain her cool manner. She said, in a low voice, "All right, Montrill, this was your brilliant idea. How do you plan to flush out the scouting party? Provided, of course, they really are somewhere in that jumbled mess. Surely, you don't intend for us to blunder around in there until we stumble across them?"

"My lady, your lack of faith wounds me deeply. Of course, I have a plan. I was going to suggest we make our way to the foot of that rock formation shaped like a tower and wait there for night to fall. I'm hoping that once the sun goes down the creatures will let down their guard. Perhaps, they'll even light a small fire that will give away their location. We can then leave the horses and proceed on foot toward them. We should be able to move more stealthily that way. Once we determine how many creatures are in the scouting party, we can either dispatch them ourselves or sneak back out and report them to General Viadon."

She stared at him, incredulous. Night would not fall for several hours. What if that beastly mountain above them decided to burst into explosive destruction before then? Would the rock formation Jorin had indicated provide them with sufficient protection against fiery rain and ash?

"Well, what do you think?" Jorin asked, sensing her apprehension. "I'm quite willing to listen to any other suggestions if this plan doesn't suit you."

She raised her chin a notch. "It will do."

His eyes twinkled mischievously, but he only nodded.

As they cautiously made their way toward the formation Jorin had pointed out, Cazlina said to Miris. *If the mountain shows any signs of exploding, I want you to leave immediately, Miris. Don't wait for me.*

The mare swung her head around and gave her a look of rebuke. *I will not leave you to face danger alone, Caz.*

Miris, don't argue with me! You must save yourself.

The mare did not answer, and as much as Cazlina exhorted her to promise, the animal remained stubbornly silent. Cazlina felt tears prick the corners of her eyes, touched that Miris could be so loyal and loving. She only hoped the mare would not die a needless death in trying to protect her. Wordlessly, Cazlina leaned over the mare's neck and gave her a warm hug.

Miris flashed a deeply affectionate look over her shoulder. *No more foolish talk*, she said, sternly.

CHAPTER 17

The sun sank slowly to the west of the brooding Mountain of Death, staining the sky with its dying light and etching the odd-shaped rock formations darkly against the brilliant colors. Except for the occasional faint hiss of escaping steam from the top of the massive mountain, silence reigned over the desolate countryside.

Cazlina leaned against the sun-warmed rock and searched the other outcroppings for any signs of Saranor's scouting party. Several feet away, Jorin was similarly engaged in vigilant observation; his tall, muscular body crouched motionless behind a pinnacle of red rock.

They had been concealed there for more than two hours, warily keeping an eye on both the disapproving bulk of the mountain beside them and the rocks in front of them. There had been no indications of life among the reddish towers and peaks. Not even a bird flew in the skies above. It was as though the mountain's rage frightened away every living being, leaving behind a desolate and empty place.

The fading rays of the sun brushed the pinnacles with burnished fingers and lengthened the shadows in the crevasses and cracks. There was almost an eerie beauty to the rugged land, if one did not look to the east where the stark, blackened stumps of the dead trees stood outlined against the flaming sky.

As she watched for movement among the rocks, Cazlina wished Yanan could have accompanied them in his cat persona. His uncanny senses would, no doubt, have detected the scouting party's presence immediately and saved them all this waiting.

She felt restless and edgy, afraid they might be wasting valuable time when they could be searching for the queen's minions. General Viadon's army could not be far behind. If she and Jorin did not find the second scouting party soon, the general might be riding directly into a trap. On the other hand, it seemed highly unlikely General Viadon would ride blindly into the area without either sending out more reconnaissance parties or awaiting word from her and Jorin.

She sighed and Jorin glanced her way. "Patience, my lady," he said.

She scowled at him. "I hope you know what you're doing," she hissed. "I feel like we're wasting our time."

"Any moment I get to spend with you, I do not consider wasted."

She stiffened. "Why must you always make a joke of everything?"

He shrugged. "Life must not be taken too seriously all the time. There is enough trouble and sorrow in the world without my adding to it." He threw her a shrewd glance. "Humor can be very calming and healing. You should try it sometime, Cazlina."

A sharp retort rose to her lips and then she stopped. All at once, her frustration and annoyance vanished and she felt the beginnings of a smile tug at the corners of her mouth.

"I suppose I *am* too serious at times," she admitted. "My brother and I both had to grow up quick when our parents died. He takes good care of me, but I still feel as though I have to prove something--how strong or brave or competent I am. I guess I've forgotten how important it is to laugh and smile, too."

She stopped, feeling her cheeks flame as she realized how foolish her words must have sounded to Jorin. She stole a glance at him, expecting to find him laughing at her, but his handsome, tanned face looked thoughtful.

"Life hasn't been easy for you, has it?" he asked, quietly.

She stirred uneasily. It felt odd to be conversing in this manner with the man who had entered her life in such a daring and precipitous fashion. Circumstances may have thrown them together, but she did not intend to bare her soul to the silk-tongued devil.

"I've managed," she said, coolly.

She turned away from him, making it clear she had no wish to continue the uncomfortable conversation. To her surprise, he seemed to accept her wishes and fell silent, once more turning his attention to searching for signs of the scouting party.

Another hour passed. The sun slipped below the horizon and shadows completely obscured the crevasses and peaks of the outcroppings. The silence became eerie and Cazlina wished she could at least hear an insect chirp, for then she would know she, Jorin and the two horses were not the only living things for miles around. Darkness settled around her like an uneasy blanket.

Something lightly brushed her arm and she jumped. Jorin's voice sounded close to her ear. "To the right. See that faint flicker?"

She looked in the direction he indicated and then she spotted it, a very dim glow in a hollow about two hundred yards away. As she watched, a shadow moved against the reddish wall partially obscured by a jagged pinnacle.

She glanced at Jorin. "The scouting party?" she whispered.

"Told you I'd find them."

She shook her head irritably, but didn't say anything. How typical of the man to gloat! It annoyed her that he had proven to be right.

Don't you say a word, Miris.

Why, Caz, I wasn't going to say anything.

Hah!

Cazlina looked back at the flickering light. She could see more shadows, but couldn't tell how many individual ones there might be. Given that the creatures in the hollow could project their shadows upon the rock wall, it seemed unlikely this scouting party contained the same ethereal beings Pharon had captured in his globe the previous night. She only hoped they would not prove to be grotesque monsters with sharp fangs and claws. With any luck, they would be humans, which would make it much easier for her and Jorin to deal with them.

She took a deep breath and glanced over her shoulder at him.

"Well, what do you think, my lady?" he asked. "Should we give our friends a surprise visit?"

She bit her lip. "I guess it's the only way we'll know how many of them there are."

He nodded encouragingly. "All right, let's go."

They left the horses concealed in a smooth, shallow cave carved out by wind and rain near the tower-like rock formation and proceeded silently on foot. Cazlina gritted her teeth and held her breath every time a stone rolled under her foot. She touched the hilt of the sword by her side, reassured by the cool touch of the metal. She expected at any moment to hear one of the members of the scouting party shout an alarm and to have a dozen attackers drop down on them from the rocks above.

Up ahead, she could barely make out Jorin's broad back as he stealthily made his way over boulders and rocks and squeezed through narrow crevasses. Cazlina followed closely on his heels, trying to be as silent as him.

This sort of thing comes naturally to him, she thought. His profession had, no doubt, taught him to move as quietly as a wraith. She, on the other hand, had no experience in such stealthy matters, and that added to the tension coiling her stomach in a tight knot.

As they drew closer to the flickering glow, it became possible to distinguish faint sounds coming from the hollow--voices, but Cazlina could not tell how many people were gathered around the fire.

A wall of smooth rock, perhaps ten feet high, loomed up in front of them, with a narrow ledge running diagonally up to its top. A few feet from the top, the ledge widened out slightly. The glow and the voices came from behind the wall.

Cazlina's heart thumped uncomfortably as Jorin stopped by the wall and put his ear to it. He nodded silently and pointed to the ledge, indicating they should crawl up it instead of going around it to take the scouting party by surprise. She stared wide-eyed at him, feeling a sudden rush of panic, but managed to force it back down and nod in agreement.

He led the way, using protruding rocks and small hollows as handholds. When he reached the spot where the ledge widened, he stopped in a crouch, his head still below the top of the wall, and looked down at Cazlina. With a silent gesture, he beckoned her to follow.

She swallowed back a lump in her throat, trying to still her trembling muscles. With the enemy just on the other side of the narrow wall of rock, she feared she would slip on the ledge or dislodge a rock, bringing the scouting party down on their heads.

Jorin made a quick movement with his head, urging her to hurry. As she began climbing, she realized the ascent was much easier than it had appeared, and soon, she was crouched beside him, her pulse hammering in her ears as the voices grew louder. She could distinguish at least two or three different tones, and to her relief, they sounded human.

"The Mist Riders are late," a man said, angrily and impatiently.

"I know," another one answered. "They were only supposed to find out if Viadon has left Terrangay and report back to us by this afternoon. What's taking them so long?"

"Trust a Mist Rider to foul up a simple assignment," the first man snickered. "The queen never should have entrusted Vax with this mission. His brain is about as non-existent as his body."

"Do you suppose they've been captured by Viadon, Cardas?"

He snorted. "Not on your life, Lorcan! Those things could hide right in front of your eyes and you'd never see them or hear them. I think Vax forgot what he was supposed to do or got lost, stupid creature that he is."

A third voice piped up. "Well, I say we give him another couple of hours and then leave. I don't like being so close to the Mountain of Death. Last night's explosion was enough to scare at least ten years out of my hide."

"Lerant won't be pleased if we don't bring back a report on Viadon," Cardas said. "And, if he's not pleased, Saranor won't be pleased."

The second man, Lorcan, asked, "What should we do if Vax doesn't contact us? I don't want to be blamed if Lerant isn't informed of Viadon's whereabouts."

"It's not our fault," Cardas pointed out, but his voice lacked confidence.

Cazlina had the impression the men feared the person named Lerant almost as much as they feared Queen Saranor. She wondered who this Lerant was that he could inspire such dread.

"Well, there's only three of us," the third man said. "Maybe we could ride toward Terrangay ourselves and find out what's happening with Viadon's army. That way, we could get on Lerant's good side and Vax will be the one in trouble."

"I think Tothe has a good idea, Cardas. It's better than sitting around here waiting for that idiot Mist Rider to come. If Viadon reaches Lerant's forces at the Jezalar Plateau without us warning Lerant ahead of time, we'll all lose our heads."

Cardas, who seemed to be their leader, said irritably, "Our orders were to stay here until Vax reports to us."

"Then, *you* stay, Cardas," the second man growled. "Tothe and I don't intend to wait here for Viadon to find us and kill us." His voice turned sly and insulting. "What's the matter, Cardas? Are you a coward? Would you sooner hide here and be routed out like a frightened animal than act like a man?"

"Why, you..."

Violent scuffling sounds and muttered curses erupted below Caz and Jorin before the man named Tothe fiercely ordered, "Put your swords away, you fools! We're supposed to be fighting Viadon, not each other. The sooner we report to Lerant, the better. Viadon may be on the move right now toward the queen's castle. We have to find out what's happening, since something seems to be delaying Vax's scouting party."

Cardas swore and spat into the dirt, "I shall not forget your insults, Lorcan. Remember that. This is not finished."

Lorcan snorted. "I'm not afraid of you, Cardas."

"I say we leave immediately," Tothe urged in an effort to divert another scuffle between the two men. "Lerant expects a report the day after tomorrow. We don't have much time."

"All right," Cardas said, grudgingly. "But, don't forget, I'm still the leader of this group. *You* take orders from *me*."

"Whatever you say, Cardas. I just want to get away from this place as soon as possible. I don't like it here," Tothe said in a placating tone.

Cazlina felt her muscles tightening in nervous anticipation. She and Jorin had to prevent the men from leaving. They could not be allowed to seek out General Viadon's location and report it back to the man named Lerant. Plus, she had to return to the general as soon as possible to inform him of the valuable information she had learned from Saranor's men, namely the location of Lerant's forces at the Jezalar Plateau.

CHAPTER 18

Jorin's thoughts seemed to be in sync with hers, for he leaned close and put his mouth against her ear. "There are only three of them," he whispered, his voice a tiny breath stirring her hair. "If we separate and circle around to either side of them, we should be able to take them by surprise."

She swallowed hard and nodded, her pulse bounding at the prospect of attacking the men, but she knew it was necessary.

Silently, Jorin made his way back down the narrow ledge and she followed, terrified she might slip and fall or make a noise to alert the men behind the rock wall. At the bottom, Jorin pointed to himself and then to the right, indicating he would go in that direction and Cazlina should circle to the left of the wall.

He disappeared into the shadows, and the darkness pressed down on her like a suffocating wool blanket on a hot summer's night. As quietly as she could, she withdrew the light sword from the scabbard at her side and tightly grasped the hilt in her right hand, trying to draw reassurance from its coolness.

Drawing a deep, silent breath, she picked her way carefully over the broken ground, squeezing between crowded boulders and trying to avoid the piles of loose, shattered rocks that lay everywhere. The murmur of the voices of the three men behind the smooth wall of rock continued and she used the sounds to guide her around to their left. The wall of rock curved slightly and she used that to her advantage, shielding herself for the first several feet, but, eventually, it petered out, tumbling into a pile of smooth, rounded boulders.

She crouched behind them and peered cautiously over the top.

The wall of rock surrounded a natural curved depression on one side and piles of boulders edged two other sides. A narrow opening in the outcroppings of red rock left the fourth side open for easy access.

The three men squatted around a small fire in the center of the depression, their backs to her. She could see them preparing to douse the flames and leave.

Desperately, she searched the shadows beyond them, wondering where Jorin had hidden himself. She had no intention of attacking the men herself without first being assured Jorin was in a position to help her.

She thought she saw something move in the shadowy crevasses beyond the men. They didn't seem to notice anything, as they continued quarrelling in harsh, heated tones, although she couldn't focus on their words very well above the rapid beating of her heart.

She waited behind the rocks, searching for some signal from Jorin and tightening her grip on the hilt of the sword. Again, she thought she glimpsed movement and held her breath, certain this time it was Jorin.

Her gaze shifted to the three men around the fire. They were still involved in their argument and oblivious to the danger surrounding them.

It suddenly occurred to her that, since the men faced the pile of boulders where Jorin waited in the shadows, it would have to be up to her to give the signal to attack. The element of surprise would be lost if Jorin had to reveal himself to her and inevitably to the three scouts.

She took a deep breath and rose cautiously from behind the boulders, hoping Jorin could see her. Slowly raising the sword in her right hand, she brought it down in an abrupt motion.

With a swiftness that startled her as much as it did the men in the center of the rock depression, Jorin leapt silently into the flickering illumination of the campfire, brandishing a wide-bladed sword in his right hand. The men gaped at him as though some kind of monstrous apparition had suddenly appeared out of thin air.

One of the men grunted as Jorin's lean, muscular body crashed into him and threw him to the ground. Jorin's sword rose and fell in the fitful light and dark liquid drenched its blade. The man lay motionless on the smooth rock floor.

Cazlina's silent rush into the depression on top of Jorin's dramatic appearance took the other two men by surprise, and instinctively she moved in on the one closest to her.

He seemed slow to react and her lighter, narrower sword came up under the clumsy, heavy blade he lifted toward her. Nervousness threw her aim off and the blade plunged into his left shoulder instead of his chest. Swiftly, she wrenched the sword out, feeling it grate on bone and sinew.

The remaining man confronted Jorin, who circled warily in front of him, his stained sword inscribing small, invisible loops in the air.

The man Cazlina had attacked bellowed at the pain she had inflicted, and snarling in rage, lurched toward her with his deadly blade. She danced out of the way, but the heavy sword connected with her lighter weapon with a resounding clang that sounded like the tolling of a gigantic bell. The power of the blow almost wrenched the sword out of her hand, and her whole arm went numb. She gasped, trying not to lose her grip on the hilt of the sword, and stumbled backward away from the charging, bellowing man, desperately searching for a route of escape. The man's sheer size and strength were too much for her. She would never be able to overpower him. Her surprise attack had only slowed him momentarily.

She heard a loud shout behind her, but dared not turn around. Her whole attention remained focused on the snarling man in front of her, his hard-bitten face set in a deadly scowl as he advanced on her. She held her sword in both hands and parried another thrust from his weapon, her entire body vibrating with the blow.

Terror and panic fanned white-hot through her veins as the brute strength of the man forced her steadily backward. She dared not take her eyes off him to see where Jorin was. For all she knew, he, too, could be lying dead next to the man he had killed, and she had to face not only the man in front of her, but the second one as well.

Her only advantage might be her lighter weight and smaller body. Her opponent was a hulking man slow on his feet. If she could keep dancing out of his reach, perhaps she could tire him and dart in to deliver a fatal blow with her sword.

She gasped as the man's weapon slashed viciously close to her face. If she had not turned her head at the last second, the blade would have cleaved her skull in two. Her mind suddenly went still behind a wall of cold, stark light.

As her attacker brought his sword up above his shoulders for another swipe, he left his chest exposed for a moment. She saw her chance and plunged her blade as hard as she could into his chest, feeling his breath whoosh over her face at the force of the blow. Warm blood gushed out over her hands and arms, but it didn't register with her senses. She was completely numb to what had just happened.

The light in the man's eyes abruptly faded and he dragged her to the ground with his weight, for she still clung tightly to the sword. She stayed that way for a moment, half-lying on the dead man beneath her; her white knuckled grip still on the hilt of the sword lodged in his chest cavity, her breath coming in short, panting gasps. The cold blankness that had descended on her flickered and began to fade away. She became aware of her surroundings once more and stared down in horror at the dead man's face so close to hers.

Shuddering, she began to push herself away from him, her skin crawling with revulsion. Strong hands seized her shoulders and she screamed, flailing out in terror.

"Cazlina, it's me! It's all right. It's Jorin."

She went still at the familiar voice, sagging in relief against the muscular body of the man behind her.

"Are you all right? Are you injured in any way?"

It took a few moments for his rapid-fire questions to penetrate her panicked mind and then she shook her head weakly. "I'm fine. I'm not wounded," she managed to say.

Jorin helped her to her feet, where she stood swaying. Her gaze slid irresistibly to the dead man lying on the ground, her sword still buried in his chest. Blood ran from the wound and pooled in the shadows by his sides.

"I killed a man," she whispered, still unable to believe it.

"I know," Jorin said, his voice quiet and grave. "It was necessary, Cazlina. They would have discovered the approach of Viadon's army and warned Lerant of our position. We couldn't allow that to happen."

Cazlina nodded silently, yet the revulsion ran deep and strong in her veins. She wondered, not for the first time, if she had made the right decision to join the rebellion. This encounter with the three men would only be the beginning of the killing and bloodshed, and she didn't know if she was strong enough to face more of it.

Jorin's strong hands tightened for a moment on her slim shoulders and then he moved away. He picked up his sword from beside the second man he had killed and came back to her. He threw a quick glance at her before bending down to pull her sword from the dead man's chest. It came out with a sullen reluctance, causing Jorin to grunt with the effort of removing it.

Cazlina shivered as Jorin placed the hilt of the sword in her hand. She refused to look at it, not wanting to see the dark blood staining its once-shiny blade.

"We have to go," Jorin said. "General Viadon will need to hear our news as soon as possible."

She took a deep breath and nodded, sheathing the sword in the scabbard at her side. She tried not to look at the three dark, lifeless shapes lying scattered about the flickering rock depression as she followed Jorin back out into the deep shadows.

As they picked their way carefully toward the rock formation where they had left the horses, she became aware of an urgent voice growing stronger and stronger in her mind.

Cazlina, are you all right? Where are you? Please answer me!

Miris, I'm here. I'm all right. We're on our way back to you now.

I was so worried. For a while, I couldn't read your thoughts and I feared the worst.

I'm sorry, dear one, Cazlina tried to soothe the mare's trembling fear. *I'm fine, really. It was a horrible experience, but it's over now and we must ride back to the*

*general's army and warn him about the queen's forces
stationed at the Jezalar Plateau.*

It surprised her to see the moon still riding, pale and
ghostly, on a wispy carpet of cloud across the dark sky.
The Mountain of Death hulked like some kind of black,
rumbling monster above them and silvery moonlight
gleamed on the patches of molten rock streaking its barren
sides. She felt as though an eternity had passed since she
and Jorin had left the horses to seek out Saranor's scouting
party.

When they arrived back at the horses, Miris greeted
her with soft, worried gusts from her nostrils and tiny
tosses of her head. Cazlina stroked her velvety nose and
murmured soothingly into the mare's flicking ears.

From the men's conversation, they were reasonably
certain no other enemy troops were in the area. As Cazlina
and Jorin prepared to ride away from the Mountain of
Death and back to General Viadon's army, she realized
she'd never in her life been so relieved to leave any one
place, especially one as desolate and dangerous as this one.

CHAPTER 19

Darnellis Viadon listened quietly as Cazlina gave her report. A slight faltering of her voice betrayed her inner emotions when she recounted the attack on the three men.

Jorin remained silent, standing beside her in the general's tent. She had expected him to gloat and take all the credit for his discovery of the scouting party near the Mountain of Death, but he did nothing of the sort. He let her report their experiences without interruption, and she found herself wondering if this night's adventure had dampened his normally flippant manner.

At the mention of Lerant's name, Viadon's mouth tightened, but he remained silent until Cazlina had finished her report. When she stopped speaking, he gazed solemnly up at her and Jorin. "You've done very well this day, both of you. I'm grateful for your efforts. The news you bring of Lerant's whereabouts is extremely helpful. Janix is a vast area and it could have taken us weeks to find out where his forces are stationed."

"How far away is the Jezalar Plateau?" Cazlina asked.

"Roughly a day's march from here," the general answered.

He rose from behind his makeshift desk and began to pace about the tent.

Pharon sat unobtrusively in a corner, his bony hands tucked up inside the voluminous sleeves of his robe. Mattius Yanan leaned against the corner of the small table in the middle of the tent, his arms folded across his chest as he listened attentively to the conversation.

"I don't think Lerant will make a move until he receives the report from his scouting party, which he is not expecting until the day after tomorrow," Viadon said. "I will send a small contingent to the Jezalar Plateau to ascertain his exact position and strength, and I will need a good commander to lead the force. Sergeant Zandorin."

The sergeant snapped to attention. "Yes, sir. Who would you like me to fetch?"

The general's lips twitched faintly. "No one, Sergeant. I would like *you* to take command of the platoon."

Zandorin gaped at him. *"Me?"*

"Yes. I want you to put together a group of ten soldiers and ride out at first light. Your mission will be to discover the whereabouts and strength of Lerant's forces and then report back to me. Do not attempt to engage in battle unless you are discovered and are forced to defend yourselves. I want to maintain the element of surprise."

The sergeant drew himself up, barely able to conceal the delight and excitement threatening to explode from within him. Cazlina could almost see his chest swelling with the importance of the mission bestowed upon him.

"It will be done as you command, General."

Viadon nodded gravely. "Cazlina and *Tan* Montrill, I would like you to accompany the sergeant on his mission. When you have ascertained where Lerant's forces are on the Jezalar Plateau and roughly how many troops he has, report back to me. I will be following behind you with the rest of the army."

Both Cazlina and Jorin nodded. "Yes, sir."

Viadon's eyes took in Cazlina's pale face and disheveled appearance. The blood of the man she had slain still stained her hands and arms. "You will be leaving shortly," he said. "I know a few hours will not be enough to completely restore you, but try to get some sleep before you move out."

She nodded and slipped out of the tent, followed by Jorin Montrill.

She still felt so keyed up from the attack near the Mountain of Death she knew she would never fall asleep. Her whole body tingled with heightened awareness and nerves. The raw pain and anguish of having killed a man had faded, but the repugnance remained as an uneasy reminder in the back of her mind.

"You seemed to have gained the favor of the general," Jorin remarked, walking along at her side in the predawn darkness. There was a questioning note in his voice, and she could sense his inquisitive gaze on her.

She smiled faintly to herself. The poor man would dearly love to know why an important person like General Viadon treated her almost as one of his captains. Truth be told, she wasn't certain herself why the general had taken such a shine to her. But, despite her gratitude toward Jorin for being there with her during the disturbing events of the night, she still harbored enough resentment toward him for his interference in her life that she was not ready to warm up to him at that moment.

"Hmm," she murmured, noncommittally, and veered off toward her tent, leaving him standing alone in the darkness with his curiosity unsatisfied.

As she neared her tent, a dark figure detached itself from the shadows near the door and came toward her.

"Caz?"

She recognized Gareth's voice, and the sight of his dear, familiar features caused the raw emotion to burst through the dam she'd built up over the last few hours. Before she knew it, she had thrown herself against his comforting chest, sobs racking her tired body and tears staining the front of his uniform, feeling very much like a small child who had been frightened by a horrible nightmare.

For a few moments, he simply held her, murmuring soothingly and stroking her sweat-dampened hair. Finally, he pushed her gently away and looked down at her, his eyes dark with concern. "What is it? What's wrong?"

She swallowed another sob, trying to get her emotions back under control. "I killed a man tonight," she said, and went on to tell him all that had happened since she had ridden out of camp early that morning, which now seemed a lifetime away.

When she had finished relating her experiences, she swiped at the tears staining her cheeks and smiled with bitter self-mockery. "A fine soldier I am, blubbering away like this. Especially after all my bragging to you and the general about how tough and independent I am. I've only killed one of our enemies and I'm acting like a weak-kneed coward. Maybe you were right after all, Gareth. Maybe I should quit deceiving myself into thinking I'm brave and strong and can handle all the bloody realities of war. Obviously, I can't."

Gareth remained silent for a moment. When he finally spoke, his voice held none of the reproach and chastisement she expected to hear. Instead, his quiet tones reflected a surprising mixture of sadness and self-recrimination. "My poor Caz. You're very wrong, you know. The only one who has been questioning your courage has been me. Even the general can see what I'm too selfish and blind to acknowledge."

"Maybe." She emitted a small, pitiful laugh.

He placed his hands gently on her shoulders and a catch sounded in his voice when he spoke again. "Don't ever think you're weak or cowardly, because that is the furthest thing from the truth. Your spirit and courage are amazing, and I'm proud of you. I know I haven't always told you that, because I've always been too busy playing the part of the big, strong brother who has to protect his helpless little sister from all the pain and suffering in the world. Can you ever forgive me for being such a pompous, insufferable brute?"

She felt the sting of tears well up once more in her eyes. With Gareth's words, the sense of closeness and love she felt toward him intensified.

True, he always considered himself the one who had to look after both of them, being the oldest and a male. But, even though he indeed acted self-important and insufferable at times, she had always known he loved her and would give up his very life to protect her from any threat, even though he didn't always say it in words.

She could not resist the urge to tease him. "I'll forgive you if you promise *not* to be a brute anymore."

He chuckled. "Now, that's going to be a hard promise to keep. I think it's in my nature to be unbearable and bossy at times. I can, at least, promise to try." His voice turned serious once more. "I'm sorry you had to go through the horror of killing a man tonight. You can see it was necessary, can't you? And, even though I'm still not happy about the idea of you placing yourself in such danger, I've come to realize I can't keep you in a safe bubble forever. With Saranor's wickedness spreading daily, there's going to be much more killing before this terrible war is over."

He touched a finger to her cheek and lifted away a tear that glistened there. "Caz, just because you feel such distress over killing that man, it doesn't mean you're weak. It means you're a decent, caring human being who abhors taking another's life. Don't ever lose that part of yourself. It's what sets you apart from inhuman monsters like Saranor and her followers." He gently squeezed her shoulders. "Will you be all right now?"

She hugged him tightly. "I think so. Thank you for the moral support, and for not saying I told you so. I don't know what I would do without you."

He laughed softly. "Remember that the next time you're yelling at me for trying to tell you what to do. Now, try to get some sleep."

He kissed her on the forehead and started back toward his own tent.

She smiled wistfully as she watched his shadowy figure weave its way through the campfires and tents spread out over the field. It felt good to unburden her doubts and uncertainties with him. The effort of trying to disguise her emotions around the general and Jorin Montrill had been very draining. Although she knew she would never be able to completely erase the memories of this night's disturbing events, Gareth's presence had helped to ease her troubled mind.

As she prepared for bed, she found herself hoping her brother's encouraging words would be enough to sustain her spirit in the dark days ahead. The attack on the three men in the rock clearing would be nothing compared to the full-scale battle that would take place when the general's army encountered the enemy forces defending Saranor's domain. The bloodshed and killing would be much more horrendous then.

She shivered as she thought of the mission awaiting her later that morning. Once again, she would be venturing into enemy territory. Perhaps, she would not be as fortunate this time to escape unscathed. Thirteen people against an unknown number of enemy troops would not stand much of a chance if they should be discovered.

Resolutely, she pushed the thoughts away. Both the general and Gareth had an extraordinary amount of confidence in her ability to face the upcoming conflict, more than she had in herself. Still, her nature would not allow her to turn tail and run when life threw challenges at her. After their parents' deaths, she and Gareth both developed independent and resilient characters. Even though that night's experience had badly shaken her, she vowed to become stronger because of it.

CHAPTER 20

Her preparations to leave took place well before Sergeant Zandorin scratched at the door flap of her tent later that morning. The few hours between her preparing for bed and the first faint light of dawn had passed in restless tossing and turning, until she had finally risen and waited on the edge of her narrow cot for Zandorin's summons. By the time the sergeant arrived, she had managed to reach a tenuous state of composure.

As she followed Sergeant Zandorin toward the horse enclosure in the predawn darkness, a restless wind kicked up dried leaves and dirt around their feet and flapped the sides of the canvas tents they passed. A narrow line of red rimmed the dark horizon to the east. Despite the effort she had made to quiet her nerves, Cazlina could not help but liken the reddish glow to the slitted glare of a monster and the wind to its fiery breath. She shivered and forced her gaze away from the troubling horizon.

As she hurried along after the sergeant, the wind suddenly buffeted her, causing her to stagger. She knew it had to be only her imagination, but she thought she could hear a faint demonical laughter in its voice. She was glad when she finally reached the horse enclosure where Miris waited patiently for her. The mare's gentle breath blew against her cheek, soothing the renewed unease that had assailed her in the short journey across the dusty field.

Cazlina's spirits lifted further when she saw that Gareth was among the small troop of soldiers preparing to leave the camp. He gave her a wink as he saddled his horse. Although she knew she should probably be annoyed the general had thought it necessary to send her brother with her to keep an eye on her, instead she felt only relief at his presence. The mission did not seem as frightening as it had before. Of course, the danger would not be lessened just because Gareth was at her side, but she knew she would be able to face it more bravely with him there.

Jorin Montrill, tightening the cinch of his saddle, looked up at her approach and flashed her one of his now-familiar grins. For once, his presence did not instill annoyance in her. Their mission to the Mountain of Death had shown her another side to the horse thief, and she found that, instead of feeling angry over his insisting he accompany her on every one of her assignments, this time she experienced a perverse comfort in knowing he would be there to help her with his strength and deft sword skills.

As the troop readied itself to depart, General Viadon came out of his tent to see them off. Not for the first time did Cazlina wonder if the man possessed superhuman powers, for it seemed as though he never slept and yet still managed to appear well-rested and alert. For her own part, she felt groggy and dull-witted, as though sleep had eluded her for an eternity. Only adrenaline and nervous energy kept her upright in the saddle, as well as a grim determination to live up to the general's, and her own, expectations of her.

Sergeant Zandorin gave the signal to leave the camp, which was already stirring to life as the small group of soldiers filed out of the compound.

The restless wind that had greeted Cazlina after leaving her tent had died down to a faint breeze that no longer held monstrous voices. The red line on the horizon had paled until only a faint rose blush stained the lightening sky. Cazlina's uneasiness lessened considerably. Lack of sleep and the disturbing adventure of the night before had left her susceptible to bizarre thoughts. No monsters glared at her from the sky or whispered malicious taunts in the wind.

Up ahead, the sergeant rode straight-backed in his saddle, his head held high with pride. Cazlina suspected this was the first major mission the man had been sent on by the general. She only hoped Zandorin had enough experience to carry out the crucial undertaking without jeopardizing the mission and the lives of the soldiers who accompanied him. On the other hand, it seemed doubtful General Viadon would have assigned such an important task to someone he had no faith in.

She glanced to her right where Gareth sat astride his horse, cantering silently beside her. He stared straight ahead, his face alight with barely-repressed excitement. This, she realized, would also be *his* first major mission, and she could see he was anxious to try out the newfound fighting skills he had learned in Terrangay these last few weeks. She felt a twinge of concern. They had promised each other they would not act rashly or recklessly in the dark days ahead, but it worried her a little that her brother's impulsive nature might get the better of him once he engaged in actual battle. She could only hope common sense and a cool head would prevail and keep him from doing something foolish that might get him killed.

On the other side of her was Jorin Montrill. He looked as calm and nonchalant as he always did, as he cantered easily along on his stolen roan stallion. Everything seemed to be a source of amusement to him, although she had to admit the previous night's venture near the Mountain of Death had shown her he could be deadly serious when the situation warranted. She shuddered to think of what the outcome might have been if he had not been with her to help dispatch Saranor's scouting party. She could only hope Montrill would display the same zeal for defending their little troop today should they be attacked and not turn tail and run at the first sign of trouble.

As though he was aware of her thoughts, or perhaps sensing her gaze on him, Jorin glanced her way and gave her a wink. She tightened her lips and whipped her head around to stare straight ahead; flustered he had caught her staring at him. For the rest of the morning, she refused to look his way again, knowing his eyes would be laughing at her and his firm mouth would be quirked in that maddening grin of his.

For the first few hours of the journey, the small troop of soldiers followed a rutted dirt road skirting a series of low-lying hills with stunted, gnarled trees marching up their slopes. The red dawn that had promised an unsettled day brought exactly that. Low-hanging clouds of charcoal gray scudded across a sky that seemed to press heavily down on the mounted soldiers. The smell of rain hung strongly in the air, but aside from an occasional raindrop pattering down on them, the storm held off.

By the time midday arrived, the troop had left the hills behind and cantered across open fields of long, brown grass. Cazlina glanced nervously about, feeling exposed and vulnerable. They were deep into Queen Saranor's domain and were approaching the Jezalar Plateau. Lerant would, undoubtedly, have many scouting parties roaming the vicinity. Instinct warned that danger lurked behind every long, swaying blade of grass surrounding the small troop. If an enemy patrol should suddenly rise up and attack them, there would be no place for them to take cover and defend themselves.

Sergeant Zandorin seemed to harbor the same apprehensions as she did, for he suddenly picked up the pace and gestured for the soldiers behind him to do the same. In no time, they covered the remaining open fields and then drew to a halt at the edge of a thick grove of yellow-leaved trees.

Cazlina failed to completely suppress a shudder as the dim, cool shadows settled around her. Her nightmare experience in the Windles' forest had left her feeling wary and nervous of all woods. Her eyes darted about, searching the underbrush for repulsive little creatures with sharp teeth and tiny, murderous claws.

She felt someone move up beside her and her keyed-up nerves made her jump.

"Are you all right, my lady?"

She glanced at Jorin and released the breath she hadn't realized she held.

He leaned forward. "I'm not totally familiar with this part of Queen Saranor's domain, but I've never heard of any creatures like the Windles inhabiting these forests. I don't think you have to worry about that here."

She felt warm color rush into her cheeks. She hadn't realized just how transparent her reaction to the forest had been. Jorin had obviously read something in her manner or her face to lead him to the perceptive conclusion that she had been reliving the nightmare of the Windles' forest, even though she had been trying her best to disguise her thoughts. Perversely, his assurances made her feel annoyance instead of relief.

She replied coldly, "I'm fine. Kindly, go away and stop bothering me."

Laughter glinted in his eyes. "Now, that's the spirit I've come to admire in my lady."

"Stop calling me your lady!"

He grinned and touched a finger to his forehead in a mocking salute before moving away.

The nice man is just concerned about you, Caz. Don't you think you were a little too sharp with him?

He deserves it for being such an intrusive pest.

Miris gave her head a small toss and blew out her breath in an exasperated sigh.

Up ahead, Sergeant Zandorin announced they would move a little further into the shadows of the forest and then stop to rest and eat. There would be no fires built and the soldiers were to make as little noise as possible. Some of Lerant's sentries might be lurking close by and the sergeant didn't want to draw unwanted attention to the troop.

Gareth came to sit beside Cazlina on the fallen log she had chosen as her seat. "How are you holding up, Caz?" he asked, in a low voice.

She leaned into his shoulder and sighed faintly. "I'm fine."

He grinned and shook his head. "Even if you weren't, you'd be too stubborn to admit it."

He glanced across to where Jorin Montrill sat on the ground, leaning back against the smooth bark of a slender tree with his eyes closed.

"What's the story with Montrill? How did you meet him?" Gareth asked, casually. But, she could hear the underlying tension in his tone and suppressed a weary sigh.

Her brother would not be satisfied until he knew every detail of how she and the horse thief had become acquainted with each other. She wished now she had not confronted Jorin quite so negatively in front of her brother in the courtyard of the general's headquarters. Even though he had not heard their conversation, her tense body language had certainly triggered Gareth's protective instincts, and she didn't doubt for a moment he would do something drastic if he thought Jorin had threatened or harmed her in any way.

Don't forget to tell him the nice man saved our lives, Miris said, helpfully, from nearby. *Then, perhaps, he won't be so upset.*

Cazlina threw her a withering look. *I should just* forget *the part about Montrill trying to steal you and his shameless interference in our lives ever since? The man is an irritating scoundrel.*

The mare snorted delicately. *Well, you must admit, Caz, he hasn't actually done anything bad to us. I think he's just concerned for our safety.*

Cazlina shook her head. Miris might be convinced Jorin Montrill was harmless, but she did not trust the horse thief one bit. He seemed determined to force himself into her life at every turn, as though his trying to steal her mare had somehow earned him the right to keep on harassing her. True, he had not actually harmed her, aside from causing her to experience strong feelings of exasperation and bad temper in his presence. But, just because he had not plunged a sword into her and stolen Miris away to add to his collection of ill-gotten livestock, that didn't mean she would allow herself to drop her guard and start trusting him or his motives any time soon.

Beside her, Gareth sighed impatiently. Cazlina bit down on her lip, wondering how much to tell him.

"Sergeant Zandorin doesn't want us to talk too much," she said, as a stalling tactic.

Gareth's eyebrow rose warningly. "Caz."

She wrinkled her nose, knowing she could not escape that easily. She would have to give him an explanation sooner or later, or he would keep hounding her until she did.

Finally, she decided it would be better for all concerned if she left out certain parts of the story. It would only serve to cause trouble between the two men, which she wanted to avoid at all costs. General Viadon certainly did not need his soldiers fighting amongst themselves, and especially not over her. She had to prove to the general she could handle herself in any situation. Compared to Viadon's campaign against Queen Saranor, Cazlina's problems with Jorin Montrill could hardly be considered significant.

She chanced a glance at Jorin. He looked to be dozing, but she couldn't tell for certain. A faint smile played about his firm mouth, which could mean a pleasant dream occupied his mind, or he found her predicament with Gareth amusing.

In a low voice, she gave Gareth a shortened version of her adventures on the way to Terrangay, even skipping lightly over her encounter with the loathsome little Windles. Her brother didn't need to hear that she and Miris had nearly been killed. Since they had survived, it seemed pointless to upset him and perhaps trigger another lecture about how she should have stayed in Rothtown.

As for Jorin Montrill's part in her adventures, he too assumed an insignificant role. She explained her hostile attitude toward him was the result of the man's infuriating belief that being young and female automatically rendered her helpless and incapable of looking out for herself. Since Gareth knew full well her fiercely independent nature, she felt certain he would find this a plausible explanation. Indeed, a large part of her dislike of Montrill, aside from the fact he had tried to steal Miris, stemmed from his smug attitude that she would surely die a horrible death if he did not protect her.

"So, there you have it," she said, bringing her tale to an end.

She glared over at Jorin Montrill, who still slept, or at least continued to appear as such. "He's just another annoying male who thinks I'm helpless. As you know, I don't like that attitude one bit."

Her brother grunted. She could see her explanation of why she resented Montrill so much had not totally convinced him, and she couldn't really blame him. But, she had no intentions of pursuing the matter any further. Gareth would just have to be content with what she had chosen to tell him.

Sergeant Zandorin passed by at that moment, glaring at the two of them. "No more talking," he hissed. "We're about to move out."

Cazlina nodded and stood up, glad Gareth would not have the chance to press her for further details.

As she moved toward Miris, she saw Jorin rise from beneath the tree and stretch leisurely. He sauntered toward his stallion, and as he passed by Cazlina, he lowered his head to her ear, his firm mouth quirked in an amused smile.

"An interesting tale," he murmured. "But, you disappoint me, Cazlina. I was certain you would give your brother a more colorful and dramatic version of our encounters. I'm wounded that I was reduced to such an insignificant part of the story." His eyes danced. "Perhaps, I should give him my version."

She glared up at him. "You weren't sleeping at all! You were eavesdropping."

He shrugged. "I can't help it if I have very acute hearing."

"Well, unless you want to see yourself run through by *Gareth's* sword, I would advise you not to say anything to him. If he knew the whole truth, you would be in very big trouble."

One eyebrow rose. "Even more so than I am with you, my lady? Then, I guess, I have to thank you for protecting me."

She smiled grimly. "If you are as smart as you obviously think you are, you would do well to remember my warning." She swung up into the saddle and turned Miris away. As the small troop of soldiers continued further on into the dappled shadows of the forest, she suppressed a heavy sigh.

Somehow, she just knew Jorin Montrill would not take her threats and warnings seriously. He certainly hadn't up to this point. Even with the added antagonism of Gareth to contend with, it seemed almost certain that Jorin would continue to treat that with the same nonchalant condescension he did everything else.

CHAPTER 21

When Zandorin's little troop of soldiers left the grove of yellow-leafed trees, they found themselves entering a wild maze of cliffs, canyons and pinnacles of black-streaked gray rock scoured and carved by wind and water. The severely eroded landscape forcefully reminded Cazlina of the barren, brooding land around the Mountain of Death; only this terrain seemed twice as daunting and forbidding.

Despite the smell of rain in the heavy air, a hot wind swept across the naked buttes and down through the canyons, flinging grains of black sand into the faces of the soldiers. They pulled the collars of their uniform jackets up, trying to shield their noses and mouths from the gritty, flying particles.

Up ahead, Cazlina could see a long, narrow plateau of black-banded rock towering almost as high as the Mountain of Death over the other ridges and cliffs. That had to be the Jezalar Plateau, she thought, and a thrill of fear raced up her spine. Somewhere in that stark and eerie landscape, Lerant and his troops awaited word of General Viadon's movements. How in the name of all the gods would she and Sergeant Zandorin's pitifully small troop of soldiers find the enemy in all that weathered rock?

Zandorin stopped his horse and sat gazing up at the imposing plateau that lay several miles away. From the dazed expression on his round face, Cazlina suspected he felt the same apprehension and helplessness at the enormity of their task. Then he straightened in the saddle, a look of grim determination settling over him.

"Everyone, dismount," he said, quietly, his eyes flicking across the bleak cliff walls and ravines in front of them. "We'll need to discuss a plan of action to find out where Lerant has his troops stationed and how many he has."

The soldiers dismounted and gathered silently around the sergeant, forming a tight circle to keep away the hot wind and blowing sand.

To her annoyance, Cazlina felt Jorin and Gareth crowding closely on either side of her until she felt almost suffocated. She elbowed both of them sharply in the ribs and they grunted, moving back a step and allowing her room to breathe.

Miris' soft breath tickled the back of her neck. *Now, Caz, don't be so prickly. They only want to keep you safe.*

Cazlina tightened her lips and clamped down on her irritation. She turned her attention back to the sergeant, who still had a worried look in his eye. She thought she could understand his feelings. He wanted to prove to General Viadon he could successfully carry out the mission assigned to him, but at the same time, he found the task much more daunting than his duties at the general's headquarters.

"Now, ladies and gentlemen, listen up carefully. You know our mission is to find out exactly where Lerant has his army and how big it is. Then we ride back to General Viadon and report our findings."

A lanky, dark-haired woman with a huge bow strung across her back lifted her hand. "Excuse me, Sergeant, but how are we going to find out how big Lerant's army is with just the thirteen of us?"

The sergeant's eyes swept the barren, wind-scoured landscape around them. "Just past those cliffs and canyons there's flat grassland spreading for several miles toward the foot of the Jezalar Plateau. The general believes that's where Lerant will have his troops stationed. General Viadon thinks this is probably the main force of Saranor's army, and the grassland would be the only place big enough to hold hundreds or thousands of soldiers. That will at least give us a starting point."

A burly soldier with a swarthy, pockmarked face grinned, revealing several gaps in his teeth. "Do you think we'll see some action, Sergeant? I wouldn't mind cutting a few of those murdering dogs to pieces."

Zandorin shook his head forcefully. "The general's orders were explicit. No engaging in battle unless absolutely necessary."

The man's grin widened. "It doesn't need to be in battle. Just a quick little nip into their camp, cut a few throats and out again. No one would be the wiser."

Zandorin glared at him. "You heard me, Kesel! We do a quick reconnaissance and then it's back to the general."

Kesel! Cazlina threw a startled glance at the burly soldier and looked away again, afraid he would recognize her as the assailant who had wounded him in the narrow mountain pass.

Behind her, Miris moved closer, her worried breath fanning the back of Cazlina's neck. *Oh, oh, Caz, it's one of those bad men from the mountains!*

Beside her, she heard a faint intake of breath from Jorin as he, too, realized the identity of the man. She felt his strong hand close over her arm and squeeze gently, but she didn't need his silent warning to keep her mouth shut. Obviously, it had been dark enough in the mountain pass to prevent Kesel from seeing her clearly; else he surely would have said something by now. But, if she spoke, he would almost certainly recognize her voice.

"We'll split up into two groups," the sergeant continued. "I'll take one group around to the east of the Plateau. It's a bit of a rough ride through these hills, but I want to make sure we come at the grassland from both directions." He pointed to the dark-haired woman with the bow who had spoken earlier. "Merinda, you lead the other group around to the west. That way is fairly easy, because you can skirt most of the canyons and cliffs. And, it's the way the general will be bringing his army, so make sure you take good note of any sentries or potential ambush sites."

He glanced up at the sky. "It'll be dark soon, which will be good for us, because we'll be able to see the torches and fires of the enemy camp. But, we'll have to use our own torches sparingly. We don't need any sentries spotting us. Keep the Plateau in sight as much as you can and stick to a southerly direction. You won't miss the grassland. Try to get as close as you can to the Plateau. Once you've confirmed the location and approximate size of Lerant's army, return to this spot. If you're not back here in five hours, I'll assume you've been captured and will return to General Viadon at once. I expect you to do the same if I fail to meet you here at the appointed time."

He looked around at the group of soldiers. "Everyone got that?" He stared hard at Kesel. "No quick nips into the enemy camp, Kesel, or I'll have you hung for insubordination."

The man glared at him, but finally nodded.

161

Sergeant Zandorin glanced toward Cazlina, Gareth and Jorin. "You three come with me, as well as Pross and Donegal. The rest of you follow Merinda."

Cazlina felt immense relief that Kesel had been relegated to the other group. She had no wish to remain in his company for any length of time in case he finally came to the realization that she was the one responsible for the bulky bandage poking out of the right sleeve of his jacket.

Within minutes, the little troop remounted and prepared to go their separate ways.

"Make sure you're back here in five hours," Zandorin reminded Merinda. "I want to be well on my way back to General Viadon before first light."

She nodded and wheeled her horse toward the looming Plateau up ahead. The six soldiers in her group followed closely, bending low over their mounts' necks in an effort to block out the blowing sand. Before long, they had disappeared from sight into the craggy canyons and ravines.

"Let's go," Zandorin said to his group, spurring his horse up a long, narrow canyon running between the bleak cliff walls.

Cazlina cantered along behind the sergeant, trying to keep his broad back in sight against the sand that found its way into her eyes no matter how hard she squinted against it. The approaching darkness made the going even tougher and the uneven ground rolled and shifted under Miris' hooves. The canyon walls began to narrow further as they rode up into the eroded range of mountains. The hot wind blew harder, flinging itself down through the tunnel of blasted rock with a high-pitched whine that beat against the ears of the riders.

Cazlina wanted this mission to be over with as soon as possible. The unease that had plagued her earlier that morning as she had made her way to the horse enclosure returned in full force as she imagined a faint demonical laughter in the wind that howled around her.

By now, they had reached the top of the ridge where it widened out into a flat table of rock strewn with fist-sized boulders. The far edge dropped away into dizzying nothingness, and the black-streaked walls of the Jezalar Plateau loomed beyond the impossibly wide gap. Cazlina wondered dazedly how they were ever going to reach the foot of that imposing butte. Yet, Sergeant Zandorin did not hesitate. He led them toward the left side of the table of rock, and Cazlina could see a wide, relatively smooth trail leading down into a maze of ravines. Up here, the flying sand had nearly disappeared, but the wind still howled like a specter around the spires and pinnacles of rock.

The trail down the mountain, although steep in places, proved to be easier to negotiate than the canyon they had used to reach the top. Sergeant Zandorin seemed to know the best route to take to avoid the rockiest and steepest parts of the trail. Of course, Cazlina realized, the sergeant had probably been one of the men General Viadon had taken with him when he had escaped from Saranor's castle, so naturally the man would know his way around the area.

Darkness descended rapidly as the small group of riders carefully navigated the trail down into the labyrinth of ravines. Despite the heavy, hot air, Cazlina shivered with nerves and apprehension. Somewhere below them, Captain Lerant's army was spread out across Saranor's domain, an army that would not hesitate to crush Sergeant Zandorin's pitifully small troop of soldiers like bugs, should they be captured. Even now, sentries hidden in the confusing maze of cliffs and canyons could be spying on the little group of riders, letting them ride further and further into danger before pouncing on them and killing them.

Cazlina frantically searched the dark shadows, hoping to spot an enemy soldier before he could leap out and pull her from the mare. Her growing panic communicated itself to Miris, who began to skitter nervously on the rocky trail, bringing them dangerously close to the edge.

With a great effort, Cazlina quelled her fear and calmed Miris with a soothing hand on her sleek neck. *Don't mind me, dear one. I'm just being foolish.*

You are not being foolish, Miris said. *I don't like this place, either. Something doesn't feel right.*

Cazlina's pulse gave a little bump. *Can you sense the enemy close by, Miris?*

I don't know what I sense, the mare said, fretfully. *All I know is the air carries an odor I don't like.*

Once more, Cazlina swept the landscape, but it had grown so dark she could hardly see the trail or Sergeant Zandorin in front of her. Behind her, she heard the reassuring hoof beats of Gareth's and Jorin's horses, but, without visual contact, it still felt as though she and Miris were alone on that dark, lonely path.

The trail began to flatten out, and Cazlina sighed faintly in relief. They must be nearing the bottom of the cliff, which meant the grassland between it and the Plateau was probably not far off. Hopefully, their reconnaissance mission would be carried out swiftly and they could return once more to General Viadon without the enemy even knowing they had been there.

It seemed strange to her that the little group of soldiers had not encountered any sentries up to this point, for surely Lerant would have posted guards in the hills around his encampment. Yet, no one had challenged Cazlina's group. Of course, she certainly welcomed the lack of enemy contact, but it bothered her a little, as well. She hoped Merinda had also encountered no danger in leading her group toward the Plateau.

Miris suddenly flung up her head, snorting urgently through her flaring nostrils. *Caz, there's something here! I can feel great danger all around us. We must hide.*

CHAPTER 22

Cazlina didn't stop to question the mare's frantic message. She spurred Miris forward, at the same time crying out urgently, "Sergeant! There's danger here. I think the enemy has surrounded us."

Ahead of her, she could dimly make out the broad back of the sergeant atop the darker shape of his horse. He stopped and turned to look back at her over his shoulder, his face barely visible in the darkness. She sensed, rather than saw, the frown of impatience he gave her.

"How do you know? We haven't seen anything to indicate the enemy is anywhere near us."

"We have to take cover," Cazlina implored, ignoring the skepticism in his voice.

She felt Miris trembling beneath her, the mare's panicky thoughts careening through her own brain. *I think it's those terrible mist things! They feel the same as the ones we almost ran into outside the city.*

Cazlina's heart gave a frightened leap, dreading another encounter with those inhuman beings. Before she could insist to Zandorin again about the urgency of the situation, Gareth prodded his horse up beside her.

"Caz, what is it? What's going on?"

She turned to him, hoping to convince *him* at least of the danger surrounding them since the sergeant seemed disinclined to believe her. "Gareth, we have to get off this trail immediately and take cover. Lerant's sentries are nearby."

Her brother's head swiveled to survey the surrounding walls of eroded rock. "Are you sure? Did you see or hear something?"

She suppressed a groan of impatience. Why did everyone have to question her? Why couldn't they just accept her word and find concealment instead of standing there exposed on the open path?

Gareth knew about her ability to communicate with Miris, and Cazlina opened her mouth to tell him the mare had given her the warning when Jorin rode up to them.

"What's this about Lerant's sentries?" he asked.

"We're in danger," Cazlina said in a rush. "We have to get off this path *now,* before Lerant's sentries swoop down and kill us all."

"You're just imagining things, girl," the soldier named Pross said from behind her. "If the enemy is surrounding us, where are they, eh? Why haven't they attacked us yet?" He made a sound of disparagement. "This is what happens when you let a flighty young girl come along on a military mission. You're just panicking for no good reason."

Cazlina ground her teeth in frustration. How could she convince these battle-trained soldiers the danger was real and not just a product of her fear and panic? She couldn't very well tell them her mare had warned her of the presence of the enemy. They would think she had lost all reason and sanity.

"I don't know why they haven't attacked yet," she said, trying to keep her voice reasonable. "Maybe they're not sure how many of us there are and they want to find out before attacking. Or, maybe they're letting us ride into a trap further down the trail. All I know for certain is, they're here somewhere, and, if we hope to remain alive to report back to General Viadon, we have to do something fast."

By now, Sergeant Zandorin had joined them, his face still holding an impatient frown. "I haven't heard or seen anything to indicate there is anyone around here besides us," he said, irritably. "What makes you so sure we're in such danger?"

"You haven't heard or seen anything, because what's here are those horrible things called Mist Riders that Pharon captured the other night," Cazlina said, crossly, forgetting for a moment that she should show respect and deference toward her superior officer in her pressing need to convince him of the danger.

Miris, can you still sense those beings around here?

The mare tossed her head. *They're closer, Caz. I can feel them almost on top of us.*

"Sergeant, listen to me," Cazlina demanded. "This is *not* my imagination. We're in grave danger. Get off this path and in among the rocks before it's too late."

"Maybe she's right, Sergeant," Jorin spoke up. "Cazlina is not a weak, silly girl given to unprovoked flights of fancy, believe me. If anything, she's a little too cautious and serious for her own good."

Cazlina glared at him, not sure if she should thank him or be annoyed at his mild reprimand.

Unperturbed by her frosty expression, he went on, "If she thinks something's wrong, I, for one, am inclined to believe her. Besides, what would it hurt to exercise a bit of caution until we know for sure what we are or aren't facing?"

Zandorin stared pointedly at Cazlina and then spun his horse around to face the downward slope of the rocky path once more. "I know of a small canyon just a few hundred yards down," he said. "We'll ride into that."

"But, Sergeant, won't we be boxed in then?" Gareth asked, in a worried voice. "Maybe that's the trap Cazlina mentioned earlier."

The sergeant shook his head. "If memory serves me right, there's another way out of the canyon on the far side. It's only an animal track, pretty narrow and rough, but it should bring us out a few miles to the east of the Plateau, which means we'll probably have to backtrack a bit."

He threw another glance over his shoulder at Cazlina. "This is going to cost us more time, girl. I hope you know what you're talking about."

Cazlina raised her chin. "Why don't we stop arguing about whether a girl could be right or not and get out of here before it's too late."

He growled low in his throat, obviously affronted at being told what to do by a young woman, but she noticed, with relief, that he began to urge his horse down the dark, rocky path.

Miris pranced nervously for a moment. *We must hurry, Caz!*

Cazlina nodded and they hastily followed the sergeant down the trail. Gareth and Jorin followed closely behind, while the other two men brought up the rear. A sense of urgency settled over the group and Cazlina wondered in exasperation if *her* warnings had finally persuaded the men, or if it had been Jorin's words they had decided to listen to because he was a man.

As they clattered down the rocky path, Cazlina whipped her head to the right and left, trying to distinguish foul, misty shapes among the dark shadows and pinnacles of rock. The keening wind, which had not ceased blowing since they had entered the maze of canyons and spires of rock, took on an even higher-pitched whine.

Up ahead, she vaguely saw the sergeant's horse stop on the path. He pointed to the left, indicating the entrance to the small canyon. Cazlina felt a small surge of relief, but, like Gareth, she wondered uneasily if they might not be riding directly into a trap set for them by Lerant's sentries. The closer she came to the entrance, the stronger her premonition became. It was disturbingly similar to the apprehension she and Miris had felt upon entering the forest of those loathsome little creatures, the Windles.

Miris obviously felt the same way for she said, worriedly, *I don't know, Caz. I don't like the feel of this.*

I don't, either, dear heart. But, we may not have a choice. If we stay out here, we'll be more exposed than if we go into the canyon. At least in there, we could split up and find places to conceal ourselves instead of having to follow single-file down this trail.

The mare snorted anxiously. *I hope you're right.*

A talus slope made up of plates of shattered rock, some as big as houses and others as small as a man's fist, provided a precarious descent from the trail into the canyon. The six riders had to proceed cautiously to prevent the slabs of delicately balanced rocks from shifting and sliding.

Cazlina's brain screamed at them to hurry before the Mist Riders caught them out on the shaky, exposed slope, but she knew one false step could send them tumbling to serious injury or even death on the canyon floor below. She gritted her teeth in an effort to quell the rising panic threatening to overwhelm her and concentrated on guiding Miris safely over the dangerous ground.

They had almost reached the bottom of the slope and a dry gully fringed with spindly alders and tamarisks when a gray shape with long trailing tendrils and twin orbs of burning orange fire suddenly swooped down on them.

Cazlina screamed and ducked, nearly losing her seat on Miris. The mare neighed in terror and skidded on a sheet of flat rock. Cazlina fought for control, barely preventing them from sliding off the edge of the rock plate and into a dangerous jumble of wind-blasted trees.

CHAPTER 23

All around her, she heard shouts from the men and frightened whinnies from the horses as more Mist Riders plunged down on them from the dark skies. Whimpering with fear, she fumbled for the sword hanging by her side and withdrew it clumsily, fighting to stay on the panicked mare beneath her.

Gray mist brushed in front of her eyes and she jerked back, gasping at the foul stench sweeping across her flared nostrils. She swung the sword frantically at the insubstantial form in front of her, but the weapon passed through the swaying tentacles as it would through air.

"You cannot kill a Mist Rider so easily, human," an unearthly voice hissed at her. "Surrender now, or suffer the consequences of my touch."

"Cazlina!" She heard Gareth frantically call her name, and looked wildly about for him.

The air was filled with gray, wavering shapes that swooped and spun like curtains of gauze threaded with burning streamers of orange fire. At first, Cazlina couldn't see any of the others, but then she spotted Gareth only a short distance away, trying to fight his way past the Mist Riders to get to her. His sword had as little effect on the inhuman beings as hers, but he kept swinging it as he urged his terrified horse toward her.

"Gareth!" she cried out in horror as a Mist Rider flew directly at her brother and obscured her view of him. At the same moment, she felt the tiniest touch of waving tendrils brush her face as the Mist Rider that menaced her before darted in close again. Although she could barely feel the unclean mist against her skin, she experienced an agonizing chill that numbed the very bones of her cheek.

Gasping for breath, she pulled away and the Mist Rider's eerily inhuman voice hissed, "That is but a small taste of what my touch can do, human. Surrender or I shall freeze the very life from your weak, pathetic body."

A high-pitched scream filled with unbelievable agony ripped through the air behind her and abruptly ended in mid-cry. Her heart lurched up into her throat as she whipped around on the trembling back of Miris to find the source of the horrible scream.

For a moment, her paralyzed brain could not make sense of what she saw. One of the Mist Riders floated up and away from a white statue of a man and a horse that glowed eerily in the darkness near the edge of the talus slope. The man's mouth stretched wide in a fixed, gaping grimace, still holding the echoes of the tortured scream that had shattered the air seconds before.

In the space of time it took to draw a horrified breath, Cazlina realized the white statue was not some bizarre sculpture of marble carved by an unknown hand in that desolate wilderness, but none other than Pross and his horse. The Mist Rider's lethal touch had frozen the man into a lifeless hulk. Everything about him--his skin, his hair, his clothes, even the pupils of his wide staring eyes-- had turned snow white and rock solid. His horse had fared no better, its muscular body twisted awkwardly, as though it had been in the midst of jumping sideways, and its lips drawn back over its teeth in an expression of agony.

For a moment, Cazlina could not breathe, feeling her heart freeze inside her chest as surely as though the Mist Rider had touched her, too, with its deadly tendrils. Dimly, she could just make out the others in her group immobilized in positions of shock, with waving shapes flitting above them.

"Stop!"

The booming command penetrated the fog in her mind, and she shuddered as sensations and emotions rushed violently back into her numb body.

The thunderous voice had come from the top of the talus slope where several flickering torches suddenly appeared. Dark shapes on horseback materialized on the edge of the slope, looking down on the frozen tableau below in the narrow canyon.

One of the riders separated from the others and started down the shaky slope, the light from his torch bouncing wildly against the rocks and trees.

"Trax! Are you completely stupid? You know the queen's orders. She wants these prisoners alive." Cold anger vibrated in the rider's rough voice.

The Mist Rider who had been tormenting Cazlina drew itself up into a tall, menacing curtain of foul mist. "Do not insult me, human! You will regret it."

The rider pulled up in front of Cazlina, flicking a quick glance toward where she sat motionless with fear on the mare. Her breath caught in her throat as cold eyes raked across her. Twin scars of ridged skin bisected the man's cheeks on either side of the faceplate of his spiked helmet, from which long strands of black, lank hair straggled out and brushed his shoulders. Across his broad chest, bands of narrow, flexible steel overlaid with hundreds of tiny, lethal-looking spikes created a formidable armor, and he wore heavy gauntlets with similar adornments. He looked the part of a cruel, dangerous soldier, and Cazlina had no doubt he would kill without mercy or conscience.

She slumped a little in relief as his icy gaze pulled away from hers and back toward the Mist Rider hovering nearby. No trace of fear showed on the man's disfigured face as he contemplated the foul creature before him.

"Queen Saranor does not tolerate disobedience," the man said, tightly. "You would be well advised to curb your repulsive appetites, if you know what is good for you."

The Mist Rider named Trax remained silent, the burning orange orbs of its eyes flickering in response to this reprimand.

By now, the rest of the riders had descended into the canyon, and, after relieving the captives of their weapons, silently surrounded them, creating an impenetrable wall of bristling weaponry, cold, flat eyes and wildly flickering torches.

The man who had addressed the Mist Rider named Trax, and who seemed to be the leader of the troop, turned in his saddle to cast his callous gaze over the five prisoners. He frowned as his eyes swept across the unfortunate Pross in his frozen, lifeless state and then his expression became unreadable once more, until his cold eyes fell upon Sergeant Zandorin. Then a chilling smile twitched his hard, thin-lipped mouth.

Zandorin blanched, shaken by the relentless gaze of his captor.

The leader of the queen's troops urged his horse over to stand in front of the sergeant. "Ah, Zandorin. How nice to see you again. I see Viadon has made you a sergeant in his traitorous army. Congratulations."

Zandorin gulped, struggling to keep his face expressionless. "Lerant."

Cazlina's head jerked up at the name. This cruel, ruthless man was none other than Captain Lerant himself? No wonder the men waiting by the Mountain of Death had seemed so afraid of displeasing the queen's soldier. Clearly, he would have shown no mercy for their failure to complete the mission assigned to them.

"That's *Captain* Lerant, Sergeant. Did the general not teach you to respect your superiors?" He smiled smugly. "Why are you here? Have you come to your senses and deserted the enemy to rejoin the queen's forces? Or, has my good friend Viadon sent you to scout out my position and strength?" He leaned forward over the saddle horn. "Which is it?"

Zandorin remained silent, a stubborn, defiant look on his face, and Lerant laughed coldly. "Such admirable loyalty, but, alas, I fear it is for a lost cause. Queen Saranor will prevail in her bid for supremacy, and General Viadon will pay dearly for his betrayal. As will all who foolishly follow his lead and persist in defying the queen."

He turned his head, and, once more, his dark eyes clashed with Cazlina's. A faint smile brushed his disfigured face when she flinched, as though struck by him. His next words chilled her to the very bone.

"The queen will be pleased to have such a succulent youth as you to feast upon."

CHAPTER 24

The prisoners were prodded back up the precarious slope to the dark trail and marched down it to where the path flattened out into extensive grassland. The imposing black bulk of the Jezalar Plateau loomed in the background. The Mist Riders swooped overhead, their foul stench stinging Cazlina's nostrils, and the rush of wind from their waving tendrils making her cringe.

Terrified and shaking, she took in the sight of hundreds of fires and flickering torches dotting the sprawling field, sending plumes of smoke up into the air to hang in a thick, acrid cloud. Raucous laughter and coarse voices floated out on the hot, heavy air, mingling with the odors of pungent cooking, horses and sour sweat. The sight and sounds of so many enemy soldiers nearly paralyzed her.

She tried to twist in the saddle to search for the comforting presence of Gareth and was rewarded with a hard cuff on the side of the head from the rough-bearded soldier riding beside her. "Eyes in front! No moving unless I tell you to."

Caz, are you all right? Miris asked, anxiously.

He didn't hurt me much, Cazlina tried to reassure her, although her ears rang from the hard blow.

She swallowed nervously, steadfastly keeping her gaze on the back of the other enemy soldier riding in front of her.

What are we going to do, Caz?

Cazlina licked dry lips, trying to quell the rising panic threatening to overwhelm her. What *could* they do? There were hundreds, maybe thousands, of enemy soldiers surrounding them and countless repulsive Mist Riders hovering overhead. What in the name of all the gods could their pitiful little group do to avoid a horrible, inescapable fate as victims of Queen Saranor's Pool of Souls? True, when Sergeant Zandorin's troop failed to report back to General Viadon, he would know something had gone wrong and would ride with all haste toward Saranor's castle, but by then it might be too late for Cazlina and the others.

Unless…

Miris, I have an idea. As soon as we are allowed to dismount, I want you to break away from the man holding you and run as fast as you can back to General Viadon. When he sees you without me on your back, he'll know something's wrong and will come to our rescue.

Caz, I can't leave you alone! I need to stay here to protect you.

Miris, dear heart, I don't like the idea of being separated from you either, but I think it's the only way to let the general know of our fate.

The mare's ears flicked back and forth in agitation and she blew noisily through her nostrils. The enemy soldier riding beside Cazlina and holding Miris' reins threw a frowning glance at the animal, and Cazlina gently patted her sleek neck. *Miris, calm down. We don't want to draw any unwanted attention to ourselves.*

But, Caz, I don't like the idea of leaving you here by yourself. Fear sparked like a wildfire through the mare's mind. *What if something happens to you before I could get back here? I would never forgive myself.*

Aware of the man's intense scrutiny of her, Cazlina stared straight ahead, trying to keep her face expressionless as she carried on the silent conversation with Miris.

We must take that chance, dear one. I don't think Lerant will harm any of us until we reach Saranor's castle. You heard him in the canyon. The queen wants her prisoners alive so she can use them in her horrible ceremony. And, you know that Gareth will protect me to his last breath.

Doubt still lingered in the mare's mind. *What if I get lost on the way back to the general? What if he doesn't understand the message I'm trying to deliver to him? What if he waits too long before he brings his army here?*

Miris, you won't get lost. You're very intelligent and brave and you know the way. Don't let panic get the better of you and you'll be fine. I'm sure General Viadon is not that far behind us. And, secondly, he is also very intelligent. As soon as he sees you've returned to him without me, he'll know immediately something has happened to our group.

I still don't like the idea, Miris said, stubbornly.

I know, neither do I. But, it's the best plan I can come up with at the moment. If we don't try to get a message somehow to General Viadon, we're all doomed.

At that moment, another voice sounded in her head, this one with a distinctly masculine timbre. *I could not help but overhear, Cazlina. Perhaps, I can help, too.*

Cazlina didn't dare turn her head to pinpoint the source of the voice, but she was fairly certain whose it was. *Is this Jorin's horse?*

Yes, my name is Veygar. I would like to help you.

How?

I, too, will escape my captor and accompany your mare on her journey back to the general. That way, she does not have to carry out her mission alone and the sight of two horses without riders might spur Viadon to greater haste.

Gratitude swept through Cazlina at the roan's offer. The idea of poor Miris running alone and frightened through the dark night and unfamiliar territory was heart wrenching, but knowing the stallion was with her on her journey would greatly ease Cazlina's mind.

Miris, did you hear? Jorin's horse, Veygar, has offered to go with you. Would you like the idea better if that were the case?

I would certainly welcome his presence, Miris said. Faint amusement threaded its way through Cazlina's fear at the note of shy coyness in the mare's tone.

Good, then that's settled. As soon as you see a chance to escape, take it and return to General Viadon as swiftly as you can.

Cazlina settled back in her saddle, a sense of relief chasing away some of her terror. Granted, it wasn't much of a plan, but at least she felt as though she was doing something to help extricate her and the other captives from their dire predicament.

They were marched through the encampment. Coarse-featured soldiers with emotionless eyes watched them pass and then ignored them, returning to their various tasks as though the sight of more prisoners had become so commonplace they were no longer a source of curiosity or attention.

Cazlina's fears returned as they were led deeper into the middle of the enemy camp. With so many soldiers surrounding them, escape would be next to impossible. She was certain Lerant would place a heavy guard around them, as well.

The prisoners were prodded toward a large cage built from thick, wooden poles driven deep into the ground. To her dismay, Cazlina could see that half a dozen dejected, slumped figures already occupied the cage. More captives bound for Saranor's castle of horrors.

Two guards stood stiffly at the front of the wooden enclosure. Their arms in the heavy, spiked gauntlets were crossed over their chests and their eyes stared straight ahead. When Lerant approached with his band of prisoners, the two men snapped to attention.

"More guests for you, Rizol," Lerant said with a smirk. "Be sure to treat them kindly."

One of the men grinned, revealing yellowed teeth. "Of course, Captain. Don't we always?"

Cazlina's heart tripped a little faster. *Are you ready, Miris? When I've dismounted, bite the arm of the man holding your reins and flee as quickly as you can into the night.*

Miris tossed her head and said grimly, *I think I will be quite happy to bite this time, Caz, even though I normally don't like to do it.*

Good girl. Be prepared, Veygar, Cazlina said to the stallion.

The roan's dour voice sounded in her mind. *I, too, welcome the opportunity to inflict pain upon my captor.*

Miris, when you reach the general, try to act as scared and nervous as you can so he'll know something's wrong.

The mare snorted. *Believe me, Caz, I won't have to act.*

Lerant brought the group to a halt and ordered the prisoners to dismount. Cazlina hesitated, her body quivering with nervous anticipation, and the man beside her gave her a hard shove. "Move it!"

She slid from the saddle and pressed herself against the trembling side of the mare, trying to soothe away the tendrils of panic skittering among the chambers of the animal's mind. *Easy, Miris, don't draw attention just yet. Wait for Veygar.*

She risked a glance toward the big stallion and saw him tossing his head and stamping his feet in impatience. Jorin, still astride him, gave the horse a quizzical glance as he swung his leg over the saddle to dismount. As soon as Jorin's foot cleared the stirrup, Veygar lowered his head and bellowed, kicking out sideways with his powerful hind legs. Jorin jumped out of the way, a look of shock on his face as one of the stallion's sharp hooves caught the left kneecap of the enemy soldier beside him, breaking the bone with an audible snap. The man screamed in agony and collapsed to the ground, clutching his injured limb.

Now, Miris!

Cazlina staggered backward as the mare bucked, her breath whistling through flared nostrils. Her head whipped around to nip sharply at the arm of the enemy soldier standing to the right of her. He yelped in pain and dropped the reins.

Both horses wheeled as one and streaked off into the night shadows, kicking out with flying hooves at anyone unfortunate enough to be in their way. The soldiers scattered, trying frantically to avoid the wild-eyed, snorting animals.

One of the men standing by the prisoners' cage snatched his longbow from his back and notched an arrow, preparing to send it flying after the horses. Cazlina's heart leaped into her throat, but before she could scream and rush toward the man, Lerant himself reached out and knocked the bow to one side.

"Let them go. There's no sense in wasting valuable ammunition. The stupid beasts will probably break their necks falling off a cliff in the dark."

He flicked a glance toward Cazlina, his hard mouth twisting in a cruel smile. "Saranor is not interested in animals. Human prey is much more to her liking."

When his goading words failed to elicit an expression of terror on Cazlina's frozen face, a scowl darkened his scarred features. He growled at the guards. "Put the prisoners in with the others."

Cazlina vaguely felt herself being jostled toward the cage. Her mind was elsewhere, fleeing through the darkness with her brave mare.

Run like the wind, dear heart! Be safe!

CHAPTER 25

Cazlina was relieved to see none of the prisoners inside the cage belonged to the group that had accompanied Merinda. This knowledge gave her hope that the second half of the scouting party would elude Lerant's sentries and be able to report back to General Viadon as planned.

Cazlina was also relieved to finally be able to get close to Gareth. With Jorin following on their heels, the three of them wound their way through the slumped figures of other prisoners to the far back wall and sank to the hard packed ground. Gareth's strong arm closed around Cazlina's shoulders as she pressed herself tightly against him. Jorin placed himself in front of her so that she was shielded as much as possible from the gloating eyes of passing soldiers. Sensing his concerned gaze on her, she didn't harbor the usual resentment she felt by his protective attitude.

"Are you all right?" Gareth whispered in her ear, his breath barely stirring her hair.

She nodded, not trusting herself to speak. She was having a difficult time maintaining her composure. Since Miris left on her mission, every thought involved images of the mare lying broken and dying on jagged rocks beneath a mountain ledge. Her fear was great where Miris was concerned, and tears threatened to betray the strength she'd shown in the canyon.

Determinedly, she pushed the terrible images away. The mare would be fine. She had a strong, stout heart and a brave companion to carry her safely through the perilous journey back to the general.

"What in the name of all the gods possessed Miris?" Gareth murmured, bewilderedly. "I've never seen her behave like that. Why did she and Montrill's horse run away?"

Cazlina glanced around the dark bulk of Jorin toward the two guards standing with their backs to them in front of the cage. "I sent them back to the general," she whispered.

Gareth drew back a little and a slow smile spread across his pale face. "Smart girl! But, I'm surprised Miris would leave you. You two are practically inseparable."

Cazlina grimaced. "It took a lot of convincing, but she finally agreed, especially after Veygar--that's Jorin's horse--offered to accompany her." Her breath caught for a moment and she lowered her head, the tears once more threatening to overwhelm her. "It feels as though my heart has been ripped in half, Gareth. I hope I've done the right thing. I would die if something happened to her."

His arm tightened around her and he brushed a kiss across the top of her head. "She'll be fine."

She nodded and sighed wearily. "It was the only thing I could think of to do. I'm hoping General Viadon is not far behind us and will quicken his pace once he sees Miris returning without me."

Gareth nodded slowly. "Hopefully, Lerant won't send us to Saranor's castle right away. That might give the general a chance to catch up to us before we reach it."

Cazlina shuddered at the thought of entering the wicked queen's castle. Once inside the walls, it might be impossible for General Viadon's army to infiltrate its fortifications and save the captives from becoming part of her obscene ritual.

Jorin leaned closer, his voice floating quietly over to them. "I admire your ingenuity, my lady. I was wondering why my stallion suddenly went berserk. How fortunate for us you possess the gift that you do."

Cazlina stared at him. "What do you mean?" she asked, warily.

He shrugged. "I know you don't think highly of me, Caz, but perhaps you underestimate my intelligence just a little. I have noticed on many occasions you seem to have an unusually strong rapport with your pretty mare. I suspect that's because you can communicate with her much like you can communicate with any of us. Am I right?"

She sighed inwardly. She had forgotten how acute the horse thief's hearing was.

Gareth stiffened beside her. "That's none of your business, Montrill!" he hissed.

Cazlina placed a placating hand on her brother's arm. "Hush, Gareth. It's all right."

And, strangely, it was. Only a few days ago she would have bristled at Jorin's discovery of her secret, but it didn't seem to bother her as much now. His tone had held no ridicule or mockery, as she would have expected. Indeed, he had sounded almost awed by the idea of her telepathic abilities.

His white teeth suddenly flashed in the semi-darkness. "You *told* your mare to bite me, didn't you?

That sweet-tempered creature would never have done it without prodding, I'm sure of that."

Cazlina lifted her chin. "It was no more than you deserved."

"Indeed, my lady, you are quite right. Anyway, I think what you've done is very clever. Not telling your mare to bite me, of course, but sending her back to General Viadon without you."

"I hope so," she said, quietly.

A hand suddenly reached through the bars of the cage and twisted her hair, yanking her head painfully back against the wooden poles. She cried out as rancid breath, reeking of onions and unclean teeth, permeated the air in front of her face.

"Well, now, ain't you a pretty one," a coarse voice crooned in her ear.

Cazlina gasped, trying to twist away from the man holding her captive, but his cruel grip only tightened in her hair and pulled her head back even further.

"Where'd you come from, eh, my pretty? How's about you and me have a little fun before our lovely queen gets her hands on you?"

Before Gareth had a chance to react, Jorin lunged forward and shoved the man hard in the chest, breaking the callous hold on Cazlina's hair and sending him sprawling to the ground. "Take your hands off her, you filthy scum!" He turned to Cazlina, his eyes reflecting concern. "Are you all right, my lady? Did he…?"

A blur of movement out of the corner of her eye caused her to cry out in warning, "Jorin, look out!"

The enemy soldier had lunged up from the ground with an enraged bellow and a fist-sized rock clutched in his right hand. The rock slammed between the wooden bars of the cage and into the side of Jorin's head before he had a chance to dodge out of the way. With a startled grunt, he dropped to the ground, blood pouring from a nasty gash on his right temple.

"No!" Cazlina scrambled to Jorin's side, her hands frantically trying to staunch the flow of blood.

As she pressed hard on the wound, Jorin's eyelids fluttered and opened. He stared up at her with acute pain in his eyes, but the ever-present twinkle as well.

"Well, I guess it's fortunate I have such a hard head," he said, weakly.

She blew her breath out in relief. "Yes, it is."

He grimaced. "I do wish you wouldn't agree so readily with me," he complained.

"Shut up and lie still."

She glanced covertly at the man still outside the cage, his coarse face glaring in at them.

"It's lucky for you the queen has ordered none of the prisoners killed," he snarled. "Or else, I'd gut you both and leave you to the scavengers."

Abruptly, he stalked off, cursing and pushing other soldiers out of the way as they laughed raucously at him.

"That was a foolish thing to do, Montrill!" Cazlina hissed. "You could have been killed."

"Yes, by Donar's breath, what were you thinking, man?" Gareth echoed.

Jorin winced as he struggled to sit up. "I couldn't stand to see that filth's hands on Cazlina. I had to make him stop hurting her."

Cazlina stared at him, puzzled once more by the contradictions in his character. He had seemed at first to be nothing more than a shallow, reckless, disreputable horse thief, who made his questionable living preying on other people's possessions, and who found life to be one amusing adventure after another. But, on more than one occasion in her brief but chaotic relationship with him, she had seen other complex sides of him. That he would risk his own life to protect her was a startling revelation.

"*Tanim* Narzin, are you all right? And you, *Tan* Montrill?" Sergeant Zandorin's voice intruded on her disturbing thoughts. She looked up to see the sergeant hovering close by, his face anxious.

"I've definitely felt better," Jorin admitted wryly, reaching up with a shaking hand to touch the gash on his temple.

"I'm fine, Sergeant," Cazlina reassured him.

A look of misery crossed Zandorin's face and he swiped his hand across his eyes in a jerky motion. "The general ordered me to keep you safe. Fine job I've done of that, haven't I?"

Before Cazlina could say anything, he fidgeted and cleared his throat. "I-I just wanted to say…well, I just wanted you to know…"

"Yes?" Cazlina was puzzled by the man's apparent uncertainty and discomfort.

"Well, I wanted to tell you I'm sorry I didn't listen to you earlier," he said in a rush, his face flushing. "You were right about the sentries and I dismissed your concerns. Now, we're in this mess and it's entirely my fault."

Although she had been frustrated earlier by the man's casual dismissal of her warnings, Cazlina felt the need now to alleviate his guilt.

"Sergeant, I don't think we stood any chance of getting away from those awful Mist Riders, even if we had reached the canyon earlier. They probably knew we were there long before I sensed them and were just waiting until we were further down the mountain before capturing us."

"Yes, well, I still shouldn't have shrugged off your warning," he muttered. "A good leader should listen to his men, or, in this case, women, when they point out something that could endanger the whole troop."

Cazlina touched the sleeve of his jacket. "You *are* a good leader, Sergeant. General Viadon would be proud of you."

His eyes brightened a little. "Do you think so?"

"Yes, I do," she said, firmly.

His shoulders slumped in dejection. "Well, I guess we'll never find out, will we? By the time the general gets here, we'll all be dead. Lerant's army will have already initiated their attack and all will most likely be lost."

Cazlina and Gareth exchanged knowing glances.

"Don't give up yet, Sergeant," Gareth said. "Maybe we'll get lucky before then."

Zandorin snorted. "Highly unlikely, lad. The gods would have to be smiling pretty heavily down on us to get us out of this mess."

"Never underestimate the gods," Jorin said, sagely, his eyes twinkling at Cazlina.

She was glad to see his natural good humor restored despite the obvious pain he must be feeling from the terrible blow to his head. Shaking her head, she reflected on the irony that, only a few days ago, she had been highly irritated by the man's persistent light-hearted attitude. Now, she was relieved to see it return.

CHAPTER 26

At some point during the long hours of their imprisonment, jugs of cool water, bowls of stew and chunks of bread were distributed among the captives. No doubt to keep them alive and healthy for Saranor, Cazlina reflected bitterly. As the long terrible night dragged on, she found, despite her fatigue, she could not fall asleep. Overriding her own panic at her current predicament, fear and concern for Miris were prominent in her thoughts.

Gareth was right. She and the mare had been inseparable from the moment Cazlina's father had given her the pretty little filly as a birthday present when she had turned five. The telepathic link between them had strengthened over the years until it almost seemed as though they were one mind and one heart melded together.

Now that precious link had been severed--at least temporarily disconnected--by the growing distance between her and the mare. She couldn't hear Miris' thoughts, but she knew with empathic certainty the mare was experiencing the same anguish and loss her mistress was. She could only hope Jorin's horse, Veygar, would provide the mare with the strong, mental support she needed to get through this harrowing experience.

Cazlina glanced down at Jorin. He slept fitfully with his head on her lap, his eyelids fluttering and his face pale. Despite the levity he had exhibited before, it was obvious he was still feeling acute pain from the nasty wound on his temple.

Earlier, she had surprised him, and herself, by insisting he lay down with his head on her lap to pillow it from the hard ground.

"Don't think I've forgiven you, Montrill," she had warned him in a whisper, as he grinned weakly up at her and complied with her order. "I would do the same for any poor wretch who has had his hard, foolish head knocked about."

"I do not doubt it for a moment, my lady. I am truly grateful for your compassion toward this particular poor wretch."

Gareth had given her a sharp, suspicious glance, but had refrained from saying anything, for which she was grateful. Trying to deal with her brother's issues with Jorin Montrill, as well as her own, seemed far beyond her capabilities at that moment.

Jorin stirred now, a low moan issuing from his dry lips. She shifted slightly, trying to ease his head into a more comfortable position. She was relieved to see the wound had finally stopped bleeding, although the sight of its jagged, blood-encrusted edges made her feel queasy and guilty at the same time, if she was honest with herself. Jorin had been injured trying to protect her, even after all the verbal abuse and angry insults she had heaped upon him ever since their first unfortunate meeting.

She sighed wearily, trying not to disturb either Jorin or Gareth, who slumped against her right side with his head on her shoulder. He, too, slept restlessly, twitching every now and then as though demons and monsters chased him through his dreams. The other prisoners lay about the dirt floor of the cage in various uneasy positions of slumber.

The hour was late, but pockets of enemy soldiers still lingered around the smoky fires, laughing raucously at each other's crude jokes or sharpening their weapons. A few stopped on their way past the cage to leer at the prisoners, and Cazlina closed her eyes, feigning sleep. She saw no more of the soldier who had grabbed her hair and attacked Jorin, nor did she see any of the repulsive Mist Riders hovering over the encampment. To her intense relief, Captain Lerant also seemed to have disappeared, hopefully finished with his goading and toying of the prisoners, and retired to his tent to prepare his battle plans against his archenemy, General Viadon.

Cazlina leaned her head gingerly against the wooden poles of the cage. The rough grasp of the enemy soldier had left her scalp feeling almost as painful as it had when the disgusting little Windle had clung to her with its murderous grip. That episode now seemed a lifetime ago, but she could still recall the abject terror and panic that had assailed both her and Miris when the horrible little creatures had attacked them in an unending nightmare. Jorin had saved her life then, too, riding into the Windles' forest at great peril to himself to drag her and Miris out of danger. And, if he could be believed, he had been prepared to come to her rescue once more when those two men, Kesel and Farzi, had threatened her in the mountains.

As though her troubled thoughts had conjured him up, a commotion suddenly ensued outside the cage and Cazlina heard a voice similar to Kesel's bellowing and cursing. She straightened, seeing a number of enemy soldiers coming toward the cage with a burly, struggling man between them. Two Mist Riders hovered overhead, their tendril-like limbs thrashing hungrily in the currents of smoky air.

The prisoner was indeed Kesel, his ugly face red and defiant as he was dragged forward. "Let go of me, you filthy dogs! Murdering scum!"

Gareth jerked awake, his breath hissing out in confusion. "Huh? What is it? What's going on?"

Jorin struggled to rise from his prone position and groaned, clasping his head as an agonized expression flashed across his pale face.

"Take it easy," Cazlina urged, and helped him to sit upright.

He leaned against the poles of the cage, his eyes closed and his brow furrowed with pain. Around them, the other prisoners stirred from their fitful slumbers, their voices confused and bewildered.

"It's Kesel," Cazlina whispered, her heart tripping with alarm. "He's been captured."

She frantically searched the encampment for the other members of Merinda's troop, but all she could see was Kesel shouting and struggling against his captors. They threw open the door of the cage and flung him inside, where he landed face down in the dirt. He immediately jumped up and rushed to the door, but the soldiers slammed it shut in his face and barred it once more.

"Lily-livered cowards!" he shouted, grasping the wooden poles and trying to shake them loose. But, they held sturdy.

He thrust his face between the poles and snarled. "Tell your loathsome queen this is what I think of her!" A huge gob of spit flew from his mouth and splattered on the chest of one of the soldiers.

The man stared down in shock at the front of his jacket for a moment and then lunged forward with an enraged roar. Before his sword could impale the defiant Kesel, an arm reached out and knocked the weapon away.

Captain Lerant, his helmet removed and his scarred face revealed in all its ugly deformity, strode forward, a smile playing about the corners of his thin mouth. He walked up to Kesel and stopped only inches away, his cold, merciless eyes boring into those of the burly man.

"Saranor will be pleased with you," he said, with satisfaction. "There is much darkness and violence in your soul she can feed upon."

"Feed upon this, you filthy scum!" Kesel growled and spat directly into Lerant's face.

A collective mutter surged through the enemy soldiers crowded around the cage, and they leaned forward, their hard-bitten faces eagerly anticipating their captain's reaction. Cazlina's heart tripped again, certain the captain would forget his queen's orders and kill Kesel himself for such an insult.

Lerant's expression never altered as the slimy trail of spittle slid down one disfigured cheek. His soulless eyes continued to bore into Kesel's.

"Trax," he said, snapping his fingers.

One of the Mist Riders swept down to hover beside Lerant, its orange eyes flickering. "What is your wish?"

The captain's thin mouth twisted into a cold smile. "I think our good friend here needs to be taught a lesson in proper social graces."

The Mist Rider flowed toward Kesel, lightly brushing one of its waving tendrils over the man's left hand where it gripped the sturdy pole of the cage door.

Kesel screamed in agony as the flesh of his hand turned bone-white. He lurched awkwardly away from the door, tripping over the legs of another prisoner and falling heavily to the ground. He stayed there, rocking back and forth as he clutched his injured hand tightly against his chest.

The captain's lips twitched. "You would do well to remember this lesson, my friend. Trax enjoys inflicting pain on mortals. If I tell him to, he will play with you all night until you scream for death. But, he will not grant it, because I have other plans for you."

He turned to the two guards by the door of the cage. "Be sure to keep this one safe, Rizol. The queen has need of his black soul."

The man named Rizol bowed. "Of course, Captain. It shall be as you wish."

"The same goes for the rest of you, as well," Lerant said, raising his voice to address the other soldiers crowding around. "No one kills or harms any of the prisoners, or you shall answer to me and your queen. Is that clear?"

The men murmured their assent.

Lerant turned abruptly and stalked away, the other soldiers falling back to clear a path for him. One by one, the men slowly returned to their campfires and stories, their interest in the prisoners already waning now that their captain's show of dominance was over.

CHAPTER 27

The moment Lerant was out of sight, Sergeant Zandorin made his way over to where Kesel sat hunched over on the ground, cradling his useless hand in his lap.

The sergeant grabbed Kesel's unscathed arm and hissed at him. "What happened? Where are the others?"

Cazlina edged closer to the two men, anxious to hear what Kesel had to say. If Merinda and the others in her group had been killed or captured too, then Miris and Veygar remained their only hope of getting a message to General Viadon about their imprisonment.

Kesel raised a startled face to Zandorin. "Sergeant, what are you doing here?"

"We were captured by Lerant's sentries part way down the mountain. What happened, Kesel? Where are the others?"

Beginning to show signs of shock, Kesel seemed not to hear him, gritting his teeth in agony as he turned his attention back to his hand. From the fingertips to the wrist, the skin and even the fingernails had turned pure white, glowing eerily in the semi-darkness. "Argh, by all the gods, it feels as though my bones are burning!"

Zandorin roughly shook the man's arm. "Listen to me!" he barked in a notch above a whisper. "Where are the others in your group? Have they been captured, too?" He flicked an apprehensive glance toward the front of the cage, but the two guards had their backs to him and didn't appear to be listening. "Dammit, man, answer me! Where are they?"

Kesel scowled at him, his ugly face twisted with pain. "I don't know. Now, leave me alone." The sergeant stared at him. "What do you mean, you don't know?" His face suddenly registered comprehension and he flushed with anger. "You fool! You deliberately disobeyed me and entered the encampment on your own, didn't you?"

"So what?" Kesel said, in a surly tone. "I didn't think it would do any harm to kill a few of the enemy and then slip back out. I wanted a little fun."

Zandorin stared at him in disbelief. "You jeopardized your comrades and the mission for a little *fun*? How in the name of all the gods did you hope to enter and leave the camp without somebody seeing you? You would have led them right back to the others."

"I was being careful," Kesel insisted. "But, unfortunately, one of the murdering dogs woke up just as I was about to slit his throat and got a shout out. Next thing I knew, I was surrounded by a dozen of them." His face darkened with grim satisfaction. "I managed to get in a few good whacks before they pinned me to the ground."

"By Orun's sword, man, how could you be so stupid? Lerant's no fool. He'll suspect you're part of a second scouting party sent by General Viadon and will send out searchers to find Merinda and the others."

He dropped his hand from Kesel's arm and ran it through his hair in agitation, shaking his head in disbelief

198

at Cazlina. She could only stare back at him numbly, just as shocked as he at the utter foolhardiness of Kesel's actions. How could he have so thoughtlessly endangered the whole mission for such selfish and senseless reasons? The last vestiges of guilt she had harbored for wounding him in the mountains blew away on the winds of her anger and disgust.

She crawled back to Gareth and Jorin, suddenly anxious to put as much distance as she could between her and the repugnant man. She didn't trust herself not to leap on him and pummel his swarthy, pockmarked face into a bloody pulp.

Gareth and Jorin had not been able to hear the whispered exchange between the sergeant and Kesel, so she hurriedly told them what had happened.

"Well, let's hope Merinda is smart enough to elude Lerant's soldiers," Gareth said, trying to sound encouraging, but the bleak expression in his eyes belied the attempt.

Jorin brought his impassive gaze back from the hunched form of Kesel and looked into Cazlina's eyes. "Methinks, perhaps, you should have aimed your sword a little higher, my lady," he said, softly.

"What do you mean by that?" Gareth asked, frowning.

Cazlina shook her head, pulling her gaze away from Jorin's. "Nothing, never mind." She tried to inject a positive note into her voice. "Merinda seems like a smart woman. I'm sure she'll be able to return safely to the rendezvous point, in spite of Kesel's stupidity."

She desperately wished she could believe her own words. Their situation had taken on a more hopeless turn with Kesel's capture; a turn that might have jeopardized the rest of the scouting party, too. Sergeant Zandorin was right. Lerant was not a stupid man. He, no doubt, had soldiers and Mist Riders out scouring the countryside for more of Viadon's spies, although it was entirely possible he had already taken that precaution after the capture of her and the others.

Over to the east, the sky had begun to glow with a pale, pinkish light, heralding the imminent arrival of dawn. The fact the rest of Merinda's group had not been thrown into the prisoners' cage gave Cazlina some small measure of hope the woman had been able to elude the captain's net of pursuers and reach the rendezvous point undetected.

Despite Cazlina's brave attempt to be optimistic, she couldn't prevent a shudder of dread from coursing through her body. How easy it had been to be fired up with courage and zeal back in Rothtown where she had been sheltered and protected from the bloody realities and horrors of war. And later, in the walled city of Terrangay, the valiant, battle-trained men and women of General Viadon's army had surrounded her, keeping her safe.

She cringed at the memory of how adamantly she had tried to convince both Gareth and the general she was capable of fighting bravely against the tyranny of the wicked queen. That bravado seemed ludicrous and false now, buried beneath cowardice and terror so strong it transformed her back into a little child. She wanted to face death with dignity, but doubt and self-mockery bit and twisted in her gut like a many-pronged spear. For all her steadfast declarations of fearlessness, all she really wanted to do was curl up into a tight, quivering ball and give in to the hopelessness of her situation.

She leaned back against the rough poles of the cage and closed her eyes, feeling the pressure of Gareth's shoulder against her own. Although she wished with all her heart he had remained safely back with General Viadon's army instead of being here with her in this dire predicament, his presence provided her with a small measure of comfort. Without him by her side, she didn't know how she would have survived to this point.

Her eyes flew open at a sound close by. Early morning sunlight streamed through the wooden bars of the cage, slanting over the stirring captives in bands of warm gold. With a start, she realized she must have fallen asleep, her mind and body finally dragged down by fatigue and fear into a brief unconscious state. An arm encircled her shoulders and her head lay cushioned against a strong chest, but the angle was wrong for it to be Gareth holding her.

She sat up and turned her head, meeting Jorin's eyes. Instead of the irrepressible twinkle she expected to see in them, there was a disturbing expression of unease in their blue depths. Despite the gravity of his expression, he looked much better than he had during the night.

"I believe they are coming for us, my lady," he said, quietly. Fear raced through her body like a wildfire and she could only stare helplessly at him. His hand reached out and touched hers, closing over the white, rigid knuckles with a warm, reassuring grip.

"I know my brave lady is still in there somewhere," he murmured, the grim expression in his eyes softening. "I'm honored to have known you, even though our acquaintance has been brief and somewhat volatile."

Before she could swallow the panic clogging her throat and answer him, Captain Lerant arrived in front of the cage in full uniform and with the spiked helmet once more covering his disfigured face. The two burly guards parted to let him pass and he strode briskly up to the door of the cage.

His cold eyes fell upon Cazlina near the back, and her heart jolted in her chest as that cruel gaze raked across hers. Beside her, she felt Gareth stiffen and move closer to shield her body with his, and Jorin's hand tightened painfully on hers. But, neither man's actions could protect her from the surge of terror that threatened to suffocate her at the captain's next words.

"Prepare the prisoners for transport immediately to the castle," he said, his eyes pinning Cazlina's in a pitiless trap. "Saranor grows anxious to meet her new playthings."

Within short order, the twelve captives were bound tightly and tossed into the back of a large, cumbersome wagon hooked up to two weary-looking horses.

With so many people crammed into the wagon, it was almost impossible to move or breathe. To her dismay, Cazlina ended up wedged tightly into one corner, with Kesel jammed against her on one side and the man named Donegal on the other. Desperately, she sought out Gareth's figure far away from her at the other end of the wagon, similarly crowded into a tight, uncomfortable position. He stared back at her with helpless anguish. She would even have welcomed the comfort of Jorin's presence, but that, too, was denied her, for he had ended up several feet away, with three prisoners between them.

She turned her head and leaned as far away from Kesel as possible, her stomach queasy with the sour stench of sweat and fear emanating in waves from his bulky body. He seemed too distracted by his lifeless hand to pay much attention to her. Her shoulder brushed against the man named Donegal and he recoiled, eyes rolling in panic. She swallowed tightly, unable to offer him even the slightest bit of comfort or encouragement.

With a bone-jarring jolt, the wagon pulled away and Cazlina was thrown against Kesel. She pushed herself away with a grimace and a shudder, hoping he wouldn't notice the revulsion that was surely showing on her face, but he didn't even glance her way. As the wooden wheels of the wagon bumped erratically over the uneven ground, the movement seemed to match the alarmed tripping through Cazlina's heart as the terrifying journey to Saranor's castle began.

CHAPTER 28

The towering presence of rock ledges and crevices utterly devoid of grass and trees was the only thing Cazlina could see as the Jezalar Plateau slid slowly past the high sides of the cart. As the sun ascended into the clear bowl of the azure sky, its warmth soon became uncomfortable and then almost unbearable. Around Cazlina, the prisoners shifted and groaned, the smell of their sweat and fear nearly suffocating her. Closing her eyes, she turned her face away from the baleful sun, willing her mind to ignore the heat blasting down upon her unprotected head and concentrate instead on images of cool, shadowy meadows and gurgling streams where she and Miris had often enjoyed pleasant afternoon and evening canters. But, the images only served to remind her of the painful separation between her and the mare and the terrible uncertainty of the animal's fate. She stifled a moan, refusing to allow herself to break down under the crushing pressure of her fear.

The journey became an endless nightmare. On one hand, Cazlina wished for it to be over so the tortuous, monotonous jolting of the wagon and the sweltering heat would stop, but the thought of what awaited them in Saranor's castle had her praying to the gods the ride would go on forever. She lost all track of time, and even the effort of trying to avoid contact with Kesel became too much for her to bother with. She let her weary, aching body slump against his, allowing his bulk to cushion her from the worst of the jolts and bumps.

It must have been late afternoon, judging by the low position of the sun, when she glanced up into the sky through half-closed eyelids and spotted something that made her bolt upright. She squinted harder and held her breath, hoping against hope the object in the sky was real and not just a figment of her fevered brain.

"Gareth!" Her voice came out in a hoarse rasp, and she feared for a moment he wouldn't hear her. But, mercifully, he did and slowly raised his hanging head, his dull eyes seeking her out.

She dared not say anything further for fear the guards driving the wagon would hear her. Instead, she pointed her chin skyward, bobbing it up and down several times. Gareth frowned, a blank expression on his face, and her stomach clenched. Somehow, she had to make him look up. She repeated the gesture, raising her eyes at the same time. When she glanced back down, she was relieved to see a faint look of understanding cross his face.

He lifted his eyes to the cloudless sky overhead and his mouth fell open in shock. Cazlina almost laughed out loud at his expression, giddy with relief she had not imagined the object in the sky. Her brother's gaze flew back to hers and she smiled, trying not to give herself away with a whoop of elation.

Several feet away, Jorin, who had been slumped against the swaying side of the cart, suddenly came to attention, glancing keenly from her to Gareth, and she realized he had noticed the silent exchange between them. As she had done with her brother, she raised her face skyward and Jorin immediately followed her gaze. Surprise and relief flickered across his face for a moment before he glanced back at her, nodding his head once.

None of the other prisoners seemed to have noticed anything unusual, nor could Cazlina detect any discernible change in the bored attitude of the two enemy soldiers at the front of the wagon.

She glanced back up at the sky, the heavy weight of hopeless dread lifting from her heart as she watched the graceful flight of the Fire Bird against the almost colorless sky. The transparent wings with their thin membranes of black, gold and blue shimmered like jewels as they beat against the air currents. As she gazed in rapt wonder, the creature suddenly gathered its wings together and plummeted downward in a swift, silent spiral, heading straight for the wagon lumbering along beneath it.

Alarm tripped through Cazlina, and she held her breath, certain the hydrith was going to crash right into them. She could just glimpse the tiny woman strapped to the narrow back of the creature, her fire weapon pointed toward the cart. The two guards remained oblivious to the danger hurtling down at them from the sky as the monotonous plodding of the horses continued.

Elation and joy turned to horror. The Fire Bird's rider seemed about to unleash the deadly fire of her metallic weapon upon the helpless and bound prisoners in the wagon, no doubt believing them to be enemy soldiers.

Several yards above the wagon, the hydrith pulled out of its swift dive, and, to Cazlina's immense relief, the diminutive woman on its back pointed her weapon at a spot just in front of the wagon. A geyser of flame spewed from the ground directly in front of the horses and they whinnied in terror, rearing up on their hind legs. The two guards shouted and cursed in alarm, finally realizing an attacker threatened them from above. While the driver pulled frantically on the reins in an effort to control the terrified horses, the other man snatched his longbow from the seat beside him and notched an arrow. Cazlina wanted to scream out a warning to the woman on the hydrith's back, but the warrior had already seen the danger.

Another pillar of fire erupted beside the wagon and the horses jerked sideways, throwing the man off-balance and nearly unseating him. Mere yards above the cart, the Fire Bird darted about in elaborate maneuvers, its jeweled wings a blur against the sky.

The driver struggled to guide the frightened horses around the blazing fires and slapped the reins sharply against their backs. The other man loosed his arrow, but it flew harmlessly by the whirling hydrith. The horses were now racing at breakneck speed across the uneven ground. Cazlina and the other prisoners were thrown roughly about, bouncing painfully off the wooden sides of the wagon and each other.

From far behind them came the distant sound of thundering hooves and clashing weapons. Bloodthirsty battle cries rent the air.

One of the prisoners pushed himself to his feet and peered over the side of the bouncing cart. "The general's army is here! We're saved!"

The other captives began shouting and cheering.

Joy welled up in Cazlina. Miris and Veygar must have reached Viadon safely and spurred him into action, as she had hoped. Or, Merinda had successfully evaded Lerant's sentries during the night. Either way, rescue had arrived just in time.

Something nudged Cazlina's mind, prodding it with an urgent persistence. Though it came through only faintly as a mere whisper of sound, she could have sworn she heard a dearly familiar voice calling her name.

"Miris?"

She tried to stand upright to see over the side of the wagon, but her bound hands and the violent jostling threw her back down. She landed in a heap on top of Kesel, who grunted and swore at her.

"Get off me, boy, or I'll knock your fool head off!"

She ignored him, pushing herself away and trying to hold on to that tiny breath of a voice in her mind. The tears she had determinedly quelled earlier now streamed down her sunburned face in a burning flood.

Miris!

The mare's cry, if indeed that's what it was, became lost in the bedlam of the unseen battle behind them, the loud beating of the hydrith's wings overhead, and the noisy rumbling of the wagon careening over the rough ground. Donegal was shouting in Cazlina's ear and she wanted to scream at him to shut up.

"Move it, man, move it! We're almost there. We can't lose these prisoners, or Saranor will have our heads," the man beside the driver shouted, and helpless frustration and dread washed once more over Cazlina.

Was rescue to be denied the prisoners, after all? Saranor's castle must be close at hand, and the Fire Bird's rider would not dare risk a direct attack on the wagon to stop it for fear of killing the captives.

Cazlina glanced frantically up at the darting hydrith and saw the tiny woman frowning in helpless frustration as the flames from her weapon danced all around the wagon but did not prevent it from careening toward the queen's castle.

"Open the gates!" the driver called.

There came the sound of massive creaking and groaning, and Cazlina twisted her head, trying to see over the high sides of the cart. She caught a glimpse of a sprawling edifice of gleaming white marble resplendent with crenulated towers and soaring spires looming up in front of them. In the next moment, dark wooden gates inlaid with intricate patterns of crystals and jewels appeared on either side of the wagon. The horses barely slowed their frantic pace and thundered into the open courtyard beyond, the gates slamming shut behind them almost before the rear end of the wagon had cleared the narrow opening.

Cazlina watched in dismay as the Fire Bird was forced to wheel away from the dozens of arrows loosed in its direction from the archers standing on the ledges above the high gates. The hydrith flew back toward the Jezalar Plateau.

CHAPTER 29

The wagon shuddered to an abrupt stop, the frightened horses still prancing and snorting as the driver pulled back on the reins. The man beside the driver jumped hastily to the ground and shouted. "Help me with the prisoners! Get them inside the castle. Quick!"

The boards at the back of the cart were ripped off and rough hands began dragging the bound captives out on to the cobbled stones of the courtyard. A man with greasy red hair sticking out of his spiked helmet loomed over Cazlina and she cringed away from him, but he easily hauled her to her feet and flung her over his shoulder. She gritted her teeth and suppressed a groan as he jumped down from the back of the wagon with a bone-jarring thud and began to jog toward a wooden door set into the white marble wall of the castle. Her face thumped painfully against his broad back.

An immense fire suddenly erupted close by and then another several feet away. Cazlina managed to lift her bobbing head high enough to see two Fire Birds circling overhead, blasting their fire weapons down into the chaos of the courtyard and dodging the arrows streaking toward them from the enemy soldiers. Beyond the thick walls, the sounds of battle and war cries grew louder and closer.

"VIADON!"

At the sound of the thunderous voice ringing out from above, all noise and movement suddenly ceased both inside and outside the courtyard walls. The man holding Cazlina skidded to a halt and froze, flinging his head upward toward the battlements far above. Cazlina pushed against the man's immobile back and craned her neck, trying to see what or who had been capable of overriding the deafening furor and pandemonium of battle with that one single shout.

Her breath caught in her throat at the sight of the figure who stood on a wide ledge a hundred feet above the courtyard, arms outstretched toward a sky that had turned as black as the inside of a thundercloud. A violent wind snapped white robes about the woman's body and twisted long, thick hair as white as snow in a whirlwind around her shoulders.

"VIADON, MY GOOD FRIEND! I SEE YOU HAVE RETURNED TO PAY HOMAGE TO YOUR QUEEN."

The clear voice, dripping heavily with mockery and venom, echoed through the frozen silence as though amplified a hundred times. The soldiers in the courtyard and lining the thick marble outer walls remained perfectly still, their wide-eyed faces reflecting fear and trepidation as they stared up at the woman on the ledge above.

Dread swept through Cazlina like a burning tide. The frightening figure could be no other than Queen Saranor. Even from that distance, the effects of the Pool of Souls could clearly be seen in the incredible icy beauty of her face and the glow of strength and youth in her impossibly tall, slender body.

Up until now, the renegade queen from the Janix domain had existed only in the bloody tales of her exploits that had run rampant throughout Regalis. Even though Rothtown was part of Saranor's realm, its remoteness in the northern region had prevented Cazlina from actually seeing her sovereign in person. And, now that she had, it was little wonder Saranor's very name struck terror into the hearts of all who heard it. No description, bandied about in uneasy, awestruck whispers in the shops and taverns of Rothtown, could even begin to compare with the ghastly reality of the woman standing on the parapet above. Evil and power flowed from her in such palpable waves that Cazlina, hanging helplessly over the shoulder of the enemy soldier a hundred feet below, could feel its malevolent touch on her skin.

"SO, MY FRIEND, YOU THINK TO DENY ME MY RIGHT AS ABSOLUTE RULER, TO PIT YOUR TRAITOROUS ARMY AGAINST ME IN A PATHETIC ATTEMPT TO DETHRONE ME? WHAT A DISAPPOINTMENT YOU ARE TO ME, DARNELLIS! WE COULD HAVE RULED THE WORLD TOGETHER, YOU AND I. I WOULD HAVE MADE YOU MY CONSORT AND ALL OF MY POWER AND RICHES WOULD HAVE BEEN YOURS AS WELL. BUT, YOU CHOSE INSTEAD TO DEFY ME, TO BETRAY MY TRUST AND LOVE."

Saranor's eyes suddenly blazed with an unholy light and a terrible smile twisted lips as red as rubies.

"THAT IS SOMETHING I CAN NEVER FORGIVE, DARNELLIS. YOU MUST PAY FOR YOUR TREACHERY, AS MUST ALL WHO SO FOOLISHLY FOLLOW YOU IN YOUR MISGUIDED REBELLION."

She raised her arms once more and the black clouds above began to boil and seethe. "KNOW THAT THE

DEATHS AND SUFFERING ABOUT TO FALL UPON YOUR HEAD ARE OF *YOUR* DOING, VIADON! I WILL SHOW NO MERCY OR KINDNESS TOWARD THOSE WHO WOULD DARE TO OPPOSE ME."

A swirling mist suddenly surrounded the queen's towering figure. When it cleared, she was no longer standing on the parapet and late afternoon sunlight once more blazed from a colorless sky.

As though a switch had been thrown by Saranor's disappearance, the courtyard came to life again as the soldiers began to renew their attacks on the unseen army outside the castle walls, and the men holding the bound prisoners once more hustled them toward the entrances into the castle.

Cazlina bit back a moan as her face smacked against the shoulder blade of the red-haired man when he jolted forward in a rush. A small trickle of blood dripped from her nose, staining the coarse fabric of his jacket.

A sudden *twang* sounded close to her ear and she stared in horror as an arrow imbedded itself deeply into the back of her captor only inches from her face. He grunted and pitched forward. Cazlina yelped in alarm as his weight dragged her down with him and her back hit the unforgiving cobblestones of the courtyard with an excruciating jolt. The breath was knocked from her lungs in a rush and she frantically gulped for precious air as the dead man's heavy body pinned her to the ground. For a moment, she lay stunned, and then began to frantically push with her bound hands at the dead weight on top of her. An eternity later, or so it seemed, she managed to fling aside one of the man's heavy arms and wriggle out from beneath him.

She lay motionless for a moment with her head resting on the ground, still trying to catch her breath and wincing at the burning pain raging in her back. All around her, bedlam reigned, from the tramp of running feet and shouting voices to the snap and crackle of fires raging from the Fire Birds' attacks. She jerked in alarm as a portion of the white marble wall of the courtyard suddenly exploded into millions of flying fragments. The men lining the ledges in that area flew through the air like rag dolls, their shrill, dying screams adding to the cacophony of battle. From the way the air above the shattered section shimmered and pulsed, Cazlina was certain Pharon was responsible for the explosion.

It took her a moment to realize she was free of her captor. When the notion finally sunk into her dazed brain, she covertly looked around. With all of the confusion and bedlam in the courtyard, it didn't appear as though anyone was paying attention to her. The bulk of the red-haired man's body hid her from view and the other enemy soldiers were focused intently on dealing with the attack of the general's army outside the walls. Pharon's explosion had sent many scrambling to shore up the damaged wall in an effort to keep Viadon's men from entering the castle.

Cazlina moved closer to the dead man's body, trying to conceal herself as much as possible, and peered over his back, grimacing at the sight of the pool of blood that soaked his jacket around the arrow still sticking straight up. She anxiously searched the noisy, frenetic courtyard for Gareth and Jorin, but she couldn't see them anywhere. Her heart plummeted as she realized they must have already been taken inside the castle with the other prisoners, for there was no sign of Sergeant Zandorin or Kesel or any of the others.

She needed to do something quick to save them, but the chances of her being able to steal through the unfamiliar halls and rooms of the enormous castle without being hindered or discovered were slim to none.

Her heart pounded in her chest while she momentarily questioned her sanity. Was she seriously contemplating entering the very place she had earlier prayed to the gods to rescue her from? Yet, she couldn't just sit there waiting passively for a passing soldier to find her and drag her away to a similar fate as the other captives. For some reason, the gods had given her this temporary reprieve from imprisonment and she must make the most of it. It would likely not last long. Someone was bound to notice her at any moment, even with the battle raging on.

Although she longed desperately for a reunion with Miris, finding Gareth was of greater importance at the moment. The comforting presence of the mare inside her head would have made the task easier, but the distance between them was still too great for communication. She would have to content herself with that one tiny, elusive thread of contact for now.

Fortunately for her, the dead man's sword lay sheathed in its scabbard on the side of the body where she crouched. Peeking cautiously over his back to make sure she was not being observed, Cazlina slid the sword part way out as silently as she could and used its sharp edge to cut the coarse ropes binding her wrists. She gingerly rubbed the raw skin, wincing at the pain of the scrapes and bruises. When the feeling had flowed back into her hands enough to grasp the sword properly, she worked it completely out of the scabbard and held it against her trembling body.

She found herself close to the doorway her captor had been heading toward before he was killed. With any luck, she could crawl to it and slip inside before anyone noticed her. What happened after that, she dared not think about, or she would lose her nerve completely. She had no idea what lay on the other side of the door. For all she knew, she could find herself standing in the middle of Saranor's throne room, surrounded by the deadly weapons and cold, remorseless faces of her castle guards, or, worse still, face to face with the queen herself. And, yet, she had to take the chance. Gareth and Jorin and the others depended on her.

Taking a deep breath to calm her shattered nerves, Cazlina lay down flat on the warm stones of the courtyard and began to slither inch by inch toward the door, trying not to bang the sword against the ground and hoping the dead soldier's body would provide enough concealment to mask her movements. Her back protested with a sharp stab of pain, but she ignored it, her attention and concentration focused entirely on the doorway in front of her.

CHAPTER 30

Although the distance to the entrance could not have been more than a few feet, to Cazlina, it seemed an almost insurmountable goal. At any moment, she expected to feel a hand reach down and haul her roughly up by her short-cropped hair and drag her off into the bowels of the castle to Saranor's hideous Pool of Souls.

To her relief, nothing of the sort happened, and she managed to reach the door undetected. She hesitated for a moment, lying perfectly still on the ground with the sword hidden underneath her in case someone should glance her way. Hopefully, she would appear as another dead body among all the others in the bloody, noisy courtyard.

She froze in terror as a loud rumbling came from close by, the sound echoing through the cobbled stones into her very bones. She risked a peek under her outstretched arm and saw a heavy wagon being pulled and pushed by several men toward the section of wall that had been breached by Pharon's spell. The wagon contained stacks of lumber, heavy nets and huge boulders, which would no doubt be used to try and repair the wall.

But, before the men could push the cart close enough to the collapsed wall and begin fixing it, several bubbles of bright light floated over the wall and landed on the ground nearby, instantly erupting into a heavy bluish mist that obscured everything from sight.

Is this more of Pharon's magic? Cazlina wondered, watching the soldiers' shadowy figures stumbling around in confusion. Adding to the chaos, enemy soldiers began yelling. None seemed to realize they were transmitting their positions to Viadon's army as well.

She pressed herself tightly against the cobblestones as tendrils of blue mist suddenly swerved her way and floated gently around her head. Images of Pross and his poor horse frozen into white, lifeless statues slammed into her brain and she cringed from the touch of the mist, terrified it would prove to be as deadly as that of the Mist Riders. But, instead, feathery fingers caressed her exposed cheek as a tiny voice breathed into her ear, *Go!*

Cazlina stiffened, wondering if Pharon was trying to tell her he had sent the blue mist to help conceal her from the enemy soldiers, giving her a chance to enter the castle without being seen.

Well, whether it was true or not, the magically induced fog *did* provide a shield and, before she could change her mind, she pushed herself upright to grasp the handle of the door, opening it just wide enough to squeeze her slim body through. She cringed as a second massive explosion took out another section of wall somewhere behind her in the courtyard.

Collapsing against one of the walls on the other side of the door, she closed her eyes, trembling in terror as she waited for soldiers to come crashing through the doorway in pursuit of her, or for guards inside the castle to swoop down. When no one assailed her, she slowly opened her eyes and glanced cautiously around.

A long, echoing corridor stretched before her, with thick pillars of pale, green jade encircled with carved vines and flowers reaching from floor to ceiling on both sides of it. In between the stone columns, niches carved into the walls were filled with golden statues and sculptures, and, where there were no openings, gigantic tapestries hung on the walls. Towering arched doorways presumably led off into other rooms or corridors.

Cazlina slid slowly up the wall to a standing position. The sword in her hands was heavy and awkward and the muscles in her arms quivered from its unfamiliar weight. She longed for the light and finely honed rapier the blacksmith back in Terrangay had given her, but beggars could not be choosers. At least, she had a weapon, which gave her some measure of comfort and security.

Cautiously, she moved forward, keeping as close to the left-hand wall as she could. Her first few steps rang hollowly on the pale, green marble and she froze in terror certain that at any moment, guards would erupt from the towering doorways and surround her. When none did, she released her breath in a faint sigh.

She tried to recall the way Jorin had moved so stealthily through the stone canyons near the Mountain of Death, his footfalls barely whispers of sound against the rocky, uneven ground. He had started each step by placing the toe of his boot carefully in front of him and then letting the heel slowly and silently drop down to touch the ground. As Cazlina started off again, she tried to repeat his actions and found her progress was quieter. As much as the horse thief sometimes annoyed and aggravated her, she had to admit the skills he'd acquired to pursue his profession were of great value to her now.

She came to the first arched doorway leading off the long, echoing corridor and pressed herself against the wall, holding the heavy sword upright in front of her. Her ears strained to hear any sounds from the room or corridor beyond. Only silence greeted her, which, after the din and chaos of the courtyard, was a blessing, but the lack of sound or voices did nothing to reassure her. A whole roomful of Mist Riders could be floating just out of sight and she would not be aware of them until it was too late.

Cazlina bit her bottom lip indecisively. Only the gods knew what awaited her beyond the doorway. With any luck, she might choose the very path that led in the direction of the dungeons where the prisoners had no doubt been taken, or, more likely, she would stumble straight into the arms of danger and death.

Heart beating erratically, she risked a glance around the edge of the doorway and breathed a sigh of relief. An empty room that might have been an antechamber for receiving royal guests greeted her. Several gilt-edged chairs upholstered in red velvet were lined up in two rows in front of a massive oak desk sitting on a raised dais. It was cluttered with papers and books, but fortunately no one sat in the high-backed chair behind it.

Not the way to the dungeons, Cazlina guessed, and tiptoed past the doorway to the other side. She had gone no more than a few feet when she caught a sudden movement out of the corner of her eye and leapt away from the wall, brandishing the ungainly sword in front of her, her breath locked in her throat.

An enormous, brilliantly colored tapestry hung on the wall before her and she was astonished to see the movement coming from it. The wall hanging depicted a battleground scene, the details and colors gruesomely realistic and lively, but the action was carried out in complete silence. In the middle of a bloody and corpse-strewn field, a tall, slender woman with flowing white hair and a long sword in her right hand sat astride a powerful white stallion. As Cazlina watched in horrified fascination,

Saranor--for it could be no other than the queen of Janix herself--bent at the waist and lopped off the head of a cowering peasant. The gory object with its wide, staring eyes and silently screaming mouth rolled under the white stallion's powerful hooves. The horse reared and kicked the head, sending it flying across the field and spraying blood and gore in every direction.

Shuddering, Cazlina tore her gaze away from the ghastly scene and hurried away, bile rising up in an acidic tide into her throat. Glancing back over her shoulder, she saw that the tapestry had stopped moving and the woman in white sat frozen in the middle of the tableau. Still reeling from the horrific display, Cazlina reasoned the scene must have been triggered by her presence in front of it and, when she had moved away, it reverted back to its inert state. What a shock visitors to the castle must receive when the supposedly inanimate wall hangings suddenly came to life in front of their eyes! Cazlina wondered uneasily if *all* of the tapestries in the hallway had this capability and vowed to avoid them whenever possible.

She continued on down the long corridor, her nerves frayed and tingling, her body so tense she thought her bones would shatter at any moment. She didn't know how much longer she could hope to wander aimlessly through the dangerous hallways of the castle before someone discovered her. Surely, her luck could not continue forever. Silently, she cursed the foolhardy impulse that had led her to enter the castle instead of seeking a way to escape it and find General Viadon.

Grim resolve made her straighten her slumping shoulders and quell the rising hysteria.

Stop acting like a weak-kneed coward! She told herself sternly. *You're a soldier in the general's army, not a young child afraid of the dark and your own shadow. You wanted a chance to prove how courageous you are, so stop sniveling and show Gareth and Viadon and, yes, even*

Jorin, that you have the moral strength to carry out this task and face whatever dangers may threaten you. Miris' stout, brave heart helped her to overcome her fears and misgivings. You must do the same now and make her proud.

Cazlina took a deep, shuddering breath. The bracing lecture had helped to dispel some of the tension and dread fogging her mind, although her white-knuckled fingers still trembled on the hilt of the heavy sword. Pressing herself closely against the cool stone of a pillar, she forced herself to calm down and concentrate on forming a plan to find the prisoners and avoid discovery while searching the perilous corridors of Saranor's castle.

The soldier who had slung her over his shoulder had been heading for this entrance for a reason. That must mean one of the branching corridors, or maybe even this one itself, led toward the dungeons that resided somewhere below the castle. Or, perhaps, the captives had already been taken directly to the queen's Pool of Souls, wherever it was housed. It was conceivable Saranor wanted to replenish the horrible talisman immediately to gain more power to fight General Viadon and his army.

Panic threatened again, but Cazlina determinedly quelled it. She needed to keep her wits and courage about her if she hoped to be of any help to the hapless prisoners.

The image of Gareth's face flashed into her mind. *I will find you, dear brother,* she vowed fiercely. *If I have to kill every person in this godforsaken castle to get to you, I will do it!*

She glanced back down the corridor the way she had come and was astonished to see blue mist seeping around the frame of the door that led to the courtyard beyond. It sped toward her, billowing out into softly tinted clouds that hid much of the hallway from view. When it reached her, it seemed to hesitate for a moment before touching her reassuringly on the cheek and then continuing to flow on down the length of the long corridor.

Cazlina drew herself up with a faint smile. *All right, Pharon, I get the message. No more wavering. It's time to move on.*

The mist felt warm and soft against her skin, not at all damp or cold as one might expect from such a fog. Then again, this was no ordinary feat of nature but one conjured up by a powerful mage. It surrounded her like a gentle, safe cocoon and made her feel less alone.

She pushed herself away from the pillar, focused once more on navigating her way silently down the corridor. Even though she still lacked a precise direction or plan, at least some of the fear and panic had been cleared from her brain, leaving her with a determination to see this dangerous task through.

Before she had gone more than a few feet, she thought she heard the faint whisper of footsteps on the marble floor in front of her. She stopped, her heart galloping up into her throat, but the sound was not repeated. No doubt, her tightly-strung nerves and over-active imagination were playing tricks on her. She started forward again, suddenly colliding with an invisible figure in the billowing mist and letting out a shocked scream before she could stop herself.

CHAPTER 31

Hers was not the only cry to echo in the corridor. Whoever she had bumped into also yelped in alarm, the two sounds mingling in a calamitous noise that was sure to bring every guard in the castle running to find the source.

Cazlina leapt backward, desperately searching the mist in front of her for the person she had encountered. As though sensing her dilemma, the blue fog parted to allow her to see a small boy with dark tousled hair and eyes wide with panic. He stared at her for a second and then disappeared.

Cazlina blinked uncertainly. The mist had not come together again to hide the boy from view. He had simply vanished into thin air, and she wondered if she had only imagined him. But, she still felt the collision of her body against his. He had certainly seemed solid and substantial enough then.

Tentatively, she reached out a hand and waved it through the air where she had seen the lad. There was nothing there. Prickles of fear raced up and down her spine as she peered anxiously into the surrounding mist and strained her ears for more footsteps. If it had truly been only a boy she had bumped into and not just her overwrought imagination, he probably didn't pose much of a threat to her. But, if an adult was with him, then she would certainly be in danger.

Now, she cursed the blue cloud that hid everything from view and made it impossible to tell if someone else was in the corridor with her. The comforting, concealing presence had abruptly become a liability instead.

A faint sound came from behind her and she spun nervously, gripping the sword tightly in both hands. Again, the mist billowed out to either side so that the boy she had seen moments ago became clearly visible once more, his wide, frightened eyes locked on the huge sword pointed directly at his face.

He started to fade before her very eyes, and she reached out hurriedly with one hand to grip his arm. "No! Don't disappear. Who are you? Are you alone?"

The boy gasped and struggled, becoming totally invisible, but Cazlina could still feel his thin arm in her grip. The sensation was eerily surreal, for it appeared as though she was grasping thin air, and yet there was solid flesh under her hand.

"You can't get away," she said. "I can still feel you, so, you might as well become visible again." She softened her tone. "I don't want to hurt you. I just want to talk to you. Please?"

The boy slowly reappeared, his slight body straining away from her. His wide eyes, a striking emerald color, stared back at Cazlina like a frightened animal's. He was just a young child, as terrified and panicked as she was, and she felt an overwhelming urge to ease his fear. Yet, she knew if she loosened her grip on his arm, he would flee into the mist before she had a chance to talk to him.

"Who are you?" she asked again.

He continued to gape silently at her, his mouth slightly open, and she wondered if perhaps he was incapable of speaking.

She lowered the sword to her side and his huge eyes followed the movement of the weapon.

"I promise I'm not going to hurt you," she assured him. "I swear on Donar's breath. Will you talk to me, please?"

He hesitated for a moment and then nodded, his eyes flickering back up to her face.

She glanced around, feeling far too exposed in the corridor despite the billowing mist. "Is there a room nearby where we can talk safely?"

Without a word, he turned and started to move off down the corridor. She followed closely, keeping a steady grip on his arm, although she loosened it a little to avoid hurting him.

He led her into a small room--a library or an office of sorts. Floor to ceiling bookshelves lined the back wall, and, in front of them, sat an oval desk with ornate carvings and silver writing implements resting on a white blotter.

Once inside, Cazlina closed and locked the door, which was inlaid with heavily lacquered panels of a reddish-colored wood. It seemed sturdy and solid, and she hoped it would block out the sound of their voices from inside the room.

Cautiously, she released her hold on the boy's arm, ready to pounce on him immediately if he should try to run away. She knew he was capable of vanishing into thin air, but she didn't know if he could walk through solid objects like doors and walls. She would have to take that chance if she hoped to gain his trust and cooperation.

The boy stood silently watching her, making no move to try and escape, and she was relieved to see his thin-featured face looked less wary and afraid now.

"My name is Cazlina," she said, smiling at him and hoping to put him at ease. "What's yours?"

For a moment longer, he continued to stare at her and then answered in a piping voice, "Niko. Niko Kesel."

She started and frowned at him, not certain she had heard right. "Did you say...*Kesel*?"

He nodded gravely. "Arman Kesel is my Da."

"Is he with General Viadon's army?"

A worried frown flickered across Niko's face. "I'm not supposed to talk about that."

Cazlina squatted down in front of him and laid her hands gently on his shoulders. "It's all right, Niko. There's no one here but us, and I promise I won't tell anyone you talked to me. You can trust me."

He still looked doubtful. "Queen Saranor forbids anyone in the castle to talk about the rebel army or even say...you know...the general's name. She gets really mad whenever somebody does and then bad things happen. Very bad things."

Cazlina could only imagine the horrors this poor child must have witnessed in a castle ruled by an insane queen and her followers. Those huge green eyes held a haunting vulnerability and wisdom far too mature for someone his age.

She bit her lip indecisively, wondering if she should tell him that his father was a prisoner in the castle and in danger of becoming a victim of Saranor's depravity.

Niko tilted his head. "I thought you were dead," he said. "When the guard fell down, I thought you'd been hit by the arrow, too."

"What? How did you know about the guard and the arrow? Were you in the courtyard?"

His expression became wary. "You won't tell on me, will you?"

She gripped his shoulders a little tighter. "I promise I won't. What did you see, Niko?"

He still looked a little uneasy, chewing on his lower lip as he contemplated whether or not to speak. Cazlina tried not to squirm with impatience, afraid she would scare him into silence if she pushed too hard. Her heart soared with the possibility that, if he had witnessed the arrival of the prisoners, maybe he had also seen where they had been taken after being brought inside from the courtyard.

To her relief, Niko apparently decided to trust her and started speaking again. "I was in the courtyard, up on the ledge near the gates. I know I wasn't supposed to be there, but I wanted to see what was going on, and, since I made myself invisible, no one knew I was there. I watched the big bird with the beautiful wings and the tongues of fire attack the wagon outside the castle walls. Then the wagon was inside and all these people were being pulled out of it. I jumped down from the ledge to get a closer look."

His eyes slid to her face. "I saw you being carried by that man. Then he got killed and fell on top of you, so I thought you were dead, too. But, you crawled out from underneath him and I followed you into the castle. When the blue mist came into the hallway and covered everything up, I thought it was all right to become visible again, but I guess it wasn't. You saw me."

Cazlina stared at him in silence, unnerved there had been a witness to her entry into the castle, even if it had been only a curious young boy.

"Why didn't you tell someone about me?" she asked, in bewilderment.

He frowned. "Why would I?"

She tried a shaky smile. "Well, I'm very glad you didn't. I was a prisoner trying to escape. I thought you would tell the soldiers so I couldn't get away."

"That's *why* I didn't say anything. I didn't want you to get caught again, because the queen does very bad things to prisoners." He tilted his head. "Why did you come into the castle instead of running away?"

Cazlina sighed wearily. "That's what I keep asking myself, too. I have this insane idea I can single-handedly save the other prisoners." Her voice caught for a moment as emotion welled up in her. "You see, Niko, my brother was also captured and I have to try to find him."

"My Da is a prisoner, too," he said, matter-of-factly.

Her concerned gaze flew to his face. "You saw him?"

He nodded and she leaned forward eagerly. "Can you help me find them, Niko? Do you know where they were taken?"

He regarded her solemnly for a moment. "I'll help you find your brother," he said. "But, I don't really care what happens to my Da."

CHAPTER 32

The boy's unemotional pronouncement left Cazlina staring at him in puzzlement.

"Why do you say that, Niko?"

He shrugged. "Da hates me. That's why he left me all alone here when he went and joined the rebel army, even though he knows I'm scared of this place and Queen Saranor."

Cazlina's heart constricted at the note of resigned acceptance in the little boy's voice. "Oh, Niko, I'm sure that's not true."

"Yes, it is," he replied. "He's always telling me he wished I'd never been born."

Shocked anger surged through Cazlina. How cruel for a father to tell his son such a thing! She already knew from her short acquaintance with the man that Kesel was selfish and nasty, with very few redeeming qualities, but she never realized the true depth of his brutality.

Niko continued, oblivious to Cazlina's revulsion and anger, "He thinks there's something wrong with me, too, 'cause I can disappear and nobody can see me." He peered shyly at Cazlina. "Do *you* think there's something wrong with me?"

"No, of course not," she said, adamantly. "I think you're a very special little boy with a very special gift from the gods."

He looked doubtful. "Well, anyway, Da doesn't think so. He hardly even looks at me or talks to me, except to yell if I don't do something fast enough when he tells me to. When I was younger, he used to hit me a lot, until I figured out I could make myself disappear. Ever since then, I just become invisible and run away whenever he gets drunk or mad."

Cazlina stared at the young boy, an uneasy suspicion tightening in her stomach. "Niko, where is your mother?"

He shrugged. "She died when I was born. I don't know where she's buried."

"Oh, you poor child!" Cazlina burst out.

She pulled Niko to her in a fierce embrace, shock and outrage consuming her at the abuse and neglect he had suffered at the hands of his cruel, uncaring father.

The boy held himself stiffly and awkwardly within the tight circle of Cazlina's arms. When she drew back, there was an apprehensive look on his face.

"How old are you, Niko?" she asked.

"Nine, I think," He shifted away from her, clearly uncomfortable with her display of empathy, and she let him go without protest.

Poor child, she thought sympathetically. *It certainly sounds as though he's not used to any acts of kindness or gentleness, especially from anyone in this castle of horrors.*

She stood up. "Surely, your father didn't leave you here alone, did he? There must be someone who looks after you."

"I look after myself," Niko said, a bit defiantly, drawing himself up to his full height and thrusting out his skinny chest.

She regarded him sadly. It was obvious from the way the grimy tunic and trousers hung like rags on his thin, malnourished body that he was not having an easy time of looking after himself, and she could only imagine the crushing loneliness he experienced every day. But, despite all of that, there was something heartbreakingly tough and independent about him that told her he had grown up very quick in a poisonous environment.

"Besides, I *do* have a friend here," he went on, his eyes lighting up. "His name is Tor, and I love him more than anything in the world. And, he loves me, too."

Cazlina smiled. "That's wonderful! I'm so glad to hear you have someone to keep you company."

"Maybe Tor can help us free the prisoners," he suggested, eagerness brightening his face.

Cazlina dismissed the idea immediately. She couldn't possibly trust anyone else in the castle. She was taking enough of a chance as it was putting her faith in Niko not to give away her presence. Perhaps, this Tor person was not a complete monster if he could forge a relationship with a lonely, neglected little boy, but that certainly didn't mean he wouldn't sound the alarm the moment he discovered she was an escaped prisoner.

"I don't think we should tell anyone else what we're up to, Niko," she said, adamantly. "Not even your friend Tor."

Disappointment clouded his face, but he nodded and said sagely, "That's all right. We don't need anyone else, anyway. We can handle this on our own."

She smiled at him, impressed by his courage and tenacity. Such traits surely must have been inherited from his mother, for certainly Arman Kesel possessed little of either.

Cazlina didn't believe for a moment that carelessness on the part of the little boy or pure coincidence had revealed him to her in the blue mist. It seemed far more likely the invisible hand of Pharon had sought out the one person in the whole castle who could be trusted to help her in her quest and had led him straight to her.

A pang of guilt pricked her conscience as she gazed down at the earnest young face dominated by huge green eyes. He looked so innocent and trusting and, by enlisting his help, she would be putting him in grave danger.

"Niko, maybe you should stay here where it's safe," she said. "You can tell me how to get to the dungeons and I'll find them on my own."

His face fell and hurt shone from his eyes. "You think I'm a coward, don't you? You think I'll get scared and run away." He drew himself up with dignified affront. "Well, I won't."

She placed a gentle hand on his tousled hair. "I know you wouldn't, Niko. I believe you are a very brave young man. But, this task is going to be very dangerous. If you're caught helping me…"

"We won't get caught," he said, insistently. "I know some secret ways to the dungeons, but I have to show you 'cause you'd never find them on your own, even if I described them to you." He thrust out his chin. "So, you see, you *do* need me to come with you."

She had to smile at his determined stance. His earlier fright and panic had completely disappeared, replaced with a dogged courage she wished she possessed. He was also surprisingly stubborn, so it was highly likely he would make himself disappear and follow her anyway.

She wanted to hug the child to her once more but refrained from doing so.

"You're right. I can't do this alone. I need a brave warrior by my side, one who knows his way around the castle and can help me fight off anyone who tries to stop us."

He looked pleased at being called a warrior. "I wish you'd let me tell Tor. He'd be really good at helping to protect us."

Cazlina shook her head. "I'm sorry, Niko. I don't think it's a good idea. You're the only one I can trust in the castle. I know you won't betray me."

"No, I won't, but Tor wouldn't, either. He's my best friend."

"I know, but it has to be just the two of us, all right? You can't tell anyone else."

He sighed. "All right."

"Good. We'd better get going before-before..."

"Before the bad things happen to the prisoners," Niko finished.

Cazlina nodded silently, her throat tight with emotion.

She put her ear to the door and listened. No sounds could be heard from the other side, but the silence did nothing to reassure her. Though she and Niko had tried to keep their voices low, someone coming down the corridor might have heard something and come to investigate. He or she could be waiting on the other side of the door, ready to strike her down as soon as she stepped out of the room.

She felt a small hand touch her arm and looked down at Niko.

"Better let me go first," he whispered. "If anybody's out there, they'll see it's just me and go away again. Nobody around here cares what I do, so they'll ignore me as usual."

Cazlina swallowed against another rush of dismay and anger. The words were delivered in such a dispassionate manner that their effect was far more devastating and poignant than any emotion could have made them. What hardships and barbaric cruelties this young child had already suffered in his few short years!

Her rage toward Kesel grew with every moment she spent with his neglected, unloved son.

She stood off to one side as Niko pulled open the door and slipped out into the corridor. In the next instant, she pressed back tightly against the wall, catching her breath as a gruff voice suddenly demanded, "What're you doing in there, boy? I nearly skewered you on my sword!"

Niko's voice trembled as he replied, "I-I heard the fighting outside. It scared me, so I ran in here to hide."

"Good. Now, get back in there and stay out of the way. We don't need a snot-nosed brat underfoot."

"Y-Yes, sir."

"By Orun's sword, where did this damnable fog come from anyway? Can't see a foot in front of my face. Folton, you still there?"

Another voice sounded close by. "Yes, Sergeant, we're right behind you. At least, I think we are. I can't see you, but I can hear you pretty good."

The first man grunted. "Right then, let's go give Viadon a good thrashing for the queen. You all know what'll happen if we don't put a stop to this rebellion right away."

The man named Folton piped up in a quavering voice, "Surely not the-the Pool of Souls, sir?"

The sergeant snorted. "What else does the queen do to those who fail her or disobey her? We'd better get a move on if we don't want to end up like those other poor fools. Out of the way, lad. Go back and hide under the desk if you know what's good for you."

The tramp of booted feet echoed down the corridor as the unseen soldiers hurried away to engage in battle with the general's troops.

Niko stuck his head back in the doorway. "They're gone."

Cazlina released her breath, her pulse hammering at the close call. If Niko had not suggested leaving the room first, she would have run straight into the arms of the enemy.

"All right," she said, a little shakily. "Lead on to the dungeons."

CHAPTER 33

They hurried down the corridor, slipping into abandoned rooms when more soldiers rushed by on their way to the battle outside in the courtyard. The men cursed the blue mist that made visibility difficult, but Cazlina silently thanked Pharon for sending the phenomenon to aid in concealing her presence within the castle.

As she and Niko furtively stepped out of yet another room and continued on their way, they passed another of the gigantic tapestries on the wall. Cazlina sensed movement out of the corner of her eye and averted her gaze, having no desire to witness what gruesome scene this one depicted.

At the end of the long corridor, a set of wide, shallow stairs spiraled downward, their risers covered in a deep blue carpet patterned with silver stripes. Niko took Cazlina's hand and led her silently down the stairs, keeping tightly to the left-hand wall. The blue fog hovered at the top of the stairs but didn't follow them down.

Cazlina wondered uneasily if the mage's magic could reach only so far into the castle.

Partway down the staircase, Niko suddenly stopped and Cazlina almost ran into him.

"What…?"

The young boy put a finger to his lips and she fell silent, straining her ears to listen for someone coming up or down the stairs toward them.

"Do you hear something?" she whispered, unable to make out any sounds.

Niko shook his head and pointed to the wall. She frowned, seeing nothing different about that section of wall compared to the rest of it. Highly polished oak wainscoting ran from the stairs to about halfway up the wall and then the rest was covered in gold-leafed silk wallpaper.

Niko pushed on the raised edge of the wainscoting and there was an audible click. A section of the oak paneling, about three feet by three feet, silently swung inward.

Cazlina stared at it in amazement. She would never have known the door existed just by looking at the paneling. But, obviously, a curious young boy left with little or no adult supervision in a castle full of uncaring people would have no problem finding secret places to hide in or explore.

Niko gave her a conspiratorial smile and slipped through the small opening into the darkness beyond. After a quick glance up and down the staircase to make sure no one was coming, Cazlina followed after him, being careful not to bang the unwieldy sword against the sides of the narrow door. When she was fully inside, he pushed the heavy panel closed and darkness fell like a velvet curtain, cutting off her sight, but only for a few seconds. A soft green glow suddenly lit up the space and she saw a tiny ball of light resting on Niko's palm.

He grinned at her in the eerie light. "I stole one of Nostrimus's luminary orbs. He'll never miss it. It's better than a torch 'cause there's no smoke."

She smiled back, once more amazed by the boy's versatility and intelligence.

"Where does this lead?" she whispered, not certain if their voices could carry out beyond the opening in the wall.

"It goes to a bedroom on the floor below, used by Agneus Molitare, the queen's chief advisor." Niko's eyes narrowed with something akin to malice and contempt. "He's a mean, ugly man. I don't like him and he doesn't like me, either. Sometimes, I'll hide behind the secret door and whisper and moan in the dead of night, or else I'll make myself invisible and stand right beside his bed, whispering in his ear. He thinks his room is haunted and the spirits will steal his breath away as soon as he closes his eyes. He's always complaining he can't get a good night's sleep."

Cazlina hid a smile, picturing the lad pressed up against the panel in the darkness, an expression of glee on his thin face as he groaned like a specter and Molitare quivered in abject terror on the other side.

"We should get going," she suggested, but before they could do so, a sound from close by nearly made her jump out of her skin. A couple of women were passing by on the other side of the secret panel on their way up the staircase, chattering nervously in high-pitched voices.

She and Niko held their breaths until they could no longer hear the women and then they stood up. The ceiling of the passageway was only about five feet high and Cazlina had to stoop a little, but Niko had no trouble standing upright. The green glow from the luminary orb lit up the plain wooden walls and floor, which surprisingly had a narrow brown rug running down its centre. Niko explained in a whisper that he had 'borrowed' the rug from a storage room and placed it in the secret passage so he could walk through it without making any noise. Cazlina once again silently praised the lad for his ingenuity.

It took only a few minutes to traverse the narrow passageway. When they reached the door that led into Molitare's bedroom, Cazlina could see reddish light shining through a tiny hole in the paneling. Niko peered through the hole. After a few seconds, he looked back at Cazlina and nodded.

"I can't see anyone in there," he whispered, "unless Molitare is hiding under the bed."

He reached up and pressed against the top edge of the secret door. Silently, it swung open about an inch or so and the young boy peered cautiously around the edge. Then he slipped out into the bedroom beyond, followed closely by Cazlina, who held the sword at the ready in case there was someone in the room.

She found herself standing in a lavish bedchamber dominated by a high four-poster bed draped in thick curtains of crimson velvet. The silk wallpaper had huge red flowers on a cream background, and even the lampshades were made of crimson silk, which explained the reddish glow.

Cazlina suppressed a slight shudder. Instead of projecting an aura of opulence and comfort, the predominant theme of red in the chamber combined with the very dark wood on the ceiling and floor made her think of a dim cavern filled with blood. She knew she would never be able to sleep in such an oppressive setting and wondered if its occupant experienced similar feelings of unease. Perhaps, Niko's midnight hauntings were not the only reason Agneus Molitare could not sleep properly in his bedchamber.

She wrinkled her nose in distaste. The room reeked of incense and some other heavy, unpleasant odor she could not define.

Niko smirked up at her. "Molitare constantly burns ghostbane, hoping it will chase away the spirits that haunt his room."

Cazlina smiled. "Something tells me it's not working very well."

The young boy snorted. "It just makes the room smell bad." He tiptoed across the floor to a dark- door set into one wall of the room. "This next part could be a bit tricky," he said. "We have to go out into a hallway and pass several other bedrooms until we get to a storage closet at the end. There's another secret panel in the closet and a ladder that will lead us down to the next level where the dungeons are. But, we shouldn't be in too much danger of being caught. I don't think anyone will be in the rooms right now. They're all out fighting or with the queen."

Cazlina nodded, eager anticipation thrumming through her veins at the thought of finding Gareth soon. He had to be in the dungeons. She refused to even entertain the thought that the prisoners might have been taken elsewhere. The close bond she shared with her brother made her reasonably confident he was still alive and well. If something terrible had already happened to him, it would surely have caused a rift in her soul as hollow and agonizing as the one she had experienced when she had sent Miris away into the dark, dangerous night.

The hallway was indeed deserted when she and the boy slipped out of Molitare's bedchamber. Most of the doors to the other rooms were closed and those that stood open showed chambers in untidy disarray, as though their occupants had left in a hurry while in the midst of doing some task. The general's attack on the castle had most likely precipitated the hasty departures.

They reached the storeroom at the end of the hallway undetected. Once inside the small closet packed with boxes and wooden crates and odd pieces of furniture, Niko handed the luminary orb to Cazlina. She watched curiously as he pushed aside a wooden crate and pulled up a narrow strip of carpeting to reveal a trapdoor in the floor. The door came up easily and without the slightest creak. Cazlina reasoned that, with the boy's propensity for stealth and secrecy, he probably kept the trapdoor's hinges regularly oiled so it could be opened and closed without making any noise.

She leaned cautiously over the opening, holding the orb aloft to illuminate the darkness. The greenish glow revealed a steep, vertical ladder descending down into a black hole that seemed to have no bottom. A sense of profound dizziness rushed through her. Hastily, she drew back from the edge of the trapdoor.

"How-How far down does it go?" she asked, trying to keep a quaver out of her voice.

Obviously, she wasn't entirely successful at concealing her trepidation for Niko glanced at her and said kindly, "Don't worry. I'll go first and keep you from falling. Don't look down and you'll be all right."

His blithe assurances did little to dispel her misgivings or give her confidence that a slight boy could prevent her from falling if she should slip off the rungs of the ladder. But, she couldn't let fear keep her from the task at hand. The dungeons--and Gareth--were too close. It would be foolhardy to turn back now when she had already come this far.

She forced a note of determination into her voice, "All right, lead on."

Niko nodded, his teeth flashing for a moment in a grin, "I've done this hundreds of times," he assured her. "It's easy. You'll see."

She rolled her eyes at him. "Let's go, before I change my mind."

CHAPTER 34

In a blink, Niko disappeared over the edge of the trapdoor. Cazlina leaned down and handed him the luminary orb. Then she sat back on her heels for a moment to bolster her courage for the first step on to the disturbingly steep ladder. She contemplated leaving the heavy sword in the closet to free both hands for the descent, but dismissed the idea almost immediately. She didn't want to leave herself defenseless against the guards in the dungeons.

Finally, she took a deep breath and swung her leg over the dark opening, feeling for the first rung of the ladder. A hand closed around her ankle and she startled, nearly crying out in shock, but it was only Niko helping to guide her foot toward the narrow step.

With both feet finally planted firmly on the ladder, she clung for a brief moment to the edge of the trapdoor, reluctant to let go. But, Niko tugged at her foot insistently and hissed up at her, "Come on, Cazlina, let's go."

Gritting her teeth, she grasped the edges of the ladder and started down slowly, keeping her gaze glued straight ahead to the wall in front of her. Whenever her foot faltered in finding the next step, Niko was always there beneath her to guide her into the right position. The sword forced her to hook her left forearm instead of her hand around the side of the ladder, making the descent slow and awkward.

A whole litany of aches and complaints accompanied her down the ladder. Shooting pains lanced through her bruised back with every tentative step, and her face burned and throbbed from having been out in the relentless sun and the hard smack against the enemy soldier's shoulder blade. Exhaustion grated through every bone in her body. On top of all that, the fear of falling still nagged insidiously at the back of her mind, no matter how hard she tried to push it away. The only comfort she derived from the harrowing experience was that the darkness in the narrow shaft, relieved only by the faint greenish glow filtering up from below, prevented her from seeing just how far down the ladder descended and gave her hope it was only a few more steps to the bottom.

At last, Niko's voice floated up to her with the welcome words, "We're here."

She sagged in relief when her feet touched solid ground once more, her legs trembling with the effort of the descent. She transferred the heavy sword to her right hand and shook the feeling back into her left arm.

In the eerie green glow of the orb, Niko grinned impishly at her. "See, that wasn't so bad, was it? You made it down in one piece."

She glowered at him in mock reproach. "That's easy for you to say, you impudent scallywag. You probably scamper up and down this ladder ten times a day. Besides, you weren't carrying a sword that's nearly as big as you are."

Seeing the twinkle in his huge eyes pleased her. Gone was the frightened, wary waif she had first encountered in the corridor upstairs. In his place, stood a typical mischievous nine-year old child on an exhilarating adventure.

It only goes to show what a little bit of attention and empathy can do to make a neglected child's eyes shine, she thought.

Looking around, she could see they stood in a narrow shaft that contained only the ladder and the faint outline of a low door in the opposite wall. As was the case with the panel that led into Molitare's room, a tiny hole near the top filtered a slim beam of light into the shaft.

Pointing to it, she said, "Don't tell me. That's another secret panel leading into another room."

Niko nodded. "The armory. Once we leave that, we go down another flight of stairs to the dungeons."

"The armory?" Cazlina repeated, nervously, lowering her voice to a whisper. "Won't that be dangerous? Surely, there'll be a lot of soldiers in there, getting weapons to fight against General Viadon."

The boy shrugged, unconcerned. "We'll just have to wait until it's empty and then slip out."

He moved over to the door and placed his eye against the hole. Cazlina slipped quietly up beside him, her muscles taut with tension as she listened intently for sounds from within the room beyond the panel.

Niko held up two fingers and she took that to mean there were two soldiers in the armory. Pressing her ear tightly against the wall and holding her breath, she could make out two voices jabbering at each other. After a moment, Niko nodded, indicating the men had left the room, presumably with whatever weapons they had come to retrieve.

Inside the armory, Cazlina was amazed at the massive array of weapons piled on shelves and counters or hanging from hooks on the walls. Swords ranged in size from light rapiers like the one the blacksmith in Terrangay had made for her to some that were even bigger than the sword she had taken from the dead enemy soldier. Lances and longbows and long wooden shafts with razor-edged blades leaned against the walls, and spiked balls on chains hung from the hooks. There were even some unusual weapons she didn't recognize, but they looked very dangerous and deadly and she shied away from touching them.

She hurriedly rid herself of the heavy, unwieldy sword she had taken from the dead soldier and grabbed a smaller one, plus a dagger with a jeweled hilt that she tucked inside the waistband of her trousers.

She heard Niko say, "Oh!" behind her and spun around to see him picking up a wicked-looking serrated blade curved in an arc, with a long wooden handle attached to one end. He swung it in experimental circles a few times in front of him.

"Niko, put that down before you cut yourself," she exclaimed.

He ignored her, his eyes dancing with excitement as he feinted right and left and slashed the weapon at imaginary enemies.

"I never saw this one before," he murmured in awe. "I bet I could really hurt somebody with this."

"Including you. Put it back where you found it and let's go."

His face assumed the stubborn expression she was fast becoming familiar with despite her short acquaintance with him. "You said I was a warrior. Well, warriors need weapons and I want this one." His eyes narrowed in fierce indignation. "Besides, you can't tell me what to do."

Cazlina bit back a sharp reprimand, instinctively knowing that forcing her authority on the lad would only make him more obstinate.

"Well, by Donar's breath, at least be careful with it and stop swinging it around. I don't want my head lopped off by accident."

He grinned, his pique forgotten, and, to her immense relief, ceased slashing at the air with the deadly weapon. She was not comfortable with the situation and could only hope the boy would have the good sense to handle the weapon carefully so he didn't inadvertently hurt himself or her.

Giving the serrated blade one last nervous look, she started toward the door. "There's another set of stairs and then the dungeons, correct?

He nodded and she felt a rush of fearful anticipation, wondering how many guards they would have to encounter before she could free Gareth and the others.

"No more secret passages?"

Niko shook his head. "From here on, we'll have to take our chances out in the open."

Forcing the disappointment and panic down, she gripped the sword a little tighter. "All right, let's go."

The door creaked as they slipped out into the deserted corridor. This part of the castle boasted none of the rich, lavish décor of the upstairs rooms and hallways. The walls and floor were built of gray stone, void of wallpaper or carpeting of any kind. Metal light fixtures placed at irregular intervals along the corridor provided poor lighting and the air had a decidedly chilly feel to it.

Cazlina shivered as they crept along the hallway, her nerves frayed by the fear of discovery now that she was so close to finding Gareth. She would gladly have scaled another steep ladder in a dark shaft if it meant she could reach the prisoners without Saranor's guards seeing her.

She and Niko had gone only a short distance when the castle suddenly trembled and an unearthly shriek rent the air. The sound intensified until it seemed to emanate from every crack and stone in the corridor, and forced Cazlina and the boy to their knees on the cold floor, desperately covering their ears against the horrific scream. It lasted only seconds, but Cazlina could still feel it vibrating throughout her body after it stopped.

Before she could raise herself from the floor and ask Niko if he knew what had caused the terrible scream that had literally shaken the castle's foundations, maniacal laughter echoed throughout the corridor, coming from everywhere at once, and then a thunderous, masculine voice shouted incomprehensible words, *"EXPELLIUM SOLIS!"*

Sudden silence descended on the corridor and Cazlina sat up, her whole body trembling from the frightening experience.

She turned to the boy beside her. "Niko, what…?"

Her voice trailed off at the look on his white face. The expression in his eyes was blank, devoid of all life. He was breathing, so the traumatic experience hadn't been fatal, but it seemed like he had retreated into the far reaches of his mind, never to venture out into the world again.

She grasped his arm, shaking it. "Niko! Niko, are you all right?"

He gave no indication he heard her. Before her concerned gaze, his tense body began to fade away into the translucence that heralded a disappearance.

She clutched his arm tighter, trying to hold him there. "No, Niko, don't go. It's me, Cazlina. Stay with me, please."

At last, her voice reached something deep inside him and he shuddered violently, his body once more assuming its corporeal appearance. His eyes flickered and focused unsteadily on her anxious face. In their depths, she could see desperation and panic and terror swimming in a sea of tears.

Compassion for him surged through Cazlina. Despite his tough and brave exterior, he was still a little boy.

She caught her breath as realization suddenly dawned on her. "Was that…?"

Niko nodded jerkily, and his voice, when he spoke, was wooden. "The queen has sacrificed another prisoner to the Pool of Souls."

The words sliced through Cazlina's heart as surely as a sharp blade would. She leapt to her feet, Gareth's name trembling on her dry lips.

"Which way?" she asked, wildly. "Which way are the dungeons?"

He shrank back a little from her fierce intensity but pointed down the hallway. "Down there about halfway. The staircase is to the right."

She began to run toward it, heedless of the noise her boots made on the stone floor and only vaguely aware of Niko following behind. An overwhelming need to make certain Gareth had not been the hapless prisoner used in Saranor's ceremony thrust all other thoughts out of her head.

Before she could reach the stairway, however, the extraordinary luck she had experienced so far at escaping detection in the castle came to an abrupt end as heavy boot treads sounded on the stone floor ahead of her and two soldiers appeared around a corner.

CHAPTER 35

They both drew up sharply at the sight of her and Niko.

"Hey, you, what are you doing here?" one of them demanded.

Cazlina hesitated for only a fraction of a second and then ran straight toward the two men, the sword held unwaveringly in front of her. She didn't even stop to think about the danger of her actions. The soldiers were merely obstacles that stood between her and Gareth and her only thought was to remove them from her path.

Surprise and shock flickered across the men's faces as she charged down the dim corridor toward them. They didn't even have time to draw their own weapons before she reached them. Her sword whistled through the air and sliced into the torso of the soldier nearest her. Blood spurted and the man dropped to the floor with an agonized cry. Cazlina immediately turned to the second man, but in the feverish pitch of battle zeal, she had forgotten about Niko. The young boy leapt past her, swinging his arced blade in a vicious circle that caught the other soldier on the side of the neck. He fell to the floor beside the other dead man, his life's blood spurting out into a ghastly pool on the stones of the hallway.

Cazlina glanced at Niko's white face. His eyes were wide and unfocused. She stepped between him and the two dead men and rested her hand on his shoulder, giving him a gentle shake. "Niko, are you all right?"

His gaze flicked upward to meet hers, and she was gratified to see comprehension in his eyes instead of the disturbing emptiness that had seized him earlier. The stained blade in his hand trembled. Cazlina suspected the bloody reality of actually using the weapon against a real person and not an imaginary enemy had been more than the child had bargained for. She wished with all her heart she could have spared him such a dreadful ordeal, and cursed herself again for permitting him to accompany her on her dangerous and foolhardy mission.

She had not reckoned with Niko's amazing ability to overcome adversity and trauma, however. His life experiences, short as they were in the corrupt environment of the castle, had no doubt inured him to all kinds of horrors, and he looked at her now with an expression of eerie maturity.

"Maybe we should hide the bodies," he suggested. "In case someone comes along before we reach the dungeons."

The shock and suddenness of killing the two men had served to dampen some of the single-minded purpose that had seized Cazlina at the mention of the Pool of Souls. Reason and cool-headedness prevailed once more, and she saw the wisdom of Niko's suggestion.

Quickly, they found an unoccupied room off the corridor, which was another storage room, loaded with boxes and crates, and, with great effort, dragged the heavy bodies inside. Cazlina turned the key in the lock and shoved it into her pocket, hoping the locked door would prevent anyone from finding the men any time soon. She bit her lip at the sight of the large pool of blood staining the stone floor and decided there was little they could do about it. There was no time to try to find something with which to wipe up the blood, and, besides, it was unlikely they would be able to clean it up enough to prevent anyone from seeing that something untoward had happened there.

"Cazlina, we should go," Niko prompted.

The sudden appearance of the two soldiers had made her reconsider her headlong and incautious rush toward the dungeons, and, this time, she and the boy proceeded down the winding flight of stone steps at a stealthier pace. Now that they were closer to their destination, Cazlina expected to encounter more guards and her pulse quickened at the thought of having to kill again.

The possibility became heart-lurching reality after they had descended about halfway down the staircase. Another soldier came bounding up the stairs toward them, brandishing a sword in one hand and a spiked ball on a chain in the other. There was no time to retreat back up the staircase. The man drew up short when he saw Cazlina and Niko cowering against the wall and his eyes narrowed suspiciously.

"What are you two doing here?" he growled.

Both Cazlina and Niko had thrust their weapons behind them the instant they saw the soldier. They pressed tightly against each other and the wall, hoping the dim lighting would help to conceal their bloodied blades and the dark splatters on their hands and arms.

Cazlina stared at the soldier, her mouth dry with fear. She had no idea what to say, but, once again, Niko came to the rescue, piping up in a scared little boy's voice, "We-We heard fighting and ran down here to hide." His voice trembled, sounding on the verge of tears. "I think the enemy is in the castle. We-We heard a man scream and saw blood in the corridor upstairs."

His quick-thinking had the desired effect. With a bellow, the soldier pushed his way past them and charged the rest of the way up the stairs.

Cazlina squeezed Niko's shoulder and smiled at him. "Good boy. Hopefully, that will keep him busy searching for the enemy."

They hurried down the flight of stairs, concerned less now with stealth than with haste. With any luck, other guards they encountered on the way might also be convinced that General Viadon's army had invaded the castle and not question them too closely about why they were in the dungeons.

The next obstacle presented itself in the form of a vicious-looking brute of a dog with a scarred face that slunk around a corner of the winding staircase and stopped only a few steps below them. A deep growl rumbled from his throat as his lips drew back over wicked teeth.

Cazlina froze, her heart thumping in her chest. "Niko, get behind me," she ordered, in a low, shaky voice. "But, move slowly. We don't want to provoke him."

Without taking her gaze off the dangerous looking animal still growling only a few steps away, she sensed the boy moving forward instead of retreating behind her.

"Niko, what are you doing?" she hissed.

She put out a restraining hand, but he brushed past it, dropping the arced blade to the stone steps and bounding down them with a joyful cry. To Cazlina's astonishment, he dropped to his knees and fiercely hugged the dog's neck. The animal responded by licking Niko's dirty cheek.

"It's all right, Tor. Cazlina is a friend."

Tor! So, this was Niko's much-loved companion in the castle? Not a person at all, but a huge brown and black dog with a puckered scar running from his right eye down to his muzzle. The animal had stopped growling, but his yellowish-brown eyes still glared at her in warning.

Tor, Niko's right. I am his friend, just as you are.

The dog's head jerked up and he whined in surprise at the sound of her voice in his mind.

She smiled. *That's right. I can talk to you.*

He growled uneasily. *Who are you? You're a stranger to me. I haven't seen you before in the castle. What are you doing with the boy? I have sworn to keep him safe, so if you harbor ill intentions toward him...*

I assure you, I mean no harm to Niko. He's trying to help me find my brother, who is a prisoner in the dungeons.

The dog's eyes narrowed. *You should leave at once, girl. It's much too dangerous here. If the guards catch you, you might very well join your brother in his prison.*

Cazlina's lips tightened with defiance. *I intend to free him. He will not become a pawn in the queen's sick fantasies!*

The dog made a raspy sound in his throat, surprisingly like a mirthless chuckle. *Your intentions are noble but very foolish, girl. Once someone becomes Saranor's prisoner, there is no hope for him or her.*

"No!" The word burst involuntarily from Cazlina, and Niko glanced questioningly at her.

"Cazlina, what is it? Are you all right?"

She struggled to get her emotions under control once more. Tor's fatalistic words seared themselves upon her soul, but she refused to believe Gareth's fate was irrevocably sealed.

"Tor doesn't think we can free my brother," she said.

The boy gave her a strange look and glanced at the huge dog by his side. "Tor can't talk."

"I can communicate with him in my mind," she explained, "and he can talk back to me the same way."

Niko's mouth dropped open. "You can?"

"Yes."

He looked back at the dog, brushing a hand gently over one of his ears. "I wish I could talk to him. I'd like to tell him how much I love him and what a good friend he is."

Cazlina smiled kindly. "He knows, Niko. He loves you, too, and wants to protect you."

She moved down a few steps toward the intimidating dog that stood almost waist-height to her and stared challengingly into his eyes.

"Tor, I intend to rescue my brother and the others with him. I know you're worried about Niko, but he doesn't have to go any further. Like you, I don't want him exposed to any more danger. I wouldn't have let him come this far, but, as I'm sure you're well aware, he can be quite headstrong when he wants to be."

Tor gave a heavy sigh. *Yes, indeed, I do know of his willful nature. I often have great difficulty keeping him out of trouble.*

"I hope you won't try to stop me," Cazlina continued, "because I *will* fight to the death to free Gareth."

She saw Niko's eyes widen but steeled herself against the dawning fear on his face and steadily held the dog's gaze with her own.

Tor drew his lips back over his teeth, but resignation colored his voice when he spoke. *You're being extremely foolish, girl. You can't hope to get past the guards and free the prisoners. But, if you insist on carrying out your mad scheme, I won't stand in your way. The boy stays behind, however.*

Cazlina nodded, relief washing through her at the thought that she would not have to harm or kill Niko's best friend in front of him. "I agree. Niko, you should go now with Tor and find a safe place to hide. You mustn't be in harm's way when General Viadon breaches the castle's fortifications, if he has not already done so."

Niko jumped to his feet, his eyes blazing. "I'm not going anywhere but with you, Cazlina! I'm the warrior who's been chosen to protect you. I want to help you free the prisoners."

Cazlina sighed inwardly. She regretted putting the notion of being a warrior into his head. He had taken it far too much to heart and she was afraid he might act recklessly in the mistaken belief he was invincible.

"Niko…"

With a look of mulish defiance on his face, the boy disappeared. Cazlina and Tor exchanged helpless looks. The dog began to stalk back and forth on the steps, sniffing the air.

He's still here, I think, Tor said. *He won't reappear unless I agree to let him accompany you. If I don't, I'm afraid he will go on by himself.*

"Niko, we don't have time to play games," Cazlina addressed the air impatiently. "We only want you to be safe. Please, listen to me and go with Tor. He'll keep you from harm, as he always has."

She jumped when the blade Niko had dropped on the steps above suddenly clattered down to land near her feet, as though kicked there by the invisible boy.

"I want to go with *you*," his petulant voice sounded behind her, "and I want Tor to come with us, too."

Cazlina glanced at Tor. The huge dog closed his eyes for a brief moment and then said. *We will both go with you; although I still think you will fail in your mission.* He gave Cazlina a menacing look. *No harm had better come to him.*

"I will protect him as fiercely as you would," she assured him.

CHAPTER 36

Cazlina shivered from the clammy touch of the air on her skin as Tor led the way down the rest of the stone staircase. In her head, prudence and reason fought a fierce battle with an overwhelming urge to rush recklessly forward and find Gareth. The dog's pace was frustratingly slow and cautious, his toenails clicking faintly on the stone steps, and she gritted her teeth, wanting to push him aside. Reluctantly, she forced herself to match the animal's stride, bowing to the wisdom of stealth.

Behind her, she sensed Niko's restlessness, too. Like her, he chafed at the slow pace and kept crowding her heels until she sent him a stern glance and a whispered reprimand.

At the bottom of the staircase, Tor stopped just before the corner, forcing the two behind him to do the same.

There is a sentry posted at the entrance to the dungeons around this corner, Tor said to Cazlina. *There is another who guards the block of cells further on.*

Fortunately, his station is not visible from the entrance, because there's a thick stone door between the two. Once we remove the first guard, we should be able to approach the second without his being any the wiser.

Any suggestions on how we can do that? Cazlina asked.

The dog glanced at Niko shifting impatiently from foot to foot, and a look of pained reluctance crossed the animal's scarred face. *As much as I hate to involve the boy, I think his ability to disappear can help us in this case. While invisible, he can distract the guards long enough for you to sneak up and knock them unconscious, or to kill them, whichever you prefer.*

Faint nausea gripped Cazlina at the thought of killing again, but she knew she would do it if necessary. Certainly, none of Saranor's minions would feel the same hesitation or trepidation about killing her if the roles were reversed.

The first sentry has in his possession a disk that is inserted into a notch in the door and turned in a specific series of patterns to open it. Tor continued. *The boy, in his invisible state, can slip through the door and use the same distraction tactic on the second guard.*

I don't have a clue how to turn the disk, Cazlina said, worriedly. *If I knock the guard unconscious or kill him, how will I be able to open the door? We could be here forever trying to figure out the right patterns.*

Tor gave her a smug look. *To most of the humans in this castle, I'm just a dumb animal, good only for kicking when the mood strikes them or for baring my teeth and threatening prisoners when they try to escape. What they don't realize is I'm actually quite intelligent and observant. Don't worry, I'll tell you the correct way to use the disk.*

Cazlina nodded, finding no fault with Tor's plan, and leaned down to whisper it in Niko's ear. His eyes shone brilliantly with excitement and eagerness.

"Don't be reckless," Cazlina warned him. "Just make sure the guard turns his back to me so he can't see me sneaking up."

The ploy worked perfectly. Within seconds, the first guard lay dead upon the stone floor. At first, Cazlina had thought only to render him unconscious, but the thought that he might awaken before she and Tor could carry out the rest of their plan changed her mind.

The disk, a small flat circle of clear crystal engraved with strange symbols, fitted neatly into an indentation in the stone door. Following Tor's instructions, Cazlina manipulated the disk in a series of complicated maneuvers until there was a faint click and the massive door began to swing ponderously inward.

A voice called out from the other side. "Bonsell, is that you? Are you bringing me more prisoners?"

In his invisible state, Niko slipped through the opening, and the second man was dispatched as silently and quickly as the first one. Beyond him, Cazlina saw a series of wooden doors with small barred windows in them. Her pulse quickened at the thought of Gareth behind one of them, and she rushed up to the nearest one, calling frantically through the barred opening. "Gareth!"

There was a rustle behind the door and then a face suddenly thrust itself against the window, startling her into a quick retreat.

"Who's there?" a quavering masculine voice demanded.

Quelling her alarm, Cazlina moved forward once more, peering into the dim cell beyond the window.

"My name is Cazlina Narzin. I'm looking for my brother, Gareth."

The bearded face at the window withdrew for a moment and she heard a murmur of voices, which fast grew louder and more excited.

"He's not in here," the man said, reappearing at the opening. Cazlina saw several other figures crowding in behind him. "Are you-Are you by any chance with General Viadon's army? Has he attacked the castle and sent you to rescue us?"

The news that Gareth was not in the cell sent a shaft of dismay through Cazlina, but she managed to give the man a weak smile. "Yes, I'm with the general and I've come to free you. Wait and I'll get the keys to unlock the door."

Determinedly avoiding the staring eyes of the dead guard, she unhooked the massive ring of keys attached to his belt and unlocked the cell door. Several men and women poured out of the cramped space, bombarding her with gratitude and excited questions. All were total strangers and none belonged to the group she and Gareth had been part of. Although she was happy to have freed them, she didn't have time for their questions. Her blood burned with the urgency to find Gareth.

Pushing her way through the crowd, she hurried down the line of other closed doors, frantically calling her brother's name. Finally, from the last cell, she heard his familiar voice cry out, "Caz?"

"Thank the gods, you're still alive!" Cazlina choked out, grabbing the bars and trying to peer into the cell beyond.

Gareth's pale, dirt-streaked face swam into view, blurred by the sudden tears that threw a gauze curtain over her vision. His strong fingers closed over her white knuckles grasping the bars.

"Are you all right? By Donar's breath, I thought I'd lost you. What happened? Why are you free? Why aren't you in one of the cells? Has General Viadon managed to get into the castle?"

She laughed a trifle hysterically. "One question at a time, Gareth. I'll answer them all as soon as I get you out of here."

Her hands shook so badly she could hardly thrust the key into the lock and turn it. Finally, after much fumbling, the door clicked open and she fell into Gareth's arms, burying her face against his chest and letting the tears that had been held in check for so long unashamedly fall upon his dusty uniform jacket. She felt his body shaking with emotion as he clung tightly to her. Other prisoners who had been in the cell with Gareth pushed their way past them with apologetic murmurs.

Finally, Gareth thrust her gently away from him, his eyes raking her face as though he couldn't quite believe it was her standing before him. "What happened to you? I lost sight of you in the courtyard when they pulled us out of the wagon. How did you manage to get free?"

"Not now, Gareth. I'll explain everything later. Right now, we need to get away from here as fast as possible, before someone comes."

He nodded. "You're right. Has the general infiltrated the castle? We felt it rocking with an explosion earlier."

Cazlina grimaced. "That wasn't the general. That was the queen sacrificing a prisoner in her Pool of Souls. I nearly died myself, thinking it might have been you."

He squeezed her shoulder in sympathy, his face grim at the news. "About an hour ago, I heard a commotion outside and one of the prisoners a few cells down said that some of the captives had been taken away. I didn't realize that's what the explosion meant. I'd hoped it was General Viadon breaching the castle's fortifications."

"It's so awful, Gareth. Those poor men and women. I hope the general can stop the queen from using more souls in her terrible Pool."

She felt a tugging on the hem of her tunic and looked down into Niko's flushed face. His eyes flicked to Gareth and he grinned. "Can I have the keys, Cazlina? We want to free the other prisoners.

"Oh, yes. Yes, of course. Here, take them."

She watched him scamper away, his body quivering with the excitement of being in the midst of a rescue operation. Tor padded closely by his side as he ran from cell to cell, unlocking each one and releasing the prisoners into the narrow outer chamber, where they milled about in some confusion and disbelief.

"Who's that?" Gareth asked.

"That's Kesel's son, Niko, and his good friend, Tor."

Gareth lifted an eyebrow. "Kesel? The same Kesel who had the hare-brained idea to have a little fun with Lerant's men and ended up with a dead hand instead?"

"The very one." Her eyes narrowed with contempt. "He left his nine-year old son alone to fend for himself in the castle when he joined Viadon's army. But, he's an amazing lad. Without him, I probably wouldn't be here right now."

Gareth shook his head, a stunned look on his face. "I have a thousand questions to ask you, but we'd better get a move on."

She nodded, and then grabbed his arm as a sudden thought struck her. "Wait, Gareth. Where are Jorin and Sergeant Zandorin and Kesel?"

Gareth searched the throng of milling, animated prisoners, but the three men were nowhere to be seen.

Alarm bells clanged in Cazlina's head and the same awful thought that careened through her brain must have occurred to Gareth as well, for an expression of unease crossed his face and he grimaced.

"We were separated into different cells when the guards brought us down here. I haven't seen them since," he said. "They must have been among those prisoners taken away earlier."

Cazlina stared at him, her breath locked in her throat.

An image of vivid blue eyes twinkling with irrepressible amusement flashed across her mind. Jorin Montrill's unwelcome intrusion in her life ever since trying to steal Miris had been a constant source of frustration and annoyance, not to mention the minor guilt that gnawed at her for deceiving Gareth about her relationship with the horse thief. And, yet, despite all that, she couldn't easily dismiss or forget the reality that the exasperating man had saved her life twice, and had proven to be a strong pillar of support on a number of occasions when she had needed him most. What did she care if she never saw the horse thief again? Wasn't that exactly what she had been wishing for since the night he had entered her life so precipitously? Why, then, did a pang of something strangely close to anguish stab her heart at the thought of that unruly, brilliant life being snuffed out?

His last words to her reverberated through her mind, his deep voice surprisingly serious and soft, *"I know my brave lady is still in there somewhere. I'm honored to have known you, even though our acquaintance has been brief and somewhat volatile."*

Cazlina swiped angrily at the unwelcome tears stinging her eyes. "You're nothing but trouble, Montrill," she murmured unsteadily, unaware she had spoken aloud until she saw Gareth giving her a questioning look.

Ignoring it, she grasped his arm urgently. "We have to save them, Gareth, before it's too late."

CHAPTER 37

Gareth gazed at her with a sympathetic expression. "It may already be too late, Caz."

She glared at him, obstinately refusing to acknowledge his words might be true. As unorthodox and disreputable as Jorin Montrill might be, he still did not deserve to meet such a hideous end; a helpless pawn in the hands of a wicked queen bent on gaining total supremacy over Regalis, and uncaring of how many innocent lives she destroyed along the way. Nor did Sergeant Zandorin, who was so full of pride and anticipation at the responsibility and trust bestowed upon him by General Viadon. In all conscience, Cazlina could not leave the castle without at least trying to determine if they still lived. As for Arman Kesel, she found herself adopting much the same attitude Niko had upon learning his father was Saranor's prisoner. She didn't much care what happened to him. His callous treatment of Niko alone made him deserving of suffering pain and torment himself.

As for Jorin...

She refused to believe he had been the victim sacrificed to the Pool. Despite everything that had plagued their relationship thus far, his image imprinted itself indelibly upon her mind's eye and sent complex emotions ricocheting through her brain.

She took a deep breath, trying to calm herself. "I know it sounds crazy, Gareth, but, we can't just leave them to suffer at Saranor's hands. If there's any chance they're still alive, we have to try and save them."

He looked doubtful. "Caz, I don't know. It's too dangerous. We should try to escape the castle and join up with General Viadon. We'd stand a much better chance with the army behind us."

"But, we're here *now*," she cried. "By the time the general's forces reach Saranor, it may be too late. She'll have sacrificed more souls and her powers will have been strengthened, maybe to the point where General Viadon and Pharon can't stop her."

A grim determination settled over Gareth's face. "You're right. You stay here with the boy where it's relatively safe, or, better yet, find a way out of the castle and get to General Viadon. He'll protect you. Meanwhile, I'll take a couple of these men here and try to find the Pool."

The condescending tone of his voice sent a surge of hot anger flushing through her veins. Balling her hands into tight fists, she thrust her face into the startled visage of her brother, forcing him to retreat a step.

"For once in your life, stop treating me like I'm a helpless child! Do you have any idea how much I endured to get here and free you? I killed three men in cold blood, and I watched as that nine-year old boy standing over there sliced the throat of another. I could have escaped the courtyard and fled to General Viadon when my captor was killed, but I didn't. I wanted desperately to find Miris and ride as far and as fast as I could away from this horrible place, but I didn't do that, either. Instead, I risked my life to *enter* this castle to try to find you, because I knew if I ran away and left you to the queen's mercy, I would die as surely as if a sword had been thrust into my heart. So, don't you *dare* suggest I go hide behind big, brave, strong men, while I let my big, brave, strong brother do the fighting!"

Gareth stared at her, stunned by her outburst. Around them, the others had fallen silent, watching and listening with avid interest and curiosity. From across the room, Niko gaped at her, his eyes wide. Even Tor's scarred face seemed to hold an expression of astonishment.

Hot flags of embarrassment rushed into Cazlina's cheeks. "I'm sorry," she murmured, unable to meet her brother's eyes. "But, I've seen far too much--been *through* far too much--to be treated like a little child who can't defend herself. Besides, isn't this the very thing that separates us from monsters like the queen--this sense of compassion and decency and honor? When someone's life is threatened, we don't turn tail and run away. We try to save that person from death, no matter how much our own lives may be endangered."

A ghost of a smile flitted across her brother's face and he hugged her to him. "Cazlina Narzin, you make me ashamed of myself. You're right, of course. We need to do everything in our power to free anyone who hasn't already been used by Saranor in her ceremony. And, when I say *we*, I mean you, too. Otherwise, you're liable to bash me over the head, stick me back in one of these cells, and go off on your own."

Several of the men and women standing around chuckled. One older man with a gray-flecked beard and hazel eyes clapped Gareth on the shoulder. "Guess you've been put smartly in your place, my lad."

"And, well deserved, too," a blonde-haired woman teased, her fair eyebrows drawn together in a mock frown.

"You're right," Gareth agreed, sheepishly. He slanted a beseeching gaze down at Cazlina. "Can you forgive me for being an insufferable, bossy brother again?"

She sighed heavily, feeling the fury ebbing away in tatters, and hugged him tightly. "Maybe this time. Try not to let it happen again."

Relief washed through her at Gareth's agreement to search for the other prisoners, and mixed in with it was a thrill of terror at the thought of encountering the queen and her Pool of Souls.

"Do you know where the Pool is?" Gareth asked.

She shook her head and looked toward Niko standing amongst the prisoners, one hand fondling the ear of the big dog by his side.

"He won't like it, but I don't think we have any other choice," she said, nervously biting her lower lip.

"What do you mean?"

"See the dog by Niko's side? He's the boy's sworn protector. He nearly bit my head off, because I let Niko accompany me to the dungeons. He definitely won't be happy with my suggestion that Niko show us where the Pool is. I don't want to place the boy in further danger, but there's no one else who can do it for us. He knows this castle inside and out."

Tor's reaction was every bit as violent and negative as she feared when she told him what she had planned. His hackles rose in a bristling mane along his back and his lips curled back over his fearsome canines. He took a menacing step toward Cazlina, and, for a moment, she thought he might attack her. With a great effort, she stood her ground, facing down the angry animal.

The boy is not to be endangered any further! I forbid it.

I understand your concern, Cazlina said, trying to keep her voice calm. *But, friends of ours are also in grave danger and we need to find the Pool of Souls before it's too late to save them.*

Then do it without Niko. I don't want him exposed to the vileness of that talisman.

Cazlina feared Tor was far too late in protecting Niko from the corruption of the queen's soul-killing ceremonies. The child possessed an endless well of curiosity and imagination, and it was unlikely the guard dog could be with him every hour of every day. As a result, Niko had already seen and heard much more than he should have. His panicked reaction to the sacrifice of the prisoner earlier seemed to confirm her suspicions he had witnessed one of the ceremonies first-hand.

Do you have another suggestion? Cazlina asked Tor. *Time is running out. We need to do something. Now!*

Frustration and indecision ran through the dog's mind and he growled low in his throat. Images flashed to Cazlina of the awful beatings and abuse the poor animal endured constantly from the inhabitants of the castle and his unhappiness in his role as an intimidating, aggressive guard of hapless prisoners--a role that clearly warred constantly with the innate social and protective traits of a dog. Cazlina suspected that was why the animal had agreed to help her in the first place. His forced allegiance to Queen Saranor could not overshadow his natural instincts. His hesitation stemmed not so much from the thought of disloyalty to the queen but from worry for the safety of the little boy standing by his side.

"Are you talking to Tor?" Niko asked, curiously. "What are you talking about? Are we going to the Pool to save the other prisoners?"

Cazlina shot Tor a questioning look and the huge dog sighed heavily. *I want to say I think your plan is foolhardy and impossible, but that would be a lie. Indeed, I admire your bravery and loyalty to your companions. As much as I want to keep the boy out of harm's way, no one will be safe until the threat posed by the queen's absorption of souls is ended permanently. We'll take you to the Pool, although I fail to see how you will stop Saranor once you get there.*

Cazlina's lips twitched with a touch of irony. *I had no idea how I was going to free my brother and the other prisoners when I came here. Then the gods sent you and Niko to show me the way. Perhaps they'll smile down on me once again.*

She hurriedly relayed the dog's agreement to Gareth and Niko and the little boy's face lit up. She wagged an admonishing finger at him. "You must promise to listen to what Tor and I say. If we tell you to do something, you must do it immediately, no questions asked. Do you understand?"

He nodded readily, but she still felt a twinge of concern, afraid his avid taste for adventure might make him reckless.

She eyed him doubtfully and he said, "I'll be good, Cazlina. I promise."

"You'd better be, or I'll have Tor drag you away by the scruff of the neck and keep you hidden somewhere until all of this is over."

The huge dog bared his teeth to emphasize her stern words, and Niko glanced uncertainly at him, his eyes wide with faint alarm. "Would you really do that, Tor?" he asked, in a small voice.

"Of course he would," Cazlina said. "He wants you to be safe. So, if either one of us thinks you're unnecessarily endangering yourself, or anyone else for that matter, you won't be allowed to accompany us any further. Do I make myself clear?"

Niko nodded silently, his face losing some of its enthusiasm.

She softened her austere expression a little and tousled his hair. "Good. As long as you realize this is not a game or a grand adventure."

Again, a disturbing maturity peeked out from the boy's eyes as he said solemnly, "I know it's not, but the queen likes to play games, and they're really, really bad games. She kills and tortures people just for the fun of it. I want to help stop her, if I can."

Cazlina smiled encouragingly at him and then turned her attention to the men and women standing around her.

"Can I have your attention, please?" she said, raising her voice a little to be heard over the hubbub of voices. "I can show you where the armory is so you can arm yourselves against the inhabitants of the castle. My brother and I would like a couple of volunteers to come with us to the Pool. Are any of you willing?"

The gray-bearded man who had spoken earlier stepped forward. "I am. My name is Paulis Mergan."

"And, I," said the blonde-haired woman, who introduced herself as Marli Darghis.

A man pushed forward from the back of the crowd and Cazlina recognized him as Donegal, another member of Sergeant Zandorin's ill-fated scouting party. He had an expression of grim determination on his face. "I want to help rescue the sergeant if I can," he said, gruffly. "He's a good man and doesn't deserve that kind of fate."

Cazlina nodded gratefully at the three volunteers. "Thank you. I think that's all we'll need. I would like to keep the group as small as possible. What do you think, Gareth?"

Now that she had established in no uncertain terms she would not be left out of the rescue party, she was quite willing to concede some of the decisions to her big brother.

He nodded. "I agree. The fewer people, the better. If the rest of you can keep the inhabitants of the castle busy and distracted, that would help us tremendously."

A thin man with bushy black sideburns guffawed. "It would be my pleasure to *distract* Saranor's minions at the end of a big, sharp sword. Lead on to the armory, girl. We have some fighting to do."

CHAPTER 38

Cazlina set a brisk pace and led the way up the stone staircase and along the dimly lit hallway to the armory. Fortunately, this part of the castle was deserted and they encountered no one, not even the guard who had passed Cazlina and Niko on the staircase. No doubt, most of the inhabitants were in the upper reaches of the castle, defending it from General Viadon's invading army.

Gareth and the others in the rescue party made short work of arming themselves with various weapons from the armory's stores. Niko adamantly refused to give up his curved weapon despite Cazlina's fervent pleas to leave it behind.

Cazlina noticed Gareth examining several fist-sized balls of a soft, yellow material that resembled a sponge. "What are those?" she asked.

When he looked up, his eyes were shining with excitement. "I'm sure these are incendiary spheres. Sergeant Brayth told us about them back in Terrangay when we were doing our training. They're made from a metal called fierenze that is very malleable and soft so it can be formed into a ball. A mage then casts a powerful flame spell into the sphere that can be triggered by these." He held up what looked like metallic coins with raised centers. "Do you realize what this means, Caz? We can use these to blow up the Pool if we can get close enough to place them around the perimeter. Thank the gods, you found the armory, little sister."

"Thank Niko. He's the one who led me to it."

Elation surged through Cazlina at the thought they might possess a weapon capable of destroying the Pool. Maybe their mission was not so hopeless, after all.

Gareth stuffed half a dozen of the innocuous-looking yellow balls into his pockets, along with several of the metal coins and then asked, "Where do we go, Niko?"

He gulped, a little boy's fear shining in his eyes for a brief moment. "The Pool is in a special room in one of the towers," he said. "We could go through the whole castle to reach it, but there's a faster way. The tower is right over top of the dungeons, and the queen had a rising platform built near them so prisoners can be brought straight up to the room. We can use that."

Gareth touched the top of the boy's tousled head. "Lead on, lad. Time's wasting."

They ran back down the staircase toward the dungeons. After everyone else had gone through the open stone door, Cazlina inserted the flat crystal disk into the indentation, and, following Tor's instructions, turned it in the pattern that would cause the door to close and lock once more. As the heavy door swung ponderously shut, she snatched the disk from its niche and slipped through the narrowing opening. Without the disk, no one would be able to enter the dungeons from the staircase side.

Niko led the way to a wooden structure that Cazlina hadn't noticed before in the shadows at the far end of the row of cells. The structure had an elaborate pulley and rope system connected to a mechanism that, when activated, enabled the circular platform to be hauled up through a wide shaft. Several heavy, metal hoops were anchored to the floor of the platform, which Niko explained were used to shackle the prisoners for the ride up to the tower and the Pool. The structure was wide enough to easily accommodate the seven of them.

Looking up into the dark shaft opening overhead, Gareth asked, "What can we expect to find at the top, Niko?"

"The platform stops at a ramp that slopes down toward the Pool. That's the only way you can go, because there are high railings on either side of the ramp so the prisoners can't jump over and kill themselves before they get to the Pool. There are usually two guards standing near the top of the ramp. "

"Well, that's just great," Donegal exploded. "As soon as we reach the top, the guards will be able to pick us off one by one. There's not a damn thing we can do about it." He glared at Niko. "Why didn't you tell us before we'd be stepping right into the arms of the enemy, boy? Or, did you just want to ride on this contraption for the fun of it?"

A surge of protective anger washed over Cazlina and she stepped closer to Niko, placing her hand on his shoulder. "Leave him alone," she snapped. "If you knew what he has been through, you'd realize he doesn't do a whole lot of things for *fun*."

"I said it was the fastest way, not the safest," Niko spoke up, defensively.

"How in the name of all the gods are we supposed to avoid being seen?" Donegal snarled. "We can't just waltz nonchalantly down the ramp waving hello to the queen and her guards and asking them to please not kill us."

"Lower your voices," Marli hissed in warning, glancing apprehensively at the opening. "Who knows how much sound might carry up this shaft to the top."

"Donegal's right," Gareth said with a note of disappointment in his low voice. "It's too risky. We'll have to backtrack and take the longer route."

Cazlina's spirits plummeted at the thought of having to battle their way through a castle under siege and crawling with the enemy to reach the Pool before more victims were sacrificed, especially when they were so close. Surely, there was some way they could escape detection once they reached the ramp?

As though in answer to her unspoken question, Paulis clasped Gareth's shoulder as the younger man turned to leave the dungeons. "Hold fast, lad, there's no need to find another way. I'll just place a glimmer spell on us before we get there and no one will see us."

Gareth stared at him. "A glimmer spell?"

The older man shrugged. "A little talent I have. I can make it appear to anyone standing near the platform that there's no one on it. Unfortunately, I can't hold the spell indefinitely, but at least long enough for us to get off the platform and conceal ourselves." He glanced down at Niko. "I take it there *is* some place we can hide once we reach the bottom of the ramp?"

The boy nodded. "There's a wide ledge and marble columns all around the Pool. We should be able to hide behind them."

Paulis nodded and turned back to Gareth. "What say you, lad?"

When her brother still hesitated, Cazlina touched his arm urgently. "We have to take the chance. We'll waste too much time getting to the tower any other way."

He frowned. "You're right, the platform it is. Here's what I suggest we do. Once we reach the top and hopefully avoid detection," he slanted a skeptical look at Paulis, "we kill the guards and then hide near the Pool until we can figure out what the situation is with the queen and the prisoners." He shrugged. "Who knows? Maybe Donegal's suggestion isn't so far-fetched, after all. Maybe all we have to do is ask Saranor nicely and politely to give up her bid for supremacy and stop using the Pool to gain power."

He grinned at his facetious proposition, but no one else shared in his amusement.

"Sorry." He grimaced. "You're right, it's not that funny. I'm just trying to lighten the mood. Once we know what we're up against in the tower, we have to free the prisoners, kill the queen and destroy the Pool."

Paulis grunted. "That doesn't sound daunting, or impossible, at all."

Gareth shrugged. "If anyone has any other ideas, now would be a good time to bring them forth."

Donegal scowled. "I don't know about anyone else, but I say we forget about the glimmer spell and come out fighting the moment the platform reaches the top. The guards won't be expecting us. We could take them by surprise."

"We don't know how many people are in the tower," Paulis pointed out. "We might be able to kill a few of them before they know what's happening, but there's no guarantee we won't be overwhelmed and killed ourselves. I say we stick with the glimmer spell."

Gareth looked at his sister. "Caz?"

She hesitated, liking neither option but knowing they had very little choice. "I think you and Paulis are right about not rushing into the tower without knowing what we'll be up against. I vote for the glimmer spell."

"As do I," Marli said.

"Me, too," Niko piped up, "although, I guess I could just make myself invisible."

Cazlina shook her head emphatically. "No, Niko, don't do that. I want to be able to keep an eye on you."

"Are there any other suggestions?" Gareth asked. When the others remained silent, he nodded. "All right, then, everyone on the platform before I change my mind."

Donegal had a disgruntled expression on his face but kept his mouth shut. It was obvious that, as a soldier trained for battle, he would have preferred a much more direct method of confrontation than sneaking around and hiding, but he went along with the majority ruling.

As the seven of them crowded on to the structure, Tor's droll voice sounded in Cazlina's mind. *What was that you said about the gods smiling down on you, girl? A glimmer spell, indeed.*

Niko pressed the mechanism that operated the rope and pulley system and the platform began to rise silently up through the wide shaft. Luminary orbs had been placed at regular intervals along the circular wooden walls so the ride was carried out in a soft green glow that reflected off the apprehensive faces of the passengers.

Cazlina glanced upward and saw flickering light filtering through the round opening at the top of the shaft. Dread spread like hot acid through her body as the platform approached the opening.

Beside her, Paulis Mergan closed his eyes and began to chant very softly under his breath. After a moment, he opened his eyes, and, seeing Cazlina's worried expression, nodded briefly. "It's done," he said, in a low voice.

She doubted his words, seeing very little difference in the appearance of the others except perhaps for a slight shimmer that outlined everyone.

Paulis whispered so that all of them could hear. "It may not look like it, but we'll be invisible to anyone at the top of the ramp. I used an all-encompassing glimmer so we can still see each other, but no one can see us."

Cazlina and Marli exchanged glances. It was clear the blonde woman harbored much the same doubt Cazlina did.

"I do hope you know what you're doing, Mergan," Marli muttered.

Paulis smiled faintly. "Trust me."

"It would appear we have no other choice," the blonde woman retorted, clutching her short-bladed sword in a tight grip.

Cazlina swallowed past a dry lump of fear, knowing she, too, had no choice but to put her faith in the man. He had presumably performed such a spell countless times before and therefore knew whether or not it worked.

"When we reach the top, we'll need to stay as close together as we can," the older man went on. "If we get separated, the spell will be broken. Once we reach the safety of the columns, then it won't matter. They'll provide the concealment we need when we become visible again. Another thing, we must be as quiet as possible. The glimmer spell doesn't disguise sound, only appearance."

The others nodded, the green glow of the luminary orbs reflecting off their anxious expressions. Niko's eyes were as wide as Cazlina had ever seen them, dominating his face. For all his amazing bravery, the thought of coming face to face once more with the queen's awful plaything must be a terrifying prospect to him.

She moved closer to him and took his hand, squeezing it reassuringly. Instead of shying away from the contact, as she feared he might, he pressed himself against her, his grip tightening on hers as his other hand twined itself in the thick fur of Tor's neck.

Within moments, the platform reached the opening at the top of the shaft and came to a shuddering halt on a level with the ramp Niko had described. Two guards standing on either side jerked to attention and looked around at the sudden clunking noise.

Cazlina froze in panic as the men stared straight at her. She feared Paulis' glimmer spell had failed. Her first thought was to shield Niko from a deadly sword thrust and she started to move in front of him. But, Paulis' hand clasped her arm and held her back. The man shook his head at her and she subsided reluctantly, her pulse racing as she stared back at the guards.

They both wore puzzled expressions and one man scratched his head as he continued to examine what Cazlina fervently hoped looked like an empty platform.

"What the…?" he muttered. "Why did this come up? There's nobody on it."

"Must be a malfunction in the mechanism," the other man said. "Galligan wouldn't send it up just for the fun of it, especially not when the queen is in the middle of a ceremony."

"Unless he's sending us invisible prisoners now," the second man smirked.

The two men chuckled coarsely at his witticism as they glanced back over their shoulders in the direction of a strange chanting sound that seemed to echo off the high ceiling of the tower room. Cazlina had to quell an overwhelming urge to laugh hysterically at their unwittingly accurate guess at the truth.

Still shaking their heads and grinning, the guards turned their backs to the platform, preparing to resume their positions on either side of it. Without hesitation, Gareth and Donegal stepped forward and dispatched the two men, lowering them silently to the floor. Paulis nodded at the others, and, with extreme caution, they all stepped off the platform, keeping as close together as possible and tiptoeing silently down the wooden ramp. Cazlina's back itched in anticipation for the thrust of a sword between her shoulder blades, but it never came. Aside from the two dead men behind them, there were no other guards in the immediate vicinity, and Paulis' glimmer spell appeared to be working as well as he had said it would.

The trip down the sloping ramp seemed to take forever. Flickering torches lined the high railings on either side, and, at the bottom, Cazlina could see the towering marble columns that extended around the circular tower room and rose to the unseen ceiling far above. The chanting grew louder, and her palms dampened with icy sweat at the thought of her first close-up glimpse of Saranor and her Pool of Souls.

CHAPTER 39

C azlina's group finally reached the bottom of the ramp and arranged themselves behind the black-veined columns. In front of them, a wide, knee-high ledge of black marble ran around the perimeter of the circular tower room, its highly polished surface reflecting swirls of strange, bright purplish light.

As Cazlina pressed tightly against the cool stone of one of the columns, the chanting stopped abruptly and a hissing sound like a thousand snakes echoed around the chamber. The eerie sound sent shivers of revulsion up and down her body, as though those very snakes were coiling and writhing against her skin.

Scarcely daring to breathe, she risked a peek around the column. She didn't know what to expect, and, at first, couldn't make sense of the sight before her.

Four stone walkways radiated like the spokes of a wheel out to a raised dais in the middle of a pool of black, turbulent water. Saranor--or at least a white figure Cazlina presumed was Saranor--stood on the dais, facing the columns where Cazlina and the others hid. Tendrils of purple light, as sharp and brilliant as a noonday sun, rose from the seething water and twined themselves around the motionless figure standing with her arms outstretched and head thrown back toward the ceiling. The queen's mouth was stretched wide, greedily sucking in the coiling wisps of light and emitting the hissing sound reverberating throughout the tower room.

As more and more of the strange light disappeared into the queen's mouth, her limbs and body stretched and shimmered, her stature growing until she was at least nine feet tall. An unseen energy whipped her long white hair into crackling spirals about her head. Cazlina watched in revulsion as the light writhed beneath her translucent skin, as though it possessed a life of its own.

And indeed it did, Cazlina thought, sickly. The life of those poor, innocent victims who had been sacrificed to the Pool, their souls and energies drained dry by Saranor. The blinding essence of their spirits eclipsed the feeble light of the flickering torches.

Behind the queen, at the end of one of the long stone walkways, two men stood watching eagerly as Saranor drank in the eerie light swirling from the black water.

One of them, a tall, thin man with a bald head and a double-pointed beard as black as midnight, possessed the same mystical demeanor and bearing as the mage, Pharon. Cazlina presumed this must be Nostrimus, the mage who had been instrumental in bringing the dreaded Pool of Souls to Saranor. His gaunt face was suffused with an unholy joy as he clasped his hands together and avidly observed the swirls of purple light being absorbed into the queen.

The second man wore robes of dark blue upon his rotund body, and thick unruly hair floated like a nimbus around his huge head. His face, even from that distance, was rendered ugly by a bulbous, squashed nose and bulging, close-set eyes. Cazlina wondered if he could be Agneus Molitare, the queen's chief advisor.

Both men's identities were confirmed a second later by Niko's faint whisper. "The tall man is Nostrimus and the ugly man beside him is Molitare."

Cazlina nodded, dragging her gaze away from the revolting sight of Saranor to search the tower room for the other prisoners. The turbulent movement of the Pool's dark waters caught her attention and she had to fight hard to stifle a shocked gasp at what was causing the water to seethe--*hands*. Dozens of white, skeletal-thin hands thrashed and clawed desperately at the surface of the water as the brilliant light spiraled from their fingertips toward the figure of Saranor. A grayish head, its mouth stretched wide in a silent, agonized scream, broke the surface, only to disappear again under the black water. More heads popped up and fell back with soft plops.

Vaguely, Cazlina heard the gasps of indrawn breaths from the others around her as they, too, witnessed the horrifying spectacle. A small, trembling body pressed hard against her side. Instinctively, her arms went around Niko's shoulders, trying to shield him from the sight of the Pool and its ghastly inhabitants. The boy buried his face in the shelter of her arms. On the other side of him, Tor's ears flattened against his big head, his anxiety and fear for Niko's sanity swirling like sharp sparks of firelight through his mind.

"Over there, the prisoners." Paulis Mergan's whispering voice cut through Cazlina's paralyzed state.

She looked in the direction he pointed, dreading what she might see. Her heart lurched at the sight of Jorin, Sergeant Zandorin and a third man who was a stranger to her. All three were still alive, their hands tied behind their backs as they knelt on the wide ledge close to where Nostrimus and Molitare stood. Zandorin and the other man had their heads lowered and faces buried in their chests as though resigned to their fate, but Jorin knelt upright, his face as carved and still as a bronze statue and his eyes staring toward the queen's figure out in the middle of the Pool. A thin line of dried blood from the wound on his temple snaked down his right cheek. There was no trace of fear in the horse thief's demeanor, only a watchful, coiled energy that seemed to permeate his body.

An odd jolt of pride ran through Cazlina. How could she have ever thought of him as a coward, or a weakling, simply because he chose to view life in a light-hearted, jovial manner? How many times had he proven to be as brave and strong as any of the other soldiers in General Viadon's army? And, now...now when he was faced with the certainty of an agonizing, soul-killing death, he met it head-on with fearless defiance.

I must save him, Cazlina thought. *I'll never forgive myself if I don't try.*

A disturbing thought occurred to her. Where was Kesel? He was not with the other three prisoners, or anywhere else in the tower room that she could see, and she wondered uneasily if he had been the prisoner thrown into the Pool earlier. As much as she disliked the man, he was still Niko's father and his death might have a traumatic effect on the boy, despite his earlier claims of indifference.

She glanced down in concern at Niko and saw him looking toward the three prisoners on the other side of the room. His eyes slid up to hers. "My Da's not here."

Despite the flat tone of his voice, shock and tears swam in his emerald eyes, and Cazlina tightened her embrace around his small body, compassion surging through her. The child was truly alone, with only a fiercely protective dog as his companion.

And, me! Cazlina thought, as a wild idea careened through her brain. *If we get out of this alive-- and we will-- I shall take this poor orphaned boy under my wing and*

care for him as though he were my own child. What
Gareth would think of such a rash decision on her part was
irrelevant for the moment. She would override any
objections he might raise, because there was simply no
other choice. Niko and Tor had both suffered enough at the
hands of Saranor and her servants. With Kesel's
whereabouts unknown, they could not be left behind to
fend for themselves when the queen was finally
vanquished and the castle rid of all its horrors.

Her heart buoyed by the thought of Niko's future
being determined, she turned to the others, who were
pressed up against the columns on either side of her.

"Saranor and the others aren't paying any attention to
the prisoners at the moment," she whispered. "Niko and I
could sneak around to the other side of the room and cut
them loose while the rest of you remain here on watch. If
something happens to alert the queen or the others to our
efforts, perhaps you can create a diversion."

"I agree," Gareth said, "with one exception. I'm
going with you. No arguments, Caz."

She nodded, knowing it would be futile to argue.

"Once you break off from the group, my glimmer
spell will no longer affect you," Paulis warned. "You'll
become visible again."

"We'll have to hope the ledge and the columns will
be enough to conceal us," Gareth replied. He pulled the
incendiary spheres out of his pocket. "While Caz and I are
freeing the prisoners, you three can place these around the
sides of the Pool. There should be enough magical fire
here to completely destroy it." He held up the metal coins.
"These are the triggers. Press them into the spheres, but
make sure you don't push down on the raised centers just
yet or you'll set off the spell and arm them prematurely.
We'll set them off right as we leave the tower and then, by
Donar's breath, run like the wind, because we won't have

much time to get out of here before everything explodes around us."

The others nodded and Gareth passed around the balls of spongy material and the metal disks. Marli held her two spheres gingerly in the palms of her hands, eyeing them as though they were going to detonate at any moment.

"Once you've planted the incendiaries," Gareth continued, "each of you work your way around to one of the walkways and wait for my signal. As soon as the prisoners are freed, I'll give a sharp whistle and we'll rush Saranor from all four directions. She won't be able to deal with all of us at once, if we take her by surprise and surround her."

"We hope," Paulis muttered.

Gareth gave him a wry glance. "Think positively, man. We have to try. We can't let her get any stronger."

"What about the mage and that ugly creature beside him?" Donegal asked.

"Once we free the prisoners, there'll be five of us," Gareth answered. "We should be able to overpower those two before they know what's happening."

Cazlina looked at her big brother with pride and love. Leadership suited him very well. He had fallen into the role as naturally and easily as though he had been planning battles and giving orders all his life.

He turned to her. "Are you ready to go?"

She took a deep, steadying breath and nodded. On trembling hands and knees, she crawled behind Gareth as he crept beneath the lip of the ledge toward the other side of the tower room. Glancing back over her shoulder, she saw Niko following closely on her heels, with the huge dog crawling along on his stomach behind him.

They hadn't gone very far when the hissing noise stopped and a voice, unmistakably the queen's, amplified to a thunderous volume called out, "NOSTRIMUS!"

An oily voice, dripping with subservience, answered. "Yes, my Queen?"

"COME JOIN ME IN THE POOL."

"What?" The mage sounded wary.

Saranor's voice turned playful. "I want you to come and stand by my side. I have a new game I wish to play."

"I don't understand, your Majesty."

"You don't need to understand. You need only to obey, mage." An ominous note crept into her playful tone.

"But…"

"DO YOU DARE TO DISOBEY A DIRECT ORDER FROM YOUR QUEEN?"

Saranor's howl of rage echoed around the cavernous chamber. The torches flared wildly in a sudden surging wind that made the marble pillars creak ominously. Although Cazlina was reluctant to see what would happen next, her gaze was drawn to the center of the room against her will.

Ropes of purple light spewed from the queen's open mouth and wrapped themselves tightly around the figure of the mage. He was lifted off his feet and dangled high up in the air, his arms bound tightly against his sides. Dark anger suffused his gaunt face.

Saranor snapped her mouth shut and impassively watched Nostrimus's futile struggles against the strangling coils of light.

"What is the meaning of this, Saranor?"

"I no longer need your services, mage," she said. "My powers far outweigh yours now. Your usefulness is at an end."

Clearly struggling for breath, Nostrimus called down, "What do you mean? I can still be of use to you. Why are you doing this?"

A terrible smile twisted her ruby-red lips. "Because, my friend, there can only be one supreme power in Regalis and that is me. You still have enough power to be dangerous, and that, I cannot allow."

"Your Majesty, I am your loyal servant and will always remain so! I would never dream of challenging your authority."

"So you say now, mage. But, the temptation may become too great for you to resist one day. As I see it, there is only one way I can ensure you will never try to wrest my rule away from me."

The mage's eyes widened as realization flooded his face. "No, don't!"

Saranor's laughter bounced off the stone walls in deafening peals as she flicked her fingers upward. The desperately struggling figure of the mage suddenly plummeted straight down toward the seething Pool below him.

CHAPTER 40

Cazlina held her breath as she watched the falling figure of Nostrimus. The white, skeletal hands in the Pool clawed at the air, as though trying to reach the mage and pull him into the turbulent black waters to join them. A mere foot above them, Nostrimus' body came to an abrupt halt and the queen flicked her fingers a second time, causing him to fly back up toward the ceiling. Then she sent him plunging downward again, only to have him halt within mere inches of the grasping fingertips.

"So, Nostrimus, what do you think of my new game?"

He gritted his teeth as he spiraled upward once more. "It is quite--*amusing*, my Queen."

"Liar," Saranor pretended to pout. "I don't believe you are enjoying it. I, on the other hand, find it highly entertaining."

"As it should be, your Majesty."

"Caz, we should go now while the queen is distracted," Gareth whispered into her ear, and she nodded.

Within moments, they reached the other side of the room, stopping at the black-veined column that stood directly behind Jorin. Not far away around the curve of the ledge, Cazlina could see the plump, quivering figure of Molitare crouched on the floor, the door to the tower room at his back. Fortunately for them, his full attention was focused on Nostrimus far above.

"Careful," Gareth cautioned. "I see a guard standing by the door."

Cazlina nodded, drawing back a little behind the column.

She turned to Niko beside her. "I need you to become invisible, so you can cut the ropes binding the prisoners. Can you do that?"

He bobbed his head in answer.

She pulled the dagger out of the waistband of her trousers and pressed it into his hand. When he started to stand up, she pulled him back down and whispered, "Wait. I want to let Jorin know we're here so he doesn't give us away when you start cutting his bindings."

She eased around the column, ducking below the lip of the ledge. Above her, she could see the rigid back of the horse thief. She flicked a quick glance toward Molitare, but the chief advisor's frightened eyes still followed Saranor's toying of the hapless mage.

"Jorin," she hissed. "No, don't move. Act like nothing's going on. It's Cazlina. I'm right behind you and so is Gareth. We've come to free you and the others."

After his initial start at the sound of her voice, Jorin's body immediately resumed its former statue-like posture, and, once again, she had to admire his ability to face any situation, no matter how strange or dangerous, with remarkable aplomb.

"Let the others know what's happening," she continued, "but make sure they don't give us away."

Jorin's head bent in a very faint nod and then he leaned slightly toward Sergeant Zandorin, speaking to him in a low whisper.

When Cazlina slipped back behind the column, Gareth said, "I'll take care of the guard."

"Be careful."

Her brother smiled and then started to make his way toward the tower door.

Niko quietly placed the curved weapon on the floor and gave Tor's huge head a pat before disappearing. Cazlina felt a breath of air against her arm as the invisible child slipped past her.

She craned her neck to see where Gareth was, but he had disappeared in the shadows beneath the ledge. The guard stood motionless by the door, his mouth hanging open as he watched the display out in the middle of the Pool. Cazlina hoped he would be so mesmerized by what was happening that Gareth could sneak up on him unawares.

She turned her attention back to Jorin and the others. The invisible Niko worked stealthily, cutting the ropes binding the prisoners' hands and ankles in short order. While the other occupants of the tower room remained distracted, the three men slipped silently off the ledge and behind the column where Cazlina waited. She glanced toward the guard, expecting to hear an outcry from him, but he was no longer standing by the door. Instead, a dark shape lay on the floor off to one side in the flickering shadows of the torch set in the wall above.

The corners of Jorin's eyes crinkled as he crouched in front of her. "Well met, my lady. What a pleasure it is to see you again."

Before she could answer, Niko suddenly materialized beside her and Jorin blinked, for once seemingly at a loss for words.

"*Tanim* Narzin, how did you...?" Zandorin's bewildered whisper broke through the amusement that filled her at the sight of the horse thief's blank face.

"I'll tell you later, Sergeant," she whispered back. "Right now, we have to concentrate on stopping Saranor."

At that moment, Gareth rejoined them and he and Jorin exchanged brief nods. Gareth wordlessly handed him the guard's sword.

Zandorin retrieved the curved weapon from the floor, much to Niko's chagrin, and Cazlina handed the dagger over to the third prisoner. He nodded gratefully. It was not much of a weapon, but at least he was not completely unarmed.

Before they could carry out the next phase of their plan, an enraged, male shout froze them all in their tracks.

"Intruders! Guards, seize them at once!"

Cazlina bit back a cry. Agneus Molitare must have finally noticed the prisoners had disappeared from the ledge and had spotted Cazlina and the others behind the column. He was standing upright now, his finger pointed accusingly at them. "Guards!"

Saranor's annoyed voice cut across his bellow. "Molitare, you are disturbing my game. What is the matter?"

Molitare's rotund body fairly jiggled with outrage. "Intruders, my Queen. They are attempting to free the prisoners."

"Then take care of them."

The man's eyes boggled. "Me?"

"Yes, *you*, you fool. Make yourself useful for a change."

"But-But, your Majesty, I have no weapon!"

"Not a wise admission, my friend," Jorin chuckled, leaping out to confront Molitare.

The queen's advisor blanched and backed away, holding his hands out in front of him to ward off the wickedly grinning horse thief.

Cazlina heard Tor growl behind her and felt something brush against her arm. She whirled to find the boy gone.

"Niko!" she hissed.

Molitare jumped violently and pitched forward, almost impaling himself on the weapon in Jorin's hand. The ugly man glanced over his shoulder, his bulging eyes wide with fright. In the next second, he clutched his right leg, howling loudly.

Jorin stood stock-still, his face bewildered as he watched the man jump around as though being attacked. Cazlina almost laughed out loud, because she knew exactly what was happening. Niko was playing his own game with the hated Molitare and exacting revenge for the chief advisor's mistreatment of him.

Both of Molitare's legs suddenly went out from under him and he landed with a painful thump on the stone floor, winded and moaning. A triumphantly grinning Niko materialized beside him, aiming one more kick at the man's side.

A loud clapping came from the middle of the Pool and Saranor said, "How amusing! What a pitiful warrior you are, Agneus, to let such a small boy get the best of you."

Leaving Nostrimus trapped in his cocoon of purple light near the ceiling of the chamber, the queen began to glide across the walkway toward the group by the tower door.

Cazlina's first instinct was to protect Niko. She ran out from behind the column to stand in front of the boy, her sword held at the ready. Growling and bristling, Tor planted himself in front of both of them, and Jorin moved to Cazlina's side, his arm pressed reassuringly against hers.

Saranor's lips twisted in a faint smile, her footsteps never faltering. "How touching that you rush to protect each other. A pity, though, that such bravery is foolish and all for naught. Don't you realize your weapons are puny and useless against my powers?" She flicked her fingers up toward the ceiling and Nostrimus jerked in the coils of light surrounding him. "See how pathetically easy it is for me to overcome my mage, who is much more powerful than any of you could ever dream of being." She tilted her head, her expression contemplative. "Although I much prefer feeding on the darker elements of a person's soul, strength and youth are also traits I seek. You will all make a fine addition to my Pool of Souls."

Cazlina stared into the queen's merciless eyes as she continued to glide toward her. She felt as trapped and helpless as Nostrimus far above her. How could they ever hope to defeat such an evil being that fed off the energies and strengths of those she threw into her awful talisman? The lightweight sword in Cazlina's hand quivered. Of what use would it be against a woman who could simply flick her fingers and reduce a powerful mage to a helpless plaything that she could do with what she willed?

Gareth gave a sharp whistle and Marli, Paulis and Donegal stepped out from behind the columns. They jumped up on to the three stone walkways behind the queen. Zandorin immediately guessed at Gareth's intentions and turned to the other man who had been imprisoned with him. "Rossio, you go left. I'll go right."

The man nodded and took off at a run to where Paulis stood on his walkway. Zandorin joined Marli on hers. The blonde woman nodded tersely at him, her gaze flicking back to the impossibly tall figure of Saranor, who turned slowly to stare at the tense figures behind her.

"How wonderfully foolish and naïve you little mortals are."

She flung out her arms and shouted up at the ceiling. "I AM SARANOR, SUPREME RULER OF REGALIS! YOU CANNOT DEFEAT ME!"

"Everybody move, now!" Gareth shouted.

As one, they all charged toward the queen, coming at her from different directions while her eyes were still trained on the ceiling.

"Stay here with Tor!" Cazlina yelled to Niko before sprinting after her brother.

Gareth and Jorin were closest to the queen, but, before they could reach her, she dropped her arms and pushed her right hand out in front of her. The two men slammed into a shimmering wall of purple sparks that rang with the sound of a sword blade clanging against a rock. Gareth staggered backward, teetering dangerously close to the edge of the walkway. The black waters beside it churned furiously. Cazlina cried out and rushed forward, but Jorin had already reached out and grasped her brother's arm, hauling him back to safety.

While the queen's attention was occupied with Gareth and Jorin, Zandorin and Marli pounded down the walkway behind her. But, with uncanny speed, Saranor whirled to face them and released two rings of light that spun in deadly arcs toward them. One of the rings hit Zandorin in the shoulder and he screamed in agony as his uniform jacket smoked, the smell of burnt flesh filling the tower room. The ring of light careened into the pillar behind him, knocking huge chunks of marble out of it. The sergeant dropped to the walkway and flung his uninjured arm protectively around his head as the deadly objects rained down upon him.

Marli swung her sword at the second spinning ring, trying to deflect it away from her. Blue-black flames raced along the length of the weapon's blade and into the hand that held it. The woman cried out and dropped the sword, clutching her wounded hand.

With a roar, Donegal charged down the walkway at the far end of the tower room, heading straight for Saranor. The queen's lips twitched in a ghastly smile as she pointed at the running man, lifting him off his feet with an invisible hand and flinging him the entire length of the walkway. He slammed into the wall at the far end with a sickening thud and then slid down it to land in a crumpled heap on the floor, his body unmoving.

Saranor whirled to face Paulis and the man named Rossio. "So, foolish ones, do you also wish to challenge me with your pitiful weapons? Come. Let us see what you can do against my powers."

The two men halted in their tracks, their faces wary and tense. Cazlina saw Paulis' lips move soundlessly and, then suddenly, both he and Rossio vanished.

Saranor's chilling laughter rang out in the calamitous air and her hand shot out in front of her. Paulis suddenly reappeared, dangling helplessly in the queen's tight grip on his shirtfront. Behind him, Rossio skidded to a stop, an expression of panic flaring across his face.

"Did you really think such a child's trick would fool me, my friend?" Saranor's voice dripped with contempt. "A simple glimmer spell is no match for my powers."

She threw Paulis away from her as easily as though he was a doll made of straw, and he slammed into Rossio. Both men tumbled and slid across the walkway, disappearing over the edge of the wide ledge.

From her helpless position behind Gareth and Jorin and the still crackling wall of sparks, Cazlina watched in dread, her blood running cold.

Saranor was right. Their fragile mortal bodies and weapons could not possibly defeat a being of such unspeakable power.

CHAPTER 41

A sudden commotion erupted on the other side of the closed tower door. The sounds of boots thudding against the ground, indistinct shouts, and the rattle of weapons caused everyone in the chamber to spin toward the door, their faces startled. Even Saranor appeared frozen for a moment, her attention caught by the disturbance. The wall of purple sparks fizzled and disappeared.

The heavy wooden door crashed open and several dark figures rushed into the room.

Jorin sprang forward and grabbed Cazlina about the waist, leaping off the walkway with her. Niko stood paralyzed by the door, his mouth hanging open at the sight of the onrushing soldiers. Jorin twisted his free hand in the collar of the boy's shirt and lifted him away before he could be trampled. Tor yelped as a hard-toed boot caught him in the side before he could leap out of the way. Cazlina was vaguely aware of Gareth flinging himself to the opposite side.

The lead figure came to a sudden halt, his eyes flying to the still white figure of Saranor standing on the walkway over the Pool.

She stared back for a moment and a slow smile spread across her face. "My good friend Viadon, how nice of you to join us for my ceremony."

Cazlina sagged with relief against Jorin's strong arm encircling her chest. It was indeed the general who stood there silently watching the queen, but, for the first time in Cazlina's acquaintance with him, she saw that his immaculate steel-gray uniform was disheveled and stained. Although some of the blotches on the cloth looked suspiciously like blood, Viadon appeared uninjured, his body held as ramrod-straight and alert as ever. Cazlina hoped the blood was from the enemy and not some grievous wound the general was hiding with remarkable composure.

Directly behind him stood Mattius Yanan, his face almost as expressionless as the general's and his eyes staring at the woman who had been responsible for turning him into a creature unable to live in the world of men. Cazlina could only guess at the thoughts that must lie behind that dark gaze.

She was pleased and relieved to see the angular figure of Pharon standing next to Yanan. The mage's eyes swept across hers and he smiled. *Well done, child.*

She started a little as the same voice that had whispered to her in the blue fog sounded in her mind. She smiled back, trying to convey her gratitude for his help in negotiating her way through the treacherous corridors of the castle in search of Gareth and the other prisoners.

Pharon's eyes left hers and flicked up toward the ceiling where Nostrimus remained entrapped in the queen's snare. The black-bearded mage glared down at him, and his hands jerked uselessly at his sides, as though he was trying to free them in order to unleash deadly spells on the tableau below.

Behind the general, several more soldiers from his army crowded into the room and came to a sudden weapon-rattling halt. A tense, expectant silence reigned over the assemblage.

Saranor's blazing eyes tried to pierce the unreadable gaze of General Viadon, but he remained undisturbed by her glare.

"So, my friend, I see you have managed to infiltrate my fortifications," she said, her voice sounding unconcerned. "I must ensure Captain Lerant is punished for his failure to stop you."

Viadon gazed at her for a moment longer and then said dryly, "I believe your captain is beyond punishment, Saranor."

For the first time, Cazlina noticed that the general held something in his right hand, hanging down by his side. He lifted the object and threw it toward the queen. As it bounced across the stone walkway and came to rest at her feet, tendrils of thick, viscous liquid flew through the air and splattered the hem of her white gown.

The liquid was blood and the object that rocked at the queen's feet was a severed head. Cazlina recognized the scarred ridges on each sunken cheek and the cold, dead eyes. The head belonged to Captain Lerant, the merciless, inhumane soldier who had captured her and the others in the mountains. The sight of the grisly object made her nauseous, but, at the same time, elation swept through her at the death of the vile man. Thank the gods he would no longer be able to do the queen's bidding and spread terror and panic throughout the countryside in his quest for prisoners for her Pool.

Saranor glanced down at the severed head, and, for a moment, rage marred the perfect, icy beauty of her face. Her eyes narrowed. "You shall pay dearly for this, my friend," she whispered, her burning gaze returning to Viadon's.

He smiled. "Perhaps, I shall, but not before the world is rid of your evil, Saranor."

Her exultant laughter rang out around the cavernous chamber. "We shall see, my friend, we shall see."

She suddenly flung up a white hand and an expanding ring of purple light streaked toward the general. Before it could reach and engulf him, it shattered against an invisible wall and spun off in a dozen different directions. One of the black-veined marble columns exploded with a deafening bang as a fragment of light bounced off it.

Cazlina jumped, her heart threatening to fly out of her chest, and Jorin's arm tightened painfully around her. She pulled Niko's shaking body closer to her own, trying to shield him as much as possible, knowing all the while her mortal body would be no match for Saranor's deadly powers.

Pharon moved around the stiff figure of Viadon, his angular face intense and watchful as he faced the wrathful glare of Saranor. "General, please ensure you and the others remain behind my shield for your protection. Do not under any circumstances move away from it."

The invisible wall rippled as the mage stepped through it.

Saranor's lip curled derisively. "So, it is you who I must battle? Hah! You are but a paltry mage. Just like poor Nostrimus here, who, as you can see, is helpless in my hands."

Pharon bowed. "Yes, I'm afraid I *am* the one you will have to defeat, your Majesty."

"So be it. I shall enjoy ripping you apart before the eyes of your good friend, the general."

The mage did not answer, but the glow of his eyes intensified.

Without warning, Saranor hissed and writhing strands of light shot from her open mouth and flew toward Pharon. His hands danced in a blur through the air. The tendrils were caught in an invisible grip that threw them high up toward the ceiling, narrowly missing Nostrimus, who struggled violently in his tight bonds.

"My Queen, release me and I will help you," he cried.

Saranor threw him a baleful glance. "I have no more need of you, mage. You shall die along with these others who dare to defy me."

While her attention was momentarily distracted by the interchange with Nostrimus, Pharon's right hand shot forward and she stumbled, her body jolted by a ball of blue light that had streaked across the intervening space in a blur, almost too fast for the human eye to see. The waters of the Pool on either side of the walkway churned in a white froth, the skeletal hands clawing at the air.

"Be careful, my Queen!" Nostrimus shouted. "Remember what I told you about the dangers of getting too close to the Pool."

"Shut up, you fool!" Saranor shrieked.

Craning her neck upward, Cazlina caught an oddly malicious and triumphant expression on the mage's face and wondered at its source.

"But, my Queen, I'm only warning you, because of the dire consequences that would befall you should you touch the black waters of the Pool."

Saranor's scream of rage reverberated off the echoing ceiling of the tower room and Cazlina's mouth dropped open as she realized what the queen's mage was doing. The dawning realization on Pharon's gaunt face told her he, too, had figured out Nostrimus's purpose in his warnings to Saranor. As incredible as it seemed, the mage was telling Pharon how to destroy the queen.

Ghastly light writhed under her translucent skin and spun out of her body in deadly strands that shattered against the columns surrounding the Pool. Chunks of marble flew in all directions around the tower room. If it hadn't been for Pharon's invisible shield, the deadly shards would have cut them all to shreds, Cazlina thought dazedly, as she and Niko crouched on the floor inside Jorin's protective embrace. Tor whimpered as pieces of stone clanged off the shield in front of them, and she reached out to place a comforting hand on his big head.

Marli and the others! Worry for their safety careened through her brain. They didn't have the protection of Pharon's invisible wall. The flying chunks of marble could kill them.

She anxiously craned her neck to peer over the ledge and breathed a sigh of relief. The blonde woman and Sergeant Zandorin had disappeared from the walkway. They must have taken refuge behind the columns once more. There was no sign of Paulis Mergan and Rossio, either, and she wondered uneasily if the two of them were dead behind the ledge. Donegal had not moved since he had crashed into the far wall.

Cazlina's attention was dragged back to the conflict between Pharon and Saranor.

She was horrified to see that Pharon's spells no longer seemed able to penetrate the immense power aura surrounding the queen. After that first ball of magic had taken her by surprise when her attention had been focused on Nostrimus, she must have strengthened her defenses, now easily repelling the mage's spells and forcing him to back up several paces.

An opaque shield crackling with blue sparks sprang into being around Pharon, and his hands again moved in a blur. To Cazlina's astonishment, his magic was no longer directed at Saranor, but rather the walkway at her feet, gouging huge chunks of stone out of it. The mage's aim could not be that bad, Cazlina thought in bewilderment, and then realization suddenly dawned on her. Because

Saranor's power surrounded her too closely and strongly for Pharon's spells to infiltrate, he had chosen instead to direct them toward destroying the walkway on which the queen stood in the hopes she would be thrown into the waters of the Pool.

Saranor staggered as the walkway heaved beneath her feet. The severed head of Lerant swayed violently from side to side and then rolled off the walkway into the Pool. Instantly, an eerie wailing erupted from the water and white hands seized the gory object, pulling it under the boiling surface.

Behind her, Cazlina heard General Viadon shout, "Pharon, look out!"

Saranor's shrieking body flew through the air and collided violently with the aura around the mage. He staggered backward, nearly falling to his knees at the sudden impact. The shield cracked and sizzled at the touch of the queen's malevolent power. For the first time, Cazlina saw an uncertain expression cross Pharon's face, and she quailed at the thought his power might not be a match for Saranor's.

Saranor threw back her head and laughed triumphantly at the sight of the mage cowering inside his crumbling shield. "See, mage! There is no way you can defeat me. I can crush you like an insect under my foot. And, that is exactly what I intend to do."

Pharon threw up his arms as though to ward off the bolts of power she was preparing to unleash on him, but, before she could do so, his voice thundered, "*UNBINDUS!*"

At the same time, he rotated his right hand and Saranor's feet lifted from the walkway, her body spinning in a circle and her long white hair whipping about her head. She shrieked in rage as the spinning grew wilder and she rose rapidly into the air.

"Nostrimus, you have seen how your loyalty to your queen will be rewarded!" Pharon shouted. "If you do not die today, how much longer do you think she will let you live? I have given you the chance to change that. Seek the path of light before the darkness destroys you."

Cazlina craned her head upward, wondering what the mage meant, and saw that the ropes of light binding Nostrimus's right hand had been severed. The mage was staring at the appendage as though he had never seen it before. When he raised his head, his eyes were narrowed in his white face. "What makes you think I won't use my powers against *you* instead, mage?"

Pharon pointed at Saranor. "Because now you know that you mean absolutely nothing to her. You were only a pawn used to obtain what she needed to gain power. She will kill you as she has all of her other hapless victims. She has betrayed you, Nostrimus. Will you allow her to rule Regalis without you by her side, after all you have done for her?"

Nostrimus ground his teeth and his eyes followed the queen's gyrating flight through the air as she neared his ensnared body.

"Don't listen to him, you fool," Saranor hissed, struggling to stop her uncontrollable spin. "Kill him! And, I will reward your actions by allowing you to live."

"How generous and merciful of you, my Queen," the mage snarled.

Fire sparked from his fingertips, striking the queen and sending her flipping end over end through the air. Before she could recover, he released another stream of flames that drove her downward toward the churning Pool of Souls far below.

CHAPTER 42

Cazlina gasped as she watched the rapidly falling figure of the queen, for incredibly, Saranor twisted around and grabbed the blazing rope of fire connecting her to Nostrimus. Smoke rose from her blackened hands and the sickening stench of burning flesh filled the tower room, but what should have caused excruciating pain seemed to have little effect on the queen.

"By all the gods, what manner of creature has she turned into?" Jorin wondered, his voice an awed whisper.

Cazlina shuddered against his broad chest, unable to take her gaze off the impossible sight. Saranor's channeling of the energies and souls of her victims had changed her into a being of unspeakable capabilities.

Nostrimus's eyes widened as the queen's relentless pull dragged him closer to her and thus closer to the black waters of the Pool. He tried to call back the mage fire he had unleashed, but Saranor's touch had changed the flames from red to purple and the spell could not be broken. When she was within a few feet of him, she reached out and wrapped her arms tightly around him, his fiery magic and her own writhing coils of light colliding in a cacophony of sparks and thunder. Locked in a macabre dance of power, the two figures fell inexorably toward the eager Pool waiting below.

The waters began to swirl faster and faster, the white hands and bobbing heads thrashing the surface. An unearthly moaning filled the tower room.

With an enormous splash that sent a geyser of black water shooting upward toward the ceiling, Nostrimus and Saranor hit the Pool and disappeared from sight. An explosion of smoke and steam billowed up amid a deadly cloud of purple fire and sparks. The moans of the soul-dead in the Pool rose to a deafening shriek.

A howling figure rose partially out of the water, and Cazlina bit back a scream.

Saranor resembled a Mist Rider, her facial features and limbs melted and pulled into elongated blurs. Instead of the brilliant purple radiance of her stolen powers, black light now writhed beneath skin that had cracked open in steaming fissures. Her long white hair had burned away to a few charred wisps on her ruined head.

Dozens of hands reached up and grasped the almost unrecognizable queen, dragging her back down into the depths of the Pool. Cracks began to appear in the columns and walls as the entire cavernous chamber shuddered and shook.

Pharon whirled to face Viadon. "General, you must take your men and leave the tower at once. You are all in grave danger."

"Is she dead?" the general asked, brusquely.

The mage inclined his head. "I don't believe even Saranor could have survived that much damage. It appears to me the Pool and its unfortunate victims have enacted their revenge on her."

Viadon nodded and turned to issue the order to retreat. One of his men dragged the whimpering Molitare to his feet and shoved him roughly out the door. The others hurriedly followed, as a choking cloud of dust filled the tower from the crumbling columns and walls.

Gareth fought his way through the retreating men to where Cazlina still knelt on the floor with Jorin and Niko. "Let's get out of here."

He staggered as a loud crack tilted the stone floor and a marble pillar close by fell over with a tremendous crash.

Jorin leapt to his feet and scooped Niko up in his arms. "Come on, Caz!"

She grabbed his arm, alarm coursing through her. "Wait! Marli and the others! They're still on the other side of the room. We have to see if they're all right."

Without hesitation, Jorin thrust Niko into her arms and commanded, "Stay here." He took off running to the right where Marli and Zandorin had been, struggling to stay on his feet as more columns toppled over and shook the tower room.

Gareth grasped her shoulder. "Don't worry, we'll find them."

He headed to the left where Paulis and Rossio had disappeared behind the ledge, leaving Cazlina standing there, bracing herself against the increasingly unstable floor and her own overwhelming panic.

Against her chest, Niko's body was stiff, the streaks of dirt outlined sharply against his pale cheeks. She tightened her hold on him, trying to allay her own fear in an effort to comfort him instead.

We must leave at once! Tor's anxious voice pounded in her head. *It's not safe here.*

I know, Cazlina answered. *But, I can't go until I know Marli and the others are safe. You don't have to stay. Take Niko and join the general. We'll follow as soon as we can.*

She lowered the boy to the floor and grasped his shoulders, looking down earnestly into his wide eyes.

"Go with Tor. As soon as Jorin and Gareth come back with the others, I'll join you."

Niko shook his head, his small hand clinging to her trousers. "No, I don't want to leave you! You'll die and then I won't ever see you again."

She tried to smile, brushing a lock of tousled hair off his forehead. "I won't die. I promised myself I would take care of you and I intend to keep that promise. Please, for once, listen to me and let Tor take you away from here to somewhere safe."

The big dog nudged him and whined and Niko bit his lip, indecision and stubbornness waging a battle on his face.

The stone floor tilted, nearly throwing them to their knees. A section of ceiling fell into the seething Pool, sending black water spraying through the choking cloud of dust that seemed to be thickening with every passing second. The unearthly wailing from the Pool had risen to a deafening crescendo.

"Niko, go now!" She turned him around and thrust him toward the door.

Tor grabbed the sleeve of the boy's shirt and tugged hard. Niko looked back over his shoulder at her with a heartrending expression in his eyes and she nearly ran after him. But, the thought of leaving without determining if Jorin and Gareth and the others were still alive and safe held her rooted to the spot. Niko would be safe with the general outside the rapidly disintegrating tower room and the thought helped her to endure the parting. She gave him an encouraging smile and waved at him to go.

As soon as he and Tor disappeared through the doorway, she turned back to the shuddering room, peering anxiously through the clouds of dust and holding her breath in an effort not to breathe in the particles, listening for the sounds of the others returning.

"Jorin! Gareth! Can you hear me? Where are you?"

A violent pitch in the floor sent her stumbling forward and she barely avoided falling face first into the wide ledge. She clung to it, her heart pounding with fear and anxiety. In the next second, she reared back in terror as a head suddenly popped up out of the water directly in front of her, its white eyes staring into her face.

It was Nostrimus. Or, at least, as far as Cazlina's terrified eyes could tell, it was the mage. He was recognizable only by what was left of his double-pointed black beard. The rest of his features had melted and fused into lumps of deformed flesh that bore no resemblance to his former appearance.

"Tell...Pharon...she...is... no...more."

The strained whisper trembling on the ruined lips died away and the head sank back beneath the surface.

Cazlina struggled with her emotions, scarcely daring to believe the evil reign of Saranor was truly ended. Did Nostrimus speak the truth? Only a short time ago, the queen had seemed invincible, so powerful that nothing or no one could defeat her. If Nostrimus had not made the choice he did and been instrumental in plunging her into the Pool to be destroyed, the world would have become a place of terror and corruption with no hope of salvation.

The sounds of coughing and retching drove Cazlina back up to her feet. In the next moment, two dim figures emerged from the choking cloud and she rushed over to them.

The tallest figure was Jorin, his entire body covered in dust as he carried the limp body of Marli in his arms. Blood matted the woman's long blonde hair and streaked across her stark-white face.

Cazlina's breath hitched on a sob. "Is she...?"

Jorin shook his head, doubling over as a violent cough racked his body. When he could finally speak, his words caused Cazlina to sag in relief. "No, she's still alive but badly injured. Part of a column fell on her. We need to get her to a healer as soon as possible."

The second dust-covered figure with Jorin was Sergeant Zandorin, his face strained. His left arm hung limply at his side, blood staining the scorched shoulder of his jacket where the ring of purple light had connected.

Gareth stumbled up beside them, Paulis Mergan's arm slung around his shoulder. The older man was pale and trembling. The trouser leg on his right side was torn and bloody, and he grimaced every time he put weight on the leg.

"Where are Rossio and Donegal?" Cazlina asked, trying to peer around her brother.

"They didn't make it," Gareth rasped.

Cazlina swallowed, tasting tears in the back of her throat. She hadn't known Donegal for very long, but the man had been incredibly brave in volunteering to help free the prisoners and in facing up to the evil of Saranor, as had the stranger, Rossio.

"Let's get out of here," Jorin urged.

"Wait, there's something else we have to do," Gareth said.

"What are you talking about?" Zandorin demanded. "We have to leave now. The whole place is falling apart."

"Incendiary spheres," Gareth explained. "They're planted all around the Pool. We have to arm them and destroy it."

The sergeant's pale face lit up. "Then, by Orun's sword, let's do it!"

"Let me help," Paulis said, trying to take a step forward. His injured leg buckled and he nearly fell to the heaving floor, his face twisted with pain.

"You're in no condition to help," Gareth said, bluntly. He turned to Cazlina. "Can you…?"

She nodded, draping Paulis' arm around her own shoulders. "I'll take him. Go, and be careful."

She watched him disappear into the cloud of dust and willed her feet to move toward the doorway, stumbling a little under Paulis' weight and trying not to think about the danger that faced Gareth and the sergeant. What if they failed to find their way back to the door in time after triggering the spheres?

Jorin studied her face. "Your brother is a very resourceful and brave man, Caz."

She swallowed past a lump of tears. "Yes, he is."

The horse thief's eyes held an expression of solemn respect as he gazed down into hers. "It seems courage runs in your family, my lady. Forgive me for ever doubting that for one second."

He turned away with Marli in his arms and staggered through the doorway.

CHAPTER 43

The general, Pharon, Mattius Yanan, and five of Viadon's men were waiting in the corridor when Cazlina and Jorin emerged from the tower room. One of the soldiers came forward and slipped Paulis' other arm around his shoulder and hurried away with the wounded man. Another relieved Jorin of Marli's limp body. Niko, who had been standing beside Yanan, ran forward to wrap his arms tightly about Cazlina's waist, nearly knocking her exhausted body over. She smiled weakly and hugged the boy back as Tor nudged her arm, his eyes relieved.

Viadon's tired eyes scrutinized Cazlina's face. "It seems you have quite the tale to tell me. It can wait until one of my healers has examined you to make certain you're all right."

"I can't leave yet, General. My brother and Sergeant Zandorin are still in the tower room. They're setting off incendiary spheres to destroy the Pool."

"Then we should leave at once, General," Pharon said, with a concerned look. "It'll be very dangerous if we remain in the vicinity when the spheres go off."

"I won't leave until Gareth gets out of the tower safely," Cazlina said, defiantly.

"*Tanim* Narzin…"

She drew herself up to her full height. "Even if you give me a direct order to leave, General, I won't obey it. My brother is in there and I refuse to go anywhere until I know he's all right."

The general lifted one eyebrow and said mildly, "I was going to say, Cazlina, I commend you for your bravery and loyalty and would expect nothing less of you."

Her cheeks flamed and she was unable to meet his gaze. "I'm sorry, sir. I didn't mean…"

He reached out and grasped her shoulder. "After what you've been through, I think I can forgive a little insubordination."

Before she could say anything further, a rumbling sound could be heard from the tower room, rising in intensity until its vibrations shook the corridor in which they were standing.

Pharon stepped forward, raising his hands. "There is no time to leave! Brace yourselves. *EXPELLIUM FIERA!*"

A series of violent explosions rocked the tower room, and a concussive wave of smoke, flames and acrid wind blew through the open doorway, passing over their heads but knocking everyone off their feet in its wake.

Dazed and winded, Cazlina lay supine on the floor with a heavy weight draped across her back. Somewhere nearby, she could hear whimpering and faint rustlings.

"My lady, are you all right?" A deep voice vibrating with concern rumbled in her ear, and an unsteady hand brushed across her cheek.

She blinked away the gray fog that had descended over her mind. "Jorin?"

The weight on her eased away and she realized the horse thief had fallen across her body in the blast.

"Thank the gods, you're still alive," he said, feelingly.

Her bones felt as though they had been pulled in several different directions at once. Aches and pains too numerous to count coursed through her body and her ears rang with a strange singing sound, but she was definitely still alive.

Alarm raced through her mind. "Niko? Niko!"

Something stirred under her out-flung right arm. "I'm here, Cazlina. My head hurts."

Relief washed over her as she saw him lying on the floor nearby, grimacing and holding his head. Around her, she could hear moans and mutterings from the others.

"Is everyone all right?" The general's calm voice cut through the rumblings still emanating from the tower room.

Fortunately, everyone appeared to have suffered little injury aside from a few bumps and bruises.

Tor crawled on his belly toward Niko, laying his huge head in his lap, and the boy hugged him tightly. Cazlina smiled in relief at the dog's survival and then a sudden agony pierced her insides.

"Gareth!" The scream wrenched from her throat and she leapt to her feet.

"Caz, wait!" Jorin tried to grab her arm, but she pulled away from him and ran heedlessly toward the doorway of the tower room, her heart pounding so loudly she could hear its deafening thunder in her ears.

She skidded to a halt just inside the entrance, unable to believe her eyes.

The tower room had literally disintegrated into a deep black hole. The entire roof was gone, blown to bits to reveal an indigo sky dotted with faint, twinkling stars. Shafts of dust-filled moonlight slanted down, filling the shell of the chamber with a dazzling glare. The Pool of

Souls had completely disappeared. The marble columns that had surrounded it poked out of the deep hole like giant toothpicks. Blue flames spat and licked at the piles of rubble and the jagged edges of the hole.

"Gareth," the name slid out in an anguished whisper.

It was impossible anyone had survived the violent explosions and complete devastation in the tower room.

"Caz, I'm so sorry."

She barely heard Jorin's somber voice or felt his tight grip on her arms. Her mind had gone numb, emptied completely of all feeling and emotion just as the tower room had been emptied of the Pool and everything in it.

Pharon moved up beside her. His quiet voice when he spoke was apologetic. "The moment you mentioned the incendiary spheres, I tapped into the mage's magic inside them and commanded the fire spells to dispel all of their power directly into the Pool instead of spreading outward to destroy everything around them as they would normally do. In addition, I placed a protective shield around all of us. If I hadn't, we would not be alive right now. The concussion of power that merely knocked us off our feet would have vaporized us instead." His eyes met hers, compassion in their depths. "I'm terribly sorry, Cazlina. I'm afraid my intervention was not enough to save your brother and the sergeant. I can sense no life anywhere in the tower room."

She nodded mechanically, not really hearing the words. A curtain had fallen across her mind, a blank backdrop upon which images of her brother teasing and scolding her played like the shadow figure shows she had often watched as a child in Rothtown. As though from a great distance, she heard his laughter as they raced each other across the spring-green meadows behind their thatched log house, his loud and colorful curses as she nicked him with a sword during one of their fencing matches, his soothing voice lulling her to sleep and chasing away the nightmares that had followed in the wake of their parents' death.

Strangely, she could not grieve. Even though the rational part of her brain told her Gareth had died in the devastated tower room, her heart and soul refused to believe it. The strength and closeness of the sibling bond linking them made it difficult for her to accept the finality of his death. Surely, she would have known the very moment when his life had fled his body, when the essence that was Gareth Narzin had ceased to exist. She had felt no such severing of the connection between them and that conviction, no matter how unreasonable and childish, kept her from sliding to the floor and giving in to a despair that would shatter her soul.

Jorin urged her away from the tower room and she went docilely.

General Viadon gave her a look full of compassion. "I know it's not much consolation, Cazlina, but I intend to bestow the highest honor for bravery on your brother and Sergeant Zandorin. Without their sacrifice, Saranor and the Pool of Souls would not have been destroyed. You should be very proud."

The kind tone was almost her undoing. It threatened to crack the thin veneer of numbness that lay over her emotions. She could only nod, afraid to speak out loud for fear her words would somehow irretrievably confirm that Gareth was dead.

The general studied her face for a moment longer and then issued an order for everyone to leave the vicinity of the tower. "I must make certain my forces have been able to wrest complete control of the castle from Saranor's followers. She and the Pool may have been destroyed, but there is still the matter of capturing her remaining servants. Mattius, take these men and check out the dungeons. Hopefully, they haven't been damaged too badly by the collapse of the tower. We'll need them for the prisoners."

"Right away, General," Yanan beckoned to the remaining three soldiers and they disappeared down the corridor.

Cazlina frowned as she followed the others to the stairway leading down from the ruined tower. Something Viadon said pricked at the edges of the curtain draped over her mind, an elusive thought that rose up like a spirit from a grave.

What had he been talking about? Saranor's servants and capturing them, imprisoning them in the dungeons...

A blaze of light suddenly burned through the haze, making Cazlina halt so suddenly she nearly pulled Niko off his feet. He looked up at her in concern.

"Cazlina, are you all right?"

The dungeons!

She grabbed Niko's other hand and leaned down to speak urgently into his upturned face. "Niko, what's the fastest way to the dungeons? No secret passageways, no ladders, just the fastest, most direct route?"

"I can show you," he said, looking startled by the wildness in her tone.

"Let's go!"

He took off at a run and Cazlina followed, ignoring the concerned calls of the others behind her. She had no time to explain, and, besides, they would only think she had gone mad, that her mind had become unhinged from grief. As perhaps it had, she thought with a fatalistic shrug, but that was not going to stop her.

Mattius Yanan and the other three soldiers looked startled as she and Niko and Tor flew past them halfway down the stairs.

"Cazlina?" Yanan called after her, but she didn't answer.

Niko led her back to the corridor with the pale green pillars and the horrific moving tapestries. The long, echoing hallway was filled with soldiers from General

316

Viadon's army, either herding prisoners from the castle into groups or attending to the wounded. It was obvious a great battle had taken place there and many of the golden statues and sculptures lay broken and scattered about the bloody, slippery floor among the corpses and the injured. Most of the enormous tapestries had been torn from the walls and slashed into tatters, their garish scenes of torture and destruction thankfully unrecognizable now.

Cazlina pushed through the soldiers, ignoring their curses and questions. A blind frenzy had seized her and she was oblivious to everything around her except the single-minded purpose that burned in her mind.

A rough hand grasped her arm, dragging her to a halt. "Hey, where do you think you're going? Get over there with the other prisoners."

Cazlina struggled to escape. "Let me go!"

"Leave her alone!" Niko kicked the man in the shin and he yelped in pain.

A dangerous glint came into the soldier's hard eyes and he reached for his sword. "Going to give me trouble, are you? We'll see about that."

Tor growled and crouched, preparing to spring at the man's throat when the general's voice suddenly cut through the danger-laden air. "Enough!"

The soldier immediately dropped his hand from the hilt of his sword and snapped to attention.

Cazlina took advantage of Viadon's intervention and wrenched her arm from the man's grasp. "Come on, Niko!"

"Caz!"

She didn't stop to acknowledge Jorin's call from behind her, her mind completely free now of the numbness that had struck her earlier and flickering with a hope she dared not express out loud.

CHAPTER 44

Cazlina pounded on the closed stone door leading into the dungeon cells, oblivious to the scrapes and bruises she was inflicting on her fists. "No, no!" she cried out in frustration.

Something nudged her hip and Tor's calm voice sounded in her head. *You have the disk to open the door, Cazlina. Remember?*

She stopped beating against the unyielding stone and took a deep breath. "Of course, I forgot I had it. Thank you, Tor."

She pulled the flat crystal disk from the pocket of her trousers and inserted it into the niche in the door. But, the intricate pattern of moves required to trigger the opening mechanism eluded her and she gritted her teeth in growing panic as her shaking hand spun the disk right and left.

"I can't remember. Oh, gods, I can't remember the combination!"

The dog's muscular body pressed reassuringly against hers. *Steady, girl, I'll help you.*

Cazlina forced herself to relax and follow Tor's instructions, trying to keep her impatience in check until there was a click and the massive door began to swing inward.

She squeezed through the opening as soon as it was wide enough to accommodate her body. As she neared the far end of the row of cells, her footsteps slowed and then finally stopped. Most of the inside tower wall had caved downward, spewing cracked blocks of stone and splintered wood out into the corridor in front of the cells. The cells nearest the collapsed wall had been completely destroyed by flying debris. Dust hung thickly in the air above piles of smoking rubble from the tower room that filled the interior of the shaft.

Cazlina sank to her knees, her body beginning to shake. Her last desperate hope for Gareth's survival dangled crookedly above a huge pile of crushed stone. A single frayed rope kept it suspended in the air, but, otherwise, the prisoner's platform was a mangled mess of splintered boards, snapped ropes and twisted pulleys.

"Oh, Gareth," she whispered, brokenly.

She closed her eyes and let her head fall upon her chest, feeling a scalding tide of grief, denial, and disbelief start to rise up through her body, threatening to smother her in blackness.

An excited voice cut through the rapidly ascending miasma.

Cazlina, come quick! I think I've found them.

Her head flew up at Tor's words and she leapt to her feet. "What? What did you say?"

Over here, near the other end of the cell block!

She turned and saw Niko and Tor standing in front of a closed cell several yards away. The dog sniffed furiously at the base of the cell door and whined while Niko looked on, a puzzled expression on his face. He glanced up when Cazlina rushed over to them.

"I don't know what's wrong with him. I think there must be something inside this cell."

She wrenched the door open, her heart pounding in anticipation.

Inside, lying on a dirty pile of straw in one corner was Gareth, his gray uniform white with dust and splattered with blood from a nasty head wound trickling the sticky liquid across his forehead and down his right cheek. The ankle on his right leg flopped at an unnatural angle, obviously broken. Beside him, Sergeant Zandorin sat with his back against the wall, head tilted back and eyes closed. Deep scratches and purple bruises marred his face and he held his injured arm gingerly in his lap.

"Gareth!"

His eyes fluttered open at the sound of her voice and he smiled weakly. "I was wondering when you would come."

She sank down beside him and carefully cradled his injured head in her arms. "Oh, gods, you're alive!"

He grimaced. "Either that, or the Other Side has celestial beings that look disturbingly like my grubby-faced, sunburned little sister."

She poked him gently in the ribs. "You're a fine one to complain about looks, dear brother. *You* look like you've been dragged behind a horse for several leagues and then dumped over a cliff for good measure."

"Funny, that's exactly how I feel, too." His expression became serious. "Was the Pool destroyed?"

"Yes. The incendiary spheres completely obliterated it."

"Good." He nodded toward Zandorin, who had opened his eyes and was watching them. "After we set off the triggers, we realized we couldn't reach the door in time. The way was blocked by too many collapsed pillars. Then I thought of the platform and we raced for it. We almost reached the bottom when the first blasts hit. We were thrown off the platform. I think I must have passed out when I hit my head."

"You did," Zandorin said, wearily. "I managed to drag you over to the door, but it was locked, so I tried to get us both into a cell as far away as I could. I almost passed out myself a couple of times, but we made it."

"I *knew* it," Cazlina said, triumphantly. "It seemed certain at first you'd both been killed in the tower room, but then I remembered the platform and hoped against hope that you would have thought to use it, too." She grimaced. "I must have looked like a madwoman to General Viadon and the others when I raced down here without telling them where I was going."

"Not at all," the general said, entering the cell and followed closely by Jorin, Pharon and Yanan. "Only like a devoted sister who firmly believed her brother was still alive. As it turns out you were absolutely right. No, Sergeant, stay as you are."

Sergeant Zandorin had tried to snap to attention, wincing in pain as he did so. At the general's command, he gratefully collapsed back against the wall.

"I'm glad to see you both survived," Viadon went on. "The Pool and Saranor are destroyed thanks to you and you will both be receiving medals of bravery for your part in their destruction."

The two men beamed through their dirt and bruises and pain.

Cazlina smiled proudly down at Gareth. "Just don't make a habit of this, please," she whispered, so only he could hear, and he grinned weakly up at her.

"I promise."

"Allow me to add my congratulations and my heartfelt relief at your survival," Jorin said, extending his hand down toward Gareth.

Cazlina glanced up at him in astonishment, searching his face for the flippant sarcasm and amusement that usually colored his exchanges with her brother. All she saw was sincerity in his eyes.

Even Gareth looked surprised for a moment and then clasped Jorin's hand with as firm of a grip as he could manage. The two men nodded at each other, a brief look passing between them, as though in acknowledgement of a silent pact that had just been made. The hostility and aggression Gareth usually exhibited toward the horse thief eased away into respect.

"I feel something of a comradeship with you now," Jorin grinned. "We both have matching head wounds. Fortunately for us, we also possess hard heads that limit the damage."

"You're absolutely right about that," Cazlina said, with feeling.

"Hey!" Gareth protested.

Jorin's gaze swung to meet Cazlina's and the corners of his eyes crinkled. "My sincerest thanks to you, my lady, for saving my poor life once more. It seems our paths are destined to cross each other whether we want them to or not. It must be the gods' will, and who are we to question the wishes of the gods?"

Now that was the arrogance she had come to expect from him!

She raised her eyebrow, ready to launch a sharp retort back at him, but found herself laughing instead. Discovering that Gareth had survived the destruction of the Pool had filled her with such relief and euphoria she found it impossible to maintain her annoyance and frustration with the horse thief. Those emotions seemed ridiculous now in light of all that she and Gareth and Jorin had been through.

"Well, now that congratulations have been extended all around, it's time to get the injured to the healers," Viadon said. His eyes caught Cazlina's and she could swear she saw a twinkle in their tired depths. "Besides, I think there is a certain horse outside the castle walls that is very anxious to see you, young woman."

Her eyes misted at the thought of being reunited with Miris. The absence of the mare's loving voice in her mind had been like a throbbing ache that had refused to go away. Seeing her again would be a healing balm that would take away all the horror and pain of the last few days.

Within a short time, Gareth and Zandorin were delivered into the capable hands of the general's healers. It turned out that the sergeant had a couple of cracked ribs in addition to his injured shoulder. How he had managed to drag Gareth into the cell was a feat not even Zandorin could explain. It was no wonder he had almost passed out a few times.

Cazlina was reluctant to let her brother out of her sight. She had nearly lost him twice in this battle, and the thought of something else happening to endanger him was a persistent fear in the back of her mind. But, both he and Jorin persuaded her he would be well looked after and she consented to leave his bedside. Niko and Tor accompanied her and Jorin as they followed General Viadon outside into the night.

In addition to the brilliant moonlight, campfires and torches lit up the trampled grounds in front of the castle where Viadon's army had set up camp. Dark figures hurried back and forth, and the moans and cries of the wounded filled the night air as they were tended to where they lay on the ground or in tents that had been erected. The enormous black bulks of Fire Birds protectively ringed the encampment.

Cazlina was astounded by the destruction that had transpired during the ferocious battle between Captain Lerant's troops and General Viadon's rebellion army while she had been inside trying to free the prisoners. The castle that had once dominated the countryside with its stunning beauty and soaring spires had suffered extensive damage. Much of the surrounding outer wall had been destroyed, blown to bits by Pharon's magic or smashed to rubble by the heavy breaching weapons of Viadon's army. Piles of debris set ablaze by the flames from the Fire Birds' weapons smoldered in the courtyard, and, outside the breached walls, the strong, sickly-sweet smell of charred grass and flesh lingered in the air.

Cazlina glanced up toward the tower where the Pool of Souls had been housed and shuddered at the sight of the roofless turret outlined against the glowing orb of the moon. The outer walls of the tower had been relatively undamaged by the incendiary spheres, thanks to Pharon's redirection of their explosive power. Although she had witnessed Saranor's destruction with her very own eyes, she couldn't help feeling that some remnant of the queen's madness still lingered about the castle.

Jorin's gaze followed hers and he said quietly, as though reading her thoughts, "She's gone, Cazlina. She can no longer harm any of us."

"Her taint is still here," Cazlina replied. "It's almost as though it's embedded in the very walls."

She glanced toward Niko, who was gazing around in awe at the destruction of the castle and its grounds, and lowered her voice. "Was Kesel the prisoner Saranor sacrificed in the Pool just before we arrived in the tower room?"

Jorin's eyes darkened with remembrance. "Yes. I think she chose him first, because she sensed the blackness of his soul and it appealed to her." His lips tightened momentarily. "I didn't like the man, but he didn't deserve such a fate. No one does."

Cazlina sighed wearily. "I was afraid of that." At Jorin's raised eyebrow, she went on to explain. "Niko is Kesel's son. He left the boy to join General Viadon's army. From what Niko told me, Kesel was never much of a father and neglected his son to the point where I think Niko was raising himself even before Kesel left. Still, it's going to be difficult to tell the boy his Da is gone for good. He has no one else to look after him, except one very loyal dog."

Jorin glanced at Niko, a sympathetic expression on his face. "Poor lad. It sounds like he's had a pretty tough life."

She nodded and then shifted her gaze back to his. "I have to ask you something. Before we freed you, when you were facing certain death in the Pool, you seemed so calm and unaffected. I was amazed by your lack of fear. How could you be so brave at that moment, knowing the agony that was to come?"

He didn't answer at first, and, when he finally spoke, his words surprised her for she had been expecting a glib explanation as he was wont to give. "I could not bring myself to give Saranor what she wanted. She lived to instill fear and panic in her victims. She fed on it, gorged herself on it. I had no intention of satisfying that monstrous appetite. If I was going to die, it was going to be on my terms, not hers. I don't think I was being brave so much as stubborn and determined not to show outward fear to her."

"It still seemed incredibly brave to me," Cazlina said. She smiled. "Perhaps you're not quite as shallow and disreputable as you like to portray."

His eyebrow rose and he pretended to look hurt. "Shallow and disreputable? My lady, you wound me grievously once more. Do you really think that little of me?"

"Don't let it go to your head, Montrill, but my opinion of you has actually changed after all we've been through. I think I may have been a little harsh on you at times. For that, I apologize."

He stared suspiciously at her. "Did you perchance suffer a blow to the head, as well? Or, perhaps, *my* blow to the head is still affecting me. I thought I just heard you apologize."

She sighed. "Don't push your luck, Montrill. I still haven't forgiven you for trying to steal Miris."

The familiar twinkle reappeared in his eyes. "Now, that's more like the Cazlina I know."

She shook her head at him and turned to follow the straight-backed figure of General Viadon as he headed toward an enclosure containing several horses. Her pulse quickened at the thought that Miris was among the other animals and she would soon be able to fling her arms around the mare's neck and breathe in her sweet, horse smell.

Halfway across the trampled grass, she suddenly stopped, her heart hammering with fear. Several Mist Riders were converging on them, their gauzy outlines barely discernible but their orange eyes piercing the darkness. She heard Jorin draw in his breath sharply as he stepped in front of her, shielding her and Niko from the repulsive creatures.

CHAPTER 45

Gⁱⁱeneral Viadon halted, watching silently as the Mist Riders approached. He seemed unperturbed by their presence and Cazlina stared at him in astonishment. Why wasn't he raising the alarm? Why weren't the other soldiers in the vicinity rushing to protect them from the deadly creatures?

One of the gray, waving shapes floated to a stop in front of the general, its orange eyes flickering. "So, human, you claimed you would destroy the queen and you did. That was a feat I did not think possible, but you have proven me wrong."

Viadon stared at the creature impassively. "And?"

The creature shrugged. "We are no longer bound to Saranor's command. As agreed upon, we will uphold our end of the bargain."

Viadon inclined his head. "You will return to the mountains of Yorill and never set foot in these lands again. If you do, you will be hunted down relentlessly until every last one of you is destroyed."

The Mist Rider's eyes burned brighter, and, although its blurred features were incapable of holding any expression, Cazlina had the distinct impression it had been angered by Viadon's words. Then the glow faded and the unearthly voice said, "That is the agreement. We will honor it."

Without another word, the Mist Riders swooped away, their wavering bodies disappearing into the indigo sky.

The general turned toward Cazlina and the others, a mirthless smile on his face. "It's fortunate Mist Riders have no sense of loyalty or obligation. They do, however, understand threats. Saranor apparently promised them permanent employment as enforcers of her laws once she became supreme ruler of Regalis. I told them that once I killed her I would tolerate no such agreement with them and they would have to return to their home in the Yorill Mountains or be destroyed alongside her. Since Trax was firmly convinced Saranor could not be defeated, he readily agreed. He's not happy I won my end of the bargain, but I believe he's smart enough to realize any reneging on his part would only mean disaster for his race. I think we can be assured this is the last we will see of Mist Riders in these lands."

Cazlina released her pent-up breath, relief washing over her at the thought that the dreadful creatures would no longer terrorize the realm of Regalis.

Caz!

Her head jerked up at the familiar voice in her mind, a voice filled with so much unrestrained joy and happiness that tears sprang to her eyes and she began to run toward the enclosure. Miris galloped to the fence to meet her, her beautiful head held high and her nostrils flaring with excited whinnies. Cazlina scrambled up the boards of the fence and into the enclosure, throwing her arms around the mare's sleek neck.

"Miris, oh, Miris, I've missed you so much!"

The mare rubbed her head against Cazlina's shoulder, snuffling softly into her hair. *As I have you. I was so worried.* Her voice turned reproachful. *Please don't ever send me away like that again, Caz. I will absolutely refuse to go, and, if you try to make me, I may even bite you, even though I generally don't like to bite.*

Cazlina smiled into the warmth of Miris' neck. *I won't, dear one, I promise.*

"If I had known of the extraordinary bond between you and your pretty mare, I never would have tried to steal her," Jorin said from behind her. "That would indeed have been an unforgivable sin."

Cazlina glanced at him, surprised by the note of self-reproach in his voice and the unusually contrite expression on his face.

The other horses crowded around them, curiosity in their large eyes. Jorin's horse, Veygar, nodded his big head at Cazlina and she left Miris long enough to hug the stallion and drop a kiss on his velvety nose.

"Thank you for taking care of Miris," she murmured.

It was my pleasure. She was very brave throughout the whole ordeal.

"That's my girl," Cazlina patted the mare fondly.

"Is this your horse?" a small voice asked from behind Cazlina and she turned to find Niko standing there, his eyes wide with admiration as he gazed up at Miris.

"Yes. Niko, this is Miris. And, Miris, this is Niko, one of the bravest young men I have ever met."

"Can I pet her?" he asked, hesitantly.

"Of course, she won't bite." Cazlina threw a mischievous glance at the mare and Miris neighed in mild reproach.

The mare lowered her head toward the boy, blowing gently against his face. His eyes widened with pleasure and he tentatively stroked her nose. "She's beautiful."

Oh, how delightful, another admirer of fine horseflesh, Miris exclaimed. *Did that handsome horse thief teach the boy how to see all the splendid qualities in a horse?*

Cazlina slapped her gently on the neck. "What a spoiled brat you are, dear one."

"Can you talk to her, too, like with Tor?" Niko asked.

"Yes, although sometimes I'm not so sure that's a good thing, especially when she scolds me about something."

Miris butted her head into Cazlina's shoulder. *It's only for your own good, Caz.*

Cazlina grinned. "Miris, I also want you to meet Tor. He's Niko's best friend and was very helpful to me in the castle. Say hello to him."

Miris eyed the huge dog standing behind the boy. When she moved slowly toward him, head lowered, Tor tensed warily. Horse and dog stared at each other for a few moments and then Miris reached down and licked Tor on the nose, almost knocking him off his feet in the process. Cazlina grinned at the startled look on the dog's face.

She's saying thank-you for helping me.

Tor's raspy chuckle sounded in her mind. *It was my pleasure.*

Cazlina dropped to her knees and planted her own kiss on the long scar marring his face. "Without you and Niko, I couldn't have accomplished what I did in the castle. Thank you, Tor. I hope you consider me a friend, too."

He licked her cheek. *You kept Niko safe, as you promised, and you were very brave in saving your companions. I thought your mission extremely foolhardy at first, but you proved me wrong. I would be honored to be your friend.*

She hugged him and stood up, turning to find General Viadon behind her, watching her with a speculative expression.

"You've been through quite an adventure, Cazlina, and shown remarkable fortitude and courage through some very difficult trials. I must confess that, when I first met you, I was a little skeptical of your ability to serve as a useful soldier in my army. Certainly, you exhibited the zeal and enthusiasm necessary to fight against Saranor's tyranny, but, at the same time, I was afraid your youth and naivety might not make you suitable for the task at hand. I'm not afraid to admit I was very wrong. You proved over and over again that I'd made the right decision in permitting you to join my army. I have no regrets in that regard, only that it was necessary in the first place. I'm very proud of you, Cazlina Narzin, and honored that you chose to join my rebellion."

Cazlina stared at him, flattered and embarrassed by such high praise. Finally, she managed to say, "Thank you, General. I'd like to say it was a pleasure, but I'm afraid that would be a lie. It actually wasn't very pleasant at all."

"That is quite an understatement." He smiled. "What will you do now? Will you return to your home?"

The question startled her. Since the threat of Saranor had ended, she had given no thought as to what would happen next. Too much had transpired in the past several days and she was still reeling from it all. Somehow, Rothtown seemed so far away, a life that had happened long ago, even though she had left it only a few weeks earlier.

Her indecision must have shown on her face, for the general said gravely, "If you have no immediate plans, I would like to ask you to remain with my army. Saranor may be gone, but there are still remnants of her forces that must be dealt with. Captain Petros is continuing to fight her troops near the Telagor Sea and Captains Spargus and

Belledar remain under attack in the north and east regions. There still remains a great deal of work to do to stop the spread of Saranor's corruption. I hate to ask further sacrifice of you, considering all you've been through up to this point, but, if you are so inclined, I would be most grateful for your continued service."

Cazlina hesitated. She glanced at Niko, still enthralled with Miris, and bit her lip. The boy deserved and needed stability and happiness in his life. Rothtown would certainly be a safe haven for him, a place where he could grow and enjoy all the mundane, carefree pursuits young boys were entitled to. She supposed she could send him there and find someone willing to look after him while she remained behind with the general, but that reeked too much of his own father's callous treatment of him. She could not bring herself to abandon him when she had promised herself and him she would care for him.

And, yet, at the same time, she wanted to be part of General Viadon's mission and rid the world of Saranor's taint once and for all, for with her followers still attacking and killing, no place in Regalis was truly safe.

"I have Niko to consider," she said, quietly. "Whatever my decision, he must remain with me."

The general nodded. "I understand."

She took a deep breath. "Gareth will kill me if I decide to stay."

Viadon's firm mouth twitched at the corners. "Your brother does appear to be very protective of you."

She sighed. "I respect and love Gareth more than anything in the world, but I can't let him make all my decisions for me. I certainly can't tell *him* what to do, and I know with absolute certainty, that once he's fully healed, he'll be itching to resume his duties in your army. Do I want him to continue to be a soldier and put himself in constant danger? Of course not, but it's his decision and I have to respect that, just as he has to accept and respect my choices."

The general regarded her with faint amusement. "It sounds to me like you may be seriously considering my offer."

"I am, but I'm concerned about Niko. Life in the army won't be any safer, or better, for him than what he had in Saranor's castle."

"Yes, it will be," Jorin spoke up. "He'll have you to look after him. That'll make all the difference in the world. And I'll be there to help protect him, too."

Cazlina stared at him. "You're thinking of staying with the army? I thought you didn't like discipline and being told what to do."

He shrugged. "Ah, well, my former life wasn't very lucrative. At least, in the army I get three meals a day, a tent to sleep in, and, best of all, the pleasure of my lady's company."

He drew her toward him and kissed her, his firm mouth gentle and warm on hers. Startled, she pulled back and stared up into his twinkling eyes. He smiled disarmingly and rested his forehead against hers. "As I said before, who are we to ignore the will of the gods?" he murmured.

Her lips, still tingling from the unexpected kiss, twitched into an answering smile and her arms crept up to encircle his waist. She sighed softly and closed her eyes, leaning into the solid warmth of his body.

The nebulous, complex emotions that had seized her when learning he had been taken to the Pool for the queen's soul-killing ceremony suddenly assumed clarity and meaning. Once, she would have bristled and lashed out in annoyance at his impudence and forward behavior. But that was a lifetime ago. Her stubborn refusal to see beyond his initial sin of trying to steal Miris had made her react with childish pique and anger and had blinded her to his other qualities. If one good thing could be said of Saranor's evil, it had taught Cazlina there were far worse things in the world than a reformed horse thief with a brazen, irrepressible sense of humor.

Oh, how splendid! Miris exclaimed. *Does that mean we're going to keep the handsome horse thief, Caz?*

THE END

ABOUT THE AUTHOR

Cheryl Landmark lives in a quiet, picturesque hamlet called Gros Cap in Northern Ontario, Canada, with her husband, Mike, and faithful canine companion. She loves dogs, reading, jigsaw puzzles, and, of course, writing novels in her spare time.

She is also the author of a fantasy novel called WIND AND FIRE and a young adult adventure called SHADOWS IN THE BROOK.

Visit her website at:
www3.sympatico.ca/cheryl.landmark